Derbyshire

A sequel to Jane Austens
Pride and Prejudice

Marie Högström

Cover design by Lena & Jon Nohrstedt

Translation by Gabriella Jönsson
translations@skymnings.com

To Lena

For whom the book was written.

To Jonas

Whose encouragement has made it possible for me to get the book in print.

Chapter 1

The butler, John Goose, put his hands behind his back and fixed his gaze on the wall in front of him. He waited patiently for Mrs Darcy to put down the sheet of paper so that he would be able to remove the breakfast porcelain in front of his mistress.

His light blue eyes had the same colour as the background of the wallpaper which bore a pattern of gold medallions.

The crown of his head had long been bald, revealing a bump he had had since birth. His bushy eyebrows reached out from where they were attached like whiskers; when they grew too long he took out his little scissors and trimmed them. The moustache was twined at the ends and the well-groomed beard measured close to eight inches in length. When he stood completely still he looked like a representation out of the Holy Scriptures (Mr Collins' words).

When John finally moved his head, he let his gaze linger on the table in front of him. The contents of the teacup had long since cooled and the black leaves had stuck to the gilded rim. The piece of bread was broken but untouched, the white crumbs spread out across the plate.

Darcy smiled and nodded in the direction of his wife. The two men watched the range of expressions that passed over her face as Elizabeth absorbed the contents of the letter. Heightened eyebrows were followed by a blush that spread from her cheeks to her ears. Her mouth opened as if she had the intention to protest, but closed quickly. At the last sentence of the sheet her pupils dilated and she quickly turned the page to continue reading.

Darcy shrugged his shoulders as he met John's questioning gaze. Neither he nor the butler knew whom the letter was from. Elizabeth's fingers hid the sender's seal and he did not recognise the hand in which the address was written.

If Darcy was not the only curious witness, he was, however, the only one of the two who had the privilege to imply, enquire, or, at best, to partake of these lines. Darcy moved his hand towards the sheet as if to snatch it from his wife's grasp. John smiled and shook his head; he looked out through the window and hid a smile when Mr Darcy leaned forward and took his wife's cup. Not until his white moustache was still once more did he meet his master's gaze. John reached out to receive the cup with both hands. It would soon be time to train a successor and it was time that he talked to Mr Darcy about this.

John Goose, the oldest and most reputable of the servants at Pemberley, had followed both the older and the younger Mr Darcy in their relations, both within and outside of Derbyshire. The customs and practices of the Darcy family members, as well as their guests, were shaped by traditions that had been passed along through the generations in the country's uppermost circle. Man as well as woman knew exactly how to relate to equals as well as those of lower rank.

As Mr Darcy's butler, John had been the first in line to welcome the new Mrs Darcy when the newly-weds had arrived at Pemberley. By anticipating the housemaid in taking off her own coat, she had provided him with information that he did not think would otherwise have been mentioned in so many words.

Mr Darcy's choice of wife had surprised him; John had never imagined that Darcy would marry outside of his sphere. He admitted that it amused him that life could still offer some unexpected turns of events despite his advanced age. Mrs Darcy was undoubtedly one of these.

His master had also - through increased conversation, a lighter temperament and more spontaneity - contributed a few unexpected but not unwelcome changes at Pemberley.

Despite belonging to an older generation John was more of a liberal than a conservative, but then he had during three generations in the service of the Darcy family seen the father's fate influence the son's.

In an effort to clear his mind, he contemplated the scenario that took place outside the newly-polished drawing room window. The wind made one of the maids clasps her skirts about her as she hastened between the buildings. A gardener nodded his appreciation at what he saw. After a few steps the woman turned and smiled in embarrassment. The man, who was still watching her, took off his hat and bowed.

He stood leaning against his rake; by his coarse boots laid a pile of yellowing leaves. A sudden gust of wind made them whirl away.

The gardener threw out his hands and shrugged his shoulders. He did not see the steward, wearing a wide-brimmed hat and waistcoat, who closed up on him with long, determined steps. The employees who had seen him hastily left the path and took another way.

John watched as the gardener seemed to sink in front of the steward. His bothered expression and bowed head revealed that he had been rebuked. When the steward had withdrawn, the man once more grasped the rake and started working at a decidedly faster pace than previously.

John's brow furrowed. If there was one thing he was in disagreement with Mr Darcy about, it was the hiring of this man as steward. His master was presumably unaware of how strict Coyle was with his subordinates.

Darcy smiled as he observed his wife once more eyeing through the letter that he now saw bore the seal of the Collins family.

"Elizabeth?" he said and gave her a questioning glance. She looked up and shook her head.

"Excuse me… The contents of the letter… I am not at all sure what to make of the marital advice I have received," she said with an earnest look. Darcy held her gaze, despite her reservations he suspected that the letter had awakened more thoughts than she had the intention of revealing. As so many times before, her reaction had immediately awakened his curiosity.

The deep breath, the hidden smile and the glance at the portrait of his aunt had not escaped him. That she had tried to divert a reaction that in the presence of other people than themselves would be seen as inappropriate, made him draw his own conclusions.

"What kind of marital advice does a woman give her best friend?" He asked innocently. Elizabeth looked at her husband and was for a moment tempted to let him partake of the contents of the letter. They were:

My dear Lizzy

Let me once more express my deepest joy and wish you much prosperity and happiness in your marriage. Mr Darcy is doubtlessly aware of the happy outcome that is to be expected in his choice of bride. My hope is that you too, my friend, experience the same in your choice of partner.

With regards to Mr Darcy's wealth, place in society and close relations I doubt that any woman could have made a more advantageous match.

To a man there is however yet another aspect that is of utmost importance to his marital bliss!

By now you can hardly be unaware of the fact that a wife's duties include more than managing the household in an impeccable manner and to represent one's husband's good name.

A wife can gain much from making herself available to her husband; the advantages are not one but many. The husband's steadier temperament tends to increase his cooperation in other matters that are close to the female heart. A gift in the form of a new tea set, a dress or a necklace can be the husband's reward to his wife's ministrations and should be received with grace and a mildly surprised expression. A suggested trip to Bath or London can also brighten up the daily life that marriage entails, or that it will entail, soon after the wedding.

The pain that is every woman's passing from virginity to fully becoming her husband's wife is a lot we all share and must endure to the best of our abilities. What every woman should bear in mind is the following: the blessing of bearing forth an heir can only be attained through one's willingness to perform what has been ordained through marriage.

If a man's wife cannot assist him in this aspect, he will soon find what he looks for outside of the house walls, or what is worse, within his own household! The servants' awareness that the master of the house is forced to go to the maids since his wife refuses him his marital rights, would be an unimaginable humiliation to bear, for the man as well as the woman.

Remember that the discomfort a woman might experience is slight in comparison to spending her life childless. If the duty feels heavy to bear despite the advantages I have mentioned remember the following: a man offers his woman security, respectability and support. In return she grants him access to her innermost, as well as producing and rearing the heirs that will carry on his name.

Mr Collins' punctuality and regular habits mean that I can calmly and with confidence prepare for what is to come. Thanks to Mr Collins' profession I have, by discreetly emphasising the spiritual victory over the desires of the flesh, been able to limit his visits to once a week.

More than once it has however been the case that we were at that time invited to Rosings Park. The honour Lady Catherine de Bourgh bestows on us through her invitations can of course not be rewarded by failing to visit her.

This thought has been of some assistance to Mr Collins' spirit during the following week's wait.

A man like Mr Darcy is, however, not likely to be used to letting anyone, including his spirit, stand in the way of what he has set out to do. I am sure you will find some means of relief with time, Lizzy.

Your friend Charlotte Collins

If the letter had not been from Charlotte but a notice in a newspaper, Elizabeth would have laughed out loud and immediately shared the contents with her husband, so far from her own experiences was her friend's description of the marital duties. What must not be forgotten was that unlike herself, Charlotte was forced to share her bed with Mr Collins, which at further consideration made her description the more understandable. Without revealing her cousin's shortcomings in the marital chamber, Elizabeth chose to highlight the advantages Charlotte had mentioned.

"I am told that as the wife of a wealthy man, I should keep in mind the benefits that an attended-to man can offer his spouse," she said and smiled.

The smile left little doubt as to what sort of attention his wife alluded and Darcy rapidly retorted:

"Something tells me that the attention you have in mind has nothing to do with household chores."

Elizabeth regarded Darcy and said after a moment's silence:

"Every woman can take care of a household, or hire someone to do it for her," she added in a low voice.

A nod in the direction of the table with decanters made John Goose aware that his master required a refill earlier than usual. Elizabeth smiled innocently as she once again met Darcy's gaze.

That her husband needed some minutes' respite to collect himself was something she both appreciated and was encouraged by. She was well aware of her influence on him, it was one of the reasons she doubted he would ever feel neglected in their marriage.

Darcy contemplated his wife in silence, it was not the first time she had with a look or a movement made him wish that they had at the moment found themselves elsewhere. He stilled her hand that touched his knee. In an effort to uphold his position in front of the servants he quickly said:

"One of the benefits of which you speak is undoubtedly the increased attachment between man and woman after they have entered into marriage."

Elizabeth raised an eyebrow and bent forward to whisper:

"I don't understand what you mean at all. What I have in mind is something else completely."

After a moment's contemplation Darcy said:

"A letter or a poem? Where he in writing has expressed and fortified his emotions," he added seeing Elizabeth's sceptical expression.

"I admit that a woman appreciates a man's protestations of love, but no one can live on words alone, however fair they may be. What worth has a piece of paper? Be it of ever so fine a quality it doesn't add up to much."

The sight of Darcy's surprise made it possible for Elizabeth to be precisely as solemn as she had imagined.

"If there was anyone I thought would value the written word it was you. Are not you an avid letter writer?" He said with genuine surprise.

"My intention is not to thoroughly discard its worth but to inform you of the real benefits we women dream about, plan for and do everything to attain through marriage, even at the cost of our own happiness," she replied secretively.

"I know you well enough to know that you are hardly describing your own character," he said and smiled. "If I am not mistaken, I am beginning to suspect what it is to which you allude."

"What I had in mind was a necklace!" Elizabeth said.

"A necklace?" He said sceptically and met her gaze. "Are you sure? There is considerably more to be won for the one who makes an advantageous match. An equipage, a pianoforte or why not a town house?" He suggested with pretended seriousness.

"A precious necklace, I should add. From a man of your rank one can hardly expect enough," said Elizabeth as her solemnity melted into a smile.

"It is my wish that you experience more advantages in your marriage than has been suggested by this well-meaning advice," he said and laughed.

"You know I do," said Elizabeth and leaned forward to kiss her husband, which made John Goose bow and hastily take a step backward.

"About that there can be little doubt," mumbled the butler to himself on his way out of the room.

Chapter 2

Elizabeth looked at Darcy and smiled.

"Do you remember when we were last on our way to Netherfield?"

"Of course I remember, how could I ever forget the happiest day in my life?" Darcy replied.

"Yes, it was indeed a great day for both Jane, Bingley and ourselves, but I must insist that there was one person whose happiness was even greater," Elizabeth said and laughed.

"No, that is not possible! Who in the world could that be?" said Darcy.

"My dear mama of course!" Elizabeth replied and continued, "she was beside herself with joy when it was clear that Jane would become mistress of Netherfield and when I then told her that you had asked me to become your wife her happiness was complete."

Darcy smiled and kissed his wife. "My happiness was and is complete, after so many months in doubt about whether or not I would ever succeed in winning your love I dare say that my happiness was greater than any other's."

"Happiness can not really be compared in this way, as it has so different a basis in each person. Look at Jane who for months loved Bingley despite almost having given up the hope of seeing him again. Was her happiness when Bingley returned to Netherfield and proposed greater or lesser than your own when I agreed to become your wife?" Elizabeth said and looked at Darcy.

"You are right, the extent of happiness can only be judged by the individual in question and stands in relation to his or her own feelings and experiences, so let us be content to surmise that we were all happy in our own ways that day," Darcy said and smiled.

Elizabeth's way of arguing and twisting and turning things amused him and had from the very beginning of their acquaintance awoken his interest.

It was now six months since the wedding had taken place, Elizabeth and Darcy had spent the wedding night at Netherfield to continue on their long travel to Pemberley in Derbyshire the next day.

Since both sisters had had much to acquaint themselves with as new mistresses of the estates that were so much larger than Longbourne where they had grown up together, Elizabeth had not met Jane since the wedding.

In the beginning Elizabeth had dreaded the task of becoming mistress of Pemberly, as it was indeed a great estate. It was one of the greatest estates of northern England and the thought that she would be responsible for, and the mistress of, so many tenants and servants had at first felt strange. Fortunately Elizabeth did not scare easily and she soon discovered that with Mrs Reynolds' help the work was less difficult than expected.

One or two mishaps did occur. Like the day when Elizabeth had given the cook the day off after a large dinner party. She had thought he deserved a leisurely evening. When

Darcy and his friend had stepped through the door she had to her alarm remembered that he had that morning mentioned that there would be a guest for dinner. Such stories occurred in the letters that were exchanged between Netherfield and Pemberley. Jane had had many a good laugh as Elizabeth was a skilful narrator with a flair for detailed descriptions of the people and the daily life at Pemberley.

Jane and Bingley stood below the big stone steps to welcome their guests, and the reunion between the two sisters and the good friends was as dear as longed for by all four of them.

"Darcy! Elizabeth! What a joy to see you again, it was much too long since the last time!" Bingley exclaimed as soon as the guests had dismounted the carriage.

"I am sorry that we have not been able to come before, but Elizabeth has had her hands full planning dinners or should I say not planning dinners for my guests," said Darcy and shot Elizabeth a teasing look.

"Dear Lizzy, I am sorry to laugh, but I couldn't but do so upon reading your latest letter. Is it really true that you forgot that you were having a guest for dinner, and that you had sent the cook home by the time he arrived?" Jane asked.

"It is certainly true, I can assure you," said Darcy and continued: "It was, as a matter of fact, I who had to excuse myself and give the servant girl some suggestions for cold dishes that I knew she would be able to prepare without any major mishaps."

"You do not have it easy, dear Elizabeth! What good fortune you have Jane, that Netherfield is only half the size of Pemberley and that my guests are only half as fine as Darcy's," said Bingley with a smile and looked at Jane.

"Lizzy, why do you not say anything to your defence when Darcy teases you thus, you are not usually without an answer?" said Jane and put her arm about Elizabeth.

"Because I am silently contemplating how to best exercise my revenge for him having exposed my shortcomings to you," said Elizabeth and looked at her husband.

"You hear, Darcy!" said Bingley. "You better be on your toes!"

"I am not afraid," his friend replied and smiled.

The company continued into the house. Jane showed Elizabeth to the rooms that had been reserved for Mr and Mrs Darcy. It was the first time in a long while that the two sisters had the opportunity to speak to each other in private. They had a good deal to say for a good deal had happened in the six months and all had not been discussed via mail.

"Are you as happy as you thought you would be, Lizzy?" asked Jane when they were alone. Elizabeth looked at her sister and smiled. "Oh, yes, my happiness could not be greater. And how about you, Jane?"

"You know I am, Lizzy," said Jane and fell silent. "When I awake I must sometimes turn around to make sure that Bingley is really there. Not until then I can let myself be persuaded that I am indeed his wife and live here at Netherfield." Elizabeth laughed and took her sister's hand. Jane had always been modest. Even since she had become Bingley's wife she had to persuade herself that her happiness was real and not a dream.

They spoke for a long while about what had happened since last, and Jane confided to Elizabeth that Mrs Bennet had grand plans for Mary and Kitty. With three daughters married, two of them very advantageously, their mother deemed that only the best was good enough for her yet unmarried daughters. Jane blushed violently when she told the following story to her sister.

Mrs Bennet had been in high spirits for several days when she heard rumours of a rich young man having made plans to rent a house in the neighbourhood. She had been well aware that one was available a mile or two from Longbourne and she had on several occasions remarked on how fortunate Jane had been to have a suitor in the immediate vicinity. Mrs Bennet had painted a fanciful portrait of how Kitty or Mary, most likely Kitty, would become the mistress of this house. That they had not yet seen or met the man in question was of lesser concern.

Elizabeth listened composedly to her sister's story and admitted to herself that the distance between Longbourne and Pemberley did not always seem too long. Jane fell silent and changed the topic.

"Lizzy, how are the family relations at Pemberley, do you get on well with Miss Darcy?"

"Oh yes, she is as kind as you and she was sincerely glad to have me as a sister-in-law. Their aunt was, however, not as pleased with the arrangement," said Elizabeth with a smile.

"But Lizzy, can you really take it as lightly as you appear to do? For my part I have to confess that I was very hurt by Caroline's former ill will towards me and her efforts to separate me and Bingley."

"Of course it would be more pleasant for all of us if Lady Catherine was not so set against me," continued Elizabeth. "For my part I dare say that I could spare the visits to Rosings, but I feel sorry for Charlotte."

"Why should you feel sorry for Charlotte?" asked Jane with some surprise. Elizabeth sighed.

"Charlotte is genuinely happy about my marriage to Darcy. She was the first to see that he had formed an attachment for me. Lady Catherine's way of speaking about us upsets her, but she dares not say anything as Lady Catherine has done so much for Mr Collins. She cannot be loyal to both of us and it distresses her," said Elizabeth and added, "despite my assuring her that I do not value her any less for this Charlotte blames herself that her position, obligations and lack of courage prevent her from speaking her mind."

"Poor Charlotte - Lady Catherine really should not say such things when she knows that you and Charlotte are good friends. But maybe it is not as bad as it seems?" Jane said hopefully.

"Oh Jane, you always think the best of people, but in this case I have to say that Lady Catherine's descriptions of me are hardly flattering," Elizabeth replied and smiled.

"If such a woman had come to see me to demand a promise that I would not enter into an engagement with her nephew, I would have granted her request out of pure fright.

Darcy has your courage to thank for your present happiness," Jane said thoughtfully.

"My courage, as you call it, is a strongly contributing factor to Lady Catherine's dislike for my person, even if her choice of words would rather be a lack of manners, respect and upbringing. You can hardly risk ending up in a similar situation as you do not possess these qualities," said Elizabeth and laughed. Jane smiled back at her and brought the conversation on to more pleasant territory.

"Charlotte herself is presently in happy circumstances I have heard," she said and looked longingly through the window.

"As is her husband - Mr Collins is mightily proud to have provided his wife with an heir," replied Elizabeth. They fell silent, looked at each other and laughed. None of them commented on the idea of Mr Collins' participation in the activity.

"Seldom have any news pleased me more than when I learnt that Charlotte is with child," said Elizabeth finally and smiled.

Chapter 3

After having exchanged confidences and gone through the most important topics, Jane admitted unwillingly that it was high time for them to rejoin the gentlemen. Elizabeth and Jane locked arms and went down to the drawing-room where Bingley and Darcy were admiring Bingley's hunting trophies in the form of some fine deer horns.

The ladies continued on their round as Elizabeth was anxious to see the ballroom from which she had so many memories. It was here she had discovered that Bingley seriously admired her sister. There were more people than herself who had thought that Bingley and Jane would shortly thereafter announce their engagement, but that was not the case and the reason would forever remain unknown to Jane. Between Darcy, Bingley and Elizabeth there was an unspoken agreement not to reveal Darcy's interference in the matter. Darcy had made an error in judgement, Bingley let himself been led astray and Elizabeth knew it all. None of this would please Jane should she find out about it, which was why it has been agreed that this would not come to pass.

While Bingley, upon the gentlemen's entrance into the ballroom, enthusiastically described the ball that would be held there at the end of November, Darcy was lost in thought. Bingley remembered the night with such joy that he planned to give a ball in his wife's honour on the same date. The thought of the previous ball at Netherfield made Darcy shudder when he considered how different life could have been if fate had willed it differently.

The conversation that had taken place between him and Elizabeth that evening had left him in no doubt about her opinions and conclusions about himself and Wickham. It was with frustration, disappointment and pain that he had established that it was Wickham and not himself who had won her sympathies.

Darcy remembered the anguish he had felt when after the ball he had repeated their conversation to himself in his chamber. It had both frightened and filled him with hope that he was capable of esteeming and desiring a woman in this way. Before that, no woman had awakened more than his liking.

Women whose skilful fingers mastered a beautiful piece on the piano had awoken his admiration for the simple reason that he himself lacked any musical talent. He had, like other men, noticed the women whose fair exterior separated them from the mass. It had been an observation on his part, but never the cause of any stronger emotions. He had wanted more than beauty.

For a while Darcy had doubted whether he would ever find the woman whom he imagined would be his future wife. Apart from awaking his admiration, respect and desire he had envisioned the intellectual conversation that would take place between man and wife, a combination that as time went by seemed more and more unlikely. One of his friends had even hinted that a man had to choose between marrying a beautiful, but less intellectually stimulating woman, or a wealthy but not quite so beautiful one.

The hope he had felt when he found what he had so long been looking for had been clouded by doubt as to whether he would ever be able to sway her opinions and feelings. The thought of losing the only woman he could imagine as his wife to Wickham had been so distressing that he had had to go down to the drawing-room to fill a glass with whisky in order to sleep at all.

"Darcy?" said Bingley questioningly which brought his attention back to his friend.

"Pray excuse me, Bingley… I did not catch that last sentence," Darcy said hastily and decided to focus his attention to the present rather than dwell on the past. At once he felt relieved and could even manage a smile.

"Déja vu," said Bingley and nodded in the direction of the centre of the ballroom. The sight of Jane and Elizabeth, who in eager conversation crossed the floor on their way towards the gentlemen, reminded Darcy of Elizabeth's earlier admonishment to him to learn to look at the past only when it gave him pleasure.

This was a convenient opportunity and Darcy smiled as he brought to mind that his first impression of Bingley's ball had inevitably given him pleasure. The moment Elizabeth and her company had entered the room he had been struck by how attractive she was, there had been no other ladies in the assembly that could measure up to Miss Elizabeth Bennet.

Miss Bingley had often teasingly pointed out that Darcy had described Elizabeth's eyes as fine. Of course it was not just the shape or colour of those eyes that had caught his attention. What had fascinated him was the liveliness and the defiance that had become apparent when she was gainsaid, or was of another opinion than that pronounced.

Darcy wondered what the two sisters had been discussing as Elizabeth studied him thoughtfully and thereafter turned to Jane with a smile. Elizabeth, who had now figured out how to respond to his earlier teasing, turned to him and said:

"Do not you think me the handsomest woman in the ballroom?" Unprepared for the unexpected question it took him a few seconds before he made an answer.

"A man always thinks his woman the most beautiful," he said, somewhat confused by her question.

If the first question had taken him by surprise, the following assertion hardly made matters clearer.

"But if I remember correctly you have not always been of that opinion. I even think you once preferred Jane to me," said Elizabeth with a sweet smile. Darcy reddened.

"What do you mean, Elizabeth?" he asked in dismay. Her statement embarrassed him in front of Bingley and Jane. What was worse, for no reason, as he could not comprehend the intention behind it. For the first time Darcy found that he wished his wife's conversation to cease, or that she had never entered upon this subject.

"But do not you remember?" said Elizabeth and looked at Darcy. He could not judge whether her gaze was serious or teasing and therefore remained silent.

"Bingley surely remembers," and with these words Elizabeth instead turned to Bingley.

"Did not Darcy once tell you that you were dancing with the only pretty girl? Your sisters were already engaged and it would be a punishment to stand up with anybody

17

else."

Darcy reddened once more and looked so mortified Jane dreaded Elizabeth had gone too far in her effort to repay the morning's derision on his part.

"Then, as Bingley tried to make you aware of me by kindly complementing my appearance, did not you answer him with the words: she is tolerable, but not handsome enough to tempt me," Elizabeth said and fell silent.

Judging by her smile Darcy guessed it had all been meant as a joke, but his feelings were such that he could not share his wife's or his friend's happiness. Bingley laughed and said, "That's right, that was precisely the words he used, what an excellent memory, Elizabeth!"

"Perhaps a bit too good at times," she replied and smiled. Darcy looked at her, his eyes were dark and his jaws set.

"Truly, it pains me that you have heard me say this, as you must understand the conversation was directed solely at Bingley."

To her surprise he had turned and left the room before she had the time to reply to him. For a moment the other three stood silent.

Elizabeth was surprised by Darcy's unexpected response, Jane heartbroken by how their eagerly anticipated time together had begun and Bingley too well acquainted with Darcy's resentfulness when he found himself to be wronged by himself or others. Finally Jane was the one to break the silence.

"Oh Lizzy, do you suppose Darcy to be very cross with you?"

"I don't know, Jane, but it is beyond any doubt that he did not appreciate my jest," she replied thoughtfully. Elizabeth admitted to herself that she had very likely gone a touch further than his pride could bear. But she had never presumed he would be so offended by her telling a story that was known to all present. On further reflection it occurred to her that Darcy may have thought that Jane had not heard the story before and was therefore embarrassed by the way he had once spoken about the two sisters. Did he really fear Jane would seriously believe that he had once preferred her to Elizabeth? She was not persuaded - Darcy knew how close she and Jane were. The idea that she would confide in her on the occasion should have come as no surprise.

Elizabeth admitted to herself that Darcy's actions at times bewildered her. Often he could uphold a calm, correct, if somber, attitude even if he was in a company that gave him little pleasure, or even tried his patience. It was when his feelings welled over that he seemed to act precipitously, without further consideration of the consequences. Many times this had, of course, been a source of pleasure for her, as his actions were driven by positive as well as negative emotions.

The first time he had kissed her was a clear example of how he had let his feelings fly in the face of etiquette. Elizabeth smiled when she remembered the morning that Darcy had confessed his regard for her and repeated his proposal. This time she had gladly announced that she wanted, even wished, to be his wife.

They had taken another few steps on their walk before he stopped. Elizabeth, who had had time to look about her, had established that they were far from Longbourne and out of sight of Jane and Bingley. Darcy had seen nothing but her. His gaze was solemn as he bent to kiss her.

The intensity and desire betrayed by his movements, firmness and sudden advance had both amazed her and filled her with expectation. It was at that moment she had realised that his decisiveness did not only amount to practical matters. When she returned his kiss she had sensed what it would be like to be Mrs Darcy.

Afterwards he had looked at her and appeared so abashed she could not help but laugh. She had resisted the temptation to point out that their friends had had time to turn round.

He had struggled to control his desire and for a moment she had wondered how far he would have gone had they been alone. His behaviour did not frighten her, but rather enticed and excited her. To assure him of her position on the matter she had initiated the next kiss. Darcy had looked at her with a gaze filled with amused surprise and relief.

"Lizzy, you must go look for him," Jane entreated her, and looked so miserable Elizabeth had to smile despite the downcast mood of the company.

"Perhaps it is better to leave him in peace for a while. Darcy will likely be in a better mood in a little while," Bingley suggested.

"I am not so convinced of that," Elizabeth replied and continued, "it is true that I have not known him as long as you, Bingley, but I feel that I have noticed his moods are not always passing. A short period of uncertainty about his thoughts and frame of mind is without a doubt preferable."

Bingley looked at Jane but said nothing more about Darcy's mood.

Chapter 4

Elizabeth went into the park where she, after some meandering, entered upon a well-known path. Here she had often strolled during the days that she had been with Jane who due to illness had spent a few nights at Netherfield. This had been at the beginning of their acquaintance with Bingley, and Elizabeth had on more than one occasion crossed paths with Darcy during her excursions. She hoped that this would again be the case.

Elizabeth stopped as she spotted Darcy leaning against the oak tree and gazing across the fields. His straight-backed pose made her suddenly unsure of herself. This was the first time since they had been married that they had parted without being in agreement, if one could call his hasty departure being in disagreement. When she had gone out to look for him she had not hesitated. Now suddenly, she did not know which would be the best way to approach him.

The slight shift in his posture revealed that he had heard her. Despite his not having turned, his movement imbued her with enough courage to go forward and put her arms about his waist. Not until she felt him relax did she come face to face with him. Their eyes met, she could see that he was not angry.

"Dearest, forgive me if I have crossed you or insulted you before Bingley and Jane, it was not my intention," said Elizabeth.

"I am not cross with you, the only one I am angry with is possibly myself," Darcy replied and for a moment turned away his gaze.

"Why is that?" said Elizabeth in astonishment. "It was I who exposed you in front of our friends?" she added uncomfortably. Darcy shook his head.

"I had no notion that you had heard that heinous comment. I had hoped that Bingley would have forgotten these words, so you may imagine my dismay when you were all acquainted with them." Darcy shuddered and continued, "I can indeed understand now that you abhorred me in the beginning. No one can feel anything but dislike for a person who makes such degrading comments upon one's person,"

Elizabeth who saw his self-reproach, snuggled into his arms. She knew that he sometimes blamed himself over things that had long since passed. If, moreover, he felt he had acted unjustly his judgement upon himself was hard and unwavering.

Darcy encircled her in his arms and although he had relaxed perceptibly Elizabeth felt that he tensed anew as he said:

"The worst is that you heard words that did not accord with my real thoughts." He hesitated before continuing: "I had noticed you even prior to the ball at Netherfield. As on other occasions you stood out from the other ladies in the room that night. It was not just your fine eyes and joyous laughter that attracted my attention. I also noticed a straightforwardness in your conversation and manner of dancing that appealed to me."

"Then why did you say what you did to Bingley?" Elizabeth wondered.

"Again I fear I must be ashamed of my former pride, but I will tell you the truth." Darcy made a slight pause before continuing, "at the time I did not want to admit to myself or my friend that I had paid attention to a woman of much lower birth than my own."

Elizabeth smiled. "Considering how some have reacted to your choice I can hardly blame you."

"Other people's opinions should be of no regard," Darcy replied thoughtfully.

"So you were unaware that I knew about the conversation?" said Elizabeth.

"There was no reason at all to assume that you were acquainted with it, I hardly expected Bingley to inform you of it," Darcy replied.

"As loud as you were speaking at the time, I almost thought it was your intention that I should hear what was said," said Elizabeth.
At the sight of Darcy's aghast expression she laughed and hugged him tightly.

"Let us not place too much weight on what has been. What do old misunderstandings matter today? I became your wife after all."

"You are right, my dear Elizabeth, it is just that I sometimes judge my former actions very harshly even if they were committed a long time ago. Every time I think back to an occasion such as this I am filled with self-accusations."

"But if no one else is judging or blaming you, you are only tormenting yourself in vain, that is my opinion at least," said Elizabeth. "Do you remember what I said to you that day when you again asked me for my hand in marriage?" She added and met his eyes.

"Of course I remember. I will put it behind me and rather remember the reply you gave me on the occasion you mentioned."

By this time he was noticeably relaxed and had regained the warm, calm gaze with which he commonly regarded her.

"Excellent," said Elizabeth. "Now let us forget that episode, but you must agree that my revenge was grim."

"Yes, undoubtedly," said Darcy and smiled for the first time in an hour.

Jane breathed freely again as she saw them walk back together; she was always ill at ease when two people were in disagreement or cross at each other. She was herself so mild-mannered that she had not even raised her voice to her family at Longbourne except for the odd occasion. Bingley too looked relieved and welcomed them with a big smile.

The stay at Netherfield lasted for the duration of three weeks and in that time the gentlemen had time to hunt and Elizabeth visit her family at Longbourne on several occasions. More than anything, however, Elizabeth appreciated the intimate conversations that there was now plenty of time to re-establish with Jane.

The only cloud in her life was that she and Jane lived so far apart, but Elizabeth put her hope in what she had heard Bingley mention to Darcy. Bingley had expressed a wish to move further north, to Yorkshire, which was the neighbouring county of Derbyshire. Thus, when at length they parted, it was with the promise to see each other again soon. Bingley and Jane planned to travel north in the near future and would then take the opportunity to visit Pemberley for a few weeks.

Chapter 5

It was with pleasure that Elizabeth received the letter that her husband handed to her on her return from her walk. Darcy, who had witnessed Elizabeth's reaction upon first receiving a letter from home, took every opportunity to be the one who presented her with the mail. With an amused gaze he had wondered if in his hand he held something desirable to her. Elizabeth reminded herself that she had that night asked him the same question - if there was anything desirable to him beneath the cover she held in her hand.

At such a distance from her family and friends, every letter that arrived at Pemberley was more than welcome. The only thing missing in Elizabeth's new home environment was the daily conversations with her sister, and the intimate words that had been exchanged between the two friends. Next to Jane's letters, Charlotte's were the most appreciated, and it was with pleasure that she noted that the neat handwriting on the envelope was that of Charlotte's.

The date on the right corner of the letter reminded Elizabeth how long it had been since she last heard from her friend. Charlotte had since her marriage to Mr Collins, regularly shared her everyday experiences at the rectory as well as the many visits to Rosings. On further consideration, Charlotte's preceding letter had been dated more than two months earlier than today's letter. Elizabeth unfolded the sheet with the leaning, flourishing handwriting that was a hallmark of Mrs Collins. She hoped that the question that Charlotte had long wanted to put to her had now been formulated.

Elizabeth looked forward to accepting the duty that she knew lay before her. Charlotte had always said that Elizabeth was the godmother she would ask to watch over her firstborn. Mr Collins' bizarre idea about asking Miss Anne de Bourgh had fortunately been waylaid by his wife.

If the first words of the letter were meant to calm the one who had been given the confidence to receive that which after careful consideration had been put to paper, the effect was the opposite. The first lines of the letter bore witness that some event of great occasion had taken place, but Elizabeth was not sure that it was something that had made her friend happy. The subsequent words clearly showed that Charlotte had not written to ask what had long been an unspoken agreement between the two friends.

Dear Lizzy!

Be not shocked by the contents of this letter, for even if the feelings of the one who writes these lines will upset you there is no occasion for worry. The reason I share my thoughts with you is that you if anyone will be able to understand them, but you also know me well enough not to judge me for what I am about to confide in you.

23

As you surely remember, I once said to you that I have never been romantic and that all I wished for my own part was a home to call my own. My marriage to Mr Collins gave me this, and I admit that the society of Lady Catherine de Bourgh has strengthened my social standing which I allow is neither inconsequential nor unwelcome. Our marriage is, as you already know, based on a mutual exchange of what the other can contribute in everything but deeper emotions. That is at any rate my view of the matter. The exchange I have experienced through my matrimony I have mentioned already. My husband has in turn obtained a good, representative wife who takes care of his home and is his companion through life and with this he is perfectly content. Do not think that I am in anyway despondent. I entered the marriage with open eyes and I am, despite certain changes of circumstance, still happy with my situation.

As you have surely heard Mr Collins mention upon several occasions we have the happiness of being invited to dine at Rosings more than often with Lady Cathrine and Miss de Bourgh. Lately we have also been included in the larger gatherings that take place at Rosings, which to my joy has given me the opportunity to make two new acquaintances that I value greatly. One is my newfound friend Miss Croft, who I may reveal is soon to be the wife of Colonel Fitzwilliam.
As to the other acquaintance I cannot really say that we are personally acquainted but rather that I wish this would be the case.
Dearest Lizzy, forgive me if I am weighing you down with confessions that I know will make you worried and thoughtful both as to me and my husband. The reason I am selfish enough to ask you to bear with this, and add further weight by asking for a promise not to confide it to anyone, not even Jane, is that my burden would be too much for me to carry, were I not to share it with anyone.
The other person I mean to mention is Mr Andrew whose acquaintance we first made six months ago. Lady Cathrine had that evening invited several guests for dinner to celebrate the beginning of the foxhunt that is held annually at her estate. Naturally all the huntsmen were informed that the finest skin was to be presented to her, and Lady Cathrine particularly wanted to inform them where the shot should hit in order to cause the least amount of visible damage on the splendid animals they intended to shoot and thereafter present to her.
Mr Andrew, who had from the moment he entered the room attracted my attention, laughed loudly at these words and promised Lady Catherine that he would be the first to present her with a fox skin.

Merely through standing there, although we had not exchanged a word or been presented to each other, his presence made me nervous. Without reason I began to worry about attracting his attention in a negative manner, I wanted him to look at me with a gaze that told that he had seen me and would very much continue to behold me.
When we were introduced and our eyes met and Mr Andrew smiled, I was convinced that everyone could see what this meant to me. From the start I told myself that my reaction was merely due to the fact that Mr Andrew, through his advantageous exterior, attracted me in a way that few men had ever done, but even to myself I must confess that

it is his entire person that enthrals and binds me to him.

The common description evoked by ladies who mention Mr Andrew is that he is handsome, in what way I will attempt to further describe as well as it is possible in words.

Mr Andrew is tall, he towers at least ten inches above the tallest man in the room regardless of company, his appearance is all that a woman could wish for; more than once I have wondered what it would feel like to have his arms around me. The eyes that often bear an amused or studying expression are dark blue in colour which is an unusual combination with the once raven black hair Mr Andrew has had. Do not now believe that he is without hair, as this is not the case, but the black hair has in places been mixed in with another shade.

A sculpture could not have made a better shape with regards to the proportions around the chin and the marked line of the jaw, the straight nose, and the teeth that although they are only close to perfection attract every woman's gaze.

When I look at him, I cannot help but think about a picture from that book in my father's library, perhaps you remember how when we were little, we read with fascination about the Indians of America. Do you remember the picture of the young beautiful man with the mouth that seemed to smile due to the upturned corners of his mouth, even though his expression was serious? Apart from the length of his hair and the brown colour Mr Andrew's features resemble those of the young Indian.

Mr Andrew's behaviour is easygoing, both in manners and conversation; but at the same time he possesses a calmness and earnestness. His voice is deep and slightly emphatic when he wants to clarify something. This, in addition to the pronounced dialect, means that I can listen to Mr Andrew's voice without difficulty in company where more than one person is speaking at a time.

This is the delineation I have managed to accomplish and I will now endeavour to persuade myself that my reaction is the same as for any woman who meets a man that attracts her more than is common. Thus I will allow myself to see and listen to Mr Andrew with pleasure but not pay too much attention to my initial reaction to his exterior. My reaction surprised me, as I have never believed myself to be romantic but I admit that I now have a greater appreciation for your reasoning about what is to constitute the basis for a marriage.

I apologise again if I have shocked you but I assure you once more that there is no occasion for worry. I will not burden your mind further but will return to my daily chores that today consist of planning a dinner for my husband and a colleague of his from the neighbouring pastorate who is joining us this evening.

With kind regards,
Charlotte Collins

It took Elizabeth another three perusals of the letter before she was fully obliged to admit that these were indeed Charlotte's words that she was reading. For a moment she entertained the thought that Darcy was playing a prank on her, so great was her astonishment at the contents of the letter and the feelings that had so open-heartedly been expressed in it.

Charlotte had, as she herself had mentioned, never prided herself upon being romantic, but had on the contrary a rather crass view of matrimony. She had mainly seen it as a way out of her family home and an opportunity to create her own home. Perhaps it was because Charlotte had never been the particular object of any man's admiration. While other women had entered into matrimony, Charlotte had remained unmarried. Not because she was in any way deficient, but rather because there had always been other women to attract the men's attention. Elizabeth was well aware of why Mr Collins had been more successful the second time he offered a woman his hand in marriage.

Elizabeth was not a stranger to the intensity of the emotions that a man or a woman could awake in the other sex. Her husband had on many occasions mentioned how his desire had been aroused early in their acquaintance and how he had in no way been able to rein in its force. Darcy had told her that he had decided almost at once to do whatever was in his power to make Elizabeth more inclined to see him in a friendly light.

She had been touched when he had described how great his fear had been that she would fall for another man, who like Wickham immediately was to the women's liking.

That Charlotte, who was a married woman, had met a man who aroused such strong reactions was unfortunate. Elizabeth wondered what would be less painful, to never have known love and thus not be in want of it, or to experience love but have to give it up.

For the first time in her life Elizabeth sat with an empty sheet in front of her without finding a single word that seemed fit for a reply.

Chapter 6

Elizabeth had never been a horsewoman; of the five daughters at Longbourn only Jane, the eldest, had learnt to ride. Kitty and Lydia had not had any other interests than men, and men in uniform in particular. Lydia had expressed herself upon the matter in the following way:

"The time a good rider must devote to becoming acquainted with and master of her horse, would be better devoted to catching and taming a suitable husband."

Mrs Bennet had listened to and fully agreed with Lydia's reasoning.

"You are entirely right, dear child; it is commonly known that a woman who has not been married by 27 cannot harbour any great expectations for walking down the aisle in the future either," upon which she had added, "considering how many beautiful girls a small town like Merryton musters, a woman cannot devote enough of her time to looking pleasant and always be seen in the right society."

"Exactly!" Lydia had cried. "I, for one, intend to go to all the receptions and balls that come my way, because I intend to be married before my twentieth birthday."

"Oh yes, dear Lydia, with your happy disposition you have good chances," Mrs Bennet had said enthusiastically. Mr Bennet had looked up from his newspaper and sighed. "Something more than a happy disposition, I think, is required to be married."

Lydia had, to her mother's joy, lived up to her expectations and at the age of 16, taken the name of Mrs Wickham.

As for Mary and Elizabeth, the former preferred to spend her days in the library, while the latter opted to stroll in the countryside. Mr Bennet, who often let his daughters do as they pleased, had let the matter rest at that.

Elizabeth had always liked to be able to withdraw from her family at times and wander alone in nature. Naturally lively and energetic, she often ran short distances to experience the freedom she seldom otherwise felt.

In society, there was always someone who studied one's posture, behaviour and slightest movement. Despite Elizabeth feeling relatively at ease in her family, she could imagine her mother's horrified outburst if she had seen her daughter behave in such an unwomanly fashion.

It was different now, for while as the mistress of Pemberley, Elizabeth could move freely about the great park, she herself perceived the impropriety of running in front of the gardeners or servants.

Elizabeth had decided to learn to ride, partly because she wanted to accompany her husband on his Sunday ride about the property, and partly because she was tempted by the speed that a galloping horse could muster. Even if it might be as improper for Mrs Darcy to gallop as it was to run across the grounds, Elizabeth thought that if it did happen on occasion, she could always blame the horse.

Darcy had hardly been surprised at her wish, and he had laughed heartily when she presented her motives. Miss Georgiana, who admired her sister-in-law's liveliness, had decided to take the opportunity to join her, as she had not learnt the art of mastering a horse either.

When the decision had been made, only the choice of teacher remained, a decision that Elizabeth felt her husband took much too long to make.

Harry Jones was without a doubt the man that Darcy would have trusted with his sister's and wife's safety. The stable master had worked his entire life at Pemberley, and had tamed and broken in all the horses of the estate. His wide knowledge of the nature of these animals had been decisive when new horses were acquired or a covering was to take place. Thanks to Harry both the elder and younger Mr Darcy had made good deals when buying, breeding and selling the young stock of the estate.

Unfortunately, two years earlier the stable master had been the victim of what was feared to be heart failure and his duties had thereby been taken over by his son, Edward. Despite his father having trained his only son well, Darcy hesitated to entrust him with the mission.

"He is too young," said Darcy determinedly and crossed his arms over his chest. This was his way of signifying that he was being serious. Elizabeth looked at him; she already knew who would be the winner of this discussion.

"Edward knows what he is doing," she answered just as decisively.

"That may well be, but he is much too inexperienced for this sort of commission," her husband continued with a lowered brow.

"Do you doubt your stable master's ability to teach two young women who have never sat on a horse to ride? If I were Edward I would be deeply offended," she said and shook her head.

"I know that he can ride," Darcy said with a hint of irritation. He was ashamed that he could not give his real reason for wondering whether Edward was the right man for the task. He turned away as he felt his face heating. When he looked upon his wife again he was composed and pretended not to see Elizabeth's heightened eyebrows.

She had observed his changing mood but chosen not to comment on it. Instead she listened to his detailed description of possible candidates. Her decision was already made, it did not matter what he said.

"Mr Slowborne has a long experience and is willing to take on the task."

Elizabeth nodded.

"Mr Wilkins gives him the highest praise." Darcy enthusiastically added. As he saw that she had nodded to one of the maids he fell silent. Darcy regarded his wife; he was well aware of her resolution.

"Coyle would probably be pleased to be asked," he said suddenly. "I was merely joking," he added as he saw Elizabeth's face.

"I want Edward to be our teacher," she said calmly. "And I am wholly decided on the matter," she added with a smile.

"Yes, so I have understood," said Darcy and sighed.

Chapter 7

Edward was a young man who would be 24 that autumn, and by gaining Mr Darcy's trust he had once more attracted the attention of those around him. As a boy, curious eyes had lingered on him as he followed his father to Pemberley. Harry Jones' decision to take his boy to the stable at such a tender age had not been the only subject of the maids' low whisperings.

Edward had not outwardly resembled his father. Unlike Harry's head, which was covered with a carpet of copper locks, Edward's hair was brown, almost black, and straight. The shadow of his thick, dark eyelashes only allowed those who came very close indeed to judge whether his eyes were blue-grey or brown, and then only on those rare occasions that his hair was newly cut. The length of the working days and the priority of his duties meant that his brown-black hair nearly always reached down to his nose. At one point, it had been long enough that he could gather it in a tail at the back of his head. Every time Edward drew his fingers through his hair to clear his vision he was reminded that it was time to visit the barber; and as always he forgot it just as quickly.

It was not just the colour and quality of their hair that differed between father and son. Edward had always been able to stay a long time in the sun, while Harry had had to cover his red skin to escape the burning pain. His father's eyes had always been blue and rounded, while Edward's were dark and oval. Edward's nose was straight and covered in freckles, while the tip of Harry's nose had bent down towards a mouth that set in a firm line as he worked. Edward's amused expression often made people look around to see what, in their surroundings, had provoked his smile; when they could not find anything they sometimes asked him what he was thinking of. He usually answered them and was sometimes surprised that some seemed to lack the ability to see the positive sides of the most everyday occurrences.

It was not until the son of one of the employees had enlightened him that he could not possibly be Harry's son that he became aware of the differences in their appearances. The unexpected comment had come as a shock. He had scrutinised his father carefully and suddenly seen what others had long been speaking of.

Edward, who had no memory of any mother, and who had grown up with a father that never spoke of his dead wife, had long taken Wickham's words for the truth. In the end, he had not been able to bear the uncertainty, but had defied the man's warning not to mention the matter to the stable master.

Harry had broken out in an echoing laughter. "Whoever made that up? It is a fantastic story," he had said and wiped his eyes. Thereupon he had looked at Edward for a long time and finally said, "you take after your mother, which no one but myself can bear witness to, that is all."

If Edward had ever doubted Harry's assurance of his origins, he had merely reminded himself of the only likeness there was to be found between them. Despite being neither tall nor of a heavy build, Edward was easy to find among the other men. Like Harry, he was easygoing and had an ability to tell stories that could tempt even the sourest of servants to laugh. He liked to see others happy and was glad to amuse them even if it meant he had to expose his own shortcomings. His own laughter was seldom loud, but was well recognised by those who sought his company.

Edward's vocal ability was one of his greatest assets. Even though his position as the stable master of Pemberley meant he was never short of means he was one of the most persevering negotiators when there were commercial transactions taking place. He was not the only one who took delight in this part of the business; he had seen that Mr Darcy amongst others observed him keenly. Despite that gentleman's silence on the matter, Edward believed that there was more than the advantageous price that amused him.

Elizabeth enjoyed the stable master's company, but then she was not a stranger to mixing with servants or workers. Even if her family at Longbourn had been among the first in the neighbourhood, the gap between the family and servants had not been as marked as among the true nobility of the country.

After her marriage to Darcy, Elizabeth had become a member of one of the most powerful families in England. Despite this, she was still the same artless person who possessed a natural ability to get along with people of both high and low origins. In some circumstances, however, she still felt unaccustomed to being the mistress of such a large estate as Pemberley.

Miss Georgiana who had been brought up in this environment, and whose education after her mother's death had partly been entrusted to Lady Catherine de Bourgh, had been reared very differently from Elizabeth.

Lady Catherine's conceit and occasionally patronizing way with her servants had, happily, not produced similar behaviour in her niece. Georgiana's behaviour was, rather, marked by prudence and bashfulness that those who did not know her well enough might misinterpret as pride. Georgiana's contacts with the servants and workers were limited, as it was her brother who took care of most of their concerns. The one exception was Mrs Reynolds, who had been housekeeper at Pemberley since before Georgiana was born. With the others, she felt rather at a loss in how to address them in any way that was not the most common of greetings. Their lots in life were so widely separated from her own.

The first time this had become apparent to Georgiana was when she, at the age of ten, accompanied her brother on a visit to a worker in his home. The poor man had had a tree fall over his leg during work with tree-felling, and the leg had to be amputated below the knee.

When the man had seen that it was Mr Darcy's son who entered his house, he had immediately stood up to receive them with the aid of his crutches. Despite having clenched his teeth, he had moaned as the newly sawed-off stump had chafed against the tightly wound dressing.

Georgiana had watched in horror as the white bandages were stained red. When a drop of blood had pushed through the fabric and fallen to the floor, she had averted her eyes.

The worker's wife had all the while hurried between the stove, her sick husband and the smallest child, and trailed a musky scent of hard work. The eldest daughter was the same age as Georgiana and had regarded her dress with a look of wonderment. The girl had worn a cotton dress. Judging by its quality, it had been inherited from her two older sisters.

Despite the clean neatness of the cottage, and Georgiana's awareness that the man was well off as a labourer at her brother's estate, she had been overwhelmed by the fact that this was as much a home to him, as Pemberley was to her.

Standing on the sturdy floor boards in what was meant to be the drawing room, Georgiana had suddenly blushed as her memory evoked the drawing rooms of Pemberley. The Windsor chairs, the carpet weaves and the mended stopped holes in the walls of the cottage stood in stark contrast with the beautiful silk tapestries, the gold-framed portraits, and the beautifully crafted furniture that were to be found in her own home.

Until that day, she had never reflected on the lives of the servants when they left the estate. Apart from a few times per annum, the maids in their white aprons and bonnets had always been at Pemberley. Not until this moment had she considered that the homes they visited on their holidays in all likelihood resembled the cottage she had just visited. This revelation made her sad, as well as scared and ashamed.

On the return to her chamber, Georgiana had remained seated for a long period of time while she beheld her personal belongings. She could not understand how her brother could let his workers live so poorly when they themselves lived in such splendour. Try as she might, she could not forget the indelible impression of the man, the woman and the children in the cottage.

Not until three days later, had Georgiana dared ask her brother why everyone could not live as well as they did at Pemberley. Darcy, who had been surprised that the visit had made such an impression on his sister, had answered her question as best he could. He had told Georgiana that she as well as he had been born at Pemberley, which was why it was their home. The worker, who had been born in the village, had his family home there. Georgiana had cautiously asked if the man would not rather have been born at Pemberley rather than in the village. To Darcy's consternation this question left him without a reply.

In an effort to show her that the servants at Pemberley had a good life, her brother had, on their next stay in London, asked the driver to go by the part of town where he never otherwise set foot. The message had sunk in: Georgiana never again commented on the living standards of the Pemberley servants, but she also never forgot the sight of London's back streets. Her inability to do anything about the injustices, hardships and misery she had witnessed there, had always diminished the happiness she should have

31

felt upon the family's visits to London. The knowledge of their own wealth had incited in her the feelings of guilt that were her constant companions.

Chapter 8

The horses Othello and Caesar had that morning been paid more than their usual attentions, all on the recommendations of the steward, Coyle. When daylight overtook moonlight Edward, who had got up a half hour earlier than usual, had brushed both horses, fed them and cleaned their stalls.

It was with a relieved sigh that he extinguished the light and sat down in the hay. The work was completed, and he would finally be able to eat. With a swift movement, he broke the bread and started to chew.

"No," he said sternly and pushed away Othello's head that had closed in on what remained of his meal. "You are a horse and will have to make do with hay," he added with a smile.

One of the stable lads strolled into the building, he yawned and grunted at the early hour. When he came up to Othello's box and saw that the hay was clean he looked about in surprise. When he saw Edward he started but found himself quickly.

"I thought it was someone else," he said hastily. He was well aware that his usually pale face crimsoned. The high edge of his scalp left no space for hair that could lessen the impression. The tiny curls that grew on top of his head were so light that they looked almost white in the sunlight. Among the men at the farm he was known as The Angel.

James was glad it was Edward and not Coyle who sat in the stall. Not that he thought the steward would put himself in a position where he would risk having to look up at his employees, but one could never be too sure. Coyle was in the habit of making unexpected inspections, something James tried not to think about as he went about his business.

This morning he had been so tired he could have got into trouble if circumstances had been different. In the future he would have to be more careful; it was not just his own happiness he risked. When he thought upon the reason for last night's few hours of sleep, he could not help but smile.

Edward stopped eating and looked at James. "So glad at this hour of the day! What can be the occasion?"

His happiness was so earnest, James failed in his attempt to look serious. He muttered as he once more felt his cheeks heat. Edward squinted at him and said with a smile:

"It's said that you have a good eye to someone close by." He paused before continuing: "Someone who works in the house." Edward drummed the piece of bread against his knee and continued to take a large bite, all the while keeping his eyes trained upon his friend. James scratched his neck in an effort to gather his wits.

"How do you know…?" He began, but stopped as he saw Edward's amused face.

"What are you doing here at this hour?" He asked instead, and sat down in the hay. He liked and esteemed Edward. Even if he was prone to horse-play, James knew he could be trusted.

"Inspection by Coyle," said Edward pointedly and threw the last piece of bread to Othello who had not taken its eyes of him since he started eating.

"Aha, I see," James replied with a smile that revealed the small space between his front teeth. "When will he be here?" He said and looked hastily around.

"When you least expect him to be," Edward replied and leaned back against the hay. He reached a hand up to pat Othello who had bent its head down and was sniffing his face.

James regarded him and wondered at him being so calm at what lay ahead. He could hardly be unaware of Coyle's dislike of him. If he had been Edward he would not have given himself time to rest. Coyle always made him ill at ease just by showing himself, he could not imagine how it would be to fall into disfavour with the steward.

"I know what you are thinking," said Edward and opened the eyes that he had closed for a while. He blinked at the sunrays that had found their way in through a crack in the wall and were now shining him in the face. A low neighing was heard from the farther end of the stable. Edward nodded towards the stall closest to the entry and looked at James.

"There are others aside from me who can tell when a storm is closing in. When Beth starts to move in her stall, I know it is time."

James frowned. "And then it is best that you take care."

Their eyes met for a moment before Edward hastily looked away. However great his confidence in James was, he did not want to speak too much about Coyle. He knew that James knew more than had been mentioned. The silence that followed was not broken until James, too, lay down in the hay.

The rustle of the hay made Edward bring the conversation around to what had happened the night before. James blushed, and although he had intended to remain silent he found that he had, at length, answered almost all of Edward's questions.

"You are quite incomparable," he burst out. "Have you not thought about becoming a detective?"

Edward laughed. "No, not until now. I had no idea that so much interesting information could be obtained if one asked the right questions. And who is incomparable will have to remain unsaid. You were not exactly unwilling to speak once you had begun."

James snorted and gave Edward a shove in the side.

"Just wait until you meet someone who means more to you than your horses."

"Sssch," Edward whispered and put a finger to his mouth. James shot up, brushed off his clothes and looked around. He had not been working there long and was well aware of his place among the employees. In no way could he risk the steward seeing him without any work at hand.

Despite listening intently, he could not hear a door being opened, steps closing in or a voice issuing commandments.

When some minutes had passed by and the silence in the building remained, he turned around. Edward, who had made no effort to rise, remained in the hay. The dark gaze that glinted through his fringe revealed that he could hardly keep his countenance.

"Be careful, I have seen such as Coyle before," said James seriously and slapped him

34

over the head with a rope.

"If you thought that stung, you better take care," he added when Edward threw himself to the side to escape the next blow. "But I wager you know that already," said James and started walking towards the exit.

Despite not being a morning person, Coyle had taken the trouble to get up at dawn to visit the stable buildings in order to inspect the stable master's work. It was no secret that he hoped to give him a rebuke. It had always been his opinion that Mr Jones had been too loose in bringing up his son. The lack of firm frames and clear boundaries evidently left its mark, which Harry through his death, had left to him to set straight.

Darcy's steward had never been married, nor did he have any children. Work had required his entire commitment, time and interest during his youth. For this Coyle had obtained standing, respect and a good pay, as well as work on the best estates in the country. When Pemberley's former steward, Mr Wickham, had passed away, Coyle had hurried to put his request forward and had been hired on his good merits.

The steward's attitude to his subordinates was characterised by his firm opinions on such matters. The absence of complaints was praise enough; too many commendations could risk making a good worker less attentive, or even lazy. In Coyle's presence work was diligently carried out, the sight of his torso that seemed as wide as he was tall imbued even the most free-spirited of young men with a proper sense of respect. If he furthermore had reason to raise his already booming voice, all other activity stopped. No matter where he had been, he had won respect, but never any friends. Coyle was, and had always been, a recluse. There were few, if any, that had anything good to say about his person.

Coyle raised his arm to take off his hat, but immediately changed his mind upon recollecting who it was he was there to see.

"Are you there?" He exclaimed instead in a loud voice. No answer, which was not surprising. Where had he got to this time? Coyle looked around.

In the stable all was still - even the horses stood with half-closed eyelids and remained silent. Slow creatures, that was his opinion if anyone had cared to ask for it.

A loud snort made his impressive moustache flutter. A black stallion looked up from its box. When it saw the stout man it closed its eyes once more. Coyle regarded the animal in disbelief. What was with the horses? But what else could one expect of a twenty-four-year-old stable master. The short steward placed both his hands at his sides and straightened his otherwise lightly bent back, upon which he cleared his throat in order to make his presence known with renewed force. His deep voice echoed through the building, a horse neighed in reply. James could not understand why Edward had not replied the first time Coyle had called out to him. He shuddered, and hastily slipped out of the building.

Some weeks prior, Othello had damaged a hoof upon stepping on a nail. This would be her first time with an unknown rider on top of her since the accident. Edward had wanted to ensure that all was as it should be before the ride. When he heard Beth he understood that the steward was already in the stable. He immediately interrupted his inspection and peered out from behind Othello.

"Sir, all has been prepared," he said and made a pause to catch his breath. "The horses are ready," he added when Coyle did not reply but stared vacantly at him. Edward wiped his forehead with his shirtsleeve and looked at him.

Coyle, who had expected him from the main building and not from one of the stalls, gave him an annoyed glance, he did not like being the one who was taken by surprise. There were few people he tolerated, let alone were friendly towards. Edward was not one of his favourites.

He did not really know why, just that he was irritated the instant he saw him. It had, however, been a bit easier since the stable master had stopped looking so unjustifiably happy. Perchance he had finally managed to instil that work was a duty and not a pleasure.

The steward did not respond to Edward's comment, instead he looked him over from top to toe. He was not pleased at what he saw. The more Coyle thought about it, the more his annoyance grew. In less than an hour Edward would be presented to Mrs and Miss Darcy, and this was what would meet them. Hair that rather than being shortly cropped fell in front of his eyes, leisurely dress and dirty hands.

"Have you not had your hair cut yet," muttered Coyle. "No, I can see that you haven't," he added before Edward had time to respond.

"It's preferable if one can see what one does, and how one looks," he muttered.

When he spotted Edward's arms he stiffened. That he had placed his hands in his pockets upset him more than the fact that the sleeves were folded up to reveal more naked skin than was proper.

"Have you not learnt anything other than taking care of animals?" Coyle hissed. Edward took his hands out of his pockets. A barely noticeable shift in his eyes was the only visible reaction. He remained silent. The two men looked straight at each other. It was Coyle who, by fastening his gaze on the loosely hanging shirt, looked away first.

"You do know that it is Mrs and Miss Darcy you will be teaching, your master's wife and sister?" He said in an exaggeratedly slow voice. It was not just his physical appearance that irked Coyle.

Unlike the other young men, Edward did not avert his eyes after having been scolded by a man in a higher position. He had a mind to shake him up properly.

Despite his father's comments on it on several occasions, it still happened that Edward's gaze rested too long on the person he was regarding. In his line of work his ability to read animals was invaluable. Edward had discovered early on that some skills could be practised on humans as well as on animals. The courage to look another human in the eyes for more than a few seconds was something most people lacked. The social codes were a welcome reason to make others or oneself lower one's gaze.

Many believed that they withheld information about themselves from the world through lowered eyelids. Even in a brief encounter the attentive could, however, gauge the degree of inner peace or the lack thereof. Coyle was definitely lacking any form of equanimity.

"I needn't remind you that it is riding lessons you will be conducting," Coyle said grimly. The words were so unexpected that Edward, to his own exasperation, blushed. With a few quick movements he pulled down his sleeves, removed some straws of hay from his shirt and pretended not to see the steward's smile.

Content to have re-established the balance betwixt them, Coyle hastily commenced the overview of the morning's work. It did not take long for him to pass his first judgment.

"The small stallion would have been a better choice for Miss Darcy, I suggest you change horses," he said and looked directly at Edward who did not let himself be intimidated by his gaze.

"As you realise, he needs to be properly brushed before being presented to Miss Darcy," Coyle added with a stiff smile.

"Mr Darcy himself picked out the horses for his sister and wife," said Edward calmly while carefully adjusting the soft leather halter. He had not been able to resist giving an answer that he knew would provoke Coyle.

The steward's smile immediately disappeared and rather than looking at Edward, he turned his gaze on the horses. Othello snorted and shook its black mane as the stable flies became too intrusive. Beth scratched with her hoof and partook of some hay from the bale Edward had provided them with. In the same moment Edward saw the sunlight fall in through the apertures and reflect off the dust that had swirled up he knew his words would not pass unobserved.

"The horses are still dusty," Coyle remarked triumphantly. "You will have to brush them again." Edward opened his mouth to protest but remained silent as the steward waved his hand in warning.

"Take off the halter," he commanded, just as Edward had put it in place. Having studied it carefully he said: "This needs polishing."

Edward bent down to pick up the halter off the ground. He felt his irritation grow. Coyle knew as well as he did that he had done a good job and that the complaints brought forward were grounded on something else. Despite not being one lacking an answer something kept him back.

"There is also hay on the stable yard," Coyle said with a smirk, as he saw the young man's expression. Edward resisted the temptation to point out that he was in fact in a stable and that hay was usually found in such a place. He had learned not to test Coyle's patience too hard.

It was with resigned resentment that he once more embarked upon the morning's chores. The thought of Coyle's insinuations about his behaviour towards Mrs and Miss Darcy disappointed and angered him. Coyle could hardly believe that he was unaware of how to treat his master's wife and sister.

He was convinced the steward made these remarks to undermine his confidence. That Coyle instructed him on the safety, equipment and choice of horses was a direct insult to his father, who had been one of the most respected stable masters in Derbyshire.

Edward's movements with the brush were fast and forceful; the dust swirled off the black horse's body and left a shiny surface. His breath increased and he felt the warmth rise in his face, he could not say whether it was the effort or the anger.

Coyle glared at Edward. "It will be a miracle if this goes well, I am glad Mr Darcy himself made his choice." Edward stopped in the middle of a movement and stared at Coyle who sneered and added:

"His choice of teacher, I mean. But it may be lucky for you that Mr Darcy has himself picked out the horses."

Despite wanting nothing so much as to throw the brush at Coyle, Edward returned to his work. The time for the riding lesson was closing in and he needed to be ready.

Although he had not wanted to admit to it, it was no longer possible to deny the effect of Coyle's presence on him. A thought that had not been there before had entered his mind. What if there was an accident? The anger he had felt was now replaced by anxiety. He wanted to blame it all on Coyle, but unfortunately he could not deny the facts. He did not know if any of the ladies had been on top of a horse before. Until Coyle had entered the building he had been clear about what was expected, secure in the choice of horses and had confidence in his own ability. It both annoyed and frightened him that the steward could so easily unbalance him.

He could not avoid thinking about what sort of horse Mr Darcy had picked for his wife. Caesar had a past as a racehorse; if Mrs Darcy's intention was to gallop, her wish would in all likelihood be granted. At the last thought he felt his uneasiness increase and concentrated instead on what to say about the other horse his master had chosen. Othello's broad back, handsome neck and bushy mane would probably please Miss Darcy.

A powerful grip around his shoulder made him look up into Coyle's blotchy face, located only a couple of inches from his own. A few drops of sweat trickled down the bulging vein of his forehead and an acrid smell of tobacco puffed towards him on the steward's strained breathing. The grip around his shoulder finally eased as Coyle used his hand to dry his face. With an expression that did not succeed in masking any of the doubt he evidently felt at the arrangement, he said with emphasis on each syllable:

"Make sure they don't fall off the animals!"

Edward remained silent; an assurance to the contrary would hardly have been either believable or served to calm any of them.

Considering how Coyle had reacted when one of Darcy's guests had been injured in a riding incident, anything was possible if something should happen to Mrs or Miss Darcy.

Edward admitted that he was becoming increasingly worried at the prospect of the arrangement. He was, however, determined to keep his calm in front of Coyle. He would find enough to criticize without his help. The steward stroked his moustache with thick hands and said in a harsh voice: "You will be held solely responsible in the event of an accident."

"I had hardly expected less," Edward muttered.

"What did you say?" Coyle asked gruffly and turned around. Edward regarded him in an attempt to decide whether his irritation was slight, moderate or serious. One had to tread lightly; even if he was not afraid, he had a great respect for Coyle and did not want to anger him. Once, he had misjudged the situation and got into trouble, something he had no intention to repeat.

"I am aware of that," he said with a greater calm than he felt and turned away.

Coyle's gaze on the clock prevented him from driving the discussion any further. Instead, he pointed to the water vat and then at Edward.

"A man should look respectable in front of women, regardless of his station." Without turning he went off with the words: "He should also behave decently." Edward watched him walk off and did as he was told once more. It was only the knowledge that Coyle could turn around that kept his countenance in place.

The water was too lukewarm to have a cooling effect and was only moderately revitalising. Until Mrs and Miss Darcy's arrival, he thought himself deserving of a break. As soon as Coyle was out of sight, he sat down on the bench that had been placed at the long end of the stable building.

Despite it being a couple of hours until the sun would be at its highest, it was uncommonly warm. The morning's labour and the rising temperature contributed to the drowsiness that became apparent when he finally gave himself permission to rest.

Chapter 9

Georgiana contemplated the young man her brother had appointed to be their riding instructor. The opposite of Darcy, who was nearly as white as the bone white shirt he wore, Edward's skin was lightly tanned by the sun. His face was covered in freckles, it was impossible to mistake him for anything else than a man who spent most of his time out of doors. The thought of her aunt's reaction to such a sight made her smile. Lady Catherine had at their last meeting noted in horror that Georgiana had several unsightly spots on her face and carefully emphasised the importance of protecting one's face from the sun. Before they had parted, Lady Catherine had presented her with a gift of a new parasol and a bonnet.

Edward, who had turned his face to the sun and for a moment shut his eyes, had not yet noticed the ladies' presence. Georgiana observed his calm breathing and wondered if he were asleep. If not, he seemed deeply preoccupied by his own thoughts and completely unaware of what took place around him. He had not heard them coming and he had not reacted when a large bird swept past with a crowing sound.

She liked his smile and his relaxed posture. The day and hour of their arrival had been planned since long. The fact that he had put himself in a situation where they noticed him, rather than the other way around, filled her with both wonder and curiosity.

Elizabeth made a sign for her sister-in-law to be quiet whereupon she looked around the stable yard. When she had ascertained that they were alone, she emitted a low, neighing sound.

In the sleeplike state Edward was in the sound taken on the character of one of the stable's horses just biting off its rope and fleeing through the gate. As a stable master, he had the final responsibility for the horses and their state of health. The thought of answering to Coyle made him wide awake and he looked about him in horror.

Georgiana looked in astonishment at Elizabeth and then at Edward, whose face betrayed that he too had been surprised by Mrs Darcy's way of announcing their arrival.

Despite not intending to frighten him, Elizabeth could not but laugh at his reaction: she had apparently underestimated her own abilities for imitation. Edward arose hastily and brushed the dust off his trousers.

"Mrs Darcy," he said and bowed. To Georgiana's amazement and relief he seemed neither annoyed nor ill at ease. His smile had been sincere when he greeted Elizabeth.

When Edward once more lifted his gaze he caught sight of Georgiana who, at Elizabeth's request, had taken a few steps forward.

It was several years since he had seen Miss Darcy up close. He was unsure as to whether he would have recognised her if they had not been introduced to each other. Her complexion was fair, he supposed she rarely spent time out of doors in the sunlight.

The curls of hair that this day was not hidden underneath a bonnet were gathered in a coif with a clasp. The humid air had made them take on another shape than that which all the ladies had them arranged in. He liked that she seemed unfazed by this. Many women would not contemplate showing themselves out of doors if they were not confident that their looks were irreproachable. Her eyes were big and brown and her gaze both serious and calm. If he were to describe her he would say pretty rather than beautiful.

Georgiana had unabashedly watched him while he slept. Despite Edward now meeting her gaze squarely she did not avert her eyes, which for the longest time had been her habit in meeting strangers. They both remained standing without anyone making a start at the customary greeting gestures. Edward pulled a hand through his hair in the same moment that Georgiana pushed one of her curls to the side. His smile was so wide that she could see that two side teeth on the upper row were pointed, the rest seemed to stand according to an invisible straight line. It was but rarely one saw people with such a smile. The artists tended to paint something similar in portraits, regardless of whether or not it was true to the original.

Without thinking, Georgiana had immediately smiled back. She liked that his smile made his eyes shine, he did not try to hide or adjust his reaction. There were too many individuals who smiled when they were not happy, or omitted to show pleasure when they felt it.

Her gaze, which had lingered at his dark eyes, finally discovered the scar on his forehead. It was not yet so old that it had begun to whiten. The narrow depression in the skin that reached from hairline to eyebrow seemed but recently to have been covered by a thin layer of skin. He would always carry it and she thought that this may be the reason he allowed his hair to grow. She wondered how he had obtained it and if it had hurt.

Edward who saw her look, scratched his forehead as he let the long fringe fall across the mark. He was amazed at her frankness and hoped she would not ask questions.

A feeling of excitement and fear possessed Georgiana as she beheld the man in front of her. This will become a problem she thought and blushed. Not until she noticed that they were both the objects of scrutiny, she hurriedly looked away.

Elizabeth observed them and felt some relief that it was she, and not her husband, who had witnessed the exchange. She was convinced Darcy would immediately have had a serious conversation with both of them. As unforgivable as it was for a woman of Georgiana's rank to be speechless in the presence of her servants, it was equally reproachable for one of the servants not to show the proper respect for his master and the family.

Georgiana's awkwardness showed that there were very few, if any, times that she and Edward had spoken to one another. As they had both grown up and spent the greater part of their lives at Pemberley, Elizabeth had assumed that they were acquainted with each other. In this first meeting she had the impression, however, that this was not the case, and decided to help them, rather than reproach them.

"Edward, Miss Darcy," said Elizabeth. Edward admitted that he did not know what was expected of him - up until now he had only been introduced to labourers. Since his gaze was still resting on Miss Darcy, he saw that she bent her head and curtsied when Mrs Darcy spoke her name. Edward bowed and tried in carriage, movement and speed, to emulate Mr Darcy when he, during his town visits, met an acquaintance.

Edward, who after an amused look from Mrs Darcy had taken his hands out of his pockets, swiftly shifted the conversation onto the topic of the impending riding lessons.

"Judging by your entry I gather that one of you are already accustomed to the stables," he said and smiled.

"My talent has misled you, I'm afraid. The only horse whose acquaintance I have made is old Nellie," Elizabeth said and laughed.

Edward who had gathered his wits again remembered that he had considered whether to initiate a direct contact between the riders and animals from the outset. At Mrs Darcy's words, he loosened Ceasar's reins and handed them over with determination.

"According to an eminently reliable source your acquaintance with Nellie was limited to once in a while feeding her a carrot," he said and gave the horse the treat that it had discovered in his pocket.

Elizabeth stroked the stable's most recent acquisition over the muzzle. Ceasar was a gift from Darcy. As soon as it had come to his attention that she intended to take up riding he had begun the search for the stallion. Edward had suggested that several of the horse owners had shown symptoms of stress at Darcy's many questions concerning the creatures.

Unlike herself, her husband had never been limited by lack of means to obtain the gifts he intended to please his dear ones. Elizabeth valued Darcy's choice to personally select the presents he bestowed upon her more than their financial value.

"Even if Jane was the only one to ride Nellie," Elizabeth told Edward, "I have on one occasion tested my skills as a rider."

"Aha! Therein lays the explanation for your unique talent," said Edward happily. After a moment's consideration, and a glance in the direction of his master's horse, he added:

"Something tells me this venture did not whet your appetite."
To his relief, Elizabeth did not hesitate to reply to his statement that had also been a question.

"To misjudge one's own talent as well as an old horse's speed can have a dampening effect, even on my enthusiasm." Elizabeth laughed, whereupon she added: "Until a few years have passed and the only thing that remains is the memory of the feeling the gallop induced."
The look she gave him made it difficult for Edward to hide his hilarity at Mrs Darcy's unspoken request.

"I will do my best to help you experience this once more," said Edward and smiled.

Chapter 10

Except for greeting each other upon presentation, Georgiana had not been able to think of any appropriate comment, but instead spent her time discreetly observing the rest of the stable master's appearance. Apart from the brown leather boots that showed traces of mud as well as hay, it was only the dust on the black trousers that betrayed that this man worked outside the walls of Pemberley.

The thought that some men of her acquaintance used a wig to keep every last hair in place made Georgiana smile when Edward, in an effort to look presentable, pushed a few strands of hair out of his field of vision. Georgiana guessed that there were more than one of the maids who appreciated Edward's presence at Pemberley and she was keenly aware that she herself would have felt the same in another context.

Although Edward had held the position of stable master at Pemberley for several years, he had only on the rarest of occasions crossed paths with Georgiana prior to this. Her education and society had often meant she spent large parts of the year outside of Derbyshire. Georgiana was, in spite of this, stunned that Edward was no more than a stranger whom she had just been presented to.

The humorous glint in his dark eyes had kept her looking at the man longer than she had intended. On closer inspection, it was not the colour of his eyes that surprised her, but the fact that she had been the first to avert her eyes. To be in the company of the servants, other than when their services were required, was something new to her. Edward's choice not to be the first to avert his eyes, as was customary with servants, made her behold Pemberley's stable master with interest.

The intensity of the gaze that for a moment had suggested recognition, which could not possibly be explained by a prior acquaintance, made her blush. During the remainder of their meeting she was, therefore, careful not to meet his eyes, but instead listened to the dialogue that had taken place between Elizabeth and Edward. At the word gallop she had squirmed, and wondered exactly what kind of riding skills her sister-in-law meant to acquire.

Edward observed the two ladies and noted that their behaviour seemed markedly different. Mrs Darcy was quick and could answer back in a way that amused him, and he understood that what was said was the truth. Mr Darcy's manners had become decidedly more easy-going since his marriage to Miss Elizabeth Bennet.

Mr Darcy's choice of bride had surprised, as well as amused and been the subject of contemplation for more than one of the estate's employees. To both Edward's and the others' surprise, the new Mrs Darcy had taken to exchange a few words with her servants whenever opportunity arose.

Thus, during one of her walks, Mrs Darcy had visited Edward in the stable building. The sight of Mrs Darcy unaccompanied by her husband had made him wonder how the latter might react to such a bold venture.

Mrs Darcy, who had observed his worry, had explained her intentions with regards to the visit. After having acquainted herself with the general condition of each of the horses, she had decided to learn how to ride, which she had also announced without first having discussed the matter with her husband.

Edward wondered if he would ever dare to ask how Mr Darcy and Mrs Darcy had become acquainted.

With regards to Miss Darcy, Edward believed that Georgiana's avoidance of eye contact since being introduced, was due to shyness rather than disdain. It had not been his intention to look at her for as long as he had. Miss Georgiana's calm and pleasant manner had surprised him. Miss Darcy had been described to him as closed and serious; few of the maids could recall having seen her laugh other than on the rarest of occasions. Other traits that had been attributed to her were a reluctance to look at servants with more than the slightest of glances, as well as unwillingness to speak to them in more than a few words.

At first sight of the young woman, Edward had guessed that the judgments that had been made on her person were unreliable. He felt both happy and proud that Miss Darcy had not only looked at him but also smiled back at him and laughed. If conceit had been a characteristic trait of Miss Darcy's, she would not have averted her eyes at the estate's stable master.

The thought that he had embarrassed her with his attention came when Georgiana once more avoided his gaze. Mrs Darcy's easy-going manner had, for a moment, made Edward forget both the ladies' as well as his own position. To converse and exchange gazes with someone outside of one's own sphere was a privilege of the upper classes. Edward, who was neither undaunted nor shy, had meant to rein in his happy nature and make an effort to behave calmly and correctly. It was, after all, his master's wife and sister that he was to teach. That he had, during their first meeting, beheld Miss Darcy in this way could not be seen as anything but improper.

Although Edward tried to convince himself that the reason he hoped they would not be scared off by this was the impending riding lessons, he sensed that this was not the entire truth. During the remainder of the lesson he had been careful not to be discovered looking at Miss Darcy. He looked forward to their next lesson.

Chapter 11

Elizabeth, who had awoken early, smiled as she opened her eyes and was blinded by the sunrays that poured into the room. For a moment she lay still and contemplated the fact that she had once more awoken to find herself Darcy's wife. Carefully, she turned around and gazed at the man who slept by her side.

His head rested against the pillow that he embraced with both arms. The dark hair took on a nuance of copper that she had not noticed before. His breaths were calm and filled the room with a light susurration. Elizabeth smiled at the thought that on their first meeting she could never have imagined him with such a relaxed countenance as she now witnessed.

After having watched him for a long while, she leaned forward and ran her hand through his dark locks and kissed his forehead. When Darcy opened his eyes and met her gaze she said: "I am sorry that I woke you, but I couldn't resist."

"I don't mind in the slightest," he said with a smile and pulled her close.

Darcy and Elizabeth both considered themselves to be just as happy as they intended. Although they both had short tempers that on more on one occasion had snapped, their feelings ran hot in battle as well as in love.

Elizabeth was nowadays accustomed to her role as mistress of Pemberley. Darcy had from the first moment given her his full support and a free hand to make such improvements or changes as she saw fit. This she had not considered necessary, as Pemberley was more than tastefully decorated. By adding a few things she did, however, intend to put her own mark upon their home.

Elizabeth liked to wander through the deserted corridors and pass rooms that were seldom put to use. Especially in the evenings, when darkness had fallen, the air of mystery around the past seemed to thicken.

The portraits that hung on the walls often caught her attention and she used to wonder how Darcy's forefathers had lived their lives in the home where she was now the mistress. Darcy had told her some things about his relatives, and there were many destinies that had been lived through within the grounds of Pemberley.

There was one room in particular that had won her liking and it was here that Elizabeth withdrew when she wanted to be alone. The room was located on the second floor, all the way down the furthermost corridor. It was a beautifully decorated girl's room with tasteful furniture and heavy draperies. The first time Elizabeth had stepped into the room she had wondered if she had stepped into a private chamber.

A shawl had been draped across an armchair, a bible had peeked out from under the pillow, and pieces of a sharpened quill had lain spread across the desk. This had made her thoughtful since, as far as she knew, none of the servants had their quarters in this part of the building.

Despite it being against her principles, Elizabeth had entered the room and closed the door behind her. She did not know what had compelled her to it, just that she had reminded herself she was Mrs Darcy and that she was in her full right to make herself acquainted with her new home.

The clothes, as well as the accessories, bore witness that the room had been left untouched for many years. It had surprised her that it was so clean, the thought that somebody dusted the room and then put every thing back in its original place made her even more curious. As she had run her hand over the chiselled desk her eyes had fallen on the sheet of paper that lay by the quill. The sheet was empty except for some figures in the top right corner. Elizabeth decided to immediately find Darcy and ask him whom the room had belonged to, and why it had been kept in its original state for so many years.

On her way out of the room she had stepped on a board that had come loose. When she bent to put it back in place she had, to her astonishment, found a pile of letters.

Elizabeth had scrutinized the yellowed letters and found an assured style of writing on their fronts. Some of them were stamped in Egypt and with growing interest she had opened the first letter, and upon having read it, she could not stop until she had read them all. In the last letter there had been a dried centipede.

The room that Elizabeth had chosen had once belonged to Darcy's father's sister, Christine, who had met with a tragic fate. Christine's and Henry Darcy's father had been a stern man with the firm view that a marriage should be based on both parties' advantageous connections, as well as a well established fortune on both sides. A powerful estate could with the right choice of bride be made even more powerful.

Since the birth of his children he had searched for fitting consorts for them both. The children's mother had not had much say in the matter, but found it best to prepare them for the destiny that awaited them. Mrs Darcy had spoken well of their intended spouses, and described in detail the fancy events they would be invited to in light of their fortunes. To further add allurement to riches, she had gone so far as to describe the life at court in London, where they would be invited as soon as they were married.

Darcy's father, Henry, was the eldest and the first to be married to the bride chosen for him. His mother was delighted that he had from the outset liked Anne, and to everyone's joy, his feelings were reciprocated. Henry and Anne Darcy had lived in a harmonious marriage and the one thing that had clouded their happiness was that they had not produced an heir.

Henry's father, who had not had much compassion, had continually let it be known that he wished to see the heir of Pemberley before his death.
Mr Darcy had even gone so far as to complain to his wife that he had chosen an infertile wife for his son.

Anne's happiness had been complete when she, after five years of marriage, had finally found herself pregnant, and when her firstborn was a son, her happiness had hardly been less. Her father-in-law was not perturbed that it had taken ten years before the next child to be born, as there was now an heir to Pemberley.

Christine had, to begin with, not been negatively disposed to her intended husband even if she disliked her father's way of controlling her life. What had made her think better of it was that during her time at Oxford she met a man whom she had come to love until her death.

Christine and David had met during one of the many events that took place in the city and from the start they had been inexorably drawn to each other. Both were adventurous and more than once they had found ways to be in each other's company more or less undisturbed. This could take the form of a visit to a nearby estate where they had joined a company of visitors despite not knowing a single one. Their self-assured behaviour had, however, convinced people that they were man and wife.

After meeting David, Christine had not been able to consider marrying another man. David had not lacked a fortune, but he was not the man her father had chosen for her and thus a marriage between them was out of the question. Despite Christine's desperate pleas, her father had remained adamant. But Christine intended to marry David - even if she had to run off with him. Her father, who had guessed at her plans, had taken the steps he had deemed necessary.

One day, Christine had received a letter from David where he mentioned that he intended to go along on a voyage to Egypt, which had long been his dream. When one of the original archaeologists, for unclear reasons, had decided to give up his place, he had been given the opportunity to go in his stead.

Christine and David had met a last time and said farewell, with the promise to be married as soon as he once more set foot on English soil. Christine had not wanted him to miss this opportunity and an avid epistolary intercourse had begun between the two. In every letter, David had expressed his longing for them to be together once more and in the last letter Christine had received a dried centipede where the number of legs represented the number of days that remained until his return.

When five weeks of spring had passed without Christine receiving any more letters, she began to worry. Soon thereafter her fears had proved true when the papers announced that the returning ship from Egypt had gone under in a storm.

It was her father that had apprised his daughter of the news. The cold way in which he had let her understand that the man she loved was dead had provoked in her a hatred that grew the stronger when she learnt that it was her father who had bribed one of the archaeologists to vacate his place so that David could go on the voyage. Even if it was not her father's fault that the ship had sunk, he had intentionally separated them and it had resulted in David's death.

The sorrow had made it impossible for her to function, and Christine had spent most of her time in her room where she had sat at the window and stared with an empty gaze at the lake that glittered in the sun, darkened with shadows of rain clouds, or was hidden under a clear skin of ice.

The day after her father had set a date for her wedding to the man he had chosen for her, Christine had disappeared. Despite an intense search, she was never found. There were rumours that she had left the country and gone to France – Christine knew that her father loathed the country on the other side of the channel.

Georgiana, who had told the story to Elizabeth, thought it was unpleasant to be in the room that had belonged to Christine. Elizabeth did not share this opinion; she had been noticeably moved when Georgiana told of Christine's fate. Elizabeth admitted to herself that she was grateful Darcy's grandfather was not alive.

Chapter 12

During one of her visits to town, Elizabeth had become attached to a red velvet canapé that she had seen in one of her favoured shops. This red canapé would be well suited for the room she sometimes took refuge in. In front of the fire and turned towards the great window its owner could peacefully gaze upon the lake and read the love letters a young man had long ago sent the woman he held dear.

There was also another letter that Elizabeth sometimes took out and read. It was the letter Darcy had presented to her on the day that she had refused his first offer of marriage. Darcy had wished her to burn the letter, as he had written it in a state of turmoil and feared that the contents would displease her. To begin with this had also been her intent, but at the last second she had changed her mind and instead hidden it together with the other letters.

Even if its contents reminded her of the prejudices she had once had against him, it was also these very lines that had made her scrutinize herself and look upon the matter with different eyes. The letter was a direct reason for the slow but steadfast change her feelings had undergone.

This day Elizabeth would, in the company of Mrs Reynolds, go into town to place a bid on the canapé. The thought that her current position brought with it almost limitless financial freedom was something she was not yet accustomed to.

When she saw that the carriage had been brought forward, she put on her coat and hurried into the yard. Mrs Reynolds let her step into the carriage before she herself took a seat. The two women got on well and respected each other. The housekeeper had on Elizabeth's first visit to Pemberley, praised Darcy as a master, brother and employer, and thereby furthered Elizabeth's growing admiration for him. Mrs Reynolds thought Mr Darcy's choice of wife was very appropriate. She smiled when she saw Elizabeth wave at one of the worker's children that hollered and ran after the carriage as they passed.

The town centre was buzzing with people as it was a market day. There were many farmers who had travelled a great distance to exhibit their well-fed livestock in the hope that one of the estate owners would place a large bid. The driver excused himself, and said that they would be forced to walk the last bit on foot.

On the way to the store they passed several salesmen. One of the men on the wagons caught Elizabeth's eye. Despite it being chilly outside, his shirtsleeves were pushed up. The man's skin was covered in drawings portraying skulls, half-dressed girls and dragons. In his mouth he had a carved pipe whose shaft was shaped like a woman's body. Before him on the wagon were fish with eyes astare. In a far corner lay a grey, slimy pile that looked like a big hand with several fingers.

"What is that?" Mrs Reynolds exclaimed and wrinkled her nose. The man turned his face towards them and smiled a smile that showed the lack of all but two front teeth. He reached out for the thing and grabbed beneath its body.

"It's a squid," he said and shook his hand so the ten arms swayed around the animal's body. He lifted one of the long tentacles and turned its underside to Mrs Reynolds.

"They're good at sucking on to anything they come into contact with. In the big oceans they can grow several feet long. A sailor who is caught in its grip will not get far."

"How horrible," said Mrs Reynolds and shivered.

Wherever they went, vendors shouted after them; some were silenced at the sight of Mrs Darcy. Elizabeth did not mind the attention or the fact that everyone was aware of her position. Even if she dressed well her clothing differed to Miss Bingley's, who always wore clothes that showed exactly what level of society she belonged to.

Mrs Reynolds and Elizabeth studied some piglets that were rooting in the muddy ground of the fenced-in area where they were kept.

"It's a perfectly splendid little pig – it would be excellent on a spit over an open fire," said the farmer happily and bent to pat the pig's round belly.

"Even if I should like to buy it I do not think it would be proper for a woman to be seen leading a pig, however well-fed it may be. We are two ladies in a carriage and any other way of bringing the pig home I cannot see, so unfortunately I will have to disappoint you by declining your offer," said Elizabeth and smiled.

"But surely you have a husband who can bring the pig," the farmer tried.

"I do indeed, but he is not currently in town," replied Elizabeth. At the same moment she spotted Edward and Darcy about a hundred metres further along the way.

The two men were scrutinizing a couple of mares, and judging by their gazes they seemed particularly interested in a handsome black horse. Its owner tried to hide his delight by putting on a formal and detached attitude. If one was too eager and showed a desperate wish to sell the animal there was usually no deal. The buyer could be given the erroneous impression that there was something wrong with the animal, since its owner wished to be rid of it in such haste.

Elizabeth watched the three men and was just about to make Mrs Reynolds aware of the company when she saw a woman close in on them. The woman wore an amber-coloured dress with a daring neckline – the shawl she bore over her shoulders was not enough to hide her décolletage. For a moment all activity seemed to come to a standstill as every man in the woman's vicinity turned his gaze on her and watched her a long time after she had passed.

Her face was, in the main, thin but took on a broader shape at the cheekbones, which were carefully marked out. The hair was black and as thick as the tail of the mare the gentlemen had recently been surveying. The eyes were dark brown, the skin paper white and the lips painted a clear red. If it had not been for the expensive habit, the worthy carriage and the two maids at her side, one would have mistaken her for a fille de joie, Elizabeth thought.

"Darcy!" Although they were standing some distance away from the gentlemen, Elizabeth could not but hear the woman's exclamation of her husband's name. Darcy looked up and, at the sight of the young woman who was hurrying towards him at such a pace that she had to lift her skirts so as not to trip over them, he laughed and welcomed her with a big smile.

An eager conversation began; the young woman gesticulated with great alacrity and, at more than one occasion, tempted Darcy into a laugh. When the exchange seemed to take on a more serious tone Elizabeth saw how Edward discreetly drew away. After a while the woman looked intently at Darcy, whereupon she removed herself as quickly as she had arrived.

Elizabeth had been so surprised by the scene that had taken place that she had not moved from the spot where she stood. Mrs Reynolds, who was wrapped up in a discussion with the farmer who had tried to sell the piglet, had not witnessed what had taken place further along the way.

Elizabeth was extremely keen to know who this strange woman was, but she admitted that she was embarrassed to reveal that she did not know the name of a woman who seemed on such cordial terms with her husband.

She watched the farmer's obstinacy with impatience: when he had been informed that it was Mrs Darcy who stood before him, his hope of selling the pig had increased. Although Elizabeth knew she was being unfair, his gestures, smiles and enthusiastic phrases increased her irritation. To put a stop to the conversation, she put her hand down her purse and pulled up a few coins that she squeezed into the farmer's dirty hand.

"Mrs Darcy," he began hesitantly when he discovered that the sum was far larger than the price he had asked. Mrs Reynolds looked at Elizabeth in surprise, but said nothing as she accepted the cord with which the pig was tied. Elizabeth pretended not to notice the glances that followed them – her only concern was to find out more about the unknown woman.

Elizabeth started towards the place where the carriage awaited them; suddenly she wanted to escape all the people who could potentially recognise her or her husband. Mrs Reynolds looked at the little pig, and then at Mrs Darcy. She did not understand why her mistress had bought a pig when she had set out to buy a canapé.

"I can wait outside the shop while you look at the piece of furniture," she said, and reddened at the thought of being seen standing on a street corner with a pig at her side.

"We will do that on some other occasion," said Elizabeth shortly. In as neutral a way as possible she tried to lead the exchange onto the woman she had seen.

"While you spoke to the farmer I saw a visitor that I thought I recognised. We have only been introduced on one occasion, and I must admit that her name has slipped my mind. If I describe her to you perhaps you could help me remember her name?"

Elizabeth was ashamed at her untruth, and when Mrs Reynolds looked at her in surprise as she described the woman she was certain her lie had been discovered.

"The face you describe could not belong to anyone but Miss Byron," said Mrs Reynolds after a while. Elizabeth said nothing further; the name Byron meant nothing to her. She had never heard Darcy, or anyone else of their acquaintance, mention this name.

Elizabeth had not mentioned to Mrs Reynolds that Darcy and Edward were in town, and she was careful to choose a direction where they would avoid bumping into them on their way back.

On the journey home, Elizabeth thought of different ways to bring up the subject with Darcy, and as the ladies returned to Pemberley before the gentlemen, there was ample time for rumination.

Chapter 13

When Darcy's carriage pulled into the front yard, Elizabeth immediately went to meet him. Darcy, who saw her approach, presently beamed at her. Elizabeth was relieved when she saw that his facial expression was filled with love and genuine delight at their meeting.

Before he had reached her, a grunting noise made him look to the side in surprise and stop in his tracks. The piglet, who was still tied to the carriage, rooted on the stone-set ground without success. Its hooves clattered without finding a grip, the animal grunted and its swaying motion made the grey-speckled tail wag.

"I see that you have been making purchases," said Darcy thoughtfully.

"Yes," replied Elizabeth, a bit uncomfortable about her impulsive decision; she hoped he wouldn't ask what the pig had cost.

"Our town visit was decided on in haste; if we had known about it an hour earlier we could have gone together," he said and looked at Elizabeth.

"Then you would not have had to put the pig in the carriage," he added with a smile.

Elizabeth listened distractedly to Darcy's account of his visit to the village. The reason they had gone was that Edward had this morning been informed that a well-reputed breeder would be at the market.

"It was lucky we went. Edward recommended me to place a bid, which I also did. The breeder said that with the right sire her chances of producing an equally handsome offspring are good," Darcy said in a pleased tone.

"Is that so," said Elizabeth and wondered what an offspring between Darcy and the beautiful woman would look like. When her husband once more began speaking of the horse business, she had to make an effort to suppress her impatience. She pretended to regard the horses that grazed further away, while she took a couple of deep breaths.

For a moment, her worrying thoughts were broken by a smile at the insight that she had become quite adept at calming down before she spoke. Some people of Darcy's acquaintance had really tested her patience, and as his wife she had to be more considered than had been her habit.

"It was odd that we did not see you at any point during the entire morning," Darcy said, finally. Elizabeth blushed, but did not want to admit what she had witnessed without making herself known.

"Mrs Reynolds pointed out one of your acquaintances who were in town – Miss Byron, I think the name was," she said calmly. Her effort to sound convincing grinded in her ears; she did not like lying to her husband.

Darcy looked up in surprise but then said calmly: "Were you introduced?"

"No, we only observed her from a distance," Elizabeth replied.

For a moment he seemed to hesitate and Elizabeth had the notion he was about to tell her something. She was therefore disappointed when he merely said: "Miss Byron is the daughter of my father's good friends, Mr and Mrs Byron, but this information you have surely already received from Mrs Reynolds."

"Yes… Of course," said Elizabeth and looked away. She realised that her reply meant there would be no further particulars on the matter.

Darcy looked at her searchingly, whereupon he led them onto the path he knew was her favourite walk. The path passed by a large meadow where, during the early morning hours, Elizabeth was almost always witness to the deer grazing that were at times interrupted by wild capering on the part of the young animals.

Although he had several matters to attend to before the evening, Darcy did not hesitate to accompany her. Elizabeth gazed upon her husband and thought of his continual attentiveness and concern about her well-being, as well as his many declarations of his strong love for her. Even if she admitted that she was more than curious as to how close Miss Byron and Darcy were to each other, she decided to try to see the matter from another angle.

What did it matter that he had conversed with and shown delight in meeting an acquaintance? Nothing, she told herself. No matter how well Miss Byron knew Darcy, it was she, Elizabeth, who was the object of his affections.

Elizabeth stopped and looked out over the meadow; the breeze of the wind made the green straws move like a billowing sea. The sun shone and when she felt its warmth on her face she closed her eyes. Darcy, who was watching her with a smile, took the hand she stretched out to him.

Elizabeth pulled him towards her and placed his arms about her waist, upon which she met his loving gaze.

"Dearest Elizabeth, how lucky I am to have you," he said quietly.

Chapter 14

Elizabeth looked at Darcy and excused herself as soon as she had finished her breakfast. Yet another letter had arrived from the vicarage and even if Elizabeth had been both astonished and alarmed by the contents of Charlotte's previous letter, she was eager to read the lines that had been sent to her this morning.

Darcy was used to Elizabeth withdrawing to read and reply to the letters she received and did not usually insist on partaking of their contents. The contents of Charlotte's letters did, however, require greater caution on the side of Elizabeth. To read the letters at the desk in the drawing room could mean that a passer-by who inadvertently cast a glance their way could happen to catch some of the lines that were only intended for Elizabeth. When she saw the Collins's seal on the envelope she always chose to retire to Christine's room, where she was certain she would be undisturbed.

Elizabeth walked with quick steps and glowing cheeks through the corridor. When she passed Christine's portrait she stopped for a moment. Christine's fate had not left her unmoved, and Elizabeth wondered what Charlotte would have to tell in this letter.

Once inside the room she carefully closed the door, broke the seal, and started to read.

Dearest Lizzy,

Once more I write to you to share my innermost thoughts; letters have their advantages as I am afraid that an oral account would make me extremely embarrassed, and prevent me from expressing myself as well as in writing. My intention not to pay too much attention to Mr Andrew's appearance has not been successful. I must unfortunately admit that he affects me more than I find proper.

There are, in particular, two things that fascinate me but also scare me with regards to my reaction to Mr Andrew. As you may have guessed from my previous descriptions of his appearance, Mr Andrew is considerably older than me, and the thought that I am attracted to a man who is only a few years younger than my own father both surprises and alarms me.
This is, however, the case, and there does not seem to be much I can do to lessen this attraction; rather, I let it continue, being careful to hide my feelings from everyone else. The fact that I, more and more, seek out Mr Andrew's company scares me inasmuch as I fear that my behaviour will draw attention to itself.
During the last visit to Rosings I found myself playing a board game I have always abhorred; the reason being, of course, that Mr Andrew's table was missing a player. Despite taking every opportunity to be in his company, I do not feel relaxed therein; my movements become clumsy and more than once the pieces fell to the floor and the contents of the wine glass splashed over when it was hastily put down on the table. When I speak to him, I feel every muscle of my face move in a way that I am convinced

immediately draws the attention of Mr Andrew and the others. The words that come out are neither intelligent nor thought-through; I often speak to him merely to have his undivided attention for a while. Of all this, Mr Collins, Mr Andrew, and Lady Catherine are, of course, unaware.

Back home, I think back on the evening that has passed and I admit that my thoughts on more than one occasion go to Mr Andrew, whose face seems etched onto my inner eye. What does he do when he comes home? What does he think about? Does he find me attractive? What would it be like to live with Mr Andrew? Is there any woman he holds dear?

My friend, Miss Croft, informed me in passing that Mr Andrew lives alone since his wife left him for another man. It was a great scandal that is still spoken of; the man his wife ran off with was a good friend of Mr Andrew. The eloping couple left the country and have neither been heard from nor seen since; it is thought, however, that they are living in France, where the man in question formerly held an elevated position at court. Naturally, I am well aware that my thoughts are only daydreams; but since they brighten my days I do not spend too much energy on trying to will them away. On the contrary, I find to my alarm that I rather encourage and sustain them.

One day, I suggested to Mr Collins that we should go for a ride to behold the beautiful landscape, which he readily consented to.

As if by chance, we drove down the road that passes by Mr Andrew's estate, and I admit I found the prospect particularly pleasing. The thought of living in such an environment with the man who fills one's every thought, made me, for the first time in my life, understand the young people who defy every convention and run away together. Do not now imagine that I have the intention to elope; once again I want to remind you that these thoughts and feelings are only on my part. Mr Andrew is happily unaware of the effect he has on me. Thank you for once more relieving my burden by sharing my thoughts.

With kind regards,
Charlotte Collins

Elizabeth took out a sheet of paper and the pen Darcy had purchased for her during his last stay in London. Despite having many thoughts on the matter, she was, once more, unable to find the right words to reply to Charlotte's letter. After having sat and stared at the empty sheet a long while, Elizabeth decided to wait with her reply for a few days. She hoped, rather than believed, that she would have had time to gather her thoughts by then.

A scant attraction to someone else than one's lawful spouse was not something to be worried about; no man or woman could wholly avoid the temptation of resting their gaze, now and then, on a person of the opposite sex. Charlotte's description of Mr Andrew's effect on her behaviour had, however, made Elizabeth sharpen her attention, and when the end of the letter revealed her friend's innermost thoughts about the man in question, she could not but be worried by the situation.

How much she would have liked to ask her sister Jane's advice on how to reply to Charlotte. Jane was always so calm and thoughtful, and would in all likelihood have been able to see things in the right context. Bound as she was by a vow of silence, this was impossible; but if Charlotte managed to hide her emotions, which seemed anything but mild, she could also be sure that her friend would hide her knowledge of the same.

Chapter 15

Georgiana who had, to begin with, mostly come along to keep Elizabeth company during the riding lessons, soon discovered that she felt genuinely at home with the horses and with Edward. Out on the meadows, she was freed from the eyes she felt were otherwise always resting on her. As the sister of Mr Darcy, she was required to behave impeccably. Before Elizabeth had come into their lives, Georgiana had stood at her brother's side and received the guests of Pemberley; thereby, she had also had the responsibility for the ladies of the company. Happily, Georgiana had now relinquished these tasks to her sister-in-law.

As for the horse-riding, she was still a beginner and it was only natural, even to be expected, that she made mistakes; this relieved her of the sense of failure she would otherwise have felt.

Edward had never doubted her ability; he had seen that she was unsure of herself, but suspected that once she had overcome her anxiety, she would become an able rider. His conviction that she would be able to do what he had instructed her to do enabled her, to her astonishment, to jump over low hurdles and steer the horse where she wanted to go. To her surprise, Georgiana had discovered that she had a good way with the animals and that even Edward beheld her in surprise and, thereafter, admiration.

Georgiana who had, to begin with, mostly been embarrassed when she was the subject of one of the others' jokes, learnt in time to make cautious insinuations, particularly when her sister-in-law made some mistake. Their teacher never made any mistakes when it came to the horses, so there was nothing to be said.

Georgiana admitted that Edward's presence made her both happy and expectant. In the environment she spent her days, it was not until Elizabeth had come into their lives that laughter had become a more regularly occurring feature. Except for Mr Bingley, there had been few persons of their acquaintance that had been light-hearted; Edward was therefore a welcome addition.

As with most of the servants, Edward's dialect was pronounced; sometimes he used expressions that Georgiana did not understand. She liked hearing him speak; his language was unspoiled. Edward had never learnt another language, and was unfamiliar with expressions that were used in a world that only the select had access to.

His ability to smile or even laugh at what other men would regard as defeats or loss of prestige, was something that particularly caught her attention.

She remembered one occasion when she had seen him being reproved by Darcy's steward after having ridden across the newly-sown grass on the Western side of the park. Edward had been sorry for what had happened and volunteered to help repair any damages that had been done. When the irate steward had turned around, Edward has whispered to his horse, Beth, "and when the grass has grown, we'll come back again."

The steward had turned back and shouted "I heard that", upon which he had shook his fist at him and wandered along.

As Edward had guessed that Miss Darcy was a woman who let few people into her life, his happiness was great when he managed to make her laugh. There were few people besides Darcy, Colonel Fitzwilliam, and Elizabeth, whom Georgiana felt she could really relax and be herself with.

When the three were no longer unacquainted, Edward could not hold his jocularity back. To his delight, the ladies did not look disdainfully at him when he occasionally made a joke or even laughed when they made a mistake. On the contrary, it made the company more relaxed and even Georgiana, who had been the first to cause his laughter, had, before the end of the fourth lesson, seemed more at ease.

Elizabeth looked at the brown pile whose contents revealed the ingredients of her horse's latest meal. The aroma of the fresh droppings made her turn her head away, upon which Edward immediately excused himself and removed the remains of the diet which all the horses of the estate consumed on a daily basis.

"Mrs Darcy, I apologise for the discomfort," said Edward. He was himself so used to the smells that it had passed him by unnoticed. At the sight of his master approaching, he left out what he had intended to point out – his own inattention to what had passed.

"The quantity – it was the quantity that surprised me," Elizabeth said in horror. Edward hid a smile and said after a moment, "Horses are big animals."

For a moment, he admitted that it was fascinating how some people only knew the parts of nature they beheld from a distance. But on second thought, he assumed any droppings were removed from Pemberley's inner courtyard before it even had reached the ground. Edward stopped an impulse to ask Mrs Darcy whether there was a special position for this task.

A look at Edward's confounded face made it impossible for Elizabeth to continue with this little charade.

"It is not the first time I have seen something like this – as you will remember, I grew up in the countryside," she said. Edward smiled and helped her into the lady's saddle, and thereafter turned to Georgiana.

Elizabeth took a deep breath of the fresh air and told herself that the feeling of nausea that had come to her on ground level was starting to let go. The dizziness that made her grab at her horse's black mane, she reasoned, was due to the small amount of food she had had this morning.

Chapter 16

Darcy liked, when he had the time, to go down to the meadow to watch the riding lessons; it was a great joy to him to see his sister and Elizabeth get on so well. He had been surprised when Georgiana had been as eager as Elizabeth to learn to ride, but he assumed that it was his wife's lively talk of her impending adventure that had enticed his sister.

One advantage of the riding lessons was that he and Elizabeth could go to the remote places he had not previously shared with anyone. The thought of showing them to his wife made him smile and increase his pace.

Ten or so yards from the stable building, Darcy suddenly spotted Elizabeth who, a few moments after having been put into the lady's saddle, slipped from the horse. His surprise at this unexpected behaviour turned to worry when he saw that she, without alerting the rest of the party, presently left them. Without taking his eyes off her, he ran the final yards to the fence by the manure heap to which Elizabeth had withdrawn.

"Elizabeth, what is the matter?" He cried in horror. Elizabeth looked in surprise at Darcy and took his hand.

"I feel a little better now, but when I was on horseback it felt as though I would fall to the ground." The truth was she had once more been overcome with nausea and felt it necessary to retire to a secluded spot.

"You are not sick, Elizabeth?" Darcy looked at her with eyes so filled with worry that she had to smile. Despite still feeling dizzy, she could not imagine that there was anything seriously wrong with her.

Darcy was not calmed so easily; he had had time to see the colour drain from her face as she sat on horseback. He had felt the blood in his veins run cold when he had envisioned her falling to the ground, never to rise to her feet again. He had not had time to call out to the others and Edward, who had been busy helping Miss Darcy into the side saddle, had not been aware of her predicament.

"No, there is nothing seriously wrong with me, but I fear there will be no riding today," replied Elizabeth.

"It is entirely out of the question," Darcy said and took her into his arms. Elizabeth who saw that he was still deeply worried, smiled and said:

"The manure heap was really an appropriate place to retire to when one feels ill."

She neglected to tell him, however, that this was not the first time she had felt a sudden spell of dizziness, cold sweat and a feeling of falling helplessly to the ground without prior notice.

Darcy looked gravely at her, and together they went up to the house. He was determined to call for a doctor no matter what his wife's opinion of her own state of health was.

He could not help but think of another woman who had suddenly taken ill. His mother had been struck by similar sudden fainting spells, and how that had ended he did not wish to think of. To lose Elizabeth was more than he could imagine; he loved her so deeply he would rather die himself than see her suffer the way his mother had suffered.

Despite being aware that bad memories had activated his strong emotions, Darcy let his behaviour be guided by his worry and fears, rather than the factual state of affairs. He had always prided himself on being a man lead by reason – the number of times he had let his emotions run away with him were easily counted.

Thus it had been until the day he met Elizabeth; after that his actions seemed to be determined by moods which had little or nothing to do with reason. More than once it had scared him that he was capable of acting in a way he had formerly looked down upon in others.

As soon as Darcy had helped Elizabeth take a seat by the open fire and asked the maid to bring her refreshments, he sent for the village doctor. Thereafter he sat by his wife's side, determined to hide his own worry by reading to her from the book they had begun to read together.

Darcy often asked his wife to play the pianoforte or sing to him, which she was happy to do. One night, Elizabeth had, to his horror, asked him to sing a verse for her. He had firmly declined, well aware of his lack of a singing voice.

Persistent as Elizabeth was, he had guessed that she would not be satisfied with this, and neither had she been. On that point he had, however, been immovable: he could not and would not sing. If it was his voice she wanted to hear it would have to be in some other way than song.

One evening as they had sat by the fire, Darcy had surprised Elizabeth by taking out his favourite book and reading to her. Afterwards, he had wondered if it was the extra glass of wine at dinner that had affected his seemingly impulsive decision. The sight of her gaze that beheld him as he read had, however, been encouragement enough for him to start another one after the book was finished.

"To be or not to be." As soon as he had spoken the words, Darcy fell abruptly silent and closed the book.

Elizabeth looked up – she saw that he was worried and thoughtful, and that he had tried to hide it from her. At two prior occasions had she witnessed the worry that now showed in his grave face and few words.

The first time was at Lambton, when he had surprised her in a state of uproar after having read Jane's letters pertaining to Lydia's elopement with Wickham. How thoughtful he had been then; even though at the time, they had not been that well acquainted.

The second time was during their first month as newly-weds, when Elizabeth during one of her walks in the park had become so enraptured by its beauty that she had lost track of time. She had sat down on a tree stump and, at the time when she should have long since been back home, she had been sitting and watching some deer grazing. It was Darcy who had found her; he had become so worried when his wife had not shown up for afternoon tea, that he had himself gone out to look for her.

Elizabeth took his hand and assured him she was feeling better; he nodded but said nothing. Even if Darcy valued his wife's opinion, it was Dr Barnes's judgement that would determine whether he would be calm or not.

Chapter 17

Doctor Barnes had not been able to come the same day as Darcy sent for him. A serious incident had occurred and he could not be spared. Since Elizabeth had rallied, Darcy let himself be persuaded that it would be enough if Doctor Barnes visited them two days later.

If Elizabeth had known in what agony of worry her husband spent the next two days, she would probably immediately have conceded to his suggestion that they send for a doctor from London.

Darcy, who saw that she was not in any immediate danger, chose to suffer the forty-eight hours that remained before help was to be had. He did not want to make her anxious by letting his worry be known. During the remaining two days he had told himself that the danger had lessened, as Elizabeth had assured him that there was nothing wrong with her. What his wife did not know was that he was aware that on more than one occasion she had had to sit down in order not to lose consciousness.

One of Elizabeth's maids had summoned up the courage to go to Mr Darcy and tell of what she had seen. The young girl had grown fond of Mrs Darcy who, from the first, had treated her well, and she had become worried when she saw her feel ill. Despite thinking she was doing the right thing, she had been embarrassed and unsure whether she was out of order. To her relief, Mr Darcy had appreciated her observations and her obvious care for his wife's welfare, even if it had meant an increase of his own worries.

At the sight of the black carriage that rolled into Pemberley's courtyard, Darcy rose to his feet, kissed Elizabeth and went to personally greet the long anticipated visitor.

Doctor Barnes did not correspond to the prevalent idea of how a doctor should look. His outward appearance did rather resemble that of a loafer than an educated man.

When he handed his hat to the butler, a head that lacked all hair was exposed. His height required him to bow his head not to smash it against the doorframe. His gait was uneven due to an ailment he had attracted during his youth. The large nose, the deeply set eyes and the pursed lips made him look severe on first glance.

Darcy's serious face and Doctor Barnes's acquaintance with his character made any unrelated remarks unnecessary.

"Darcy, take me to your wife," said Doctor Barnes after they had greeted each other. The two men were well acquainted, even if Darcy fortunately had not needed to call on the doctor for his own sake before. Darcy was grateful that the doctor took his worry seriously, and that rather than making conversation had asked to be allowed to focus on the matter at hand.

Having been present on those occasions the doctor had been called for the servants' sake, Darcy was not unfamiliar with the equipment he carried with him.

In the left breast pocket of the black waistcoat he was wearing, hung a golden watch that was used to measure the heart rate. The doctor's bag contained a wooden cone for listening to sounds from within the body, a blood-letting set, scalpels of varying sizes, cotton dressings, as well as the most commonly used medicines.

When Darcy opened the door of Elizabeth's chamber, he wished to himself that Doctor Barnes would not have to use the blood-letting set. Darcy remained, at Doctor Barnes's request, outside the room while the examination took place. It was no comfort to him that a maid was present at his wife's side. He could not judge which situation was worst; to stand by the doctor's side and try to interpret from his facial expressions when he found what he was looking for, or to sit outside and imagine the worst.

Not knowing what the verdict would be put him in a morose frame of mind. When he thought about the various illnesses he knew about, his worry increased. Neither fever, pneumonia, plague, bloating or a distasteful disease where the victim bled to death, were curable.

The thought of blood was something that made Darcy shiver, as it reminded him of something he had witnessed in his youth. His father had, during one of their rides, shown him the estate's properties and future possibilities. During this excursion they had become the witnesses of an exceedingly unpleasant incident.

It had started when, through the clatter of hooves and baying of hounds, they heard a sound they had a hard time identifying. In the belief that it was a wounded animal, Darcy's father had first chosen to ignore the sound and let nature have its way. At the sight of his son's reaction and inability to concentrate on what had thereafter been said, he had, however, reconsidered and steered his horse in the direction of the sound. As the distance had decreased it had become apparent that it was a human being's desperate call they had heard. Darcy could still recall the feeling of discomfort at not knowing what they would be confronted with on arrival.

A man had come running towards them as they rode into the clearing. They had fought to catch his words as his breathing was hard and erratic. It became clear, however, that when felling one of the great oaks, one of the workers had had the misfortune of ending up beneath it and his leg had been crushed. Darcy recollected that his father had given the man instructions and thereafter urged his horse further along. He had told his son that if this was the man's final hour, their presence was of the utmost importance.

Darcy did not believe he would ever forget the sight of the accident. The great oak's weight had held the man pinned to the ground and every effort to move it had effected a sound that made even the most hardened of the men turn their eyes away. They had all had to witness his agony without being able to diminish it.

The doctor had arrived on his black horse after what had seemed like an eternity. He had jumped to the ground and taken out the tools from his great leather bag. If the man had cried out before, the sound when the doctor cut into his leg was indescribable. The alcohol the men had poured into him and that, for a moment, had made the man choke, had made his words hard to distinguish, which Darcy thought all present were grateful for. He had heard about amputations before, but had up until then been spared witnessing one with his own eyes.

Darcy could still remember the bone saw's quick movements against the leg, the blood that had coursed like a river from beneath the tree trunk, and the five men's steady grips on the man's upper body that had risen any time one of them loosened their hold. The smell of burning meat had thereafter not only been associated with roasted pig for him, but also with the doctor's singeing of the vessels from which the blood had poured forth.

Against all odds the man had survived not only the fall, but also the amputation and the convalescence. This had made the men respect their master the more, as he had sent for a doctor that was good enough to be his own.

Two months later Darcy had, at his father's request, together with his sister visited the man in his home to notify him that after long and trusty service, he need not be worried about his wife and children's future support.

That Doctor Barnes on this occasion would have to use his bone saw was not something Darcy feared. For a moment he relaxed, the thought of other's misery did undeniably lend perspective to his present situation.

Chapter 18

When twenty minutes had passed and Doctor Barnes had still not come out of the room, Darcy rose to his feet. He intended to enter the chamber and raised his fist to knock on the door. At this very moment, the door was opened and the two men instinctively stepped back as they had been near colliding at the threshold.

When thus the opportunity arose to interpret Doctor Barnes's facial expression, it was from Elizabeth that Darcy sought his answer.

Through the open door he saw Elizabeth tucked into the great bed; she looked at him and a smile spread across her face. Darcy hastened to her side so eagerly he forgot all about Doctor Barnes. A smile could not be a sign that she had been given ill tidings. Darcy sat on the bed by his wife's side.

"Dearest Elizabeth, tell me that all is well with you, I cannot bear the thought of losing you."

"Losing me! Dearest, why would you say such a thing?" she asked and took his hand. Darcy squeezed her hand and beheld her for a while before replying.

"I could not but see all the events of the stable yard, and ever since I have not had a moment of peace, the thoughts have haunted me day and night."

Elizabeth hid a smile as she saw that his worry was real and said quietly:

"Doctor Barnes assured me that nothing ails me and that the attacks of the last weeks are nothing out of the ordinary."

"Attacks! Do you mean to say you have suffered for so long without letting me know about it?" Darcy looked alarmed and stared at Elizabeth.

"It has happened on a few occasions prior to this, but as I saw no reason to worry I let the matter rest," she replied calmly.

Darcy looked shocked and said: "But how could you neglect to tell me of such a grave matter, you know you are dearer to me than anything in the world.

"Which is precisely why I did not want to cause you pain by making you worry about nothing," she replied and smiled.

"But only a doctor can judge this, you must know that, Elizabeth." Darcy was still upset and Elizabeth found it best to hastily tell him the truth.

"This is very true, but in your alarm you have forgotten to ask what Doctor Barnes had to say," she said.

When it occurred to him that for the last minutes he had not paid any attention to Doctor Barnes, Darcy looked ashamed for a moment. It was unfortunate, but understandable, that he in his relief to see that Elizabeth did not seem to have received any severe news, he had forgotten about the doctor he had been so anxious to bring to the scene.

Darcy looked at his wife, and when he saw the familiar glint in her eyes his consternation increased. The expression was the same as she bore when she teased him, which made him uncertain as to whether she was serious or in jest.

"What did Doctor Barnes say?" He finally asked. Elizabeth's gaze was both amused and serious when she replied.

"Doctor Barnes said that for some time to come you will have to show more than your usual forbearance with me and show great consideration, as well as wait upon me in every thinkable way, as my mood may come to show you sides of me you have never before been aware of."

"What do you mean? Elizabeth, tell me at once what is the matter!" Darcy's tone was stern, and Elizabeth, who sensed it was due to his worry, did not dare to tease him any longer, which for a moment had seemed tempting.

"We are with child, Doctor Barnes even suspects there is more than one!" she said instead, with a smile.

"What??" said Darcy and thereafter fell silent, his worry had been so great that he had not even considered that his wife, rather than having a deadly disease, could have come down with anything less serious, and even less that she could be pregnant.

Not that it was in any way improbable. Darcy knew he was lucky to have Elizabeth as a wife. Unlike some men, he did not feel that marital bliss afforded pleasure only to him.

Elizabeth, who had observed him, could not help but laugh at his expression. After a while he turned his gaze back on her.

"Did you just say there will be more than one child?" he questioned her.

"Twins affect their mother's health considerably more than one child; Doctor Barnes seemed quite certain," Elizabeth explained.

"Oh," said Darcy and added, after a moment's silence, "I suppose if it's two boys we will have to divide Pemberley in two."

"I have always believed it is the firstborn's right to inherit the estate, but I can see your reasoning. If the children are so alike that even their parents have difficulty telling them apart, the question of who is firstborn does indeed become complicated," said Elizabeth and smiled. Darcy gazed on her and said in a serious tone.

"I wonder what kind of temperament a mixture of the two of us will produce. I fear our children will be entirely out of control."

"Yes, there is a great risk, with their mother's impudence and their father's stubbornness and pride, they cannot but be unendurable," said Elizabeth with a laugh.

As Elizabeth's predicament did not yet show, they decided to wait a while before making their happy news public. Georgiana was, of course, immediately let in on the secret, and was thereby given an explanation as to why Elizabeth could not continue with their riding lessons. Georgiana received the news with great pleasure, as she was herself a youngest child she had rarely been in close contact with infants.

"Oh, Elizabeth, is it really true there will be more than one?" she said and smiled.

"After what Doctor Barnes said, we have reason to expect so," answered Elizabeth.

"But what if there are more? I heard speak of a woman who had four children at once," Georgiana said in alarm.

"In that case you shall have to help us find names for them all – your brother and I clearly have very differing opinions as to what constitutes a fitting name for a child. You see, he has in all earnestness informed me that he thinks Bartholomew would be a fitting name for a boy,"

Elizabeth could not keep back a laugh. "Bartholomew Darcy, it does indeed sound very honourable, does it not?"

Chapter 19

The effect of Elizabeth's indisposition was that she was forced to give up her riding lessons. Darcy had taken for granted that his sister's lessons would also come to an end; any other alternative had not occurred to him. Georgiana had been as aware as her brother of the impropriety of being alone in the company of a man who was neither her father, her brother or her betrothed. To her delight it was Elizabeth who, through pointing out Georgiana's progress and natural talent, had finally persuaded Darcy to consent to letting the lessons continue for the time being. Taken aback by his wife's argument that it would be a shame to interrupt the learning that had begun, he had given his permission.

"Where is Mrs Darcy?" Edward said thoughtfully, and looked around, the first time Georgiana came alone to the stable building.

"Elizabeth will not be able to join us for a while," she replied and nervously straightened out her blue dress. When she saw Edward's surprised face and noticed he was about to say something, she added quickly: "She will recommence her lessons at a later time."

Her brother had decided that the reason for Elizabeth not being able to continue with her riding lessons was something that would remain within the family. Georgiana hoped that Edward would be content with this answer and not ask any more questions. At a direct inquiry, she knew she would not be able to tell an untruth.

"When?" said Edward who had reached for Othello's reins, which had slipped down along her side. Georgiana's silence made him look up. When he saw her hesitation he put the reins aside and looked straight at her.

"I saw Doctor Barnes was here this week. Is Mrs Darcy ill?" he said with a frown running down his forehead.

Georgiana squirmed; if there was anyone she would have liked to confide in, it was Edward. Finally, she shook her head and went up to the horse by his side. As she didn't know what to say, she grabbed a brush and started stroking Othello over the withers. Edward looked at her in surprise, Miss Darcy had never before taken part in any of the stable chores.

"I will not ask you questions you cannot answer," he said thoughtfully. "Just tell me if Mrs Darcy will be fully recovered." Georgiana, who saw his concerned expression, nodded. With a grip around the brush she drew a long stroke over Othello's muscular breast. The horse shuddered, threw its head and started trampling about the box.

"You're holding it upside down," said Edward and nodded to her. Georgiana looked at the brush, turned it about and found it looked the same at both ends.

"I'm sorry," he said with a smile as she met his gaze. "I couldn't help myself."

It was only the thought of how improper her behaviour would seem that kept her from throwing the brush at him. Edward, who saw her expression, laughed and pretended to duck.

It was not until it was time to go outside that the meaning of Georgiana's prior statement seemed to dawn on him.

"Has Mr Darcy given you his permission to come alone?" he said suddenly and looked around the building.

"No, but I do not think he will mind," said Georgiana unconcerned, and took hold of Othello's reins.

Edward stared at her, she could now see that his eyes were dark brown.

"Wait a moment," he said and stepped into her path. "Do you mean to say your brother does not know you are here?"

Georgiana shook her head and avoided his gaze; it had not escaped her notice that he sounded uncertain.

"I don't know that it is a good idea to go out without Darcy's permission," Edward said seriously and wiped his hands on his trousers.

"What could happen?" Georgiana replied and met his eyes. Without noticing, Edward took a deep breath and sighed.

"Well, I don't know, but I suppose he would not be very pleased if it came to his attention."

Georgiana looked uncomprehendingly at him.

"No, it is possible he would not be pleased, but what does that matter?"

Edward scrutinized his hands and cleared his throat. Her idea of what it meant to be out of favour with Mr Darcy was clearly not the same as his. After a moment's silence he looked at her.

"You are joking with me," he said and pulled his fingers through his dark hair. Georgiana smiled and raised her eyebrows and took a few steps forward so that Edward had to back into the stall to be out of Othello's way.

"Miss Darcy," he called as they came out onto the stable yard. She spun round so quickly it took a few moments for the blue dress material to settle around her legs. Georgiana felt the warmth within become apparent on her cheeks and throat. Every time he said her name she thought how much she liked to hear him say it. She wondered how it would feel to have him call her by her first name.

"Are you quite sure Mr Darcy is aware of…" Georgiana's face made Edward smile and continue the sentence with the words "that I intend to ask your assistance with inspecting Othello's hoof."

"It is possible he would have something to say about you using me as a stablehand," said Georgiana, who had waited to say anything until she was sure her voice would carry. She stroked Othello's mane to the side. "But I will be glad to help you all the same," she said and smiled.

"Very well," said Edward and showed her how to hold the horse's leg in order to facilitate the work. When he supported her arm with his hand so that she could find the right grip, she held her gaze fixed to the black leg that was being inspected.

Edward left her side and positioned himself opposite her, grabbing the hoof in his hands. With her hands around the bent leg she observed his work.

"Is it heavy?" he asked after a while.

"No," she replied although her arms had begun to tremble. The effort she had to put into holding the horse's leg still was nothing compared to what she had seen Edward do in his line of work.

By being early for her lessons, she had witnessed the bringing in of the hay, cleaning out of the stalls and the breaking-in of young horses. Despite it seeming to require more than one man's strength, she had often seen Edward carry out the chores on his own. Unlike some men of her acquaintance, he was not afraid to become sweaty or dirty. If she remembered correctly, he had even said that the pleasure after a day's hard work was worth the effort of the moment.

Since becoming acquainted with Edward, she had begun to re-evaluate her ideas of poverty equating to misery. If riches alone made people happy, Lady Catherine de Bourgh should be one of the happiest people in England. Despite her fortune, however, she did not seem pleased about anything. Perhaps a beautiful house, an over-flowing dinner table, handsome clothes and a fortune was not the only road to happiness. Some people would never hope to partake of that which was the privilege of a select few; perhaps one were, in such cases, forced to find other sources of happiness.

Georgiana admired Edward's joie de vivre and positive outlook, which seemed so strong despite his not having many advantages in life. To her, he was more man than the most well-educated of men. She liked that he was strong and she liked to watch him work, especially when he was not aware of being observed.

Georgiana studied his tanned arms that had become visible as he folded up his shirtsleeves. She also dared to look at the white linen fabric against his chest and the thin leather thong around his neck. In the light of the sun, the dark hair proved to be blacker than she had noticed before.

If I reach out my hand now I can touch him, she thought when she saw the strands of hair that almost obscured his sight.

She wondered how it would feel to be really close to him, closer than when he helped her onto her horse. The feeling was so overpowering that she had to focus on what his hands were working on, in order to collect herself. The thought that Lady Catherine would have found her looks and thoughts improper made her blush.

When Edward looked up to say something their heads collided. His hand went to his forehead. Georgiana, whose hands were busy holding Othello's leg, remained still.

"Were you hurt?" he said and met her eyes.

Georgiana shook her head. "No," she said. "You got the worst knock, I think."

"And a good thing too – one bruise more or less won't matter to me," said Edward and smiled.

Georgiana returned his smile; she knew that when breaking in the stable's newest addition, he had been thrown off and contracted several bumps and contusions.

Chapter 20

Despite Miss Bingley being careful to hide her dislike about Darcy's choice of wife, she could not reconcile herself to him having chosen Elizabeth over her.

Style, elegance, breeding and the sense to behave in a ladylike manner, both in her own house and in larger companies, these were just a few of the qualities she deemed herself in possession of, but found Elizabeth utterly wanting. To make the list longer, Darcy's lack of judgement more evident, and her own vexation greater, Miss Bingley usually added a lack of any valuable acquaintances, fortune, as well as musical abilities or foreign languages.

The one acceptable explanation Miss Bingley could find for Darcy's satisfaction in his choice of wife was to be found in a closer inspection of her former rival's complexion, movement patterns and eating habits. Mrs Darcy's strategy to continually stop to admire the view on walks in the park, sit down to untie the laces of her shoes, and strolling at a leisurely pace, had not escaped Caroline's notice. The scant meals and the increasingly prevalent snacks that were brought forward at the most unexpected of times, confirmed her suspicions. Elizabeth had not succeeded in hiding her pregnancy before Miss Bingley's scrutinizing eye.

The apparently advanced state seemed to suggest that Elizabeth had, at best, saved herself until her name had changed from Bennet to Darcy. Even if Darcy was a gentleman, he was still only a man. If their child had been conceived outside wedlock, the reason was to be found in his wife's character. Qualities like willingness, recklessness and a free spirit had made him listen more to what kind of response this stirred in him, than to what reason stipulated. With time he would come to see how this overlook, or denial, of other failings in Elizabeth's character could threaten him in other, more important, contexts than the bed chamber.

Caroline did not doubt that Darcy was proud to produce an heir. This presupposed, of course, that Elizabeth bore him a son, which, considering the Bennet family history, was not very likely. Elizabeth would in all likelihood bear as many daughters as she herself had sisters.

Another comforting thought was that Elizabeth would grow larger and larger, become more and more ungainly, and be forced to wear garments that masked her condition.

She, on the other hand, would keep her slim figure, move as gracefully as ever, and attract the men's, maybe even Darcy's, eyes. As time wore on and his wife's pregnancy progressed, he would, in all likelihood, come to view her and Caroline in a new light. In time Elizabeth would not be either capable or willing to give him what he demanded. Perhaps he would then welcome another woman in her place. Caroline determined to immediately inform Georgiana that she intended to visit her for a few weeks the coming autumn.

Miss Bingley smiled and felt better at once. "Let us see, should I wear the red or the orange dress?" she asked her reflection.

"The red shows off the fact that I, unlike some, have a waist – but the orange accentuates my décolletage." An annoyed frown appeared as she remembered that pregnant women tended to be more well-endowed in that area. The choice of garment thus fell on a golden dress with dramatic waist shaping, and space to fill out what nature had not endowed her with.

A glance through the window made her aware that Darcy was in the courtyard. It was largely in her own imagination that Miss Bingley received the greater part of the attention, acknowledgement and admiration she insisted others bestowed upon her.

Her unwavering self-confidence had not been smashed by the fact that the man she had secretly looked upon as her husband had chosen another woman. In her vanity, she decided to cross his path, as if by accident. If it did not become immediately apparent to him, he would, given time, come to realise his erroneous choice. The passion would falter. Darcy would regret that he had not valued other qualities in a woman than her willingness to share his lust.

Regardless of who he had chosen to be his wife, this lady would happily have shared his bed. If not from burning desire, then to repay all the advantages that came with the title of Mrs Darcy. That he had chosen a woman without connections could be a sign that his thoughts were improper. Caroline blushed slightly at this thought and felt a frisson of pleasure.

Chapter 21

Darcy smiled as he beheld the two women approaching. Georgiana's gait and movements were, despite her consciousness of them, light and relaxed. The light-heartedness that had appeared during the last weeks became especially apparent when he saw her conversing with Miss Bingley, in whose company she had always before seemed rather taciturn.

The slight smile that was now her constant companion made Darcy aware of how other men might look upon his younger sister. Georgiana was not anymore the shy, quiet, pretty girl she had always been described as, but a young woman whose increasing confidence in herself was mirrored in the mixture of calm and joy that she exuded. This realisation made him at once surprised and melancholy. It was only a matter of time before Georgiana would leave them to create a home of her own. It was both his own and Elizabeth's wish that she would not settle down too far from them, when that day came. This made him go through the neighbouring estates' sons in his mind, in Derbyshire as well as Nottinghamshire.

His musings were interrupted by Miss Bingley's exclamation, which was followed by a blush as she became aware that he had not only noticed her stumble, but also the sound that she had uttered in the sheer alarm at having tripped. Her proud carriage, however, as well as her usually powdered white skin, returned quickly. Miss Bingley once more looked upon the world through eyes that first after having gazed upwards, fell on the object or person in front of her.

Darcy raised his eyebrows in surprise when the two ladies chose to walk across the lawn rather than taking the stone-laid path to his present position. As Elizabeth had once suggested, Miss Bingley was not in the habit of letting her exclusive soles trod uneven ground. Besides which, he had believed they intended to join him.

Humility was hardly a quality he would have ascribed to himself before meeting Elizabeth, and it was not until much later that he had become aware of other people's lack thereof. Despite Miss Bingley's shortage of this characteristic, no man could deny she was both elegant and possessed of clean, noble features. With her height, Miss Bingley was a woman who was noticed in a crowd - her long, slim figure often drew the men's eyes.

The thought of taking Miss Bingley as his wife had, however, never occurred to him. Despite them at one point having shared the same opinion in a number of matters, and her being seen as an eligible match, he had never been able to endure her company in private.

Miss Bingley had never been very adept at, or made much of an effort to hide the expectations she had had. The attention she had paid him had not escaped any of their acquaintances.

Even if Bingley, despite his sister's pressurising, had never meddled in her scheming,

Darcy believed his friend would have been delighted if a marriage had been the final result.

Miss Bingley flushed with shame. Rather than eliciting Darcy's admiration, she had made a fool of herself. She had lost control of her movements. Her foot had slipped, the shoe flown off, and her body tipped forwards so that she had been forced to touch the ground in order not to fall on her face.

The sticky, brown earth disgusted her; despite having wiped her fingers they were all rough. The worst of all was, however, the sound she had emitted. It had not been an alarmed exclamation, but an unidentifiable noise she had not recognised herself. A woman did not sound thus.

To win time and regain her pride, she had chosen to redirect their course. Her humiliation had quickly turned to anger. If they had been inside, her shoes would have clattered against the floor. She was determined to visit her shoemaker and reprimand him for his insufficient heeling. If the heels had been properly attached, she would never have slipped. The gardener, too, deserved a telling-off for failing to remove twenty detached leaves. Perhaps it was also time to change seamstresses. She would never have lost her footing if the dress had not been so long she could have stepped on it.

The lawn willingly let its blades of grass be trampled by the determined steps that led the ladies further and further away from the house of Pemberley.

Georgiana walked on in silence as she waited for the arm she held to relax. Miss Bingley did not notice her preoccupied gaze and covert smile. The soughing of the wind made Miss Darcy turn her eyes upwards to observe the detailed crowns of the trees. The leaves with the weakest holds detached and whirled away. She followed a leaf with her eyes while she looked around.

She was well aware of the area of the park they were presently in. Edward had taken her to this place during yesterday's ride. It was he who had taught her to see what had always been before her with new eyes. He had taken up a leaf and asked her to describe it. Thereafter he had given her the leaf, raised her arm to the sunlight and asked her to describe what she saw from the vantage point of the little larva. At once, the leaf had taken on shifts in colour, contours and texture she had never before noticed.

The wind that once more swept over the grounds made Georgiana close her eyes and listen to the soughing that occurred when thousands of leaves rustled and thereafter shivered on their stems. At the same time, Miss Bingley held onto her bonnet to preserve the position of its feather. The other hand pressed down on the skirt fabric that due to its sheerness had a tendency to be lifted by the wind.

"The winds of Derbyshire are a curse for those women who wish to remain respectable outside of their homes," she muttered through gritted teeth, and regretted that they had left the courtyard that was shielded from wind due to the large stone building. Rather than easing her mind, their detour had increased her vexation.

Miss Bingley's sandalettes were now muddy and wet, added to which she was cold and convinced that her appearance by this time was far from presentable.

Chapter 22

The sight of the young man who suddenly appeared in their vicinity made Miss Bingley jump. The similarly surprised expression on the man's face revealed that he too had been taken aback by their presence. He found himself quickly, however, and greeted them with a smile. Caroline cursed herself for not immediately realising it was one of the servants who had come in their way. This youngster did not even try to hide his delight at what had occurred.

"How dare you prowl about in the park in this way, do you not have a job to take care of?" she sputtered angrily.

The man stopped and a slight blush spread across his face. He still regarded Miss Bingley, but no longer smiled.

Despite Georgiana's hopes that she would from a distance catch a glimpse of Edward, she had been unprepared when he suddenly appeared in front of them. Miss Bingley, who saw her redden and try to collect herself, was in a good mind to tell the young man that she intended to mention his behaviour to Mr Darcy.

Already at a tender age, she had discovered that mentioning the master's name on such occasions was an efficient way of dampening saucy persons who seemed to forget their place and take obscene liberties. It was understandable that Georgiana felt embarrassed in front of her guest, when one of Pemberley's servants displayed such a lack of proper respect for their station in life.

Georgiana's joy at seeing Edward had quickly turned to a wish that they had taken another way and never happened upon him. Miss Bingley's behaviour made her stomach knot and she felt once more the heat in her face. Despite wanting to put her hands in front of her face or look away, she could not take her eyes off Edward and Miss Bingley.

Appalled and paralysed she observed what took place: Miss Bingley's disdainful eyes, her wrinkled nose and demonstrative step backwards; Edward's silence, his inscrutable gaze and acceptance of the situation, despite it doing him an injustice.

Even if the grounds belonged to Darcy, it was Miss Bingley who had steered them into an area where the servants had full access as often as they liked. She dearly wanted to tell him that it was they, not him, who had turned up where they were not expected. In spite of this, she remained silent.

Georgiana was well aware that the situation she found herself in prevented her from speaking freely. The shame over her own behaviour was greater than the shame she felt over her friend. Miss Bingley was, and had always been, insensitive. She herself neglected to do the right thing because she was afraid of the consequences. Georgiana could no longer endure to meet Edward's eyes.

"I apologise if I frightened you. My horse is resting and I took the opportunity of taking a stroll in the meantime," Edward said. His voice was calm and did not reveal whether he was affronted or annoyed.

Miss Bingley straightened her neck and let go of her bonnet whose feather immediately sprung up and reinforced the impression that was a distinguishing feature of her personality. With her eyes trained on the spots on Edward's coat, she said:

"If I remember correctly, the stable building is situated behind the main building." With a nod that could not be misinterpreted, she added: "I expect you can find your way home."

When he did not immediately obey her order, she was, for a moment, frightened. What kind of man did not do as he was told when Miss Darcy was around? The fear soon became anger and Miss Bingley, who was never the first to look away, said: "If I did not express myself clearly before, I want you to leave us alone."

Aghast at the words and the tone they had been delivered in, Georgiana had the outburst Miss Bingley would later that night refer to.

"As you see, Caroline, it is my brother's horse that stands over there among the trees. The breaking-in of new horses takes place away from the others," she said and looked at Edward. Despite her anger, Georgiana saw the importance of remaining calm; never before had the choice of vocabulary that would remain only in her thoughts been so great. To control herself, she had to ball up her fists until she felt her nails leaving little indents in her skin.

The sight of Edward, who despite his grave expression, regarded her calmly made her own anger fade for a moment. Georgiana who still felt hurt for Edward's sake, was convinced that she would herself in a similar situation be devastated. His ability to endure unjust attacks and cynical comments without taking it to heart was further proof of his strength. That he, being one of the younger servants, had been through this several times before did not enter her mind; her brother always treated his servants with respect.

"Edward, be so kind as to take Elizabeth's horse back to the stables," Georgiana said without looking at the lady by her side. She swallowed and added: "Darcy wants to know if the wound is still healing as it should." To tell Edward what to do in front of Miss Bingley made her despise her own actions.

"Since when is Mrs Darcy Elizabeth in front of servants?" said Miss Bingley shortly. "Does your brother know you are so well acquainted with your male subordinates?" she added and looked at her friend.

Georgiana flushed violently but found it best to remain silent. It was in no way remarkable that she herself called Elizabeth by her first name; to do the same in front of Edward was something even her brother would disapprove of. Out of all of their acquaintances, it was Miss Bingley who had seen and pointed this out. Suddenly she saw her own actions through this lady's eyes.

The feeling had been so strong she had reacted immediately. The words had just come; for once, she had not thought through what she was going to say. Miss Bingley's observations were correct; she had not behaved as should be expected of her. Instead, she had acted in a way that none of their acquaintances could fail to take note of. The thought that through her reaction, she had exposed the feelings she harboured for Edward made her immediately turn her gaze away.

She had been careful to hide her looks, daydreams, and the joy she felt in Edward's company, in front of her brother and Elizabeth. It was not until this moment that she realised the seriousness of the situation, and the possible consequences if she did not succeed in this.

Georgiana knew Miss Bingley's character more than well. Even if she did not think she had done anything wrong, her worry soon lapsed into terror. Restlessness, anxiety and nausea made her wish she could escape from it all.

Miss Bingley's gesture of taking Georgiana's arm, clearly signalled that she intended to take the shortest way back, without delay. It was with mixed emotions that Georgiana made her company.

Chapter 23

During the rest of the walk Georgiana did not utter a word. All her energy went into looking unaffected by Miss Bingley's effusions at what had passed. The grip around her arm had tightened. She could not escape.

A beige satin glove against a light yellow sleeve with white laces. Two friends walking side by side. It almost looked as though they were melting into each other. She felt Miss Bingley's well-tended, narrow fingers through the fabric. The diamond ring had turned askew and was chafing against her under arm.

The touch made her queasy, she wanted to shake off the nasty fingers and not have to feel Miss Bingley's arm against her body. She wanted to move freely, she had never liked having people rub up against her person. Especially not persons who were not of her intimate acquaintance. The physical closeness made her unable to escape the piercing scent of eau de cologne that her friend had sprayed onto her décolletage. She turned away and tried in vain to evade the scent she would for ever associate with Miss Bingley.

Miss Bingley's last words had been spoken loud enough for Edward to hear what was being said. Georgiana was convinced this had been her intention. When for a second she had met Edward's gaze, she had blushed with shame. Not even to a servant who had done something wrong did one speak thus. Miss Bingley had been both impudent and disrespectful.

"I have never seen such ill manners. To remain standing in the same place as if we should have moved for his sake." She had let the words hang in the air before she had turned to ascertain that they had not passed unnoticed. Thereafter she had continued in an even shriller note.

"Did you see his face when he spied us? As if he thought it was funny. Not to mention the way he looked at me, straight in the eyes."

For a moment she had regarded Georgiana. Her eyes were both reproachful and covetous. She had paused, pinched her lips and with a supercilious expression added:

"I have never been witness to a servant behaving in such an indecent manner. It would never have occurred at Netherfield. As far as I am aware, Darcy has never had any trouble with his minions before. But there have been considerable changes during the last year. When the man of the house is not at home, someone else is in charge."

To catch her breath she pretended to regard a flower that had peeked out of the ground in front of them. Georgiana had wanted to stomp the little plant, step on it and crush it.

"That is why a man's choice of wife can never be too well considered," she had said finally and looked significantly at Georgiana.

She had searched her eyes every so often, and every time her voice had toned down. While Miss Bingley's anger subsided, Georgiana's discomfort increased.

"I abhor you," she had thought, and flinched at the idea that her eyes had revealed what she felt. When she had reached out her hand to accept one of the yellow flowers her arm had trembled. She knew what awaited as soon as she was alone.

As soon as they had made their way back to the house, Georgiana excused herself and headed off to her room. When she saw that there was no one in sight she ran up the stairs; she could not escape fast enough. After having confirmed both once and twice that the door was properly locked, she sank down along the wall, pulled up her knees and held her head.

Her tears were silent: she never cried so that anyone heard. She did not know why, it had always been thus. She was the one who comforted, not the one who was comforted or even admitted to others that she had been hurt, or was sad or in despair.

When she thought of Edward, how much she liked him, how she had behaved, how he must feel and how she herself felt, her crying intensified. A passer-by would have been able to hear a muffled sniff if he or she stopped to listen intently, but this was highly unlikely. For a moment she wished someone would come by, discover and hold her. At the same time, she wanted to be alone with her pain. Even if someone had been by her side it would not have lessened. As with the pain from a blow, a fall or a broken leg, grief could not be shared. People could imagine, recognise, and at best, understand. Even if they offered comfort, she would be alone in the feeling, as well as the agony of putting up with it and enduring it.

It could never be as she wished. She was well aware that she, as other people, had a choice. If she followed her emotion it would cost her everything and there would be no turning back. Surprise, terror, accusations and exile was what she could expect. She would be regarded as lacking in judgement, discretion, taste and common sense. Because she felt, because she liked and wanted to be close to a person who was not seen as right, good enough or appropriate for her.

Her behaviour was unforgivable, she had let Edward be humiliated without interfering. She could have stood up for him, she could have told off Miss Bingley. They had been in her, not Miss Bingley's, grounds.

She should have acted differently. Georgiana pressed a hand against her belly to dampen the dull ache. Her eyes welled up anew. She drew a breath to clear her airways that were already clotted with tears. Her throat burned, it ached when she swallowed.

It was not right, it could not be right that one should deny oneself thus. Why did she have the ability to feel and experience such pleasure, if at the end of the day it was denied to her. That it was herself, through her own decision, who would ensure that this was the case, was too painful to think on.

Chapter 24

When Elizabeth returned to her chamber she immediately espied the letter that lay on the writing desk; the handwriting could not be mistaken and Elizabeth sighed. She wondered what kind of thoughts this letter would contain. With every letter she had received, her friend's admiration for Mr Andrew seemed to increase, and Elizabeth could not but wonder how it would all end. Despite Charlotte's insisting that she was content with her situation, Elizabeth did not feel convinced.

The words spoken, but also what was not expressed but only vaguely detected by the reader of the letter, supplied another view of reality than what Charlotte intended. If Elizabeth had had reason to worry before she read the letter, she was no less calm after having read Charlotte's third letter.

Dearest Lizzy,

Yet again I ask your pity and patience by sharing my innermost thoughts. Despite my thoughts and actions being such that I should now no longer speak of them, I cannot alone harbour all these emotions. As I mentioned in my last letter, I sometimes allow myself to daydream, but I admit that it happens more often than is proper. My thought has also turned to whether another marriage would have given me a better chance of happiness. I do, however, admit that had it not been for my marriage to Mr Collins, I would not have made the acquaintance of Mr Andrew, and thus not have discovered how attraction can affect a person's thoughts and actions.

My own reaction makes me remember how your husband acted when you visited us at the vicarage that first time. Do you remember how Darcy immediately visited at his arrival to Rosings, and how he sometimes came unannounced? This eager, restless and evident seeking to be in the company of the person one desires, cannot but be detected by an observant eye. Fortunately, few people are attentive to that which does not directly concern themselves.
The knowledge that Mr Andrew will be present at some event can be felt in my body hours before we meet. My cheeks glow, an anxiety can be seen in a slight worry on my part, and my eyes seem to take on a shine that is characteristic of a woman in love. It became apparent to me when Miss Croft at a social event exclaimed – Charlotte, you are positively glowing!

My preparations for such events attest in a high degree to my emotions. Never before have I taken such care when choosing and trying on the dress I intend to wear for the evening. The colour that will best emphasize my blue eyes, the cut that will accentuate the parts I am most proud of, all this and more is carefully considered before I finally make my choice.
My wardrobe has after a few town visits been fortified with three exquisite dresses. For

the first time I have chosen colours that through their intensity immediately call attention to them. It was a pleasure to walk through the shops and feel the materials, observe the colours and fantasize about whether or not I would look best in the mulberry or apricot dress. Both suited me very well, and to Mr Collins's horror I arrived home that day with two dresses; but when I had explained that only the best was good enough to wear at Lady Catherine de Bourgh's dinner parties, he readily agreed and encouraged me to immediately acquire another one.

By varying my wardrobe at the occasions Mr Andrew visits Rosings, I hope he shall discover something new and attractive about my person. It is no secret that a woman first attracts a man's attention through her exterior, whereupon he notices her personality.

It does not take much to make my night complete: a few minutes' worth of conversation with Mr Andrew, a smile intended for me, or the most desirable – that I have made him laugh through some story or commentary.

Whether Mr Andrew suspects my feelings for him shall remain unsaid, our eyes meet on more than one occasion during an evening. This becomes especially evident at dinner when we are often seated opposite each other at the table. At board games I try intentionally to take up a similar position that again will give me the pleasure of meeting Mr Andrew's eyes. What the expression in his eyes mean I cannot say with any certainty, I do not know either whether he looks on other women in this way.

What I cannot deny is that Mr Andrew looks at me, his gaze steady and sometimes lingering, so that on more than one occasion I have been the one forced to look away. Not because it has been my wish to do so, but for fear that someone will see the admiration that shines through my eyes.

Despite my anxiety, I should mention that I have become more and more relaxed in Mr Andrew's company; his comments and treatment of other people have long since awoken my respect and devotion. In his character there is a goodness which compels Mr Andrew never to speak disparagingly about his fellow human beings. In these times, when both ladies and gentlemen of the wrong class are objects of condemning commentary, Mr Andrew's sense cannot but invite admiration from the lady who holds him dear.

Our intercourse, at those times we have played at board games, dined or danced together, has been marked out by a genial mood, where I dare to suggest we have felt at home in each other's company. My quest for his presence, by offering my company at a board game, has been received with delight. Mr Andrew has also willingly supplied me with information on such subjects where I have to my consternation been unenlightened.

Even if these thoughts and occasions give me pleasure, I am of course tormented by the same, as they remind me of the unseemliness of a vicar's wife desiring a man other than her husband, even in thought.

Sometimes I wish that Mr Andrew would suddenly notify us of his engagement to an unknown lady; in this way it would be easier for me to move on and tell myself that my dreams are unattainable. At the same time I am, selfishly, happy that he is not engaged, or seemingly attracted to any other lady; some of his gazes fall, thus, on me instead.

It is high time to finish this letter whose contents have surely made you catch your breath more than once. Dear Lizzy, thank you once more for you unwavering friendship and your patience.

Yours faithfully,
Charlotte Collins

Elizabeth folded up the letter and gazed upon the lake that, untouched by human destinies, glittered when the sun reflected its beams on its surface. Charlotte's situation seemed to have changed character over the course of the last weeks; from having been attracted to Mr Andrew's exterior it was now evident that her friend was infatuated with the man in question. Whether Mr Andrew returned any of Charlotte's regard was not clear, but it was obvious he liked to look at her – only Charlotte herself could interpret what his looks meant.

How ill-conceived must not Charlotte's choice of husband now seem to her; that she, after having fallen in love, could be happy in her situation at the vicarage was beyond Elizabeth's understanding.

That Charlotte would elope with another man was not very likely; her friend was much too reasonable to risk what she knew with certainty she had, for something as insecure as a relationship with a strange man. Such a measure would mean that Charlotte, for a moment of intense happiness, risked being left and thereby devastated: financially, emotionally and socially. Despite her dreams about Mr Andrew, Elizabeth did not believe Charlotte was prepared to gamble her whole existence.

As her friend, she believed that an announced engagement between Mr Andrew and another lady could help Charlotte regain her balance; Elizabeth hoped, therefore, that this would soon come to pass.

A knock on the door made Elizabeth jump; after having hastily put the letter into the desk drawer and gathered her wits, she opened the door.

"I am sorry to interrupt your letter-writing, but I could not fail to observe that the hour of our guests' arrival is imminent," said Darcy and smiled.

The letters, whose contents had taken up Elizabeth's thoughts, had made her for a long while unaware of the hour; she was thus shocked when Darcy told her what time it was. Darcy saw her face and said:

"The contents of your letter must really have captured your interest; if I were not so secure in your love I would almost have suspected that you had a secret admirer." Elizabeth laughed and wrapped her arms around her husband.

"Unfortunately I must admit that you are right – the letter was from the vicarage. Mr Collins admits he still harbours deeper feelings for me and wonders if deep down I do not regret that I once rejected his proposal."

Darcy's laughter made Elizabeth smile, apart from liking to see her husband happy and knowing that she was the reason for his felicity, she was also glad that other people nowadays regarded him as less grave and enclosed.

Chapter 25

It had long been decided that Georgiana was to spend a few weeks in London. Darcy had, a few months earlier, received a long letter from Mrs Alcot wherein she invited his sister to spend some weeks in her company. Mrs Alcot's house was situated in the most distinguished part of the city, just next to the big theatre. Furthermore, Mrs Alcot assured him that Miss Darcy would be introduced to many eligible young men who had both fortune, judgement and wit. Darcy, who treasured all of the above characteristics, and who was well acquainted with Mrs Alcot, had no qualms about letting his sister stay with her. He had thus immediately given his consent, and the date for the commencement of her journey had been set for two months later.

Georgiana was well aware that this was her last riding lesson together with Edward. It was not until now, when she was on the cusp of leaving Derbyshire, that she realised how happy she had been for the last months and to what degree she would miss all that she associated with Pemberley.

Elizabeth, who had since her arrival made Pemberley so alive; her brother, who was always so thoughtful and protective; the beautiful environment around the lake and the fields; the brown mare who had become Georgiana's favourite horse. Most of all she would come to miss Edward.

The society in the circles she would move in the coming weeks was so unlike what she had become used to for the last couple of weeks that she could not look forward to what was to come. Georgiana knew very well that Mrs Alcot was an amiable lady who only wanted what was best for her, but she never felt at her ease in distinguished society where the ladies were expected to entertain the other guests with song and music. Neither did she, like other women, delight in the opportunities for courtship that such occasions meant. Her shyness brought with it a feeling of discomfort rather than excitement.

Georgiana thought about her brother and the time when Elizabeth, together with her uncle and aunt, had come to dine with them at Pemberley for the first time. Darcy's eyes when he had beheld Elizabeth that night had shone with happiness she had never before seen in him.

His letter several months later, wherein he had announced his engagement to Elizabeth, had likewise expressed complete joy. After their marriage, she had been astounded to see his former reserve, restrain and correct behaviour ease up, and also how he sometimes even allowed himself to jest in a way similar to his wife. With all her heart, Georgiana wished that she too would one day become the object of a man's affections in the way that Elizabeth was to her brother.

Despite her lower position in life, he had taken Elizabeth to be his wife, for the simple reason that he loved her.

The difference between the two sisters-in-law's situations was that Elizabeth could really be sure of Darcy's love, while Georgiana was forced to meet a man of her own birth and rank to be able to trust in this. Despite only being nineteen, she had already, in much too cruel a way, been made aware of the falsehood that a young woman with a large fortune risked to meet, in the form of young men looking only for the comfortable life such a match would bring them. These thoughts made her deeply depressed – her history with Wickham had made her doubt many men.

Since Miss Georgiana Darcy belonged to one of the wealthiest families in England, she seldom met men who could disprove the conclusions she had drawn much too early in life. In the company of Edward it was different; their situations were so markedly different that she after a while had been able to feel relaxed with him.

Darcy commented once on the positive effect the riding lessons and the company of horses had on his sister. Did not Elizabeth agree with him that Georgiana's eyes held a new glow, and that her behaviour had become easier, even in others' company than their own?

Elizabeth did not say anything but she wondered to what degree this change was only due to the horses. An infatuation seldom did any harm; often it meant instead exactly the changes in mood that Darcy had just pointed out; but Elizabeth hoped for Georgiana's sake that this infatuation was not anything serious. Not that she believed Edward was anything like Wickham – she felt intuitively that the former was well aware of his position in life, and would not abuse the trust the Darcy family had put in him.

A match between the two was naturally unthinkable. Despite Darcy having married below his station, Elizabeth came from one of the most distinguished families in Merryton.

A stable master and his master's sister were, however, as far apart as it was possible on the societal ladder. Elizabeth chose not to tell her husband what she thought she had noticed between them.

Chapter 26

Several hours after Edward had begun his day's work, Georgiana went in the company of Darcy to the stable master's lodge. They walked side by side across the lawn. Several of the servants passed and greeted them with a bow or a curtsy. Darcy nodded to the maid-servants and the gardener. Georgiana did not see them.

She had not seen Edward since their meeting in the park and she wondered how he would react when they saw each other again. The closer they came to the stables, the more her worry rose. Although they were strolling at a leisurely pace, she was already glowing. Her heart beat quickly and the pining ache in her stomach grew. She kept her eyes trained on her feet. Was it fear she felt? How could she be afraid when there was nothing to fear? Perhaps it was the uncertainty about what was to come. She did not know yet what would happen. She pushed away the thought of how much she liked Edward; at the moment, it hurt too much to think about.

Darcy's conversation passed her by, and it was not until he stopped and demanded her attention that she really saw that he was there.

"Are you feeling well?" He asked gravely. Her gaze had been vacant and she did not appear to have heard anything he had said. She nodded.

"If you are too tired to go for your ride, I will let Edward know," he said and searched her pale face. She shook her head, looked him in the eyes, and answered quickly:

"There is nothing the matter with me." As he still looked doubtful, she turned the conversation onto a subject that she knew would divert his attention.

"When does Mrs Alcot expect me?" As she had predicted, her brother immediately seemed easier.

"Already a week ago. She protested when she heard that you could not come until the third. She had intended to commence your stay there with a ball that was held on the second," he said and smiled. Georgiana nodded. It took some effort to pretend to be interested in his talk of the impending visit to London. All she could think of was Edward.

She saw him before they had come up to the building. He had taken out the two horses and stood next to them. Darcy nudged her and nodded in Edward's direction. Both the animal and Edward stood perfectly still; his hand stroked the white star on the horse's forehead. The large animal lowered its head and closed its eyes. Edward leaned forward and rested his forehead against its body.

No one could doubt that he gave the horses his full attention and care. Georgiana had heard rumours that he slept in the stables when there were foalings.

Her stomach lurched, but she neither could nor wanted to take her eyes off him. Like the horse's black mane, Edward's dark hair shone in the sunshine. He had gathered it in a leather thong that made the hair rest against his neck. She liked when he did this; it allowed her to see more of his face.

Then he noticed them. She felt her heart beat against her tightly laced stays. Georgiana regarded Edward as he greeted her brother, thereafter it was her turn to receive his greeting. She swallowed hastily when she noticed that he looked at her in the same way that he always did. He did not appear to be either angry or disappointed.

The worry she had felt was gone; she was surprised at how quickly it was overtaken by relief. It was as though the last few hours had not existed. All that counted was the joy she felt. By now she knew him well enough to be able to trust her impression. His treatment of her gave her courage. She wanted to talk to him about what had taken place in the park, explain why she had acted the way she did. Ask his forgiveness.

Georgiana waited impatiently for her brother to return to the house and leave them alone. Darcy's unexpected suggestion of accompanying them took her completely by surprise. She quenched an impulse to ask why when she realised how strange it would sound.

Her brother had always been satisfied to walk in the park or along the meadows. It had become a habit they had all grown accustomed to. Georgiana's and Edward's eyes met hastily before he turned to Darcy:

"Sir, give me a few minutes and I will immediately prepare your horse for you."

Georgiana looked at her brother and blushed as she found herself wishing he had chosen another day to join them. She realised that neither she nor Edward would be able to stop Darcy from doing what he intended. There were neither argument nor reason for him not to join them.

After saddling Darcy's horse, Edward returned seemingly unperturbed, which, however, was not the case. Like Georgiana he was well aware of his inability to turn the situation in the direction he wished. For the first time, Darcy's immediate presence confounded him. Edward was such a stranger to this emotion, he decided to do everything to behave as correctly as possible.

The ride commenced in silence with Darcy taking the lead, followed by Georgiana and finally Edward on his brown mare, Beth, whose name came from Edward's father having read Shakespeare's tale of Macbeth. Beth, who since she was a foal had been cared for by Edward, was one of the calmest and most stable of Pemberley's horses. Since her first riding lesson, Georgiana had been allotted the origin of this happy predisposition, in Beth's mother, Othello.

"I see what Elizabeth has told me is true – you have become an excellent rider," said Darcy and looked appreciatively at Georgiana. The joy she felt at her brother's praise, and the hope that he would thereby observe what a good teacher Edward had been, was eclipsed by his next sentence:

"Your stay at Mrs Alcot's comes at a happy time, as I think Edward will agree that you are no longer in the need of any riding lessons."

The words that had been meant to please both his sister and Edward had rather the opposite effect. Edward looked quickly at Darcy, taken aback by the sudden realisation these words had brought on. The information that he had succeeded in his teachings was received with mixed emotions.

The naivety of his former presumptions about continued riding excursions together was suddenly obvious. To be a riding teacher was one thing; to ride together for pleasure was the privilege of the fiancé, not the stable master.

"Miss Darcy has become an excellent horsewoman," was all that Edward could bring himself to say. Darcy nodded approvingly; Edward could not judge whether it was in approbation of the answer he had received or the observation that had just been made.

"I would really rather stay here at Pemberley... Especially now that the surroundings are so pleasant and I have just learnt to ride," said Georgiana, and blushed when she saw Darcy's surprised face.

"It is evident from Mrs Alcot's letters that she looks forward to your arrival and will arrange your stay in the city admirably. London is undoubtedly an environment that will differ from Pemberley. But I am convinced that Mrs Alcot can arrange a trip to a neighbouring country estate if you ask her," Darcy said comfortingly.

"Pemberley is at its most beautiful in the summer; on that matter we can agree, but a city too has its advantages," said Edward, without feeling fully convinced as he had never been to London. Georgiana's sceptical face made him add what he knew to be true:

"Apart from Mr and Mrs Darcy and the guests that will on occasion visit Pemberley, there are only Mrs Reynolds, the kitchen and chamber maids, and the gardeners here. A city undoubtedly offers more variation in terms of society," Edward said and smiled.

"Well spoken, Edward – a change in society is needed, and for you, Georgiana, a stay in the society outside of Derbyshire is of particular importance," Darcy added thoughtfully. Georgiana understood very well what her brother hinted at, but could not, however much she wished it, give him the reply he expected of her.

"But that is exactly it," said Georgiana and gave all her attention to Othello's ears that for a moment had pointed backwards. "I do not feel comfortable in the society of people who are unknown to me."

Edward regarded her for a long time before he said:

"Many are apprehensive about meeting new people, but remember that every one you know today were once strangers to you."

Darcy, who was unused to hearing Edward offer his opinions in other matters than concerned the horses, scrutinized him. The stable master expressed himself in a way that was uncommon among the servants; but on further thought, the employees were seldom given the opportunity to express their opinions in general matters. Neither they, nor their employer, expected this.

Edward, who had been listening to Georgiana, had for a moment forgotten Darcy's presence; this gentleman's look had, however, quickly reminded him of the situation. He abruptly fell silent, well aware of having overstepped the limits of his station. That Mr Darcy had witnessed the relaxed dialogue that normally took place between him and Miss Darcy immediately put him on his guard.

Edward had not forgotten Mr Wickham's hasty retreat from Pemberley a couple of years earlier. Even if no one knew for certain the reason for this, there were stories of the man in question having shown Miss Darcy more attention than her brother saw fit. If Mr Darcy had rejected his father's protégé, who had been as close to him as a brother while growing up, then Edward did not doubt the outcome for his own part, should he fall into disfavour with his master.

Beth reacted instinctively to her rider's tensed leg muscles and increased her speed from a leisurely to a steady pace. In an effort to calm both himself and the mare, Edward placed his hand on its shoulder. The horse's pulse seemed to beat as quickly as his own.

The sight of Georgiana's confused face reminded him of Coyle's words. The steward had, on one particularly irate occasion, said that Edward's lack of consideration would one day lead him astray. It was the first time Edward himself had questioned the characteristic that he had seen as his greatest asset. What use was his spontaneity, if he risked putting both himself and those he cared for in jeopardy?

Georgiana anxiously awaited her brother's reaction to the straightforward communication that had taken place. It was acceptable to exchange a few words with the servants if the subject pertained to their work tasks; to converse in a deeper sense was not.

The realisation that she had revealed her private fears and thoughts in front of one of the servants suddenly became clear to her. Her greatest fear in respect to Darcy's reaction was the fact that she had, without reflecting over it, spoken to Edward as to an equal.

The conversation during their earlier rides had gradually gone from pertaining merely to the horses; to neighbouring subjects like other interests; to finally encompass more topics than Georgiana could remember ever having shared with any person. After a few minutes' silence without any reprimands from her brother's side, she relaxed. Darcy seemed to have his attention trained on a figure at the outskirts of the park.

"I think that Georgiana is referring to the up-coming season and the people she will be introduced to there," Darcy said suddenly and looked straight at Edward. Neither of the two to whom the comment was made said anything. Darcy interrupted their thoughts by turning around and steering his horse straight towards them.

"Edward, escort Miss Darcy back to the stable building where I will meet you as soon as I have exchanged a few words with Coyle."

"Certainly, Sir," said Edward, amazed by his master's sudden and unexpected decision.

The silence that fell was intentional as well as desirable to both parties. Since Darcy had withdrawn, Edward was once more free to converse with Miss Darcy. However, the words that had been spoken gave him no peace of mind. Not until the distance between the first rider and the two remaining behind had increased further, did Georgiana say:

"I felt insecure in your presence as well, at the beginning, despite our different backgrounds."

Edward regarded her as he thought over his reply. By now he was all too aware that he would, in the future, have to watch himself in the company of others. Before he replied he turned to assure himself that Darcy was out of earshot.

"Personally, I did not feel the least bit of nerves over spending several hours alone with you. Particularly not when I thought about who would be held responsible if there were any incidents," he added and smiled. Georgiana smiled back but said nothing.

"Well, if we are to be serious; what is the purpose of your visit to London?" said Edward gravely.

"The usual, I expect: go to parties, exhibit myself and be scrutinized and judged and forced to play the pianoforte to strangers at gatherings." Georgiana finished with a sigh. The sigh had not been intentional but was her body's spontaneous way of underlining her words.

Edward beheld her and was for a moment struck by how different their worlds were. More often than not, he chose to disregard these differences. Not because he did not see them, but because their accordance, confidence and agreeability in each other's company made him feel happy.

"I am sorry to smile, despite having received the impression that the situation holds little enticement for you. But to me the idea of parties and gatherings does not sound all that unpleasant," he said and discreetly slowed his horse down further.

"Yes," said Georgiana and smiled, "to entertain others would most likely not be a problem to you."

"My opinion is that the response from the listener is that which gives pleasure. Is that not how it is when you play?" he asked.

"I mostly feel uncomfortable by all the attention being focused on me," Georgiana said and blushed suddenly.

At times she wondered what Edward thought of her. To put up with being the focus of everyone's attention when it made her awkward seemed suddenly a low price to pay for being in the grandest environments, eating the finest foods and listening to the best musicians, as well as conversing with interesting personalities. To complain about such matters to someone who had never set foot in a ballroom seemed an utter display of selfishness and ingratitude. She reddened and looked away.

"Think about someone you like and play to that person; see the rest of the company only after you have finished playing," said Edward.

Georgiana looked up in surprise. "I have never thought about that," she said thoughtfully. "I have only seen everyone and thought of how unbearable I find it to have them all looking at me."

For a moment she imagined the happiness she would feel if Edward was among the company; if that were the case, she would be more than happy to play. The knowledge that this was something that would never happen was not the only reason she felt herself capable of this.

Since their first meeting, Edward's presence had made her feel safe and frivolous. One of the things she admired most about him was his way of speaking to her like a person. Most other people chose their words, gestures and actions with regards to it being Miss Darcy rather than Georgiana they were in the presence of. Before she could speak, Edward said: "I will miss our conversations."

Chapter 27

Georgiana had not responded to his statement about expecting to miss their conversations. Edward did not imagine, either, that the loss for her part would be close to what he himself experienced. The truth was that he appreciated Georgiana's company more than he wanted to admit to himself. Through her, he had learnt a great deal about the upper classes and he was amazed at how mild and humble she was, despite living in such luxury. Georgiana had shown him a new side of himself; Edward had, for the first time, discovered the joy of getting to know another human being in the deeper sense and not just in the relaxed, superficial way he was accustomed to.

In the village he was known for being a happy man who always managed to lure people into laughter, and it was commonly known that he spread good humour wherever he went. Despite this, he had sometimes felt lonely without knowing why.

In the beginning he had told himself that the fact that they came from such different worlds decreased the tension that would otherwise have been likely to arise between two young people of the same age. Neither Edward, Georgiana, nor any other person of their respective acquaintances had, when planning the riding lessons, had any reason to fear that the two would develop any stronger attachment for each other. If the thought had been put forward, it would have been seen as improbable, absurd, and even laughable. It was precisely the improbability of the thought that enabled them, after having become acquainted, to speak to each other without continually thinking about the rules that regulated the relationships between men and women. Because of this, they had also discovered the pleasant feeling of being accepted and liked by a person for just who they were. They had spoken about everything except this.

Edward tried to convince himself that what happened was for the best – for what good could come of him becoming too attached to Miss Darcy? That he already liked her more than was proper was something he tried to forget about as well as he could. He would never dream of revealing his feelings; he had nothing to offer her and their situations in life were as far removed from each other as was possible.

No one could deny that one or two defied the conventions and married a man or a woman of a somewhat lower standing. The consequences of such a love match, however, left neither the parties nor their surroundings unchanged. A partner of a lower standing was bad enough, no position in society at all was unthinkable.

To voluntarily lower oneself from the rank one was born into usually meant a loss of respect, distinction and social standing.

The one who had managed to marry above his or her station in life was met with distrust, rejection and envy.

When he caught himself thinking along these lines, he used to remind himself of the unlikelihood of Miss Darcy seeing him as anything else than he was: Pemberley's stable master. He had always been and always would be their underling.

Despite this, he could not keep himself from wondering if, under different circumstances, he would have been a man to awaken her interest and love.

They rode in silence, each one preoccupied in their own thoughts, both well aware that every step brought them closer to the stable building.

Edward found this last lesson, which due to Georgiana's growing proficiency mostly came to resemble a riding excursion, much too short. He did not know when she was to return to Pemberley, and even when this occurred the likelihood of her having the same inclinations was not very high. The regret at the amount of time that would pass before he would see her again had been replaced by a sense of futility at the realisation that this would probably never happen again.

Georgiana saw the stable building closing up with a sense of sadness and excitement. Apart from the picture she had drawn of Edward in secret, she had decided to bring another memory to recollect during her stay in London. Whether this would make her time there easier or make the longing greater, she could only speculate upon. Despite the risk of the latter, Georgiana had decided to go through with what she had determined to do already at the outset of their excursion.

When she gave Edward her hand for him to help her down from the saddle, he looked at it for a while before he grasped it. Apart from the strength of his hand, she also experienced the warmth of his skin and the caution of his touch.

The upper classes wore their gloves regardless of weather, and after what Edward had heard from the maids, even indoors. Georgiana's removal of them had not passed him by unnoticed. He had liked feeling her skin against his, even if it had only been for a short moment.

"Miss Darcy…" Edward said, at the same time as Georgiana began her sentence "Edward…".

Before either of them had time to go on, the unmistakeable sound of hooves could be heard from the black stallion that appeared around the corner with its rider. Georgiana blushed as she once more wished her brother had been elsewhere.

"Good to see you are already here, I should have been more observant of the time," said Darcy and alighted from his horse.

"Elizabeth will be wondering what has become of us," he added and handed Edward the reins.

"I would like, once more, to mention the skills my sister has acquired as a result of your efforts. Your father has succeeded well in his task to make you a worthy successor of his good name," said Darcy and smiled.

"Sir, I am pleased to hear that," Edward replied and accepted the reins.

"Georgiana, we will have to make haste. Elizabeth has something she wants to speak with you about," Darcy said and gestured for his sister to follow him.

There was no time to for goodbyes, no words to say in confidence. Georgiana looked at Edward and thereafter at Darcy – she knew she had to do as she was told.

When Edward saw Georgiana wander away towards the lit house, he wished for the first time in his life that he was someone other than the stable master at Pemberley – or that Georgiana was someone else than Mr Darcy's sister. He had always been content with his life and had never felt any envy towards those who were wealthier. Even if he lived simply, he never wanted for anything. Now he felt a strong wish to be close to the woman he could otherwise only observe from a distance, even for just a couple of hours.

In his mind he had tried to find any acceptable reasons for Mr Darcy to defy etiquette and moral dictates and let them ride together in the future too. He was, however, well aware that his feelings clouded his judgement in this matter and he had not mentioned these thoughts to Darcy, whose opinion he did not even have to guess at.

The love he felt and that he had, for the longest time, tried to convince himself was a mere infatuation, he was no longer able to deny.

Georgiana's choice to not only present him to Miss Bingley, but also to justify and defend him, had given him hope that she respected and maybe even thought well of him. At the same time as this pleased him more than anything, the pain was equally great.

Chapter 28

Georgiana sighed and dried her tears, whereupon she went down into the drawing room determined not to let Darcy and Elizabeth see her unhappiness. This was her last night in Derbyshire and they would spend it at Mr Wilkins's who had invited them to a masked ball.

Darcy and Mr Wilkins had spent the greater part of their time at university together, and a close friendship remained between them.

Mr Wilkins was tall and well built, and the minute he stepped into a room all the ladies' eyes were on him. His facial features were prominent and more than one lady had compared his visage with the common description of Egyptian pharaohs. According to the findings and paintings the explorers had made, the pharaoh was an uncommonly handsome man. Mr Wilkins's shiny black hair, the light brown tone of his skin, which was not due to the sun, as well as his hazel eyes, made him attractive to many.

Unfortunately, the women's interest seldom lasted. When they had, to their delight, been introduced to Mr Wilkins, they soon found that he hardly spoke to them. Except for a few words and nods in response to their questions, he did not speak unless it was absolutely necessary. The lady in question soon felt uncomfortable and humiliated by the lack of interest he showed in her and hastily found some reason to absent herself. Most young ladies with a reasonably pleasant exterior almost always expected a certain encouragement, and to be ignored in this way hardly made them inclined to think kindly of the man in question.

If the vain women had only shown some patience and not demanded instant acknowledgement, the reason for Mr Wilkins's taciturnity would soon have become apparent. To his great chagrin, Mr Wilkins stuttered and therefore often chose to remain silent among those he did not know. The knowledge that he was among friends who did not patronize him or choke back a giggle whenever he repeated himself, made him stutter considerably less in their presence.

Darcy had on several occasions hoped that Georgiana and Mr Wilkins would take a liking to one another, and he had brought them together whenever the opportunity arose.

Mr Wilkins and Georgiana understood each other well as they both felt insecure due to the scrutinizing and evaluation that constantly took place in the circles they moved. Despite soon becoming fast friends and searching out each other's company, there was never any attraction between them.

Darcy was happy to find they exchanged letters. What were assumed to be love letters were, however, rather two friends' honest confidences. Georgiana knew all about Mr Wilkins's despair at ever finding a partner and Mr Wilkins knew about Georgiana's feelings toward Edward.

The idea of the masquerade was not just to entertain the party and increase the tension among those gathered, but gave Mr Wilkins a chance to blend into the crowd, for once. The first time he had been to a masquerade he had, to his joy and astonishment, discovered that behind a mask he could converse freely with the ladies. Of course his troubles had not disappeared but made themselves felt, even during the masked ball, on more than one occasion. The feeling of unrestraint had, however, made a lasting impression upon Mr Wilkins and he had decided to arrange his own masked ball as soon as he had the opportunity to do so.

This was Elizabeth's first ball since she had become Darcy's wife and she felt happy, as well as proud and excited. Happy and proud to be chosen by the man she had come to love so dearly. Excited to be meeting Mr Wilkins, of whom Darcy often spoke.

A masquerade was an exciting event, but Elizabeth could not help feeling sorry that Mr Wilkins had to hide behind a mask in his own home in order to feel comfortable. Her thoughts were interrupted when Georgiana put on the white, pearl-strewn mask with almond-shaped holes for the eyes. Elizabeth had a feeling her sister-in-law was relieved to finally be covering her face to the world. She sensed that Georgiana was not happy, and she could very well imagine the reason for this.

Georgiana, who only looked forward to the masked ball because it gave her an opportunity to meet her good friend, was, this evening, as happy as Mr Wilkins to be wearing a mask. The mask could hide her face and spare her the effort of trying to smile all the time.

She regretted that she had not told Edward how she felt; perhaps he believed that she did not care for him at all. Her leave-taking had been nothing but formal, and except for her tone of voice, there was nothing in her behaviour to reveal her true emotions. Once, Georgiana had turned around and looked at Edward, and for a moment, she had almost gone back to him.

Elizabeth stepped out of the carriage and looked up at the great house that seemed enormous in the light of the many torches that had been lit. Two tall pillars at the entryway reinforced the height of the building, and if the architect had wanted to transport the guests to ancient Rome, he had succeeded. Darcy, who saw her face, smiled and gave her his arm as they wandered into the drawing room where they were greeted by their host.

Mr Wilkins welcomed them with the utmost cordiality and when he looked at Georgiana his smile grew wider; a fact that did not escape Mr Darcy who looked contentedly at his wife. Elizabeth returned his smile and hoped that his expectations would come true, even if she herself did not feel as convinced. The line behind them kept growing and Darcy, Elizabeth and Georgiana went on into the ballroom. Mr Wilkins could not yet join them as he was expected to welcome his guests.

The ballroom was filled with people and Elizabeth observed with great interest the creations that those present were wearing. Most were wearing beautiful, colourful clothes and masks that matched their costume in colour and shape.

The masks served their purpose more than well and only when someone lifted it the true identity of the guest was revealed, unless one knew on beforehand what the guest would be wearing. Elizabeth admitted to herself that even without the masks she would probably not have known many of the guests. She was therefore happily surprised when Colonel Fitzwilliam suddenly appeared behind a gilded mask that matched the gold buttons of his uniform. He let it be known that he intended to dance with both the ladies, if he had Darcy's permission to do so, he added with a smile.

"Of course, but as the husband I have, undoubtedly, a prior claim to the first two dances, and even if I should wish to have my dear wife to myself all night, I will, for your sake, give up two dances," said Darcy and laughed.

"That is most kind of you," Colonel Fitzwilliam replied and took Georgiana onto the dance floor.

Georgiana thereafter danced with Mr Wilkins and only in the company of her two dance partners, Elizabeth and Darcy, did her mood seem to alleviate.

Darcy looked for more acquaintances that were then introduced to his sister, but as it could not escape him that she was uninterested in the men in question, he finally gave up. He hoped that her unwillingness to make new acquaintances was due to her being content in the ones she had already made, and it was with delight he saw Mr Wilkins once more taking her onto the dance floor.

Chapter 29

Elizabeth was, when half the evening had passed, the witness to two extraordinary events; one of which sparked her curiosity, the other her alarm. Darcy and Elizabeth had just begun the first of two dances when Elizabeth saw a man approaching Georgiana.

The man stood still a long while right in front of Georgiana without speaking to her. First, she squirmed and seemed bothered by his presence. A couple that danced by bumped into Elizabeth which made her turn her eyes on the couple, who rather than dancing should have remained seated. The man was so unsteady on his feet he had trouble lifting one leg without losing his balance. His wife blushed and endured the guests' gazes; it was obvious the man had drunk too much. However much the wife wanted to leave the dance floor, she had to remain – her husband wanted to dance, thus she was expected to stand up with him.

When Elizabeth once more let her gaze drift to Georgiana, she saw that the two youngsters had started to converse. What awoke Elizabeth's curiosity was that the man made no attempt to lift his mask and reveal his identity. This either suggested that Georgiana knew him well, or that the man in the silver mask wanted to remain anonymous.

A man of lower rank who had entered into a conversation with Miss Darcy without first having been introduced to her, had good reason to want to keep his mask on. Mr Darcy was quite adamant about which families were to be given the honour of having their sons introduced to his sister. Mr Wilkins was, of course, aware of his friend's position and obeyed his requests in this matter as well as other important affairs.

At long last Darcy too became aware of his sister and the young man, and when he saw Georgiana laugh his curiosity was instantly sparked.

"I wonder who it is that Georgiana is speaking to," Darcy said and looked at Elizabeth.

"Funny you should ask, I was just about to ask you the same question," she replied. Darcy observed the man musingly.

"If one were to judge by his habit, I would guess it is a school friend of Mr Wilkins." Another look at the man in question made him add: "Mr Wilkins has always been interested in the theatre – his friend seems to share this penchant."

Darcy had found the man's bow theatrical. When he had bent forward he had with a quick movement kept his wig from falling to the floor. Elizabeth, who had had time to observe a nervous gaze from the man in question, was convinced that the near mishap was due to a too large wig.

During the half-hour that Darcy and Elizabeth had danced, the two youngsters had remained in the same place and continued their conversation. Darcy, who for more than one reason was eager to be introduced to his sister's newfound acquaintance, waited impatiently for the music to end.

As soon as the last violin had quietened, he took Elizabeth's hand and led the way across the dance floor. When he found that Georgiana and her companion had left the room, his consternation was great.

"I had thought she would await us," he said with disappointment. Elizabeth nodded and looked around among the couples that were taking up their places on the dance floor. Perhaps they were to be found there.

She shivered in delight when she heard the well-known chords of her favourite piece of music. Suddenly she spotted Georgiana. Before her stood the youth she had spoken to; both of them were stock-still. When the sound of the music increased the man bowed and took a step forward. This time, however, he was rather more careful in his bows. Georgiana inclined her head, held out the fabric of her gown and curtsied. Elizabeth noticed that she smiled all the while as she beheld the man in front of her. When with the next movement he switched partners, she followed him with her eyes.

"Your sister is dancing," she said and nodded in their direction. Darcy followed her eyes with curiosity.

"Well then. If Georgiana is dancing and is happy in her partner, I can wait another half-hour to find out who he is," he said.

The man was dressed in dark blue, with a white waistcoat with round silver buttons. On top of his head he wore a grey-white wig of the same model that the judge of the high court wore. His face was well hidden by a silver mask.

Darcy, who was convinced they would join them after the dance, was surprised when he saw them continue with the two following dances. When he and Elizabeth took their place among the dancers, Georgiana and the man in the silver mask were suddenly gone. This was curious indeed, as one seldom left the dance floor after one dance. When the man asked, it was always for two dances. Darcy had counted their dances, and he was almost certain they had ended on an uneven number. He looked around but could not spot his sister anywhere. He began to feel rather ill at ease.

When he and Elizabeth stepped off the dance floor, Georgiana and her partner showed up once more and began another dance. Darcy stared at them and once more tried to cross paths with them, but as soon as the dance had concluded they were gone. After a while he thought he began to see a pattern.

"I am almost getting the feeling it is not a coincidence that we never stand by the side of the dance floor at the same time as my sister," Darcy said and added, "I admit that my curiosity by now is great – her actions seem to suggest I have reason to be even more curious."

Elizabeth did not know what to think, other than that Georgiana had met a man who had sparked her interest, and she was glad for her sake. Georgiana's infatuation with Edward had probably not been more than a passing fancy, and if it had increased her faith in men, she could only be glad of it and hope for a prodigious result.

"She is, in all likelihood, only shy. If we let her come to us, I am sure your curiosity will be satisfied before the end of the night," Elizabeth said and laughed.

Chapter 30

The second important event of the evening was of the less pleasant kind as far as Elizabeth was concerned. Darcy and Elizabeth had discussed whether Colonel Fitzwilliam's choice of partner was a good match for him. During the night, he had announced his engagement to Mrs Croft.

Suddenly, Elizabeth had felt as though they were being observed. When she looked around, she discovered a woman in a ruby red and golden dress, who regarded them. Over her shoulders she wore a thin shawl that looked to be spun from golden threads. Her figure was long and slim, and she was a head taller than most women in the room. The raven black hair was kept in place by several golden hair clips, which struggled not to give in to its weight.

When the woman pushed her golden mask with red streaks to the side and looked at Darcy, Elizabeth discovered that it was the same woman she had seen at the market.

It was the first time that Elizabeth saw Miss Byron at close quarters; at the market she had only just been able to make out her face, which she now saw clearly. Miss Byron smiled at Darcy and Elizabeth noted that the smile made her even more beautiful, and also, that her eyes were darker and more lively than her own.

Elizabeth, who soon thereafter turned her attention to Darcy, saw that he immediately reciprocated Miss Byron's smile. His gaze was so replete with fondness that it cut her to the quick. Judging by his facial expression, her presence seemed to make him surprised, as well as happy and amused.

Despite the last encounter having given Elizabeth pause, as well as the fact that Darcy had not mentioned it to her, she had not sincerely found any reason to worry. She had been convinced of his undying love and dismissed the idea of Miss Byron being anything else than an acquaintance.

Elizabeth looked away and tried to dispel the thoughts the woman aroused in her by beholding each of the orchestra members and their instruments in turn.

How well acquainted were Darcy and Miss Byron in reality? What did she, Elizabeth, really know about Darcy's previous history with women? Nothing, she admitted to herself. What she knew was that she had been the object of his affections for the last year. Who had been so before, and to what degree were his previous affairs a matter of indifference to him? Had he at any point been unhappily in love and been forced to move on and find love in another place, even if he really still loved the woman he had never won?

Even if Elizabeth told herself that her feelings were unfounded, her body reacted so violently that she could not deny the fact that she was jealous. Her reaction was both unexpected and unwelcome, as she had always been of the opinion that jealousy was a vice grounded in low self-esteem. Once more, she realised that her prejudice fell back upon herself. It was easy to speak about a weakness of character, as long as it was not oneself that had been put to the test.

Miss Byron was headed towards them, and Elizabeth steeled herself to appear unaffected; she was glad that her face had until now been covered by a mask.

"Darcy!" The woman reached out her hand. Darcy took it and held it for a moment.

"Angelina! As always you surprise me; neither Georgiana nor myself had expected to have the pleasure of seeing you tonight," Darcy said and met her eyes.

Elizabeth stared at Darcy, the unconstraint he showed this woman astounded her. Not until the day she had consented to be his wife had he spoken thus with her.

"My dear, that I surprise you is hardly newsworthy. I had, however, expected you to surprise me with a visit before your wedding took place," said Miss Byron and pulled back her hand.

"It was also my intention, but the reason for this, I thought we had discussed once and for all." After these words, Darcy regarded Elizabeth for a while, whereupon he introduced the two ladies to each other.

Elizabeth felt annoyed, ashamed and in turmoil. Every word that Miss Byron had spoken seemed to have some special significance. My dear, she had said, as if they were on particularly familiar terms. She had also said that she wished Darcy had visited her before the wedding. What could this mean? That she had changed her mind and had wanted to tell him she loved him back, and that he was not to marry any one else?

What increased Elizabeth's anxiety was that her husband had called Miss Byron by her first name, and immediately struck up a conversation.

Elizabeth was well aware that her thoughts increased the burden of those insecurities that already weighed on her. She forced herself to look at the thick gold ring on her right hand. When Darcy had given it to her she had weighed it in her hand: she had never before held anything so precious. Despite everything, the ring was a reminder that it was she who was Mrs Darcy, and no one else.

As Mr Darcy's wife, it was expected of her to behave accordingly, and that she conversed with every guest her husband introduced to her. A comment on the number of guests, the impending dinner, or the orchestra, felt beside the point, but had to be spoken with a smile.

Before Elizabeth had time to decide on any of the three topics, however, Miss Byron spoke.

"There is a matter on which I need your advice," she said and lowered her voice to a whisper, and looked at Darcy. He looked doubtfully at Elizabeth and seemed for a moment not to know how to act.

Would he leave his wife to step away with another woman, or would he inform Miss Byron that he had no secrets from his wife, and that if she wanted to tell him something, they would both be privy to the information? Elizabeth waited to see what his decision would be, as did Miss Byron.

"It is obvious you have not yet told your wife who I am," said Angelina and looked at Darcy, who looked embarrassed.

"Naturally I will tell her the truth, there has just not been the opportunity for it yet," he said and looked ill at ease. Miss Byron laughed and shook her head.

"My dear friend, opportunities are created. When will you tell your wife how things really stand. Now that you are married, she has a right to know," she said and turned to Elizabeth.

"Will you allow me to borrow your husband for the next two dances?"

"Of course," Elizabeth replied, although she had more than anything wanted to scream NO and take Darcy as far away as possible from this woman.

When she saw them step onto the dance floor, an uneasiness presented itself that grew when she thought about what they could be talking about. If Colonel Fitzwilliam had not come up to her, she was sure she would have left the room presently. Instead, she gathered herself and asked with forced calmness:

"Who is the woman Darcy is dancing with – they appear to be on rather familiar terms?"

Colonel Fitzwilliam looked at her and smiled.

"That is Angelina, Sir Byron's daughter." When Elizabeth still looked questioning, he added: "Sir Byron was a close friend of Darcy's father."

"Indeed." was all that Elizabeth could bring herself to say, even though the answer had not surprised her.

When she saw Miss Byron smile at Darcy she felt sure that this would have been another eligible match, as far as his parents were concerned. This union appeared, however, to have had a better chance than the one Darcy's mother and Lady Catherine had once hoped for. Darcy seemed genuinely taken by the woman in front of him; she had never seen him so relaxed with anyone but herself and Georgiana. Elizabeth wondered how many of those present were disappointed that such a union between Miss Byron and Darcy had not taken place.

Her thoughts were so occupied by Darcy and Miss Byron that she had not noticed the appearance of Georgiana. Not until she was standing beside her and for the second time spoke her name did Elizabeth wake up from her ruminations and turn to the side the sound had come from. She looked straight into a pair of brown eyes that shone with joy. Elizabeth studied her sister-in-law and noted that she looked happier than she had done in a long time. When she thought about it, she had not seen Georgiana laugh for several days. Now she smiled at Mr Wilkins and pressed his hand. If she had studied Mr Wilkins' expression she would have discovered that his eyes were alight with calm and reassurance. The reason for his happiness was hardly anything that Elizabeth could imagine.

Her thoughts still revolved around Miss Byron and she waited impatiently for an opportunity to ask Georgiana about her.

"Is Miss Byron a close friend of the family?" she said finally when Mr Wilkins looked out across the dance floor. Georgiana was at once guarded and avoided her eyes as she replied.

"Yes, her parents were close friends of our father. Mr Byron was like a brother to him."

Elizabeth looked at her sister-in-law and thereafter at Miss Byron and Darcy who were still dancing.

"Then how come she has not been a guest at Pemberley and I have never heard you speaking about her before?" she said, her voice acquiring a certain sharpness.

Miss Byron whispered something to Darcy who lighted up and took her hand. Georgiana squirmed and met Elizabeth's eyes.

"If my brother has not spoken of his relationship to Miss Byron, I do not want to be the one who does it in his stead."

Elizabeth felt despair and disappointment; no one seemed to be able to or want to give her any clues. She was married to Darcy, but where was the joy in that if there was another woman he held dear? Until this day she had been convinced that Darcy had never before loved anyone as much as he always said he loved her.

The man with the silver mask drew closer to the company, but seemed for a moment to hesitate when he saw Mrs Darcy. Georgiana beamed and this made his mind up: he joined their little party. Mr Wilkins greeted him with happiness and Elizabeth observed absentmindedly that the man in silver in all likelihood was one of his close friends.

Too pre-occupied by her own thoughts she did not pay much attention to the conversation that took place. Elizabeth could not let Darcy and Miss Byron out of her sight, and the more she saw the more she despaired. Judging by Darcy's relaxed and artless ways with this woman, they appeared to be more than friends.

Miss Byron was narrating something with great alacrity and his expression announced that the topic was one that pleased him in the highest degree. Elizabeth wanted to escape as far away from the room as she could, but at the same time, she found it difficult to leave. Just as she had excused herself as she felt she would soon burst into tears, the music stopped and Darcy and Miss Byron returned to the company.

"Elizabeth! Please stay, Miss Byron has something she wants to announce to her friends," Darcy said and stood himself in her way.

"I did not know that Miss Byron and I were friends," Elizabeth replied shortly.

"What do you mean?" Darcy replied.

"A friend is someone one knows well, and if I am not mistaken, I only know Miss Byron by name," said Elizabeth.

As soon as she had spoken the cutting words, she wished she had taken a moment to calm herself. The sudden insecurity and fear that her husband harboured feelings towards the beautiful Miss Byron had made her defend herself rather than cry.

The moment after she felt defiant as well as mortified. Mortified, as Elizabeth was not unaware that her harshly spoken words had been impolite. Defiant, as the lack of information about their relationship had left her to draw her own conclusions.

Darcy looked thunderstruck and regarded her for a moment. Filled with self-reproach at her thoughtless actions, Elizabeth left the room. Apart from having behaved without proper respect towards her husband, she had done so in front of his friends.

Her straightforward manner had often worked in her favour. When Lady Catherine de Bourgh had tried to dissuade, beg and command her to promise that an engagement to Darcy would never take place, she had been able to stand up for herself and not been frightened into silence. This time, she wished, however, that she had had more of Jane's calm and thoughtful manners.

If Darcy had ever had any doubts about her ability to blend in to the sphere she had been brought into by marriage, this evening would be ample evidence. The realisation would, however, be coming too late. Against more than one of his acquaintances' advice, he had trusted his good judgment and married a woman well below himself in life.

Chapter 31

The ballroom was filled with clusters of chatting people, and a couple in the first flush of infatuation, who stood with their backs to the others and only seemed aware of each other. The girl was blond and dressed in a light blue muslin dress, the man wore a bottle green jacket that, in combination with his red hair, suited him very well.

Elizabeth had noted that the red-haired man was the man who, during the evening, had been mentioned on several occasions due to his engagement to a merchant's daughter in town. Some of the more distinguished guests did not speak to the girl. Elizabeth, who could imagine the young woman's feelings and fears, had at the start of the evening made her acquaintance.

The girl had been more than happy, and had had to restrain her emotions. Elizabeth had been the first to come forward in order to be introduced to her. The girl's intended husband had communicated the same happiness, but also a feeling of gratitude. When he learnt that it was Mrs Darcy who had made their acquaintance, his esteem for Elizabeth increased further.

By involuntarily hearing a conversation between two women, the young couple caught Elizabeth's attention anew.

"Young people of today are much too easily guided by their emotions. The importance of preserving the family honour, traditions and good name seems of little importance," one of the women said and nodded in the direction of the red-haired gentleman.

"It is the more regrettable that the parents give their permission. If the children are lacking in judgment their fathers must show them the way," the other replied.

"A man should trust more to his intellect than to his emotions in his choice of wife. A suitable woman is not impossible to find – a neglected mansion is much more difficult to restore, and esteem once lost is gone forever," her friend retorted.

"Next I expect we will see one of the maids dancing by," she added, and they both burst into laughter. Elizabeth shivered and wondered if the young woman would find it worth the effort to be met with the kind of attitude – openly or ill-concealed – the two women had just exemplified. The husband's part in the matter was of utmost importance for her future happiness. Darcy had always stood by her side, and Elizabeth felt a sting of unease when she remembered his facial expression at her last words.

Darcy observed his wife at a distance. Her forceful reaction had for a moment stupefied him, and before he had time to gather his wits she had left the room. He was not unacquainted with the emotion he suspected lay behind her anger. In the beginning of their acquaintance, it had been exceedingly painful to witness Elizabeth's indifference to him, while she looked upon Wickham with admiration and interest.

His awareness that Elizabeth, during the ball at Netherfield, had put an extra effort into her choice of coiffure and dress to please Wickham, had provoked the same feelings in him that he thought he had just witnessed in his wife.

The group of people around Mrs Darcy immediately dissipated as Darcy drew close. He bowed and exchanged a few words with those gathered, before excusing himself and his wife.

"My dearest Elizabeth, you are not jealous, are you?" he said, as he took her arm and lead her out of the room. Darcy stopped and took her hands in his.

"Elizabeth, I do not know what you are thinking, but I can assure you that whatever it is, you are mistaken!" Darcy smiled and looked at her. "Besides, there is only one woman for me, and no one else is comparable to her."

"I assure you that you are alone in finding the situation amusing," said Elizabeth who saw his smile.

"Forgive me, my dear, it is just that the lady you are jealous of is my sister," Darcy said seriously.

"Your sister? Are you in jest?" Elizabeth stared at him.

"Naturally I had intended to tell you, but I had thought to save it for the next occasion that we were all gathered. Neither Georgiana nor I knew that Angelina would be coming here tonight. I was also certain that Georgiana would have told you everything while you were observing our dance."

"She did not," Elizabeth replied, still uncertain but beginning to feel somewhat easier. She was still shocked by his words. She had never heard of any other sibling than Georgiana. Regardless of what scandals would now be unearthed, it was nothing in comparison to what she had feared.

"I understand if you are astonished, but I will now immediately inform you of the entire matter," said Darcy and smiled. He lead her aside to a settee in one of the drawing-rooms next to the ballroom, and when they had sat down, begun to tell the story of Miss Angelina Byron.

"As you are aware, our mother died before Georgiana was two years old." Darcy paused before continuing, "My father was struck with grief and hired a nanny and a governess to care for Georgiana. Leona, the governess, was the one who came to be close to him, and it was with her he spoke about his sorrow.

Leona was a strong woman who quickly won our trust, and I must say, she handled me, who was more than stubborn at the time, very well. Naturally our mother's death had affected us all. Leona, who never tried to be anything else than the governess she was, in time succeeded to fill some of the emptiness our mother had left behind. After a few years, my father discovered that he had come to regard Leona as part of the household and more. Their love was not uncomplicated, and was at first kept secret: you can imagine the reaction if it had become known that the owner of Pemberley had a relationship with his children's governess."

Elizabeth looked at him and could more than well imagine the difficulties both of them had to endure. Darcy chose not to comment upon what he assumed was an expression of recognition; instead he continued his story.

"Inside the walls of Pemberley, we lived almost like a little family, even if my father and Leona were careful to be discreet about their emotions in front of the servants.

Sometimes our father took us on travels as far as southern England, Scotland or Wales. What could be more natural during such excursions, than to bring one's children's governess? To Georgiana, who was so young when our mother died, Leona soon became a mother figure. It was not an easy task for our father to explain to a girl of three years old why the woman who, in so many ways, acted as such, could not be addressed as 'mother'.

My father's love for Leona was so strong he planned to marry her. He knew that this would mean a break with those who could not accept his choice. What prevented him in the end was our grandfather. As soon as he found out about the wedding plans, he informed his son that a marriage would leave him without his inheritance. If he chose to marry a common woman, Pemberley would fall into his nephew's hands. My father had no other choice, out of consideration for his two children's future economic security, than to cancel his plans to take Leona as his wife. That he could not marry her, however, did not mean he meant to abandon her. My father was at Leona's side when Angelina was born. He never forgave his father for having denied him marriage to the woman of his own choice. Leona did not survive the birth of her child."

"How dreadful for your father to lose two women within the space of a few years!" Elizabeth exclaimed and looked at Darcy.

"Yes, it was undoubtedly a hard blow to our father, and after Leona's death he also grew much graver," Darcy said.

"It must have been a great loss to you and Georgiana," Elizabeth said quietly.

"Georgiana was inconsolable; she was too young to understand that both her mother figures had so suddenly disappeared. I believe it is these events that have made her the calm and cautious creature she is. I was fourteen years old, myself, and at that age I mostly felt anger at the injustice that some were permitted to live, while others died."

Elizabeth looked at him and took his hand; her eyes were filled with tenderness and all the anger she had felt a few minutes ago had melted away.

"Thank you for telling me this. I am ashamed of my own behaviour and I ask you to overlook what happened. I must admit that the thought that you held someone else dear devastated me." For a moment she cast down her eyes but then looked up anew and met Darcy's gaze.

"I was selfish enough to wish that you had never previously loved a woman thus strongly."

"There has never been, and never will be, anyone but you, Elizabeth," Darcy said and squeezed her hand.

After a few moments' silence Elizabeth asked: "What happened to Angelina after her mother had died?"

A few of the guests had stopped to admire a painting in the room where Elizabeth and Darcy sat, and Darcy waited until they had moved on before he continued.

"Despite his love for the child, my father saw the unreasonableness of bringing up three children on his own, and he made the decision to let Angelina grow up with Mr and Mrs Byron. As I have previously mentioned, they were very close friends of my father, and who could better care for his child than a friend that was as close to him as a brother? Mr and Mrs Byron had for many years tried to conceive in vain. Two children had been born but had died within the space of a few hours. Their sorrow had been great and my father's decision gave them great joy.

Angelina grew up as Mr Byron's daughter and only myself, Georgiana and our sister know the truth. Naturally we did not find out until years later. My father revealed everything to me just at his deathbed, and he asked me to wait until Georgiana was fifteen before I told her we had a sister.

My father wanted us to know the truth, not least because Angelina has no siblings, and it was his wish that all three of us would find support in each other the day our parents died.

The reason for Angelina being here tonight is that she has entered into an engagement with Mr Wilkins. This pleases me immensely, even if I must admit that Angelina's announcement caught me by surprise. I did not know they had grown fond of each other. I suppose I had not been very attentive, as Georgiana's exchange of letters with Mr Wilkins led me to believe that there was something to expect out of this contact. This was probably also the reason for Mr Wilkins to wait in declaring his feelings for Angelina."

Elizabeth blushed as she remembered that she had rejected Miss Byron when this lady had been about to reveal her good news.

"Forgive me yet again: what will Miss Byron think of my behaviour towards her? How will I be able to meet her eyes after having suspected her of being after you?" The thought that she had likewise suspected her husband's intentions made Elizabeth all the more ashamed, but of this she said nothing.

"How could you have known that Angelina is my sister? I'm sure she will understand," Darcy said and smiled.

Chapter 32

Elizabeth looked at Darcy with eyes full of love and accompanied him back to the waiting party. Miss Byron smiled when she saw them draw near.

"Did you really think I was after Darcy? He is handsome, of course, but I prefer an exterior that is purer in style," she whispered and looked admiringly at Mr Wilkins.

Darcy looked at Mr Wilkins and smiled. "My friend, it is my hope that your engagement to Miss Byron is a well thought-through decision."

"I can ass.. ss.. assure you it is," said Mr Wilkins and returned his smile. Elizabeth, who felt relieved that all misunderstandings had been cleared up, regarded Miss Byron's face to see if she could find any similarities between her, Darcy and Georgiana.

Miss Byron, after having laughed a while at the notion of being a rival to Elizabeth, entertained her sister-in-law for the rest of the night with stories about those present. With a not entirely discreet finger she pointed them out, one by one.

The corpulent man who was there with his mistress, in the belief that no one would recognise them in their outfits. Further along was the merchant's daughter who had met the red-haired young man when he was doing business with her father. The young man had become smitten with the sweet blonde girl who had that day attended her father's shop, and he had intended to do everything to win her heart and become her husband.

In a dark corner was a young couple who had married merely to please their parents. Due to the marriage, two of the largest estates in England had been joined. Their marriage was not a happy one and one of the reasons could be found here at the masked ball. Angelina nodded in the direction of a young man in purple-black costume with a black mask covering his face. It was the man who had been the young woman's true love and her eyes continually strayed in his direction and revealed whom her heart belonged to.

When Angelina came to the silver-clad man, she fell silent for a moment and then turned to Mr Wilkins.

"Who is that? I have never seen him before."

"Th.. that's Jud.. Judge Jackson, as you see," Mr Wilkins replied with such conviction that the party did not question the validity of this assertion.

Elizabeth could not help but think of her sister Lydia when she heard Angelina's detailed accounts of the guests' fates in life. Angelina was clearly spontaneous and uninhibited, even if she, as opposed to Lydia, knew when it was not proper to be quite so outspoken. Among those closest to her, to which circle Elizabeth after her marriage to Darcy also belonged, she allowed herself, however, to be just as openhearted as she liked.

Darcy explained that the Byrons had given her a good upbringing, but as she was the only child, and so dearly longed for, she had, at times, been given too free a rein.

For Mr Wilkins it was undeniably a good thing to have such an obstinate partner. By means of her eager questions and stories that contained holes that only he could fill in, she forced him to speak in front of the whole company.

When they finally left the masquerade, Elizabeth admitted that it had been a successful evening, after all. She looked at Georgiana, whose happiness seemed to have been replaced by gravity. Her face was turned away from them and most of the time she sat and looked out through the carriage window. Elizabeth was unsure whether she could really see anything. The darkness enveloped the carriage and there were few places where a glimmer of light showed the outlines of cottages or buildings. They travelled great stretches without seeing any human habitation. Georgiana's eyes were distant and she seemed absorbed in her own thoughts.

Darcy attempted to make her reveal who the man in the silver mask had been, but she only replied that it had been a friend of Mr Wilkins. When he brought up the matter again, somewhat later, and asked whether she was previously acquainted with the man she had danced with, she nodded. Encouraged by her reply, he asked whether she thought they would see each other again. Georgiana looked at him and replied she was sure they would.

"What is his name?" Darcy asked, and felt a certain amount of frustration over not having had his curiosity allayed; he was more than eager to have the man's identity revealed. Georgiana did not answer him, and he was just about to repeat the question when he met his wife's eyes.

Elizabeth shook her head and smiled forlornly. Darcy deliberated on it and decided, finally, to be content with the information he had been given. With time he was sure he would find out who the man was. The tumult around Elizabeth and Angelina had made him forget to ask Mr Wilkins about the matter.

Elizabeth, who during the evening had heard many stories of marriages of all kinds, looked at Darcy. She was grateful she had been allowed to marry the man of her own choice. What if her parents had rather forced her to marry Mr Collins, who had been the first man to offer her his hand?

Elizabeth shivered and was convinced that such a match would, in all likelihood, have driven her to madness or even to escape from her husband. Darcy, who saw her face, wondered where her thoughts were.

When she shared them with him, he laughed heartily. He could very well imagine her capable of running off; he did not, however, think that Elizabeth, with her strength of mind, would have let the situation go as far as to driving her to madness.

Chapter 33

Mr and Mrs Darcy's relationship to Lady Catherine de Bourgh had, during the first months of marriage, been rather cool, to say the least. Despite her having tried to prevent it, Darcy had chosen to marry Miss Bennet. At first, Lady Catherine had refused to accept Elizabeth as being the mistress of Pemberley, and quite some time passed without any contact between them at all.

As time went by, Lady Catherine de Bourgh had, however, realised that there was not much she could do about it. Even if she was still of the opinion that her daughter's intended had made a highly inappropriate match, Elizabeth was Darcy's wife and would remain so.

There were several reasons for the eventual thaw in the frosty relations, but of utmost importance was an event that occurred that spring.

One morning a letter arrived to Pemberley addressed to Mrs Darcy. Elizabeth was ill at ease when she received the letter; for what reason she could not determine, as none of her closest relations were in a situation to provoke her anxiety.

Judging from the seal, the letter was from Hunsford, and when she bethought her friend's blessed condition, her worry eased for a moment. Naturally, the letter would be from Charlotte, wishing to relay the good news that she had given birth to a longed-for child.

Elizabeth knew very well how great her friend's happiness had been when it became evident that an addition was to expected to the vicarage. More than one had noted that after years of marriage, she did not show any signs of producing an heir. Despite her friend only having mentioned the matter in passing in one of her letters, Elizabeth had suspected the matter haunted Charlotte more than she admitted.

Mrs Bennet had, in a letter a couple of months ago, confided in Elizabeth that Lady Lucas was greatly worried her oldest daughter would remain childless after having entered into marriage at such a high age.

Elizabeth's first reaction, when she had opened the letter and discovered that the handwriting belonged to Mr Collins, had been astonishment. The first line of Mr Collins' epistle confirmed the worry Elizabeth had felt upon receiving the letter.

Dearest cousin Elizabeth,

I write these lines with great sorrow, although a small glimmer of joy is a comfort in the situation I find myself in. Last night, a month before her estimated arrival, our daughter breathed her first breaths of the air our Lord surrounds us with.
Charlotte struggled long, and for a while the midwife feared the child would not be born thereby extinguishing both itself and the mother.

In all haste, and to our salvation, Doctor Monteau arrived, whom I am forever indebted to for having saved me from becoming both childless and a widower. My wife has, however, lost most of her spirits, and Doctor Monteau cannot deny that the outcome is uncertain.

At Charlotte's request, I ask you to come to us, as she wishes to have you by her side, perhaps for the last time.

With respect, your cousin Mr Collins

The colour drained from Elizabeth's face as she had reached the third sentence of Mr Collins' letter; thereafter she had difficulty making out what it said, as she was overcome with shock. She noticed that her arm shook and that she was cold despite the fire nearby. Elizabeth put the letter down and wrapped her shawl more tightly around her. She could not imagine worse tidings than these. It would have been preferable if it had come to Mr Collins' attention that Charlotte harboured feelings for another man. Even discovering that Lady Catherine had found out would have been preferable to this news.

Charlotte was not yet thirty years old, she could not die now and leave her newborn daughter. How would Mr Collins manage a child on his own?

Elizabeth cried for her friend, the newborn and Mr Collins – it was in this state that Darcy found her.

In the middle of her sorrow, Elizabeth noted that he was once more as considerate as he had been when he found her in a state of distress at Lambton. At the time it had been Lydia's elopement that was the reason for her tears. Now she knew that his questions about the practical details were steps towards taking necessary action. Then she had thought it was the last time she would see him; now she knew that his hasty retreat was out of a wish to be of use to her.

As soon as Darcy had found out what had upset his wife, he had removed himself in order to deal with the practical details. He always became very focused and knew exactly what to do when something serious occurred. Darcy had left it to John to bring Elizabeth a glass of wine; he knew that despite her distress, she would not want to lose a minute. On his way out of the room he bumped into Mrs Reynolds and asked her to bring out Mrs Darcy's trunks. He knew every minute was valuable and the transport to the vicarage could not leave soon enough.

Darcy felt cast down: however unwilling he was to send his wife alone in this condition, the situation was such that he could only leave Pemberley two days from now, at the earliest. He had, however, done what he could, and if he hurried his business he could, perhaps, reach the vicarage half a day sooner than estimated.

They would undoubtedly bump into Lady Catherine during their stay at Hunsford. Elizabeth's mention of a doctor by the name of Monteau had revealed that his aunt had personally become involved in the fate of the Collinses. Doctor Monteau was well known and skilled, but not even he could decide over life and death. In this case one could only think and hope that everything would be for the best. Charlotte lived and there was every reason to hope for a favourable outcome, something he also intended to communicate to his wife.

When he returned to the sitting room it was empty. Darcy went up to the table and took the letter that remained there. With a swift movement he crumpled the paper and threw it into the fire: ill tidings were not something to keep.

He found Elizabeth and Mrs Reynolds in the vestibule; Elizabeth had recovered enough to dress for the journey. By her side were two trunks: Darcy did not ask whether she had packed them herself.

After Elizabeth had assured her husband that she would not be in too much distress, travelling as she was with her maid and two male servants, they parted after a long embrace. Her gaze was clear as she beheld him: it pained her that they would be forced to be separated. She found it sad to be parted from him when he was in London on business and at this moment she wished to be with him more than ever.

"I will do my utmost to be in Hunsford by Wednesday," said Darcy. Elizabeth nodded.

During the journey Elizabeth tried her best not to think about what awaited her on her arrival at the vicarage. It was hard to think about anything else, partly due to her strong worry, but also because she had nothing else to focus her attention on. The darkness made it impossible to read, the uneven road woke her the moment she nodded off. The company limited the topics for conversation.

She could not but picture the horrific scenario of finding an inconsolable Mr Collins, a dead friend and a motherless child. She hoped dearly to arrive in time.

The long journey meant that Elizabeth arrived at the vicarage just before midnight. Mr Collins met her at the gate and greeted her with the usual polite phrases. He bowed and thanked her for so speedily having granted his wish of paying them a visit.
Her cousin was noticeably shaken: Mr Collins, who with his long-winded speeches had attracted the Bennet sisters' narrowing eyes and choked laughter, was noticeably quiet. From the gate to the house he did not utter a word.

Lady Lucas, who had been by her eldest daughter's side since the day before the birth, embraced Elizabeth as soon as she stepped through the door. The only sound that could be heard in the house was the baby's crying.

Although Elizabeth was tired, she insisted on immediately going in to Charlotte. Mr Collins nodded and Lady Lucas showed Elizabeth to the room wherein Charlotte lay.

"He hasn't slept for two nights," Charlotte's mother whispered to Elizabeth.

Lady Lucas opened the door to the chamber; all that was visible from within was a candle burning at the far end of the room. Elizabeth dared hardly look inside for fear of what she would find there. When she stepped into the room the maid, who had been sitting by Charlotte's side, immediately moved away.

"Dearest Lizzy, you cannot know how happy I am to see you," Charlotte smiled weakly and reached out her hand for Elizabeth who immediately rushed to her side.

"Oh, Charlotte," Elizabeth could not finish the sentence as she was overcome with emotion and instead she hugged her friend. To hear her speak and see that she was still alive had immediately lessened her worry. Elizabeth looked at Charlotte and noticed that she was pale and noticeably worn-out. That she smiled when she heard her daughter scream was, however, a good sign.

"Are you in much pain?" Elizabeth wondered and looked worriedly at Charlotte.

"Lizzy, I am not in the least bit of pain, I only feel a great tiredness," Charlotte replied quietly. When she had listened a while to her daughter's small cries, she said calmly:

"Lizzy, nothing can make me regret my daughter: the knowledge that she will be cared for is all…"

"Charlotte, you won't die," Elizabeth interrupted her with greater conviction than she really felt.

"None of us hold sway over this. I would still like to ask you if you will be the godmother of my child," said Charlotte with tears in her eyes. Elizabeth nodded, whereupon neither of them spoke for a long while.

After a while Mr Collins came in with the little girl and Charlotte took her into her arms. This must undoubtedly be the best remedy, Elizabeth pondered as she studied mother and child together.

When Elizabeth had closed the door behind her, and the maid had taken up her place by Charlotte's side, she asked her cousin:

"How is she, really?"

Mr Collins recounted what Doctor Monteau had said – the next days would determine the final outcome. It would then become clear whether the body would manage to recuperate after the great losses it had suffered. Rest, strengthening concoctions, and warm meals had been recommended. Doctor Monteau himself would be with them the following day.

"I have every confidence in him. When Lady Catherine was informed of Charlotte's condition she immediately sent for her own doctor from London. She said that no one but Monteau could be thought of," said Mr Collins with a weak smile.

"That was considerate of her," Elizabeth said.

"Yes, I cannot thank her enough, and tomorrow you will have the opportunity to do so as well," her cousin said with a yawn.

Elizabeth was tired and had so many thoughts in her head that she could only observe that she had not seen the lady since her visit to Longbourne, when she had had the intention to dissuade her from marrying Darcy. She was too tired to think of how Lady Catherine would react when she was forced to meet the woman she considered the reason for her daughter's unfortunate marital status.

Considering the circumstances, she hoped there would not be a scene. However much Darcy's aunt may dislike her, it was Charlotte's well-being that had to be every visitor's foremost consideration.

Chapter 34

The following morning, Elizabeth barely had time to finish her breakfast before she heard the sound of her mother's voice through the window. It was indeed Mrs Bennet who was hasting through the gate while she exclaimed:

"Oh, Mr Collins! My dear Mr Collins, how misfortune has struck you!"

Mrs Bennet had, as soon as she heard the news from Mrs Long, decided to depart for the Collins's abode, despite not having been invited there by the family. Mr Bennet had of course been against this idea; but his wife had been impossible to dissuade because, as she claimed:

"My dear, in their devastation they have of course not had time to send us a formal invitation, however I am convinced that I will be welcomed with open arms."

"Yes, if you think they intend to invite the whole world to partake in their misery, you are probably right," Mr Bennet had replied.

"The whole world! What do you mean?" Mrs Bennet had continued in an irked tone of voice. "You forget that we are practically part of the family! Is not Mr Collins our children's cousin? Your own brother's child!"

"If I am not mistaken this is indeed the case, on this point we may agree," Mr Bennet had replied. Mrs Bennet had continued her reproaches in a wailing voice.

"It really should be you who goes, as Mr Collins' own father is dead, but as you refuse it falls upon me to represent the family."

Mr Bennet had looked at his wife and shaken his head.

"Mr Collins will surely welcome you as if you were his own mother."

"He most certainly will," his wife had replied. Mr Bennet had realised that further arguments would be in vain, and had shrugged his shoulders and continued into the library, closing the door behind him. If his wife intended to make a public display of herself by arriving uninvited to ogle the Collins's misery, then it would be up to her to do so.

Elizabeth blushed as she saw Mr Collins' surprised face, and she understood immediately that her mother had come uninvited. She hurried out to meet her mother and confront her about the impropriety of arriving unannounced in this way, without any special invitation.

"Oh, Lizzy, have you heard what misery has befallen Mr Collins?" her mother exclaimed when she caught sight of her daughter.

"Mama, what are you doing here?" Elizabeth asked in a controlled voice and took her mother aside.

"What am I doing here? What does it look like I'm doing? I am here to give the Collins family my support and see if I can be of any assistance,"

Mrs Bennet responded. Elizabeth doubted her mother would be any support, or be able to offer any assistance, but she said nothing of this and continued instead to ask why she had not announced her arrival on beforehand.

"There was no reason to do so, I came as soon as the carriage could be brought forward, and that, my child, is a sign of true consideration of one's dear relatives. How will Mr Collins be able to take care of a child on his own?" Mrs Bennet said mournfully.

Before Elizabeth could reply she continued: "Mr Collins can of course remarry, and in his situation it would also be particularly advisable. Mary has always had more patience with him than the rest of you, and in that way, you know, Longbourne would not be lost to us."

Elizabeth stared at her mother, unable to believe what she had just heard. With an icy voice she replied:

"Charlotte is not dead."

"No, no, my dear Lizzy, no one can hope more than I that she will be fully recovered – I'm just saying if," Mrs Bennet said hastily.

Elizabeth could not understand how her mother could show such an utter lack of propriety and feeling, with no other consideration than her own expectations. How her own daughters had been able to acquire any sense at all was almost a miracle when one further considered the circumstances. Her mother was often thoughtless, but this was almost too much for Elizabeth to bear.

She was likewise angered that her father had not stopped his wife from going – he, more than anyone, should have seen the impropriety of her visit. Elizabeth felt faint, but thought that if Mrs Bennet could at least have the sense to be quiet upon the matter of which she had just spoken, the situation could hardly be aggravated.

An equipage drew near, and Elizabeth immediately felt lighter as she thought on how her husband had hurried to be at her side. When Darcy had married her, it had meant he had to endure her family every so often, thus her mother's presence was not of great importance in that respect.

Besides, Mrs Bennet's attitude to Darcy had gone through a miraculous transformation on the day she found out that he had proposed to Elizabeth. The negative statements she had passed on him before were all but forgotten. Mrs Bennet could not really remember ever having disliked Darcy and she could not speak highly enough of him to all acquaintances and passing strangers.

"My second eldest daughter Elizabeth is married to the richest man in Derbyshire, Mr Darcy is the name and he has ten thousand a year."

If the newfound acquaintance did not have time to interrupt she continued: "His aunt is Lady Catherine de Bourgh, the owner of Rosings Park, and frequently guest at court."

Darcy had taken his mother-in-law's sea-change with composure and on one occasion had asked Elizabeth if she thought his mother-in-law would have been quite so enthusiastic had he been less wealthy when he asked for her hand. Elizabeth did not think so, but despite her mother's behaviour she did not want to admit the importance of money to her altered manners, and replied that even if that had been the case, her mother would surely have come to like him once she had become acquainted with him. Despite her mother's at times embarrassing praise, Elizabeth preferred it to the cold and even rude conduct she had formerly shown Darcy.

Mr Bennet had, to his delight, discovered that Elizabeth's judgement when it came to Darcy had been proven right: he was, when one got to know him, a sympathetic and kind man who was also generous to his family and servants. Mr Bennet also saw that Elizabeth was genuinely happy in her marriage, and that was to him the most important aspect of the matter.

There could be no doubt that Darcy loved his daughter deeply. Mr Bennet had come to these conclusions after his visits to Pemberley where he often went out fishing with his son-in-law and thereby had the chance to get to know him better. Mr Bennet had also, during the evenings, observed his daughter and Darcy and found that their marriage was built on mutual love and respect, which, he admitted, his own marriage did not contain, and for that matter never had.

Mrs Bennet continued into the house where she was met by Mr Collins and Lady Lucas who held the little one in her arms. As soon as Mrs Bennet stepped over the threshold the child began to cry frantically.

Elizabeth felt that she needed to regain her balance before facing Charlotte and explaining to her what Mrs Bennet was doing at the vicarage. Naturally she would never hear a word of what Mrs Bennet had said, but she would rather repeat her mother's prior statement, that she had thought she might offer her assistance and support to the Collins family in their time of need.

Elizabeth lingered at the door to welcome her husband and to calm the emotions her mother had stirred with her heartless plans for the future of Mr Collins. Although they had only been parted for a day and a night, it felt like an eternity and she longed to be comforted by Darcy's embrace.

Chapter 35

Elizabeth studied the carriage that could now be seen speeding up to the vicarage. The six horses were urged on by a driver whose hat and great-coat were of the same colour as the black animals in front of him. The equally black carriage was not Darcy's but bore, to Elizabeth's disappointment, Lady Catherine de Bourgh's coat of arms.

For a moment, Elizabeth entertained the thought of running away. If the situation had seemed grim before it now appeared quite unbearable. But then she remembered that Charlotte's condition was so incomparably worse than her own that for a moment she blushed over her selfishness. Elizabeth hurried into the house before the carriage had reached its destination; she had no desire to confront Lady Catherine alone.

"Charlotte, how are you today?" asked Elizabeth when she sat down by her friend's side and took her hand.

"I have not had time to judge, as I have just woken up," said Charlotte and smiled.

"Oh, I did not mean to wake you," Elizabeth exclaimed and added ashamedly: "The discovery that the carriage was that of Lady Catherine de Bourgh, rather than my husband's, made me go aside rather than welcoming the equipage."

"No one who knows how Lady Catherine has behaved towards you could blame you for that. You are always welcome in here, I am glad to see you," Charlotte said calmly.

Elizabeth looked gravely at her friend and took the damp cloth to wipe her forehead.

"It was very selfish of me not to ascertain whether you were awake before I stepped in, but the thought of meeting Lady Catherine distressed me more than I had expected." Charlotte, who saw her downcast face, smiled and said: "You are Darcy's wife now, Lizzy – not even Lady Catherine can deny that any longer."

Before either of them spoke again the door was opened and the maid announced in a thin voice and with a nervous glance over her shoulder:

"Lady Catherine de Bourgh and doctor Monteau."

Lady Catherine was dressed in a black cape over her dark blue dress and wore a black creation on her head that made Elizabeth frown at the unsuitability of visiting Charlotte in what looked like a mourning costume.

A small, corpulent man with round glasses, white upturned moustaches and a white monk's tonsure round the otherwise bald head, tripped with short steps in Lady Catherine's wake.

Doctor Monteau nodded at the harangue of French words Lady Catherine spouted forth. That Lady Catherine took the liberty of instructing the doctor in his work was hardly something that surprised Elizabeth who, due to a sudden impulse to burst out laughing, had to look quickly towards the window.

Lady Catherine stood quite still for a moment and beheld Elizabeth before turning her eyes on Charlotte. Elizabeth met her gaze but stayed calmly by Charlotte's side. Doctor Monteau went up to Charlotte and felt her forehead, listened to her pulse and her heart. Furthermore, he asked how her night had been, which he did by turning to Lady Catherine and in French asking what he wanted to know.

Charlotte, who had full confidence in Rosings' owner, turned to the older man and answered him in the language she commanded. The dialogue between Charlotte and Doctor Monteau thus took place through Lady Catherine, who was the only one of the women in the room who spoke French as well as she spoke English.

The corpulent man removed himself to give further instructions to Mr Collins and see that everything was right with the girl child.

Thus Elizabeth, Lady Catherine and Charlotte were left alone in the room. Silence fell, and a long while went by before any of them spoke. Elizabeth still held Charlotte's hand and Lady Catherine, who had dragged over an armchair, watched the two friends in silence. Both Elizabeth and Charlotte found it best to remain quiet and it was after another long moment that Lady Catherine broke the silence with the words:

"Charlotte, you should listen to me carefully for what I have to say could be fateful to you and if you wonder with what right I speak so confidently on the matter, without having any medical knowledge, I will at once enlighten you upon that matter."
Lady Catherine looked for a moment at Elizabeth and continued after a while's thought.

"When Miss Anne de Bourgh was born I was myself in a state similar to your own. In reality, I was worse, and if it had not been for Doctor Monteau I had not been here today. Monteau has been trained on the continent and there they use a potion for blood loss that, given in the right amount, will help the body that has been depleted to refill. This may mean that you can keep your own life, but you will not, thereafter, be able to give life." After these words, Lady Catherine fell silent.

Elizabeth regarded Lady Catherine. She wondered what had made her share her private affairs so openly. She had had every right to ask Elizabeth to leave the room, but she had chosen not to. Lady Catherine looked at Elizabeth with squinting eyes: she could not yet make herself call her Mrs Darcy.

"I see what you're thinking, but circumstances such as these undoubtedly overshadow one's own slights."
Much more was not said between the ladies, and when Doctor Monteau once more entered the room in the company of Mr Collins, Elizabeth chose to remove herself.

She assumed that the gravity of the situation had brought Lady Catherine to reconsider, and if it could bridge the schism between them, she would be accommodating. She was already grateful that through Lady Catherine her friend had received the best possible medical care.

That Charlotte would not be able to have more children seemed a low price to pay in exchange for her life. Elizabeth now understood why Rosings would not go to a male heir as a patrilineal inheritance. Lady Catherine had, after the birth of Miss Anne de Bourgh, known that there would not be a male heir to Rosings Park, and her husband had changed the legal matters accordingly.

Chapter 36

Mrs Bennet had spent the last hour on the following activities: commiserating with Lady Lucas over her daughter's misfortune; convincing Lady Lucas that said daughter would be completely recovered; and asking doctor Monteau so many questions that eventually he could not be bothered to offer a reply. Finally Mrs Bennet had stubbornly maintained that since she had herself given birth to five daughters, she knew best what was the matter with the girlchild when she cried.

Lady Lucas was tired, partly from worrying about her daughter, but also with the responsibility for the little one who seemed disturbed about not being with her mother. Mrs Bennet's ideas of being a support and offering assistance were, as Elizabeth had feared, rather products of her mother's wishful thinking.

In the tumultuous state of the vicarage, no one had noticed the carriage that rolled into the yard until the door was opened and Darcy appeared at the threshold. For a moment, the room fell silent. Elizabeth was flooded with joy and immediately went to greet him. Mrs Bennet's attention was immediately turned on her son-in-law, which gave Lady Lucas a chance to withdraw a while for a well-needed rest.

Darcy looked at Elizabeth: he could not judge whether she was happy or sad as her expression held such a multitude of feelings that he could not, with any certainty, determine which was the prevalent one. If he should dare to hazard a guess, it would be that while Elizabeth's concern for her friend contributed to feelings of happiness, hope and love, the presence of the other persons at the vicarage produced only irritation, anger and bitterness.

He had hoped to arrive before Lady Catherine. When they had driven into the yard and he had seen her carriage, he had hoped for his wife's sake that the confrontation between them had not been too spiteful or dramatic. His aunt could, when she wanted to, be very adverse and bitter, and her way of expressing her grievances could be—to say the least—cutting, as Elizabeth had experienced before. Naturally, now was not the time to investigate the matter, but he was convinced that he would be informed of all the details at a later time.

Darcy stood with his arms around his wife when the door to the bedroom was opened and Lady Catherine stepped into the sitting room. He noticed that his grip around Elizabeth's shoulders tightened. Normally he did not doubt his wife's ability to defend herself. Unlike other times, however, she was now in a vulnerable position. He remembered all too well what the doctor had said about stress being unhealthy for both mother and child.

It was several months since he had met or even spoken to Lady Catherine. He noted that his aunt looked the same, apart from her hair having greyed a bit around the forehead.

Her face was as stern as usual and she pursed her lips lightly when she saw that Darcy and Elizabeth remained close together. For a moment he imagined her forcing herself in between them. He therefore had trouble hiding his astonishment as she said:

"After several weeks of deliberation, I have decided to invite you and your wife to dine with me at Rosings Park, and as you are here now, perhaps Thursday would be convenient?"

Lady Catherine, who saw that Darcy was about to speak in order to, she supposed, express his deepest gratitude, waved her hand to fend off further discussion.

"Then it is decided, let us not speak more of the matter." With those words she swept out of the Collins's home.

Through the window they saw her brushing off her cape, going down to the carriage and taking her seat without once turning around. Elizabeth and Darcy looked at each other; as there were others around they kept their expressions serious.

Elizabeth and Darcy stayed for some time in Kent. When Elizabeth spent time with her friend, Darcy took the opportunity to make errands to a neighbouring town. Even under the circumstances, they felt it was best to restrict the time spent in the company of Mr Collins to meal times.

Elizabeth, who had hoped that he would have become more thoughtful after the recent trying events, soon saw that this was not the case. Her cousin's loquacity, the intricate descriptions and elaborate compliments, increased daily as Charlotte's health grew stronger. It was a matter of days before Mr Collins was back to his old self again.

Charlotte's state stabilised, and with time it became apparent that she would be fully recovered. As Lady Catherine had predicted, doctor Monteau told the Collins that there would be no more children born at the vicarage. Charlotte took the news well, as did her husband, despite having hoped to bring forth a son to carry on his calling.

The little girl who was to be christened Margaret Elizabeth – after her grandmother and her mother's best friend – rested in her godmother's arms. Elizabeth regarded her intently as the baby floated in and out of sleep.

Despite her tender age one could distinguish her future features. She had inherited neither Mr Collins's round cheeks nor his hazel eyes. The girl's eyes were a deep blue like her mother's. The hair that on first appearance seemed a dark brown was, on closer inspection, almost black; something that seemed to have gone unnoticed by everyone but Elizabeth. But then it was only Elizabeth who had had cause to reflect on the fact that Mr Collins's daughter did not resemble her father in the least.

She would have liked to discuss the contents of Charlotte's letters with her. But as her friend did not touch upon the subject, Elizabeth could not bring herself to broach the subject of Mr Andrew.

The dinner at Rosings had, to Elizabeth's relief, gone better than expected: no one had been overly talkative, but there had not been any unkind words exchanged either. Elizabeth was well aware that Lady Catherine de Bourgh had taken a great step in inviting them to dine with her in her home.

When Elizabeth studied Miss Anne de Bourgh she could not detect any signs of the young woman having suffered any heartache at having lost her intended husband. Her eyes, when they had rested on Darcy, did not look any different from when she regarded her other cousin. Elizabeth had almost thought she saw relief in her eyes when she looked at Elizabeth and Darcy.

Elizabeth admitted, however, that the accomplishment of the arranged marriage would have secured Miss de Bourgh a husband. She could rather understand if Lady Catherine was worried that her daughter would never marry. Miss Anne de Bourgh was not lacking in wealth and at least—to some men— this would compensate for her utter lack in other womanly attributes, such as beauty, charm and accomplishments. Even if Miss de Bourgh were married, Elizabeth did not think there would be many heirs to Rosings, as anyone could see that Miss de Bourgh's health was not what one could wish for.

Elizabeth could not help but think about what would happen to Rosings Park if Anne de Bourgh remained unmarried or childless. Perhaps it would go to Mr and Mrs Darcy? Elizabeth had to stop herself from laughing out loud when she imagined how Lady Catherine might have answered to such reasoning a year ago.

Darcy, who had seen her expression, guessed that her thoughts, if spoken out loud, would not be taken kindly. He had decided to interrogate her about them as soon as they were alone.

When Elizabeth saw that Charlotte had regained some of her normal colour, and had enough strength to have the little one with her for most of the day, she decided that it was time for her and Darcy to take their leave. Partly, she felt that the little family needed time to themselves to bask in the newfound happiness that the birth of their daughter and Charlotte's restoration to health had brought; partly she felt there were too many people gathered together at the vicarage.

Chapter 37

Georgiana had arrived at Pemberley a day before Darcy and Elizabeth were expected back from their visit to the vicarage. Never before had the sight of the great stone house been the cause of such rejoicing. Every day in London had been agony. The more she had tried not to think about Edward, the more she had been reminded of him.

Already the first evening a man had caused her thoughts to thus escape. Mr Cricks, who habitually charmed women with his words, had counted on adding Miss Darcy to his collection.

He had not expected anything but success, no women had up until now rejected him. If there had, at any time, been any hesitation, he had played his trump. He was a physician, and as such, he had an advantage over every other man in the company. He knew more about physiology than any other, and he was happy to share his knowledge with those assembled.

At first, the women pretended to be shocked, some even appalled. Those were the rules of the game and he knew them well. Their glowing cheeks, muffled giggles and excited eyes always made him feel powerful and invincible. The wondering, curious and envious gazes of the other men spurred him on even more.

His repertoire was well rehearsed. As if by chance, he had placed himself by Georgiana on the balcony. He had lighted a thin cigar and blown a curl of smoke into the dark cool air. Through the slow, flourishing motions of the smoke, his thoughtful gaze suddenly alighted on her. The expression in his eyes changed from one of surprise to that of appreciation when their gazes met. He quoted some well-chosen words from Shakespeare's Macbeth, in muted tones.

His expression turned to horror when he discovered that Georgiana's eyes had turned away from him.

A young woman who had witnessed it all giggled aloud whereupon Mr Cricks cast her an angry glance. It was the same woman who, a few months earlier, had been so taken with him that she had been prepared to defy her father. She had cried, begged and finally threatened her father that she would run away if that was what it took. Her father had remained unbending. He was well aware of Mr Cricks' eye for the females. He had been the same in his youth. Despite not wholly having abandoned these habits, it was not something he wished for his daughter in marriage. As he had predicted, their quarrel had not lasted long. It had taken three weeks before Mr Cricks' interest in his daughter had faded.

Mr Cricks' hope of sparking Georgiana's interest was futile. She had forced a smile and asked him whether he might instead read something from Hamlet. At the sight of Lady Alcot's surprise she had hastily explained that she preferred this work to Macbeth.

At home, at social gatherings, among the people, everywhere there seemed to be things that reminded Georgiana of Edward. During one of the plays, a horse had appeared among the sets. In one conversation the breeding of horses had been discussed.

In a shop in the northern part of town she had spotted a dark-haired man who resembled Edward. She had been so sure she had entered the shop and approached the man. When he had turned round she had averted her eyes in embarrassment and cursed her own insipidness. She had very well known that Edward would never enter a gentlemen's tailor shop. Edward had never been to London.

When the pain had been too great she had, through sheer effort, managed to force her attention onto what presently took place around her. For some minutes, the actors' clothes or lines had managed to distract her. But as soon as she had stopped focusing, the thoughts had returned. Sometimes, she did not even notice it. Often, it was someone in her surroundings who, through a question or comment, called her attention.

The summer weeks had seemed like days compared to the weeks she spent in London. When she was finally back at Pemberley, she looked forward to, but also agonised over, seeing Edward again. Happiness at once more being in that company she did not wish to be without. Agony at her feelings perhaps not being reciprocated. Fear of the consequences if they were reciprocated.

Despite Georgiana longing to see her brother and sister-in-law, she was grateful for the day that remained before they would be reunited. Her excitement, anxiety and worry would have been hard to conceal, and she feared that Elizabeth would have been able to determine her predicament without much effort. The thought of how her brother would react if he knew of her feelings for Edward was too frightening to even bear thinking of.

Not even the familiar surroundings and the safety of her chamber made her relax. This night seemed interminable. The long journey finally took its toll, and she awoke at dawn of the day whose events she had time and again imagined.

It was the first time she wandered through Pemberley's corridors without meeting a servant or hearing the sound of the kitchen-maids' preparations for the day's meals. When she was a child, the silence had scared her. On the occasions when Georgiana had awoken and had to rise, she had seen to it that she dropped something on the floor. It had calmed her to see the servants hurrying in. It was not until she knew that someone else in the house was awake that she could go back to sleep. What she had not paid attention to then was that the silence revealed sounds that were otherwise masked by the noise of footsteps, voices and those activities that always took place within the walls of Pemberley.

The little pointer pup pricked its ears when Georgiana passed the piano room. He happily abandoned his place by the fire and ran to meet her. She rolled up her handkerchief into a ball and threw it along the corridor so that he wouldn't expose her. There was a rasping along the wooden floor as Hamlet went after his prey. When he returned to repeat the procedure, he was met by a closed door. Georgiana heard a disappointed whimper but hurried on, despite a stinging conscience.

To make sure no one was outside, she lingered a few moments at the threshold before continuing out into the misty morning. When the heavy oak door closed behind her with a thump, she was sure the whole house must have woken up. She looked hastily around, pulled her shawl tightly around her shoulders and head and quickly crossed the lawn towards the stable building. The ground was still wet with dew and the mists of the meadows had yet to clear away.

When she had come half way she suddenly stiffened and stared at the grove by the side of the house where the servants' quarters lay. A movement had caught her attention, she was almost sure it had been the figure of a man. She just hoped it was not Darcy's steward. Although he always behaved impeccably when they met, she always felt ill at ease afterwards. She felt her heart rate quicken when she realised that she could not think of any plausible reason for her being in this place at this hour.

Edward was already at work. This time of day was the calmest of those hours he spent at Pemberley, and therefore appreciated for the quietude and peace it brought him. He had always been an early riser. Besides, he also liked to see the surroundings awaken to a new day. As for the horses, they were always awake when he arrived. He had never managed to surprise them even though he had tried several times.

As always, he started his work by brushing Othello. During the days of the riding lessons it had given him more pleasure than otherwise: Othello had never been as well-groomed as she had been then. Every time Edward looked at the horse he thought of Miss Darcy. Sometimes he caught himself once more preparing the horse in the way he had done during those weeks the riding lessons had taken place.

Georgiana was well aware that her presence in the stable building at this hour of the day was highly improper, not to say unacceptable. During those weeks she had spent in London her thoughts had daily returned to where she was now standing. Now that she was there, a feeling of excitement filled her, as well as defiance and fear that kept her silent.

She beheld Edward's careful strokes over the horse's black body. The familiar laughter when the horse rummaged for oats in his pocket made her smile. She had missed his laughter. Before she had met Edward, she had not considered how different laughter could sound, depending on who it came from.

There were the formal chuckles that occurred during business deals. The forced sound that was intended to disguise humiliation. The ingratiating clucking of men or women around those whose favour they wanted to win. The twittering when the one they held dear spoke to them. The near-scream of little children before they were quietened down by their parents. Despite her collection having grown during her stay in London, she had not found any whose laughter resembled that of Edward. Edward never considered whether he laughed too loud or too low or if the situation was the right one for it.

When Edward turned to reach for a brush he caught sight of her.

"Miss Darcy!" he exclaimed, with such happiness he immediately blushed.

That he had been surprised to see her was obvious. She could see how he fought to hold back the questions her visit gave rise to. He looked at her and smiled, shook his head a little and laughed. Georgiana smiled, his reaction did something to appease her own agony.

For a long while they beheld each other in silence, the only sound was Beth's snorting from the stable. Without any watchful eyes on them, they dared let each other see the happiness they both felt.

Despite the space between them, the air seemed to bind them together. Edward felt a strong urge to go up and embrace her. He did not, he knew too well that such initiatives could never come from his side.

During Georgiana's stay in London, he had done everything to restrain his feelings so that they only encompassed the deepest friendship. He was well aware of the purpose of her visit to London. He had tried to prepare himself for Georgiana returning to Pemberley as another man's fiancée. So that he could be informed of the news without any displays of emotion, he had forced himself to think about it. It had not lessened his sorrow. Neither had it made him reconcile himself to the idea that she was unattainable to him, but available to the one who had enough money.

When he had turned around to look at her again, the same feelings were aroused that had previously filled him with such pleasure. The reaction had been instantaneous and so spontaneous that he had not even had time to think about resisting it. What kept them apart was, however, unchanged. She was still Darcy's sister, and he was still their stable master.

The sun began to climb over the horizon. Within an hour, the maid who was the first to rise would wander over the stable yard to collect the eggs that were delivered at the gate. The butler, John Goose, would go out and smoke his pipe before carefully polishing the buttons of his coat. The stable boy, James, would, five minutes later, saunter into the stable and finish the morning's work.

Edward saddled the two horses in silence. When he gave her the rein their hands touched, and he had to force himself not to hold onto her hand. Although they kept the proper distance, he was almost sure they had both sensed the same thing. He doubted that such a force could arise from only one person's wishes. Georgiana looked away and blushed.

When they wandered over the grass rather than the gravel, she wondered if this was how criminals felt. The feeling scared as well as excited her. She glanced at Edward. He looked so serious, she felt an urge to say something unexpected.

129

When Othello suddenly neighed, he looked at her and smiled. They hurried their steps. After a while, Georgiana could hear her own breaths. The social gatherings and lack of exercise of the last couple of weeks had dramatically decreased her new-won strength. She had been shocked the first time she noticed the difference. She could not be sure, however, if the warmth and shortness of breath were only due to the pace.

When they had arrived at the meadow, they let the horses take them into a quick gallop. The sound of eight hooves thundered against the ground. Georgiana shut her eyes and for a moment gave herself up entirely to the movement. She felt the wind on her face, opened her eyes and saw the landscape flowing past. Although the muscular body moved at a speed that surpassed what she had hitherto been accustomed to, she was not scared. With Edward she always felt safe: by trusting to his words she had conquered many of her anxieties. He had instructed her well, and the horses had reacted to her manoeuvres as he had foretold.

If they rode quickly, perhaps no one would see them. Although neither of them spoke about it, they rode as far from the grounds as they could. Neither of them were unaware of the likely consequences of their actions. They chose not to think about it, neither did they discuss the matter.

When they had reached the ruin, Edward leaned back, upon which Beth immediately slackened her pace. Othello did the same without Georgiana having to repeat the movement.

Edward looked at her appreciatively. At her arrival, her hairstyle had looked fit for a party. The ride through head wind had, however, ruffled both her hair and her habit. The hair clasp hung loose, and the fair curls had come undone and flowed around her face. He thought she was prettier than ever, and would have liked to tell her so. Instead he said: "I am very glad that you came and visited me."

His respect for her grew every time she did something unexpected: there were many times that her actions had surprised him. He was well aware of her role in society and what duties it entailed. He was touched that she risked everything for his sake. He did not bother to conceal how he regarded her, it was no secret that he liked her.

"I am glad that you were glad," Georgiana said and undid the last of her hairpins and shook her head so that her hair fell over her shoulders. She liked the way he looked at her. Although she had, on many occasions, worn the finest dresses and jewellery, she had never felt as beautiful as she did now.

"Well, how was London? Did you have to sing and play as much as you feared?" Edward asked, finally, with a smile, and focused his eyes in the distance.

"Yes, but I made a mistake on purpose, and after that no one asked me to play any more," Georgiana replied. Edward looked at her but could not determine whether she was serious or not.

"Did you really? That was very brave of you," he said and smiled.

"Did you think I would dare to do something like that? No, I was joking," she said and laughed.

"I have heard that you play beautifully. Unfortunately, I have not had the pleasure of determining it for myself, but have to rely on hearsay," Edward said.

"You are too kind, but I would gladly have played to you if you had been there," Georgiana said and looked embarrassed.

"And I would have liked to have been there, if I had had the opportunity," he replied and smiled.

"But I am very glad that you are here," he added and patted Beth's neck.

Edward had been anticipating Miss Darcy partaking in other activities than riding on her return to Pemberley. Until this day he had reconciled himself to it. At any rate, it was what he had told himself during those weeks they had been apart. All he now wished for was that they would spend some time together. To be close, and yet separated, was more painful than if she were somewhere else in the country.

Although he was still in turmoil from the feelings their meeting had provoked, he was eager to know whether Georgiana had entered into an engagement or not. Although his prospects were as dire as ever, he wanted to know. If she were not engaged, it would mean that she stayed at Pemberley over the winter. Considering the circumstances, that was good enough for him.

"Did Mrs Alcot manage to persuade all the rich men to offer you their hand in marriage?" Edward thought he managed to ask the question in a light, carefree manner.

"Not all of them, only Lord Malcolm from Sussex," Georgiana replied.

Edward turned his face away, he had not wanted her to see his reaction. He had no right to feel disappointed, or think of his own wishes. He should he happy for her, and yet he could not but wish the man had not proposed. A lord, he thought; then there was no other question but when the wedding would take place.

Georgiana who had observed his reaction, added hastily: "But I turned him down."

Edward looked at her in disbelief. "You turned down a lord?" he said doubtfully.

"I did." The answer was as devoid of emotion as if he had asked her whether she thought it would rain in the afternoon.

"Miss Darcy, please don't joke about such a matter as this," he said in a grave tone of voice.

"I am not joking," Georgiana said and met his eyes. Edward's expression spoke of confusion, doubt and relief. She had an impulse to take his hand, and it pained her that she could not do as she pleased. After a moment's silence, Edward spoke.

"But how could you say no to a lord?" His voice carried sincere surprise, even if she also thought she could detect some relief.

"I don't love him," she replied and looked away. Edward regarded her with admiration and doubt.

"Is that reason enough to say no to such a man? What is Mr Darcy's opinion on the matter?" he said and held his breath, without noticing it himself. He wondered how Mr Darcy would react when he was told of his sister's decision.

131

For a moment Georgiana was unsure: she was convinced he would dislike her rejecting such an advantageous match. Especially as the man in question was a good man with many admirable qualities. The only thing that was wanting was her love. When she thought on narrating the event to her brother, she felt suddenly ill at ease and replied:

"He will not be pleased, but he won't force me to marry against my wishes." She hesitated a moment, then took a deep breath and added:

"Besides, there is already someone else."

Edward looked at Georgiana and slowly his eyes were filled with the happiness she had been used to see in them, and that she had liked from the very beginning.

"Does he know?" he asked and fell silent. Georgiana met his gaze and nodded.

They did not speak. Once again she noticed how beautiful she thought he was. The sun's reflections made his brown eyes shine. She had often been fascinated by how people with a smile could turn from plain to beautiful, from invisible to radiant.

If someone smiled it almost always provoked a response from the receiver. She had always liked people who were generous in their joy. Her own shyness had many times kept her from smiling. It was not altogether easy to disregard the precepts she had been given as a child. As time had passed they had become rules and truths. The thought that it was improper, irresponsible and lacking in character came so quickly that she had stopped herself before she had had time to question the verity of this.

With Edward it had been different from the outset. Her reaction had come before the thoughts. It had not scared her. She had thought it was as it should be, and for a moment she had felt a strength and an invincibility she rarely experienced. She had felt alive and liberated.

Edward had had reason to think that she liked him – to his delight her expression revealed that her feelings ran deeper than that. At that moment, his only thought was to be happy that his feelings were reciprocated.

He was well aware that he only borrowed her for the time being, and that, in the environment they were in, she could be nothing more than a friend. With time, some other man with a fortune would enter upon the scene. This knowledge could not dampen the joy he felt in that moment. Georgiana's decision to refuse Lord Malcolm's proposal undoubtedly meant that she would stay at Pemberley until the leaves had fallen.

Edward was well aware that however much Georgiana liked him, a union between them was impossible. His hope that they would see each other every so often had, however, increased dramatically with this visit.

Chapter 38

When Elizabeth and Darcy went off the next day, Elizabeth felt elated.

"I would never have thought that I would leave this place in such a pleasant state of affairs." During their journey she related the events of the first morning at the vicarage, even if she excluded some details.

"In hindsight one can perhaps laugh at it, but at the time the thought of my mother and Lady Catherine under the same roof was not amusing in the least," she said with a shiver. Darcy deliberated a while, then he said:

"If you felt insecure about meeting Lady Catherine alone, you could have informed her of your company."

"I told you I was alone," Elizabeth said and looked questioningly at him. Darcy placed a hand on her stomach.

"What I mean is that you were not alone; if I remember correctly there are two other persons present in this carriage," he said and smiled. Elizabeth laughed.

"Lady Catherine would probably have received the news with utmost delight."

To herself, Elizabeth admitted that she had not thought much about her own happiness during the last days, apart from when she held the baby in her arms. Neither she nor Darcy had thought about divulging the news in the circumstances of their visit.

Elizabeth shivered when she thought of how Mrs Bennet would have reacted if she had found out about the pregnancy. She would, in all likelihood, have completely forgotten about Lady Lucas's and Charlotte's predicament, and without a thought of their feelings, she would have praised her future grandchildren and her son-in-law.

"Oh, Lizzy, to think that there will be two of them, I am convinced they are both sons!"

"Darcy, I knew there would soon be an heir to Pemberley – what else could one expect from a man like you!"

"Mr Collins, have you heard about the happiness that awaits my dear Lizzy: she is a strong girl, and with her good health even a twin birth should not be a problem!"

"My dear Lady Lucas, have you heard that I too have the joy of expecting grandchildren, although in my case there will be two rather than one. I am quite certain it will be two boys!"

Elizabeth did not think she had ever seen Darcy laugh as much as when she mimicked her mother's outpourings. When he had regained his countenance, he said with a smile:

"And you are fully convinced that this is how Mrs Bennet would have chosen to express her joy?"

"There is no doubt in my mind," Elizabeth replied. Despite her delight at having amused her husband with her narrative, she was even more relieved that the pregnancy had not been revealed to her mother during their stay at the vicarage. Elizabeth knew her mother much too well to doubt the outcome of such a revelation.

After a few hours' drive they spotted Pemberley through the avenue of verdant oak trees. The oaks that had been planted by Darcy's great grandfather were by now of imposing height and more than two armfuls around. Elizabeth recollected the first time she had visited Pemberley and marvelled at the beauty of the surroundings. Darcy pointed in the direction of the meadow where two riders were galloping past.

"If I am not mistaken, Georgiana arrived last night. Riding seems to have become a major interest of hers, or she would not have gone out without awaiting my approval," said Darcy and frowned.

"It surprises me that she would take such a liberty, being fully aware of our impending arrival, rather than having the patience to wait a day," he continued and looked at his wife.

Elizabeth did not speak, but she observed that Georgiana's stay in London had not lessened her interest in horses or in Edward. Like her husband, she was surprised by Georgiana's audacity to go out riding unchaperoned with a man. Perhaps it could be explained by the fact that they had arrived at Pemberley a day early: Georgiana did not expect them until the following day.

Georgiana was not to be seen until dinner. When she stepped into the room she embraced them both and expressed her delight at being back at Pemberley and seeing those who were closest to her. If Georgiana was surprised that they had arrived at Pemberley ahead of schedule, she hid it well. Darcy looked at his sister and observed that the London visit had done her good. Georgiana was in much higher spirits than she had been when she left Derbyshire.

Mrs Alcot's latest missive to Darcy had contained certain allusions, which he hoped were the reason for the glow and joy that Georgiana exuded.

"How nice to hear your stories about London; it was so long since I was there myself," Elizabeth said and added: "The latter was of course a hint to your brother that he must take me there as soon as possible, so that I may stroll about and admire the latest fashion and spend some of his money." Darcy, who had been observing his sister's and wife's happy reunion, decided to hold off questioning Georgiana about what he felt was a most improper conduct from a woman of her rank.

At times he forgot that his sister was more than ten years his junior. Perhaps it was unjust to expect her to have the same impeccable judgement as him.

Georgiana smiled. "But first I want to hear about your journey: how is your friend?"

"Oh, Charlotte will, to my great delight, be fully recovered; she has a wonderful daughter whom she has named after me," Elizabeth said.

After a short account of the state of affairs at the Collins's, Georgiana felt impelled to ask her brother if he had seen their aunt and to inquire after her health. She did not know exactly how to pose the question. Lady Catherine's opinion of Darcy's marriage was hardly unknown, and she was afraid of hurting Elizabeth by bringing up her aunt.

"Did you see Lady Catherine during your stay in Kent?"

Georgiana asked and blushed. "I mean, I suppose it could hardly be avoided."

"We saw her, indeed," Darcy said and looked at Elizabeth. "But I will leave it to my wife to recount that story."

"Well," said Elizabeth as they sat at the table, "We have yet to hear a word from you about London, but I will help you along by asking a few questions." Georgiana at once turned serious, but replied courteously to Elizabeth's questions.

Yes, they had been to the theatre on several occasions. She had, indeed, been to many fine parties. Mrs Alcot had introduced her to some of the most eligible young men in town. Yes, Mrs Alcot lived in one of the finest areas of the city and the house was very beautiful and admired by those who passed it. She had, indeed, been forced to play in public.

Elizabeth, who thought she sensed her sister-in-law's predicament, chose not to ask any questions about whether Georgiana had met any man of particular interest to her.

Darcy, who had listened to their conversation, said suddenly: "Georgiana, is there nothing in particular you would care to tell us?"

Surprised by the sudden question, she jumped in her seat and looked at her brother. For a moment, she was unsure of what it was he wanted her to tell him. She was convinced that there were several things he did not want to hear.

Very few carriages came down the long road to the beautiful but solitary Pemberley. Approaching guests were expected, and no one had to spend any time on guessing who it would be stepping out of the carriage. During her ride, Georgiana had seen the carriage approaching the estate, and for a moment hoped rather than believed that they had unexpected visitors.

As Elizabeth had guessed, she had not expected Darcy and Elizabeth to return until the following day. Despite the anxiety she felt at having to answer for her behaviour, she was sure that nothing could have made her act differently. Her brother's expectant gaze made her suddenly realize what it was he was referring to.

"Lord Malcolm asked me to marry him, and I refused him," she said and rose to leave the room.

Darcy looked at Elizabeth in astonishment; his sister's reaction had surprised him. He had had every reason to believe that she would be pleased by his question.

A few days prior, Darcy had received a letter from Mrs Alcot wherein she had described the various assemblies his sister had attended and the men who had been introduced to her. With utmost delight she had informed Darcy that there was one gentleman in particular who had shown Georgiana great attention. Apart from a vast fortune, pronounced intelligence and a perfectly amiable manner, the man in question went by the title of Lord Malcolm.

Mrs Alcot's expectations for Georgiana had been summarily surpassed, and she was convinced that Lord Malcolm would ask for the girl's hand in marriage before the week came to an end. Georgiana had received his attentions in the calm and mild-mannered way that distinguished her. Apart from a slight absent-mindedness that Mrs Alcot interpreted as being a sign of the girl's shy nature, she was convinced that Georgiana would give her consent.

Elizabeth did not know what to say when she heard Darcy recount the contents of Mrs Alcot's letter, but she offered to go in search of Georgiana and speak to her.

For a while, Elizabeth remained standing outside of Georgiana's chamber before she knocked on the door and stepped inside. Georgiana dried her eyes that immediately filled with tears as she saw her sister-in-law.

"Elizabeth, do you think my brother will be very angry with me for having rejected Lord Malcolm?"
Elizabeth sat down at her side on the bed.

"Why do you expect Darcy to be angry with you for having refused a man you do not hold dear?" She put her arm about her, which increased Georgiana's tears. After a while, she said in a quavering voice:

"But Lord Malcolm is a very rich man, and what woman would refuse a man with a fortune greater than her own?"

Elizabeth smiled.

"A woman who does not love a man should not, unless it is absolutely necessary for her survival, consent to marry him just because he is rich."

"But no man of great fortune expects to be rejected when he proposes," Georgiana said sadly.

"Perhaps your brother was once of that opinion, but I think I can promise you, my dear, that he will not be angry with you for that reason."

"I do think you are mistaken," Georgiana said despondently.
Elizabeth leaned closer and whispered:

"The first time Darcy proposed to me, I rejected him for precisely that reason."
Georgiana looked at Elizabeth and exclaimed in astonishment:

"You rejected my brother! I had no idea!"
Her consternation was so obvious that Elizabeth could not hold back a smile.

"He must have been very surprised," Georgiana said finally and frowned. Elizabeth nodded.

"It is hardly something he would choose to talk about. As far as I'm aware, only my sister Jane knows about it," she said.

"But why?" Georgiana began and then stopped herself. "I'm sorry. I did not mean..." she said and blushed.

"I had promised myself that only the deepest love would persuade me to enter into a marriage, and at the time of your brother's first proposal, my feelings were not such," Elizabeth said and smiled. "But to both our happiness, my feelings soon changed in character."

"Yes, no one who sees you now could fail to notice how much you mean to each other," Georgiana said and fell silent.

"Knowing a person's true character and mind can give rise to feelings one did not think were possible or even in existence," Elizabeth said. After a moment's deliberation, she raised her eyebrow.

"Although when it comes to Mr Collins, I am convinced that my feelings in any situation would have remained the same."

These words made Georgiana smile. Mr Collins seemed to make the same impression upon any woman who crossed paths with him, and she knew more than well what her sister-in-law was referring to.

"I suppose you are right. Given time one can come to love a man of good character," Georgiana said thoughtfully.

"The trouble is, there is already a man whom I hold dear," Georgiana whispered and lowered her eyes. At these words she sank back and dried her cheeks to mask that new tears had begun to fall.

"The thought of this man makes you unhappy, I see," said Elizabeth and stroked her hair. Georgiana lifted her head and looked straight at Elizabeth.

"It is the thought of my brother's reaction that makes me unhappy," she said.

Chapter 39

Georgiana was pleased that Darcy had not been aggravated by her decision to reject Lord Malcolm's proposal. However, that was all she had to be pleased about. Her decision to reveal her feelings for Edward to her brother did not please any one of those involved. If she had known the outcome, she would have chosen to remain silent.

While Elizabeth did not appear to be surprised by her revelation, Darcy's consternation was the greater. At first it even seemed as if he thought she was jesting.

"Edward?" For a moment he had looked puzzled. "Mr Edward Hardin from Cambridge?" Darcy smiled when he found the name he was looking for. He had long been worried about his sister's future happiness. Even if it was not the first man he would have thought of for his sister, he was happy that she had taken an interest in anyone. Although it was a long time since the affair with Wickham had taken place, Georgiana had ever since shown a visible lack of interest in the men who had been introduced to her. Darcy had assumed that she was deeply hurt by the fact that Wickham had singled her out for her fortune, and that she therefore lacked faith in other young men. If Edward Hardin could arouse her feelings, he would happily welcome him at Pemberley.

"You have my consent, although I must admit that I had not guessed at any stronger feelings between the two of you," Darcy said and smiled.

Elizabeth's raised eyebrows reminded him that his wife had only recently been introduced to the family's social circles. It was unlikely that she would immediately recollect Mr Edward Hardin, his estate Whitmore, and the man's distant relation to Bingley.

"Elizabeth, you remember Edward Hardin who was introduced to us at Bingley's ball? Edward's father, Mr Herald Hardin, was the cousin of Bingley's father..." Darcy fell silent.

The look that was exchanged between Elizabeth and his sister did not pass him by. Another glance from Elizabeth revealed that he would soon be let in on something his sister had already told her sister-in-law.

Elizabeth's calm was not the cause of his worry; instead it was the lack of any witty remark that made Darcy frown. Georgiana did not lift her eyes from the steak in front of her as she replied to his unspoken question. Her words were as few as her voice was apprehensive.

"It is not the Edward you think it is," she said quietly.

Darcy immediately began to rummage through his memory for any men of their acquaintance who went by the forename of Edward. He was readily amused by the guessing game that started off.

"Mr Edward Eton," he said hopefully. Georgiana looked away and shook her head.

"Mr Edward Conolley," he continued with assumed indifference. The Conolley family were undoubtedly rich, but personally he had never been much for their way of life. The father was a spender, and had, in all likelihood, passed the habit on to his sons. This time, Georgiana's denial offered some relief.

"Mr Edward Francis," he said and leaned back to regard his sister, whose posture once more told him he had guessed wrong. For every name he mentioned, Georgiana looked more downcast.

An older brother's guesses as to the name of his younger sister's intended was a measure of what kind of man he thought himself capable of welcoming into the family. During her stay in London, Georgiana had had the opportunity to meet many men of consequence; perhaps the man was of a higher standing than any of them had imagined. Knowing his sister's modesty, shyness and calm demeanour, Darcy assumed that her embarrassment and gravity suggested that this was the case.

"Sir Edward??" He said with a raised eyebrow and encouraging smile. Once again, Georgiana solemnly shook her head.

"It is not the Edward you think it is," she whispered and looked at her brother.

Darcy's astonishment was genuine: he had named every acquaintance and vague connection by the name of Edward without success. Due to the royal family's penchant for the name, it was common in every class of society. Darcy paused. An impulse to laugh made him look at Georgiana who with great precision cut her cutlet into pea-sized pieces.

"Pardon me for saying so, Georgiana, but if I did not know you better, or knew your standing, one could almost think you were referring to Edward... who works in the stables..." he added when no one around the table spoke.

The absence of laughter at the obvious irony of such a statement made him put down his cutlery with such force that they clattered against the porcelain. The silence around the table confirmed the unthinkable. He had not misheard. His sister had just told him she harboured feelings towards the stable master. Even if she had not said so in so many words, the insight had struck him with full force.

Suddenly it all made sense to him. Georgiana's great interest in learning to ride, Edward's serviceability and outspokenness in matters that did not pertain to riding. The two youngsters' excursion the day he and Elizabeth had returned to Pemberley. In hindsight, he could not see how he had been so blind.

Darcy stared at his sister without managing to say a word. He cast Elizabeth an angry glance to judge whether she was an accomplice. To his relief, he found that until recently, she had been unaware of what had gone on.

The thought that he had let Edward and Georgiana continue the lessons on their own made him livid with rage. The anger directed at himself was mixed with feelings of guilt at his lack of clear-sightedness. He had not in the least suspected that there was anything else than an interest in horses that made Georgiana's visits to the stable-building so frequent.

Once again his sister was preyed upon by a gold-digger, and like the first one, this man was well-aware of Georgiana's circumstances, her fortune of £30,000.

Not since he had become aware of Mr Wickham's intentions for Georgiana had he felt such a strong emotion. The thought of how Edward had betrayed his confidence in him, had exploited every opportunity that had come his way, and had even, on several occasions, been alone with Georgiana, almost made Darcy loose his composure. If Edward had been within reach, Darcy was sure that he would have attacked him. He had to sum up all his reserves of reasons to decide to wait until the next day before he took the necessary steps.

A sudden thirst made him aware that his wine glass was in dire need of refilling. His worry increased as he discovered that there were no servants in the room. He was forced to bite into the bone of his cutlet to remain composed.

Georgiana observed her brother from under her fringe; her lack of appetite resulted in a nervous shuffling of the cutlet on her plate. Darcy did not speak a word and neither Elizabeth nor Georgiana wanted to challenge destiny by asking him to share his thoughts. The rest of the meal was thus partaken of in perturbed silence. To Georgiana, Darcy's controlled anger was more frightening than those outbursts of rage she had, on a very few occasions, witnessed in him. The thought of what kind of measures her brother would take made her feel ill, and she knew she would lie sleepless for some time to come.

Georgiana remembered Darcy's last outburst of rage well: there were more than her who thought the man got what he deserved. Due to her history with Wickham, she had felt a particular sympathy for the young housemaid, Joan, who was the same age as herself.

Joan was a timid girl from Lambton, who thanks to her uncle's word had obtained employment as a housemaid at Pemberley. Joan's uncle, the owner of Lambton Inn, had taught her the importance of correct behaviour, a calm demeanour, and good service. The secret was to always remain one step ahead, to be aware of the guest's or master's needs before he himself became aware of them, and to fulfil them.

A guest's gaze that was lifted from the table should, before it returned to the table top, rest on a pint of beer served from a woman's hand. Similarly, the warm look of a patroness at her husband was the signal to let the mistress know that her bath was ready. This was some of the advice Joan had been given by her uncle, and to Mrs Darcy's delight she had practiced them well.

The change that had taken place during the autumn was therefore noticeable. More than once, Mrs Darcy had to remind Joan of her duties. One morning, Elizabeth had to sit for half an hour at her mirror before Joan arrived to prepare her hair; another day she had forgotten to take Mrs Darcy's muslin dress down to be ironed, which was unfortunate as it was to be worn the same night.

In the company of Elizabeth and other women, Joan had carried out her duties, but as soon as a man had appeared she lowered her eyes and fell silent. It was true that a woman often lowered her eyes when faced with a man she was unacquainted with, but not to meet their eyes more than hastily was more than propriety dictated. The sight of how Joan had jumped and dropped the tray she was carrying when Darcy's steward passed by, had made Elizabeth sharpen her attention. For a moment, Elizabeth had suspected that Joan had fallen into disfavour with the steward and was therefore nervous in the company of the correct but dour-looking man.

The butler's discreet entrance into the sitting room the next evening had, however, produced a similar reaction, which made Elizabeth realise that it was time to speak to Mrs Reynolds, who was in charge of the servants within the walls of Pemberley.

Joan, who had been broken-hearted at being called in to Mrs Reynolds, had assured her that she would take more care in the future. The value of the glasses that had been crushed when she dropped the tray surpassed more than a month's wages, if she was only given a second chance, she would work them off, even if it took her a year.

Mrs Reynolds had been in service long enough not to dismiss a young woman's change in behaviour patterns as single incidents unconnected to each other. On being asked if she was with child, Joan had looked up in shock and shook her head. Even if this was not the case, Mrs Reynolds had noticed that the question was justifiable. A relationship between a male and a female servant at the same workplace was not acceptable; if it did occur one of them had to leave their employment immediately, which had happened on a few occasions at Pemberley.

Anxiety about such a situation would have been justified, but not the fear that Joan showed proof of. Mrs Reynolds had looked at the girl for a long time, well aware that the answer to the next question was fully dependent on how it was posed. Mrs Reynolds was not unaware of what took place on some of the estates in the country. Pemberley had always had a good reputation among the maids; here one was expected to do one's job, and nothing more.

"Is it Mr Herring who has bothered you?" Mrs Reynolds had said suddenly. Mr Herring was the latest employee at the estate; his place was in the laundry, which was an unusual place for a man.

"My task is to relieve the women of the heavy work that the carrying of wet laundry entails," he had explained to those who made fun of his position. This was in part the truth: the sight of the laundry maids working was another reason. Mr Herring had in his former workplaces not contented himself to look, but given free reins to his desires. To his consternation, none of the laundry maids at Pemberley had welcomed his advances.

Mr Herring had never been at a workplace where not a single solitary female was ready to fulfil his desire.

The weeks of unwanted celibacy, the frustration and the burgeoning doubt as to whether his manhood was intact, had made him act in a manner that was alien even to himself.

Contemplating his situation, he had one night been surprised by steps in the laundry room. From his shielded spot, he had observed the young woman who had taken down

Mrs Darcy's dress from the line of drying clothes. Suddenly he had found himself at her side with the single thought that she had used the dress as an excuse to come and see him. The lack of responsiveness to his touch he had seen as a confirmation of the girl's shyness, her resistance a sign of long suppressed eagerness.

Joan, who had been lulled by the security offered within the walls of Pemberley, had been taken unawares by the man's sudden attack. After the shock had subsided, she had beaten and kicked the man until he finally relinquished his grip. The darkness had meant she had not been able to distinguish his features, and even if Mr Herring's place was in the laundry room, it could have been any one of the male servants who had molested her.

Mr Darcy's knowledge of the matter had not passed anyone by unnoticed. Not for a moment did he think that any of his old servants could perform such a deed, and his suspicions had immediately alighted on Mr Herring. Darcy had personally made Mr Herring answer for the information that had come to his attention.

The sight of Mr Darcy among the steam from the big tubs, had made every laundry maid freeze in their movements. Mr Herring's look at his black-clad master had reminded him of a cartoon he had seen in the magazine Gazette. The article had been on a warmer place where people who had committed a sin risked ending up after death. Mr Herring had at the time laughed at the superstitious people who believed this. That morning, neither he nor anyone else in the laundry room had laughed.

The outburst of rage that Georgiana had feared would be the outcome of this evening, too, did not occur. The dinner and the silence had been interrupted when Darcy had thrown the bone of his cutlet onto his plate, risen from his chair and left the room. Before he had passed over the threshold, he had turned and said:

"I hardly need to explain to you why such a match is entirely out of the question."

Chapter 40

Edward saw Darcy approaching the stable building with determined steps and for a moment he had a terrible premonition. After a while, he calmed himself. It was the time of month when Darcy customarily came down to the stables to discuss impending purchases or sales of young animals. The calm turned once more to worry as he saw Darcy's facial expression that was resolute, to say the least. His posture was visibly stiff and his gaze so dark that Edward, for the first time, was scared by his master.

Darcy was clad in black boots, a great-coat and a top hat. Edward did not think he had come to ask for his horse. His misgivings proved true when Darcy stopped in front of him, and in a loud voice declared:

"I have come to speak to you." A look at the workers who were in the building made them lower their eyes and hurriedly finish their tasks. The farmhand who had witnessed the scenario up close, quickly made himself scarce for fear of being included in Darcy's wrath.

Mr Darcy was rarely angered. Among the servants it was well known that when this did happen, he was not an easy man to deal with, and it was best to keep out of his way. To be the one who had caused his distemper, and to remain alone in the area, made Edward more uncomfortable than he could have imagined.

"Sir, as for yesterday's ride, the responsibility is entirely mine," he said as calmly as he could muster.

"As you must understand, I am not here about any riding excursion!" Darcy said gruffly and stared at him.

"The events of yesterday are mere trifles in comparison to what has come to my attention," he continued bitterly. Edward, who did not know how to respond, remained silent.

"Would you be so kind as to inform me of your relationship with Miss Darcy," Darcy said, and looked challengingly at him.

Edward's gaze was steady when he looked at Pemberley's owner, who had been his employer for many years. "Sir, we are good friends," he said and swallowed.

"Would you define the term good friends to me," Darcy said coolly.

Edward blushed in anger and dismay when he understood the underlying implication of the question. His voice held traces of bitterness when he replied:

"Sir, if you think I have in any way behaved indecently, I give you my word that this is not the case. Miss Darcy will tell you the same." Darcy looked at him and snorted.

"My sister's opinion is not relevant under the circumstances," he said coldly.

Before Edward had time to reply, his master's accusations continued:

"I am also well aware of a woman's precarious situation when she is alone in the company of a man, miles from any prying eyes. Especially if the man in question is only looking to his own needs and takes liberties far beyond that which is acceptable for a man of his social standing."

While Darcy spoke, his voice rose until it began to take on the character of a roar: it was as if each word that was spoken made him angrier. Edward, who could not for a moment believe that what was happening was true, remained speechless. When Darcy took a step forward, he backed away instinctively.

"Remain in your place while I'm speaking to you," Darcy bellowed. Edward looked at him quickly, before turning his eyes away. It was the first time he did not know how to act in front of his employer. If he looked him in the eyes, it would be seen as provocative; if he avoided eye-contact, the result was the same.

Although the cool morning made him shiver, he was aware of sweating despite his thin clothes. With a sick feeling, Edward remained frozen in place. They were alone in the stable yard, and would remain that way. The farmhand had in all likelihood warned the others to keep away unless they wanted to fall into disfavour. Each man was his own best friend, when it really came to it. They all had families to provide for, and could not jeopardize their positions to save someone else's hide. One was loyal to one's master. A salary weighed heavier than gratitude, which was all a colleague could offer in return.

Edward was not unaware of the rifle that rested on Darcy's shoulder. Although he had never been known to use violence against his labourers, he could not but wonder why Darcy was carrying a rifle if he had no intention of going hunting. He admitted that he had grossly underestimated the danger of being alone in the company of Miss Darcy.

For what seemed like an eternity to Edward, the two remained standing in the yard. His lowered gaze meant that he could not see what Darcy was doing. Although he tried to convince himself of the unreasonableness of his apprehensions, he could not refrain from listening intently after the clicking sound of the trigger.

Darcy looked at the young man in front of him, and reflected for the first time over the power his position brought with it. Experience had taught him that kindness was not always the most efficient way of dealing with undesirable situations. Although Wickham had been compensated richly to stay away, he had, through his wife, continued to make his existence felt.

For a moment, Darcy considered taking measures he had always despised in other estate owners. If he made a formal complaint at court, he would never again have to think about Edward accosting his sister. Elizabeth would never forgive such an action, however, and neither would his sister.

"Do you love Miss Darcy?" Darcy said abruptly and with such sharpness that Edward jumped. Taken aback by the direct question and its character, he remained silent.

"Yes," Edward said finally. Darcy's answer did not take long, and his voice now held the utmost formality.

"You can hardly be unaware of your standing in life, and that you have nothing to offer Miss Darcy. If you permit me to ask: what is your own opinion in the matter?"

Edward did not reply; his shoulders sank and he looked out across the fields. The reason he had answered truthfully to Darcy's questions was that he, as his master, valued honesty. He realised, suddenly, that this might have been a mistake. His only wish was that it would not cause Georgiana any suffering; if that was the case he would have lied without a hesitation. Darcy's question had surprised him to the extent that he had replied without thinking of the consequences.

"I am well aware that I have nothing to offer Miss Darcy," he said finally and looked away. To hear himself say what he had always known saddened him, and he did not want Mr Darcy to see it.

"On that point we are in perfect agreement, then," Darcy countered with a tone of voice that did not admit to contradictions.

"Finally I have a question that demands an honest reply. Have you had the intention of eloping with Miss Darcy? Her personal fortune is not something you can be entirely unacquainted with."

Edward looked at Darcy, he felt deeply insulted by the characteristics that had been ascribed to him. Even if he had understood that his master would be upset if he found out about the liberties they had taken the previous day, he had never imagined he would be so cruel. What hurt him the most was that Darcy, despite their long acquaintance, believed him capable not only of indecency, but also carrying out an elopement with Georgiana. For a moment his fear subsided, if it was the last thing he did he would tell the truth.

"However much it would contribute to my own happiness, I could never act in a manner that brought Miss Darcy into disfavour with her family and sullied her good name. Sir, even if I cannot deny my feelings for Miss Darcy, it hurts me that you think me capable of the accusations you have launched at me," Edward said doggedly.

"After having abused my trust, your feelings are completely irrelevant to me. I want you to leave Pemberley and I need hardly add that you will not be welcome back," Darcy replied and turned to leave.

As soon as Darcy had uttered his last words, Edward had left Pemberley in haste. It was only with every ounce of self-possession that he managed to remain standing and receive the reproach Darcy had levied at him.

Naturally, he was not unaware of Georgiana's fortune. Darcy had insinuated that this was the basis for his feelings for Miss Darcy. Nothing could be further from the truth. Edward had often wished that her fortune had been less substantial, as it might have improved his non-existent chances.

In the moment, the experience of the stable yard had only frightened him. When he thought back to it afterwards it also brought him grief. Not that he had been unaware of it before, but only now was it completely clear to him how alone he was.

There was no one prepared to rush to his defence, speak up for him or be of assistance. Edward missed his father more than he could remember ever having done before. When he remembered all the times he had admired his father without telling him so, he had to focus on something else until he had regained his composure.

What would become of him now was unknown. In his distress, he could not think about the future, or how he would thereafter earn his living. In comparison to others in similar positions, his income as a stable master at Pemberley had been more than generous. Edward was grateful he had inherited his father's carefulness and thriftiness. Like his father, he had saved a certain amount each month for future investments.

Edward's father, who had worked at Pemberley for over thirty years, had for as long saved part of his salary, and, just before his death, he had bought a little house in the village. The house was small, but decidedly more pleasant than the cottage Edward had grown up in, and his father had been justifiably proud the first time he had shown his son their new abode.

For a moment, Edward considered his alternatives. To look for work as a stable master at any of the neighbouring estates was out of question – he could hardly count on any recommendations from Mr Darcy. He would probably dissuade any future employers.

To continue in the line of work he had been trained, he would have to go as far away from Derbyshire as possible. With luck, he could, by giving proof of his skills, win his new employer's trust before any ill-humoured rumours reached him. Edward could, however, not keep himself from wondering whether his new employer, if indeed such a rumour reached his ear, would not choose to believe Mr Darcy, rather than his new employee. His courage failed him when he considered that the former was the more likely.

Another alternative was to go to the continent; if he sold the house the income would cover any travelling costs and lodgings until he had found an appropriate position. The continent had never before held any allure for him; but as it now looked, there were not many alternatives.

He could possibly join the army, but that would be a breach of all his principles. As he was so attached to both humans and animals, the thought of ending up on a battlefield made him queasy.

There were many ships sailing to far-away countries, and young men often went to sea. Edward had never been to the sea. The only water he had seen were the lakes they had passed when travelling on some business.

The alternatives were as few as they were unsavoury, and if his father could have seen his son's plight, he would have been aghast. Stricken by a sudden sense of futility, Edward was unable to rise from bed, or put any thought into action. He felt no hunger, no tiredness, no desire to do anything, and this was completely out of character.

Chapter 41

Coyle had been surprised by Darcy's decision to replace Edward. Even if he had himself, on several occasions, reprimanded the young stable master, he had never had a thought of dismissing him. Once, he had, however, threatened him with those very words. He remembered it well; it was one of the few times he had completely lost control of his temper.

Mr Darcy had on the occasion invited a few friends to the annual foxhunt that was being held in the neighbouring forests. It had been one of the largest events that Coyle had been entrusted with since he had begun his service at Pemberley. He had taken his task very seriously. The reception, the choice of rifles, the horses and the hunting grounds had been planned out in minute detail.

Coyle had chosen the most fitting of the servants to take on the various areas of responsibility. Edward's task had been to prepare and ready the horses so that they were fit for each of the important guests.

Up until the fateful event, all had gone according to plan. The guests had returned in good spirits after the first day. The laughter had not gone unnoticed by the ladies, and the story that had amused the gentlemen had soon come to everyone's attention. One of the couples had, for the rest of the evening, had to put up with more or less discreet commentaries with the accompanying laughter of the rest of the party.

Mr Morris, who had promised his wife a fur collar, was the only one who had had any luck with the hunt. When he had encountered his prey, he had shot an extra round into the air and signalled for the men to come closer. When they had joined him, he had, in a loud voice and lively gestures, made an account of his own hunting prowess. Thereupon he had, with determined strides, gone up to the shrub where the fox had taken its recourse. With the one hand he had pushed the twigs aside, whereupon he remained standing and stared in front of him. When he had finally dragged the animal out of the shrubbery, everyone knew immediately that Mrs Morris would be going without her fur. It had not passed anyone by that the poor fox was mangy.

Mr Darcy had praised Coyle for the success of his arrangements. What occurred the following day was, therefore, most unfortunate for every one concerned.

The oldest man of the party had, when his horse suddenly reared, fallen off and broken his leg. The choice of horse had been based on the riders' own accounts of their merits. Mr Wilbur, who had denied and refused to acknowledge his fear of horses, had, as on so many other occasions, insisted on being a more experience rider than he was. The shame of having fallen off made him affirm that it was the horse's temper that had been the cause of the incident. At the sight of the badly wounded leg, Darcy had promised that the horse would be taken care of so that no other person would come to harm.

Coyle had been embittered by the incident; it had been unavoidable that he, too, would be cast in a bad light. Mr Darcy's decision to remove the horse had been the right one; people who were insulted, hurt or angered had a need to be justified. A new horse, as the old one was untrustworthy, had been a low price to pay in exchange for Mr Wilbur's confidence.

A few hours later, Coyle had visited the stables to settle his account with Edward. He did not intend to give in until all his questions had been answered. The first question he had intended to ask was how he could have chosen such an unreliable horse for an old man. Why had he not followed his heed to assure himself that the horses were well balanced? Was he aware of the consequences of his lack of judgement? A bone fracture in an old man could be fatal. If the man died, had he thought of who would be held accountable? Had he thought of the consequences for this man? Had he used his head at all?

Already on his way to the stable building, Coyle had been convinced that Edward would try to escape blame. He had imagined what replies he would receive to his questions. Edward had always put the horses before himself. He would assure Coyle that there was nothing wrong with the horse, and take the blame himself. If he were prepared to face the consequences, Coyle would see to it that he did, too. He had known what he would do, and he had looked forward to it.

The anger that had built up all the way to the stable building, culminated when he had seen the animal still standing in its regular place. It had not been the first time that Edward had refused to follow orders. As he had pictured this scenario, Coyle had done nothing to dampen his rage.

The stable master had not looked up as Coyle approached; instead he had bent even closer over the horse's leg that he was examining. Coyle viewed this as further evidence of his lack of respect for his superiors.

When Edward had not answered when spoken to, either, Coyle had lost his control. He remembered the heat of his skin, the pounding and soughing through his head. The impulse, the will, and the satisfaction at having gone to attack.

"How dare you!" he had growled, and pushed Edward with such force that he had knocked both his head and his arm against the wooden wall.

When Edward had looked up, his shocked expression had revealed his astonishment at both the pain and the attack. Coyle had not given him time to explain whether he had heard him enter the building or not. In the state he was in, not even an excuse could dampen his anger; he had wanted nothing but an outlet for it.

Before Edward had time to reply or stand up, Coyle had taken a step forward, whereupon the stable master had backed into the corner of the box.

It was the first time that Edward had shied away from him; Coyle recalled that in his anger, he had enjoyed the experience. The defiance he usually imagined seeing there had suddenly been gone.

Slowly he had taken another step forward. The walls had prevented Edward's escape. In what had looked to be an attempt of an evasive movement, he had put up his arm and

148

for a moment bared the deep cuts the coarseness of the wall had effected on him. The quick breathing, the grimace and the hasty lowering had revealed that his left arm was seriously wounded. It was, however, the sight of the gaping wound on the forehead that had prevented Coyle from attacking him anew. Bloodshed could give the impression of a more damaging wound than was actually the case, and in his position it was better to be safe than sorry.

The pain in his arm had stopped Edward from immediately noticing the blood. When he looked down at his shirt that was stained red on the one side of the chest, he had hastily pressed his unhurt arm against his forehead. He had not said anything, not even when Coyle had pointed at him and hissed that his days at Pemberley had come to an end. Coyle had left him in uncertainty, and in his irate state, he had thought that Edward had got what he deserved.

It was Mr Darcy that later that night had informed Coyle that he had given Edward permission to retain and try to cure the horse that was wounded. Darcy had explained that Edward had assured him that the horse had been in an excellent state that morning. He had pointed out that as he himself had bred and fostered Beth, he knew that she was neither moody nor tempestuous. On closer inspection, he had also found that she was limping. A wound could heal; for an unruly horse, however, there was but one option.

When Darcy with a smile had recounted Edward's commitment to the horse, Coyle had looked away.

He had never commented upon the incident, and had pretended not to notice Edward's scratches. Coyle had not expected anything else than that Edward would explain his wounds as a result of having fallen off a horse, either.

If Mr Darcy had been thus indulgent with his stable master on an occasion when one of his friends had been badly wounded, the damage Edward had caused this time must be of the worst kind imaginable, to warrant his immediate dismissal. Despite wild guesses, Coyle had not been close to the real reason for this decision.

Through an unannounced visit to Darcy's office, Coyle had, however, been witness to part of the conversation that had occurred between Mr Darcy and his wife. They had apparently been of different opinions in the matter they had discussed; Coyle's consternation when he understood what it was about had been complete. That Edward, like all young men, found Miss Darcy attractive was to be considered natural; to forget his position and confess this to her brother was madness. Coyle could still not understand how Edward could put himself and Miss Darcy through this.

Chapter 42

Darcy, who had intended to suggest a stroll in the park, only needed to glance at his wife to realise that the little pointer would have to do as company. Elizabeth, who longed for her sister's and Bingley's company, had already passed by the sitting room window several times in the hope of seeing the carriage draw up.

Bingley's and Jane's visit was more than longed for by both of them. The atmosphere between Georgiana and Darcy had been tense since she had revealed that she had feelings for Edward. Elizabeth hoped rather than believed that the addition to their party would disperse the gloom. The conversations, social interaction and activities of the last few days had not brought any joy to any of those involved.

Since Georgiana's discovery that Edward had been replaced by a stable master from Yorkshire, she had not spoken a word to Darcy. She knew her brother too well to ask why Edward was no longer at Pemberley. Despite Georgiana having been part of, on Darcy's request, the activities of the last few days, she had been no more than physically present. The questions put to her had been answered in a despondent voice, and eyes that after a quick glance at the person in question, had been stuck in the distance.

John Goose had, on one occasion, turned around to see if anyone had stepped into the room without him noticing.

Georgiana's way of withdrawing and hiding her feelings of sorrow, despair and regret, which in all likelihood she felt, was harder to witness than the scenarios of weeping and acting-out that Elizabeth had been used to at Longbourn. Mrs Bennet had rather escalated than tried to dampen the emotions that had been upset or hurt. Neither had her mother been unwilling to accept support, comfort and help. If she had not immediately been offered this due to her behaviour, her complaints about the lack thereof had fulfilled her wishes.

Elizabeth's efforts to approach her sister-in-law had resulted in Georgiana excusing herself and leaving the room. It had always been Elizabeth's strong conviction that it was a cruel world that could separate two people who loved one another, for the simple reason that one of them was lacking in fortune. To discuss the matter with Darcy was futile; on this matter, his opinion was crystal clear.

"Even if my actions hurt my sister, I am fully convinced that my actions are in moral agreement with the dictates of our forefathers' and my own convictions. In other matters I may be susceptible to your inducement, Elizabeth, but in this matter my decision has been made and I have nothing further to add."

Elizabeth could not, as things stood, do much to help Georgiana, and she found it best to remain silent.

Elizabeth saw Darcy stroll off with the happy pointer that eagerly fetched a stick in the hopes that his owner would play with him. Elizabeth smiled as she remembered her husband's surprise when he had received the black little pup that she had handed over on his birthday. The dog had quickly won Darcy's affection and he followed him faithfully wherever he went. Hamlet was as affectionate and happy when Darcy returned after a few minutes' absence as he was after several days' absence. The name he had given the little pointer pup had not been up for discussion, as Darcy had been firm that it was indeed a suitable name for a dog.

Finally, Elizabeth spotted the longed-for carriage roll into the yard, and she hurried to meet her guests.

"Oh, Jane! Bingley! If you knew how glad I am to see you!" Elizabeth said and embraced them both.

"The pleasure is all ours," said Bingley heartily and looked around. "But what have you done with your husband?"

"Darcy is out walking Hamlet," Elizabeth said and smiled at her husband who approached with hasty strides.

"I am sorry not to have received you properly," Darcy said and welcomed his guests with the same enthusiasm his wife had done. After a few more heartfelt phrases of greeting, as well as accounts from the travellers concerning the journey, the party withdrew into the house. Darcy led them through the sitting room, the music room and the gallery, and finally into the dining room where the new arrivals would take their morning tea.

Elizabeth, who saw Jane's wonder at the big house with the tasteful décor whispered:

"Now you see why, on my first visit here, I decided to become the mistress of Pemberley." Jane looked at Elizabeth and smiled.

"It is a very beautiful house and the knowledge that you married its owner out of love must give him great happiness."

"Yes, there is no doubt as to that; few women would have declined becoming the mistresses of such a house, however they felt about the man in question," Elizabeth said and laughed.

After a while, Elizabeth asked her sister about their parents and sisters at Longbourn. Elizabeth looked at Jane and prepared herself for a while's entertainment in the narrating of her mother's marital plans for her two remaining daughters.

"What happened with the young man that our dear mama hoped to acquire as a son-in-law? Did he choose Kitty or Mary as his lawful wife?"

"Dear mama," Jane said and told Elizabeth the whole story.

As soon as it had been confirmed that the young man had rented the house that lay just outside Meryton, Mrs Bennet had encouraged, demanded and insisted her husband to visit its new inhabitant. Mr Bennet had, to begin with, been averse, but finally given in and listened to his wife's entreaties, and when he returned in the evening he could relay the good news that Mr Williams intended to visit them the following day. As expected, Mrs Bennet had been overjoyed and in detail prepared the dinner that they were to tempt their intended son-in-law with.

To her great happiness, Longbourn was the first place the young man intended to visit, and as no one had yet seen him, it would be Mrs Bennet who could walk into town the following day, and tell everything about Mr Williams. Mary and Kitty had been presented with new dresses, which were slightly more expensive than what their budget really allowed. Mrs Bennet had reasoned that one had, in some situations, to see to the future consequences rather than the short-term discomfort that might arise from such expenses.

Mr Bennet's comment on Kitty's latest acquirement had signalled his opinion in the matter.

"To live on water and bread, so that one's daughters can have dresses worthy of a lady at court, undoubtedly imbues one with a sense of discomfort."

Mrs Bennet, who for a moment had been disgruntled, had put her chin up and firmly averred:

"If one of our daughters is married to Mr Williams, the dress will have been worth its price many times over."

To start with, everything had seemed to go according to plan. Mr Williams had arrived on the hour, and courteously presented Mrs Bennet with a bouquet of flowers, which immediately had made Kitty chortle. Kitty had decided that as soon as Mr Williams had gone away again, she would sit down and write a detailed letter to Lydia, wherein she would describe the awkward young man who visited their home. If it continued in this way, she and Mary would never marry.

Mr Williams was young, but so dense even Mrs Bennet had looked up in surprise as she had listened to his monotonous voice.

"Our dear papa said that he would happily had welcomed Mr Collins as his son-in-law, if he had had to chose between the two of them," Jane said, and continued her story when she saw Elizabeth's raised eyebrows.

Kitty and Mary had been carried away by Mrs Bennet's outpourings on the fabulous Mr Williams, and could not be other than severely disappointed when the young gentleman was neither attractive to listen to nor to look at. Mrs Bennet had even so been prepared to overlook these failings, as the young man had a fortune, but after half of the dinner had passed, this was proven to be another false hope.

"When mama found out that Mr Williams only had £400 a year, she removed herself with the excuse that she was suffering from a sudden headache," Jane said quietly.

"How terribly rude of her; how could she behave in such a manner!" Elizabeth exclaimed.

"You are right, Lizzy. Even if Mr Williams was both dense and lacking in fortune, he did not deserve to be treated that way," Jane sighed.

Mrs Bennet had not shown herself again that evening, and the day after she had omitted to walk to Meryton. A few weeks later she had had every reason to regret her decision to put Mr Williams off in such a manner.

The reason he had not been able to claim a fortune greater than £400 a year at the time of his visit was that he had not yet turned eighteen. By Lady Lucas, Mrs Bennet was informed that on his eighteenth birthday, Mr Williams would come into the sum of £20,000, which was his birthright. Furthermore, Mr Williams had the same day become the owner of an estate in Devonshire, that had previously belonged to his aunt, who had passed away without any heirs. When Lady Lucas finally let it be known that her own daughter, Maria Lucas, was engaged to be married to the young Mr Williams, Mrs Bennet had not wanted to hear more.

"One can hardly keep oneself from laughing," Elizabeth said when Jane had finished her story.

"Does one dare to hope that this means our dear mama will become more thoughtful in the future?" she said and shook her head.

"I believe so," Jane said.

"I am not so convinced, I'm afraid. Considering her rejoicing at Lydia's match, I daresay anything's possible. While we are on the topic of Lydia, I wonder if she has contacted you? It was a long time since I received a letter wherein she kindly informed me of her financial situation and reminded me of my own," Elizabeth said and looked meaningfully at Jane.

"I admit that the letters arriving at Netherfield contain similar hints, though not phrased in that direct manner," Jane replied.

Lydia had since her marriage to Mr Wickham been in a constant need of monetary reinforcement, which she usually obtained through her two sisters. Mr Wickham was a man who had always lived beyond his means, and his judgement in this matter had not improved noticeably since he entered into marriage. As the topic was not a source of any joy to any of them, it soon turned to a discussion of Pemberley, and all Elizabeth's chores that she nowadays carried out without incident.

Chapter 43

Jane observed Georgiana in silence. Although she smiled, responded to questions, and at Bingley's request played two pieces on the pianoforte, it seemed that the smile as well as the music-making was forced. The very first evening at Pemberley, Jane had asked her sister what ailed Miss Darcy.

"What more than one woman has experienced, on account of her love for a man," Elizabeth had replied after a moment's silence. Jane knew Elizabeth well enough to suspect that Elizabeth was conflicted as to whether she should keep her husband's family business private, or whether she should confide in her sister as the two had always done.

Jane did not ask again, and received Elizabeth's look of gratitude. They were both well aware that their entries into marriage had meant that some of the confidence that had once existed between them was now reserved for man and wife.

Bingley had with his good humour, his amiability and positive outlook on life, not noticed what his wife had immediately observed. During dinner, he began conversing on a subject that made three of those present look up and hastily arrange their facial expressions.

"Miss Darcy, it has come to my attention that you have become an excellent rider. What a good notion, to learn to ride!" Bingley said enthusiastically.

If Darcy was surprised, he did not show any sign of it, but kept the grave face he had worn when discussing the current hostilities in Europe. He nodded and raised his glass to propose a toast. Bingley gripped his glass, spun it and sniffed the red, tantalising liquid. He took a deep breath and a mouthful, which he swirled around in his mouth before he swallowed.

"An excellent wine, Darcy," he said appreciatively, and smiled with teeth that had taken on a purple-red tone. Darcy smiled at his friend's enthusiasm.

"I will relate your words to Mr Wilkins, who has been kind enough to pass onto me some of the French wines he obtained during his travels."

Bingley nodded, took another sip and said: "Quite extraordinary. Say what you want about the French, but they do know how to make wine." Darcy's hope that the conversation would thereby turn to French wines, was quenched as his friend turned to Georgiana.

"Now that you have learned to ride you must come out with us," Bingley said happily. Georgiana nodded mutely, which encouraged Bingley to continue: "we should perhaps take a turn tomorrow."

Darcy looked down at his empty glass, and noted that he had drunk quicker than etiquette prescribed. He did not know whether it was to obtain the calm a glass of red wine could offer, or whether to escape from the questions he would prefer to avoid.

Elizabeth glanced at Georgiana who, in an attempt to hide the tears that threatened to break out, coughed as though something had caught in her throat. John Goose immediately provided her with a glass of water, which she gratefully accepted. Unaware of his friend's sombre expression and Georgiana's blush, Bingley turned to Elizabeth.

"The truth is, I told Darcy a long time ago that he should encourage Georgiana to learn to ride. At the time, however, he thought it was too dangerous," Bingley said and laughed.

"Tell me, Darcy, who was it that you finally entrusted with teaching both Miss and Mrs Darcy these skills?"

Elizabeth, who more than well understood how insufferable this situation must be to Georgiana, regarded her husband as he said, shortly, "Mr Jones."

"Mr Jones, the stable master! Of course, I should have known," Bingley said and smiled.

"Then I understand that you feel at ease. He seems a trustworthy fellow."

Darcy did not respond to this, and Bingley felt the necessity to explain further.

"It was he who recommended Bianca to me, a fine specimen indeed. One seldom sees such a clear marking, and such excellent behaviour."

Darcy avoided his sister's gaze as he replied to his friend. "Mr Jones passed away two years ago. It is his son who has taken over his work."

"Oh," said Bingley and fell quiet as he did not know what to say. Georgiana, who had not said a word to her brother during the meal, suddenly said:

"If I am not mistaken, Edward has been replaced." Bingley looked questioningly at Darcy, but did not, to Elizabeth's relief, extend the question further.

"Is that so?" was all he said. Darcy met his sister's gaze but said nothing. The intensity, anger and her sudden decision to let him see what her previously downcast eyes held, surprised him.

Jane's eyes wandered between Elizabeth, Mr Darcy and Miss Darcy, to finally settle on the last. It was not always an easy task to uphold the façade at all times, when one's thoughts were occupied elsewhere. Memories that one wanted both to remember and to forget were continually made fresh by surrounding commentary.

When Jane had still been uncertain about Bingley's feelings, Mrs Bennet's tactless exclamations about his absence from Netherfield had made her so forlorn, she had had to excuse herself and leave the room. Jane thought she had observed that Mr Darcy's mention of the stable master had provoked a similar reaction in Miss Darcy.

Bingley was unsure of what had taken place between Darcy and his sister. He did, however, know his friend well enough to realise that the conversation had touched upon a sensitive issue. In an attempt to clear the oppressed atmosphere, Bingley smiled.

"There are few things that give me greater pleasure than to behold the world from horseback – or what do you say, Darcy?"

"Although I share your pleasure, I admit that there are one or two other activities that give me equal satisfaction," Darcy said in an attempt to change the subject.

Elizabeth kicked her husband under the table, whereupon Darcy looked at her, uncomprehendingly. Despite the miserable situation, Darcy smiled when, after having looked at his wife for a while, he added: "For my part, fencing has always been a great passion."

Georgiana stared at her brother. Her black pupils seemed to have expanded and overtaken the colour of her eyes. Not even the light from the candles could make the dark go away; instead they revealed the paleness of her complexion. The reddened lips were pressed together; she took quick, shallow breaths through her nose. Elizabeth could see that her hands made fists in her lap as she spoke.

"What is it that brings you pleasure?" Her voice was no longer calm and relaxed, but shrill. Even if it was, no doubt, controlled anger that threatened to surface, Elizabeth thought that Georgiana could any minute burst into tears. Seeming to sense this too, Georgiana fell quiet and looked out the window. The sight of the green meadows seemed to give her strength. When she spoke again, her voice was stronger and more formal. Her tone was that of one speaking to a criminal.

"What is it that gives you pleasure?" she repeated before she answered the question herself. "To pierce your opponent with your rapier? To decide whether someone will live or die? To see the face of someone who has realised that the game is lost?"

Darcy's smile evaporated, his face became expressionless. He seemed to have lost his powers of speech. That he did not succeed in hiding his consternation, gave her a certain relief. She knew he felt inadequate when he was at a loss for words in front of his friends, and she felt a grim satisfaction to see him thus.

For those who were seated at the farther end of the table, or were engaged in conversation, her voice had hardly been audible. One person in the company had, however, heard her well enough. As the faithful butler he was, John Goose had not heard the exact exchange between Mr and Miss Darcy. Instead, he calmly announced that there was cognac for the gentlemen in the library.

Chapter 44

Two weeks after Jane and Bingley's arrival at Pemberley, a missive arrived addressed to Mr Darcy. The company had just settled down to dinner when John Goose excused himself and handed Darcy the letter. Darcy and his wife exchanged a look; John would not have interrupted them unless it was something important.

Darcy put down his cutlery and broke the seal; it was a small sheet that only seemed to contain a few words. Elizabeth watched him tensely as she mentally accounted for the whereabouts of those closest to her: the message she feared most was a message of death. Neither she nor Jane were unaware that their parents were becoming old.

"Good grief!" Darcy exclaimed, which made the others look up when they heard the tone of his voice.

"What has happened?" Elizabeth asked in alarm and put down her cutlery.

Darcy handed her the letter.

"You may read it yourself, the letter is from your sister Lydia."

Elizabeth blushed, as she had sternly forbidden Lydia from turning to Darcy when the Wickham family were in need of money. Darcy had done more for Lydia than either she or Wickham deserved, and the thought that she wrote to him to ask for more embarrassed Elizabeth.

Darcy nodded to John Goose, who left the room. When the doors were closed he turned to his wife and said:

"I think you should let Jane and Bingley partake of the contents." Elizabeth, who was by now seriously worried, looked at her sister and began to read. The letter was indeed from Lydia and was addressed to Darcy.

My good Mr Darcy,

Although I know it will upset Lizzy, I must ask you for your assistance, as I have no one else to turn to. My only hope is to our kinship through my sister's marriage, your financial means and your mercy on our situation.

My dear husband is hovering between life and death, and the only thing that can prevent his wife from becoming a widow and his children from becoming fatherless is the help I ask of you.

My dear Wickham was, unbeknownst to me, challenged to a duel – he was forced into it due to the old debts that the man in question wanted to settle. Wickham survived but was seriously wounded; his future health depends on him receiving medical attention.

As you may perceive, our situation is not such that we have any means for this. If you would be so kind as to assist us, I promise Lizzy I will never trouble you again.

With kind regards,
Lydia Wickham

"A duel!" Jane exclaimed in alarm and took Elizabeth's hand. She looked at her sister with eyes that were wide with dread.

"Poor Lydia, she must be beside herself with worry. So far from everyone she knows." Jane fell silent and looked out through the window. "Oh Lizzy, I feel I am to blame."

"How can you even think you have anything to do with it?" Elizabeth said distraughtly. She looked at Jane who was pale and stared emptily in front of her.

The uproar within her dampened immediately and her voice was calmer as she said:

"Naturally, I think what has happened is dreadful, but it is almost as bad that you would take responsibility for what has happened. Lydia alone is responsible for the choices she has made and how these have affected her life."

"I am thinking that Wickham was forced to duel because Lydia did not dare to ask her family for help," Jane said quietly.

"Jane, if that is the case, then we are all to blame." Elizabeth gave her a hug.

"Do you sincerely believe Lydia would not dare to ask us for help? I can assure you that your worry is unfounded; the contents of this letter are proof enough," she said and shook her head.

When Elizabeth had regained her composure and read through Lydia's letter once more, she felt that her sympathies for her sister were mixed with annoyance at Wickham's recklessness. Her sister's situation was pitiable, and the end to it that Lydia was expecting could forever affect her living conditions.

Elizabeth felt the most sympathy, however, for Wickham's two little children whose futures were jeopardized because their father could not keep away from the gambling that drove him to borrow more and more money to cover his escalating stakes. However much Elizabeth disliked Wickham's characteristics and way of life, she did not wish him this misfortune.

"Oh, Lizzy, what are we to do!" Jane burst out in tears. Elizabeth looked at her sister and said: "Naturally, we will go to Lydia. We have not a moment to lose."

For a moment she wondered what Darcy's position would be on having to confront Wickham again. Since Lydia's wedding, the two men had not had anything to do with each other.

Lydia had on one occasion visited Pemberley, but this had been when her husband had been away.

Over the years, Wickham had committed a number of wrongs against Darcy. Apart from the planned elopement with Miss Georgiana, he had slandered and vilified Darcy wherever he went. At the beginning of her acquaintance with the two men, Elizabeth had thought that Wickham spoke the truth, and treated Darcy as the scoundrel he appeared to be.

Although Elizabeth was now Darcy's wife, she still blushed to think how she had let herself be misled. Her behaviour towards him had been marked by impertinence, irony and distancing. Wickham's malicious talk had clouded her judgment and been one of several contributing factors to her rejecting Darcy's first proposal. In spite of this, he had loved and continued to love her. Added to all this, Darcy had spent a considerable sum on persuading Wickham to marry Lydia.

Elizabeth did not doubt that he would once again prove his goodness towards Wickham, Lydia and – thereby – herself. When she met his eyes, she understood that this assumption was correct; Darcy regarded her with such warmth that it immediately brought her relief.

From the two men's conversation, she understood that they were discussing how best to arrange for a speedy transport. The journey was not an inconsiderable distance, and it was necessary to make one, possibly several, stops along the way.

The departure was to be the next day, and it was decided that they should travel in Bingley's carriage. The carriage was already equipped for a longer journey, as Bingley and Jane had planned to travel north after their visit at Pemberley.

The contents of the letter had dampened everyone's spirits, and as the journey was to start in the early hours of the morning, they soon separated for the night.

Chapter 45

Elizabeth was glad when it was time to rise; she had not slept many hours during the night. Aside from the worry about the impending journey's destination, she felt deeply uncomfortable about having to leave Georgiana at Pemberley. She did find some comfort in knowing that Colonel Fitzwilliam had responded to Darcy's request to travel to Derbyshire as soon as possible.

Jane had not slept much either, and the two sisters exchanged a look of deepest understanding.

The first half of their journey was conducted in silence, as the passengers were all pre-occupied with their own thoughts.

It had been unanimously decided that Mr and Mrs Bennet would not be approached on the matter. Mrs Bennet's reaction could be predicted by everyone, and it was felt that Mr Bennet had had enough sorrows concerning Lydia.

Jane thought of Wickham and his gunshot wound; she could not vanquish the image that had come to her during the night in a dream. Despite great efforts, she could still see Wickham lying in the green grass, which had been stained red by his blood.

Bingley was amazed that Wickham had survived a duel; it was not often one heard of such feats. A duel nearly always ended with one of the parties dying on the spot that had been picked for the meeting. It was probable that the man who shot Wickham had pulled his weapon before it was time, with the intent of hurting or killing without risking his own life. It was unlikely that Wickham, who was a skilled shooter, would have lost a duel.

Elizabeth's thoughts went to Lydia, and she wondered whether her sister's love for her husband would outweigh the miseries she was put through for his sake. Lydia had, by becoming Mr Wickham's wife, had to move far away from her family and her friends to escape the bad reputation her husband had got in her home county. Furthermore, her father would never be able to repay more than a fraction of the sum Darcy had spent on paying off Wickham's debts. This had been imperative to bring about the marriage.

Additionally, Lydia was forced to write to her sisters to beg for money, which Elizabeth assumed must be humiliating. Lydia was, however, not one to ponder things; she usually shrugged her shoulders at what would have filled her sisters with shame or shyness. The fact, however, remained that the risk was still great Lydia would become a widow before the age of twenty.

Elizabeth looked at Darcy to try and guess his thoughts. His way of looking at her the previous night had convinced her of his commitment and interest in solving the problem as best they could. Although she told herself she was imagining things, she now had the feeling he was not as keen as the others to reach their destination.

Some time during the morning, a change had occurred, but Elizabeth was hard put to say exactly when it had happened.

It had not passed her by that Darcy had finally looked annoyed to hear the others mention Wickham's name. His eyes that had first been warm became more and more distant as the hours passed. Every time someone had mentioned Wickham's name, it had looked as though he had experienced anew the pain that Wickham had caused him through his actions and dealings.

Elizabeth understood more than anyone what a sacrifice her husband had made by once more hurrying to Wickham's and Lydia's rescue. In spite of this, she could not help feeling a little disappointed by his reaction.

Darcy had sat quietly for a long while and stared out through the window, and judging by his facial expression, his mood was not the best. Bingley, who knew his friend well, cast a worried glance at Elizabeth.

Darcy looked at Elizabeth and said, finally:

"What did Lydia mean by saying you would be upset by her asking for my assistance?" Before she could reply, he continued with a certain sharpness to his voice: "And what did your sister mean by saying that if I assist her now, she would never again trouble you?"

Elizabeth, who felt ill at ease by his questions, understood that she had to answer her husband. Lydia had on several occasions written to Elizabeth and more or less requested money. Elizabeth, who could not deny that her own situation was so much more prosperous than her sister's, had not had the heart to deny Lydia what she asked for. Naturally, she had not asked Darcy for money, but had used the money allotted to her for her own personal expenses.

On their marriage, Elizabeth had been given a smaller sum by Mr Bennet, but this money had long since been spent. The money she had for her own expenses came from her husband. The thought that she had supported Lydia and Wickham with his money, despite the large sums he had already spent on them, could hardly please him.

"Lydia has, on occasion, asked me for money, and I have satisfied her request," Elizabeth said, and met his gaze.

"Is that so," Darcy said, and cast his wife a dark glance. His scowl was so severe that an old woman walking down the road shied away as their carriage passed and Darcy looked out through the window.

"Perhaps you do not think that the sum of £10,000 that Wickham was given to pay off his debts and make a home was sufficient. Am I meant to support the man until my dying day?"

Darcy's voice was bitter and his face had taken on the sternness Elizabeth remembered from the beginning of their acquaintance.

Bingley, who did not know the precise circumstances of Lydia's wedding, looked at Darcy in surprise, which did not escape the attention of either Elizabeth or Jane. Darcy glared at them and turned away.

Jane looked unsurely at Elizabeth, who reddened both with anger and shame. What did he mean by speaking in this manner in front of Bingley and Jane? Her reply was swift and her tone so sharp that Jane looked up in alarm.

"By decreasing my own personal expenses, I have been able to supply Lydia with what was necessary to build the foundation for a secure living for the two of them, and I assure you, this money only covered the most basic expenses."

"Like gambling once, or maybe twice or three times a week," Darcy said sarcastically and continued: "You think you have helped Wickham through your support, but in reality he has been able to continue his former bad habits, secure in the knowledge that the money from Pemberley keeps rolling in."

"Lydia has not only turned to Elizabeth in this matter," Jane said in an attempt to lighten her sister's burden.

"All the better for Wickham; then he will have had even more money to squande and even less reason to change his ways," Darcy replied.

"Darcy, Elizabeth had only the best intentions, you must understand that," Bingley said in an attempt to break the tension.

"The best intentions for whom? Hardly for my own part, as I seem to be forever linked to Mr Wickham!" Darcy said and glared at Bingley who chose not to speak further.

Jane looked out through the carriage window to catch some clue as to their whereabouts. It was twilight and all she could see were fields, a few trees and some cottages. She had no notion of how far it was to the inn where they were to spend the night.

The roomy carriage had begun to feel much too constrained, and she wished they would soon arrive. She began to feel ill at ease, hers and Bingley's attempts at mediation only seemed to make the situation worse. There did not seem to be any hope of reconciliation between Elizabeth and Darcy either, they were both too embittered.

Jane, who knew her sister's straightforward ways, hoped that Elizabeth would not say something she might regret afterwards. Her words could become too sharp when she was angry.

Instead, to her horror, she heard Elizabeth say:

"Why did you even come on this journey? Apart from your economical support, there is hardly anything you can contribute with."

"Lizzy, please, can we not end this discussion," Jane begged, and had to check herself to the utmost not to burst into tears. Both Elizabeth and Darcy had a hot temperament when they were confronted with things that upset their emotions, and Jane wished for a moment that they had possessed more of hers and Bingley's calm. Although they had their disagreements, they would calmly discuss the matter until they had reached a solution they could both abide. Jane could not imagine herself and Bingley in a situation similar to this. If she had not known Elizabeth so well, Jane could hardly have imagined two people becoming so furious with each other.

Elizabeth did not hear her, as she was too wrapped up in her strong emotions. At first, she had been embarrassed that Darcy had started this discussion in front of Bingley and Jane. But now it had gone so far that her own anger overshadowed all, even the impropriety of arguing in front of others.

Darcy, who had looked out through the window and cast a glance at Bingley when spoken to, now looked at his wife for the first time in a long while.

"It would hardly have been proper to send you alone, but I admit that I would rather have foregone this journey," he replied through gritted teeth.

"Perhaps that would have been best; it would have sufficed with Bingley and Jane as company," Elizabeth retorted swiftly.

"My dears, will you not stop quarrelling and instead think of poor Wickham who, despite all his sins, is seriously hurt," said Jane in a last desperate attempt to put an end to the argument between Elizabeth and Darcy.

"Of course I can think of Wickham," said Darcy. "My thought will no doubt be that it was a shame he was merely hurt."

Jane drew a sharp breath and Elizabeth flinched at the brutal words her husband had spoken. For the first time, she was unsure of how well she knew him. She could not help but wonder whether Darcy's former good will towards Wickham had only been a necessary sacrifice to win her favour. Did he, in reality, detest Wickham to such a degree that he was sorry he had not died in the duel? Elizabeth did not know what to think, but she felt strangely empty inside and for the remainder of their journey she did not glance once at Darcy.

When the carriage stopped at the inn, there was more than one of the travellers who were grateful that the journey had come to an end for the day. Elizabeth could not dismount soon enough, and she waited impatiently while the servant girl displayed the rooms that had been allocated to Mr and Mrs Darcy.

As soon as this had been done, Elizabeth turned to Jane and Bingley with the excuse that she intended to withdraw for the night and would not join them for dinner. She did not see how Darcy reacted to this, as she did not deem him worthy of a second glance.

This was the first night that they had gone to bed separately due to anger, and even if Elizabeth neither wished nor thought that Darcy would come to her chamber, she did not feel good about the day having ended as it did.
His cold attitude towards Wickham was partly understandable, but to wish him dead was unforgivable.

Even if Darcy had taken the first step towards a reconciliation, she was unsure if she could have accepted and truly forgiven him. Elizabeth prepared for yet another sleepless night. When she crawled into bed she cried, for the first time during her marriage, over her own misfortune.

Darcy was angry, disappointed and hurt, and he did not expect to sleep that night either. As his wife had guessed, he had begun to tire of Wickham. When he had considered all the abuse and shame he had had to endure because of this man, he had felt he had done more than enough for him.

Although he had always helped Wickham, this gentleman had been consciously and studiedly malicious to him. Apart from having lost vast sums of money to him over the years, he had nearly lost his sister to the man. Additionally, the man's influence had predisposed Elizabeth to dislike him at the beginning of their acquaintance.

Despite all this, he had once more intended to do what he could for his wife's sister. Darcy felt disappointed that Elizabeth had not indulged his negative feelings; she could hardly have expected him to take on the task with delight. It was one statement in particular that had grated at him. Why did you even come on this journey? Apart from your economical support, there is hardly anything you can contribute with.

Even if he was aware that money had been a contributing factor when he had, through his previous efforts, won part of her heart, he did not want to believe that Elizabeth had chosen to marry him out of anything but love.

Her actions upon their arrival at the inn had devastated him. Despite the harsh words that had been exchanged between them, he had hoped for reconciliation. He had had to master himself to the utmost not to let Jane and Bingley see how disappointed he had been when she, without looking at him, had excused herself and gone to her chamber.

For a moment, his gaze had happened to touch upon Jane's, and, judging from the expression on her face, he understood that she had discovered what he had tried to conceal.

Darcy's anger at Wickham had increased again; he had now also managed to shatter the happiness that up until this day had been complete.

Chapter 46

Jane had been lying awake for a long time, thinking about her sister and Darcy who were in separate rooms, alone in their misery. It pained her that they had not reconciled before the end of the day; judging by Darcy's expression when Elizabeth left them, she had understood that this had been his wish. Bingley had tried to comfort her by waking hopes that both Elizabeth and Darcy would be in a better mood after a night's sleep.

Neither Elizabeth nor Darcy had slept a wink during the night and neither of them spoke when they all gathered for the departure. Jane and Bingley found it best to remain silent, and only spoke a few words between themselves during the remainder of the journey.

Elizabeth was not, however, as mad as the day before, and she admitted to herself that her feelings, which had been in a vacuum the night before, were slowly beginning to reveal themselves. She still refused to meet Darcy's eyes, but only looked at him when he did not notice. As he spent most of the time looking out the window, there was plenty of opportunity to observe him without him knowing.

He still looked stern and solemn, but the anger she had witnessed in him last night seemed to have lessened in strength and his posture was not quite so reserved. If he would take the initiative of reconciliation, she would not be quite so unwilling to forgive him.

Darcy felt less hatefully disposed towards Wickham, but he was still deeply angered. Although Elizabeth refused to meet his gaze, it did not escape his attention that she looked at him, and that she did so only when she thought he did not notice it. As for his feelings towards Elizabeth, he was still hurt and the fact that she did not yet seem to want to reconcile their differences hardly made him less downcast. Darcy did not mean to take the initiative towards reconciliation as long as she refused to meet his gaze.

The hours passed for the most part in silence; Bingley tried to strike up a conversation at some points, but when Darcy only nodded distractedly, he gave up. That Elizabeth did not reply with more than a few words, either, was a very bad sign, according to Jane. It was with some irony that Bingley observed that the most light-hearted thing to occur during the journey was the driver's announcement that they had reached their destination.

Jane, who was the first to dismount the carriage, was welcomed by Wickham's youngest son who, in an attempt to try to hide from his older brother, sought escape behind her skirt. Elizabeth regarded the child, who screamed as his brother found him and pinched him hard. In an attempt to divert his attention, she took the little one's hand and asked him where he lived. The child stared at her, broke free, and ran towards the house.

The building was a small stone building, but particularly pretty. Apparently the one who had had it built had wanted to give the impression of greater wealth than he had, and so had combined fine design with simpler building materials. The garden was splendid, with several large apple trees whose branches were heavy with fruit as no one had had the time to relieve them of their burden. Elizabeth could not imagine either Lydia or Wickham performing this kind of garden work, and rather than paying a gardener, their money had been used elsewhere.

"Lizzy! Jane! How happy I am to see you!" Lydia called in a loud voice and ran towards them. Lydia embraced her sisters and was so eager to show them her house that Elizabeth wondered if her sister had forgotten the reason for their visit.

"Oh dear! I was so happy to see my sisters I completely forgot to greet you properly," Lydia said laughing and welcomed Darcy and Bingley. Thereafter she turned again to Elizabeth and Jane.

"Oh, how wonderful that you are finally here! I just wish you had brought our mother; she would so very much like to see how we're doing. Isn't our house beautiful?" Lydia said and laughed.

Jane looked at Elizabeth and assumed that her sister was as surprised as herself to find Lydia as gushingly joyful as ever. The letter she had written to Darcy had communicated desperation, and Elizabeth wondered to see the feeling lessened so quickly.
It was Jane who finally asked the question they had all waited to have answered.

"Lydia, as you must understand, we are very worried about Wickham. Please tell us how your husband is doing," she said and prepared for the worst.

"He is rather tired, what else can one expect after a duel!" Lydia said and smiled sweetly.

"Lydia, will you please explain to me how you can be so frivolous when your letter to Darcy suggested you were on the brink of ruination."

Elizabeth was upset and for a moment she wondered if the whole duel story was just a joke from her sister's side. Had it all been invented to make them come and visit her? Lydia was surely aware that Darcy would never have thought of visiting them otherwise.

"Naturally you should be worried for your husband. Even if he has survived, I assumed he is badly wounded," Elizabeth said sharply.

"I was worried," Lydia said and for a moment her face became serious before she continued: "When I had word that he had been shot, I was almost hysterical, but that evaporated as I understood that he had survived."

After those words she turned to Darcy and continued: "I was a little worried before I knew that you would come, but I knew you would help me and now I am not in the least bit worried."

Elizabeth glowered at Lydia. When she remembered the expressions used in the letter, her anger increased. By insisting that Darcy was the only person who could prevent her future misery, Lydia had put him in an awkward position. No matter how he acted, it would be at the cost of his self-respect, and to the detriment of his finances and his wife's opinion of him.

Elizabeth did not think that Lydia was unaware of the troubled relations between their two husbands.

"Is Wickham badly wounded?" Jane said hastily when she saw Elizabeth's face.

"Jane, he was shot! Of course he is badly wounded," Lydia said dramatically. The sight of Jane's alarmed face encouraged her to continue. Lydia had always liked drawing attention to herself through her person, words or actions.

"There was blood everywhere. His shirt and trousers were soaking. There is still a spot on the floor in the hall. However much I had scrubbed at it, it won't go away. And when I took off his shirt and saw the wound…"

Jane grabbed her husband's arm, by now she was visibly pale. She swallowed and took a deep breath to ward off the feeling of nausea.

"Lydia," Elizabeth said sharply, "I think that's enough of the details."

Lydia, who was pleased at having captured everyone's attention, now looked uncomfortable. She would have liked to have told them what a human being looked like beneath the skin; she was sure none of them had ever seen an open wound before.

For a moment she thought about continuing her story anyway; she could not imagine they would be uninterested in such a subject. Jane had always been a bit squeamish, but the others could stand to listen to a description of something she had had to witness and handle as best she could.

A look at Elizabeth made her unwillingly steer the conversation onto another topic.

"We owe the farmer who found him all our gratitude, and as soon as we can afford it, we will give him a goat. Unfortunately we do not at present have a penny to spare, but of course you know that since I wrote to you." Elizabeth blushed and avoided looking at Darcy. The tiredness of two sleepless nights and the worry that they had not yet reconciled their differences made it hard for her to know whether to laugh or cry. A goat!

"Wickham is inside the house and he wants to meet you all," Lydia said as the company wandered up along the pathway. At the doorstep, she suddenly stopped and turned to Darcy.

"I almost forget, I meant to say: Wickham especially asked to see you at once,"

Elizabeth looked at her husband whose expression remained composed. Their eyes met. His dark gaze was steady and he regarded her quietly. When she saw the expression in his eyes, she wished nothing more than that they would be friends again. Darcy turned away and followed Lydia to the room where Wickham was.

As soon as her husband was out of sight, Elizabeth began to ponder over what they could be speaking of. What could Wickham have to say to Darcy that the others couldn't hear?

Were Mr and Mrs Wickham in need of a large sum of money? More money than Lydia had managed to derive out of her sisters? Did Wickham find it best to turn directly to Darcy in such a situation?

Elizabeth looked up; the best thing had, of course, been to lure them here. To describe the situation in writing would not, in all likelihood, make the same impression. If they all saw him, the prospects of the Wickham's prayers being answered were greatly increased.

It was undoubtedly so that he was unable to provide for his wife. Even if Darcy did not budge, his wife would surely let herself be persuaded, and thereafter convince her husband to help the unfortunates. Elizabeth was convinced that this must be the state of things, and she was outraged that Wickham would lower himself thus, after all that Darcy had done for him.

"Lydia, can you tell me what Wickham's intentions are with this private conversation?" Elizabeth asked and looked at her sister.

"I really don't know," Lydia answered indifferently and shrugged her shoulders. Elizabeth, who was more than eager to know, tried to conceal her impatience without succeeding. "But what did he say the matter was about?"

"He never said, and you should know that I have questioned, nagged and begged him to tell me. I was naturally very curious," Lydia said.

"Yes, it is peculiar, but I am sure Wickham has an acceptable reason for not revealing the matter to you," Jane agreed.

"I think not; he's just strange, but he has been since the incident," Lydia said and frowned.

"What do you mean that Wickham is strange?" Elizabeth said and studied her sister with earnest interest. Lydia's way of describing her husband had captured her attention.

"At first, he mostly slept, but when he awoke again, he was not at all himself. He is so serious and doesn't speak much either," Lydia said with a sigh.

"You cannot forget that Wickham was close to death, perhaps that is what has made him serious," Jane said quietly.

"But he survived! Shouldn't he instead be as happy as I am?" Lydia exclaimed. Elizabeth looked at Lydia and could not help but smile; her sister was the same no matter the circumstances.

"Some solemnity will hardly hurt Mr Wickham," Elizabeth said in a low voice and looked at Jane.

Chapter 47

Lydia proudly displayed her latest addition to the household to her sisters: a tea set whose cups and saucers had been hand painted on the continent. Elizabeth wondered at her sister's priorities when it came to the couple's expenses, and she was just about to question Lydia on the matter when the door was opened and Darcy stepped into the room.

"Wickham is asking for you," he told Lydia.

When Lydia had left, the room fell absolutely silent. Elizabeth, who stood with a hand painted cup in her hand, looked at her husband. Bingley looked at Jane, and in unspoken agreement they both left the room.

During all of the preceding evening and morning, Elizabeth had avoided the possibility of reconciliation. Now that she wished for it, she did not know quite how to effect it.

Their eyes met and for a moment they both remained standing in the middle of the floor. Elizabeth beheld Darcy, who seemed completely calm. The gaze he had given her before going to Wickham came before her again. At that moment, she had understood the extent of the sacrifice he had made to come on this visit.

Elizabeth regretted her previous harsh words and lack of understanding of him not being as eager to take on this task as the others. Again he showed, through action, the greatness of his love for her. She was warmed inside, both from the response this awoke in her, and from the blush she felt over having refused to meet his eyes for so long.

Darcy, who saw her bashfulness, reached her before any of them had time to speak and took her into his arms.

"Dearest Elizabeth, forgive me my surliness these last days; let us be friends again," he said and looked at his wife.

Elizabeth, who was too overcome to respond at once, crept into his embrace and felt his arms wrap around her body. When she finally looked up and met his gaze, she discovered that Darcy, too, was deeply moved.

"Of course we are friends again, but I must beg your forgiveness for my anger and stubbornness these last days," Elizabeth said quietly.

"It has been many hours since I forgave you," said Darcy.

A light blush spread across her cheeks when she bethought her own resentfulness. It was not until a few hours ago that she had been ready to forgive.

"Let us agree on one more thing," Darcy said and looked earnestly at her.

"What is that?" she said and smiled.

"Never to disagree again would perhaps be asking too much, but let us promise each other never to part for the night without having become friends again."

Elizabeth answered his gaze and said with a smile:

"This I can promise without difficulty. A night like yester night is not something I would like to experience again. I have never before felt so distraught."

"You were certainly not alone in your distress – I could not close my eyes for a minute and forget our argument – but let us forget about that now," Darcy said, whereupon he looked around and bent down to kiss his wife.

After a while he looked at her again.

"And what do you think Wickham had to say to me?" His expression was so inscrutable that for a moment it gave her pause.

"By now I am too well acquainted with Wickham's character to think anything but the worst," Elizabeth replied.

"This time, however, I believe you are mistaken," Darcy said and motioned for her to sit down.

"What do you mean, was there anything more than his finances he wanted you to sort out?" Elizabeth said in alarm and looked at Darcy. He shook his head and took her hand.

"No, that is not why I wanted you to sit down. The whole matter is very curious and I think it will take a while before I have told you the whole story," Darcy said and smiled. His voice was calm as he told her what he had heard.

"Already during his seminary studies, Wickham began to borrow money. His habits meant the sum he had procured from Pemberley was soon insufficient. Not unexpectedly, he neglected to pay back what he owed. He had not intended to return to that part of the country, and the likelihood of again meeting the man he had borrowed money from seemed therefore slight."

Elizabeth looked up and was about to protest when Darcy silenced her by continuing.

"During the autumn that Wickham was at Oxford, he could not resist the temptation of gambling. He was in desperate need of money and let himself be persuaded to go to an illegal gamblers' club. When he stepped into the smoky locale that was situated in one of the more dubious parts of the city, he observed that most of the men looked either alcoholic or criminal. Any doubts that occurred were dampened by his conviction that this would be his lucky night. He was right – already in the first hand, he had won big. The more he won, the harder it became to quit.

After a while, he noticed that one of the men was following him with his eyes, but he dismissed it as being the result of the man never having seen a uniform up close before. Although the man stared intently at him, he was not to be frightened off. It was not until the man confronted him and demanded his money back that Wickham recognised him. It was the same man he had once borrowed a vast sum of money from. To pretend to be unaware of this was not difficult: the man's face was badly ravaged by pox scars. He was almost unrecognisable.

To escape the man, who, he understood, would not let him get away, he ran out the back door. It was hard to leave the entire sum he had won, but Wickham understood that this was a matter of life and death. He left Oxford the same night, determined never to return. He had no plans to remit such an old debt. He was sure the matter was once more over."

Elizabeth shook her head. It was incomprehensible to her that he would have thought such a simple solution would be feasible in the long run. Darcy nodded approvingly.

"The man was, however, determined to call in his debt and Wickham underestimated his abilities. When he one day turned up in his garden, Wickham understood that he was caught. If the gaze that the man watched the children with had not revealed him, his gestures certainly did. The knife that he used to clean his nails with was an instrument intended for slaughter. As Wickham was in want of cash, there was nothing to do but to agree to the duel the man demanded. Of this, his wife was naturally unaware.

As soon as they had reached a secluded spot, the man pulled his weapon and shot him in the stomach. Wickham fell to the ground and saw the man run away.

He was left to bleed to death. The fear he felt overshadowed anything he had previously experienced. He was sure that this was the end, not just for himself but for his family as well. The thought that the man would not be satisfied with this, but would also harm his wife and children made him mobilize his last strength. He crawled out of the forest grove and down to the road that ran a few hundred yards away.

A farmer, who, by chance, was passing, became aware of his situation and rushed to his aid. On his arrival home, he was so tired and worn by the shock that he slept for three days.

During the days he had been awake, he had had opportunity to ponder his life. When he looked back on it, he saw, for the first time, what misery it had brought to others. Or rather, it was the first time it made him ill at ease.
His wish for reconciliation with those who had been injured by his former misdeeds steadily increased,"

Elizabeth looked up, her gaze was now milder. "And the first he came to think of was you?" Darcy nodded.

Wickham had sincerely asked his forgiveness. He had expressed his understanding that forgiveness for all the misery he had caused was impossible. He had also given his word that from now on he would live as a gentleman ought.

Darcy, who had entered the room in an embittered frame of mind, had at first heard his narrative without much interest. But as it progressed, he had discovered to his surprise that Wickham seemed changed in more ways than one.
As he had watched him, he had found that the impertinent and scornful glint in his eyes had been replaced by a deep earnestness and a certain thoughtfulness. For a moment, he had wondered if this was another trick to procure money. Somehow, he had still felt that what he observed was genuine, however unlikely it seemed.

"I admit that it all transpired as I had least expected it to do. Wickham surprised me with his changed ways and his different wishes," Darcy said and smiled.
Elizabeth returned his smile and related the conversation with Lydia.

"It certainly sounds too good to be true, but I suppose even Wickham can change for the better. Lydia mentioned something of his altered frame of mind. Her word for it, if I remember correctly, was that her husband had become strange."

Elizabeth, who was eager to hear more of what had passed between the two men, asked, after a moment's silence: "Did you forgive him?"

"Not at once. I thought that if he was really sincere, he would feel the consequences of his actions. I think he did, as well. He had not counted on my forgiveness. But of course, I forgave him in the end."

"Who have you forgiven, Darcy? Is it Elizabeth who has regained your favour?" Bingley said as he entered the room and surprised Elizabeth and Darcy who had stood up with their arms around each other.

"Oh, Lizzy, how glad I am to see you together again," Jane exclaimed with such joy that both Elizabeth and Darcy laughed. It had not escaped either one of them how badly Jane was affected by their quarrel. Elizabeth was glad to once more be able to delight her sister by relating the conversation between Darcy and Wickham.

"Is it really true, Lizzy?" Jane said and embraced her sister whereupon she turned to Darcy.

"Who could have thought it would come to this? Imagine, that Wickham has finally seen the error of his ways and taken responsibility for it!"

For obvious reasons, Wickham could not be present at dinner. During the course of the evening, they all took turns visiting him in his chamber. Elizabeth was the last to go. She was curious to see whether Darcy's description would be consistent with her own impressions. Wickham half sat up in bed and looked up at her with a smile as she entered the room.

"Dear sister, how glad I am to see you," he said and reached out his hand to her. Elizabeth came to greet him and sat at his side.

Wickham sat quietly for a while, and then said: "Darcy has been kind enough to forgive me the wounds I have caused him. I don't deserve it, and can never repay what he has done for me. He has forgiven me, but I will never be able to forgive myself."

"We must all pay the price for our actions," Elizabeth said.

"You are right, and when one has been forgiven, the thought that one has wounded, hurt and betrayed those who should have been afforded one's love, respect and friendship is a small price to pay," Wickham said.

"This is true, but let us now be happy that everything has turned out for the best, and that we may now count on welcoming you as guests at Pemberley," Elizabeth said and smiled. Wickham looked at her with a sincerity she had never seen in him before.

"If Darcy does me the honour of inviting me to Pemberley, I will be pleased to come," he said calmly.

During the two weeks that the company stayed with Mr and Mrs Wickham, they all had time to see that Wickham had indeed been remarkably transformed. His previous recklessness had been superseded by thoughtfulness. Rather than making fun of others as soon as a thought struck him, Wickham now scrutinized the person or situation intently before making a comment. Even if his judgments were not always positive, they were never studiedly malicious.

All welcomed the change; the only person who had some trouble adapting to it was Lydia. Even if she was glad that her sisters and their husbands now socialised with them, she sometimes missed the happy, reckless and spontaneous man she had married.

One change, however, meant that she was willing to overlook the rest. Prior to the duel, Wickham had seemed more and more indifferent to her, and despite her efforts, she had not been able to effect much change. After the accident, he had once again shown her the attentions that had preceded their matrimony. This time, his feelings seemed marked more by affection than adventure and lust.

On departing, Darcy invited Wickham and Lydia to visit them at Pemberley. Elizabeth, who had observed her husband through the carriage window, could not but feel proud, both of him and of Wickham.

When Wickham had sincerely asked for forgiveness and shown remorse at what he had done, Darcy had immediately forgiven him, which once more showed his goodness. Elizabeth was again overwhelmed with joy at being Darcy's wife and her eyes clearly showed her feeling as he looked at her, his face immediately lighting up.

The long journey had begun, but in the happy mood that now prevailed, the distance seemed insignificant.

"On second thought, a duel may not be such a bad thing, especially if the person in question survives," Elizabeth said and looked at Darcy.

"But if I am not mistaken, your opinion was rather different when we set out," she added and squinted her eyes.

"No, no, do not start arguing again, I beg of you," Jane said in alarm. Darcy laughed.

"Don't worry, Jane, Elizabeth is only teasing! But if Wickham can change to such a degree that he asks my forgiveness, it is not so strange if I change my mind and prefer him to survive a duel."

Chapter 48

When Coyle awoke, and yet another morning felt the raw humidity of the room, he felt he would rather stay in bed for another couple of hours. That such a thought even entered his mind made him immediately alert, and he pulled the cover from his face.

During his entire professional life, he had always prided himself on being a morning person and disdained those who had complained about beginning the day's work in the early hours.

Coyle spent the following minutes looking for signs of illness. When he had confirmed that there was nothing amiss, he looked confusedly about the room. The sight of the fire having burnt down made him shiver. With a sudden surge he sat up, climbed out of bed and began moving it closer to the fireplace. The chill of the floorboards made him curse and hurriedly pull on trousers, shirt and waistcoat. He looked at the bed and pulled it back to the place where it had always been. He did not understand why he had thought it should be elsewhere.

Breakfast consisted of two pieces of bread eaten standing; the mouldy part of the bread went into the flowerbed in front of the servants' quarters. The fog this morning was so thick that Coyle, if he had not known the way, would have had to grope his way forward. After a few yards, he turned around and headed for the stable building.

Pemberley's new stable master was experienced and had quickly become at home in the chores Edward had previously carried out. Coyle no longer had to be concerned by lack of discipline and youthful recklessness. To check on one minion less had lessened the burden of his work.

The new stable master was his own age, and thereby had Coyle's full confidence. As was his wont, he examined the boxes, the animals and the common areas with a critical gaze. Unlike the case had been during Edward's time as stable master, he found nothing to remark upon. The halters hung on their hooks, the floor was swept and the horses fed.

A wet breath of air down his neck made Coyle turn around, whereupon he looked straight into a pair of black eyes. The tufts of hair around the hooves, the black leather halter, the resting pose of the horse – Coyle immediately recognised Beth, the little mare that Edward had wanted to keep despite of its injury.

For a moment, he remained standing. For some inexplicable reason, he felt ill at ease. Perhaps he was falling ill after all. Did he not feel the cold more keenly than usual?

A glance at his watch indicated that it was high time to move on. He felt relieved. Before he had had time to find the stable master to announce his retreat, a loud whinnying made him flinch. The latest addition to the stable, a large, black stallion had reared, whereupon the youth that had lead him had dropped the rope that held him.

With ears turned backwards, roving eyes and steaming breath, the stallion signalled that it was safest to keep out of its way.

James turned hastily and shut the door to the stable. When he saw Coyle, he set his jaw. He could imagine what the consequences would have been if the horse had got loose and left the property.

Coyle was not unaware of the power that came with his position, and at first he took a certain pleasure in watching what took place. Judging by the man's age, his work experience was limited and the horse's unpredictable movements were not an insignificant danger. To clear the way and ensure he was not hurt, Coyle backed into the nearest box.

For a long while, the two were unable to do more than stay put and watch the stallion's mad race through the stable building. Not until his right leg began to tingle – something that often occurred when he remained in the same position for too long – Coyle moved.

The youth showed uncommon courage or foolhardiness. Coyle was completely taken aback when he suddenly left his place by the wall and stood in the middle of the walkway.

The horse reared again, neighed and flattened its ears. Coyle shook his head. By approaching the animal from the front, the risk was great that the man would be struck in the head by one of the hooves that were still in the air.

Just as the steward was about to enlighten the man about the whip that hung on the wall, he saw something that further surprised him. The youth bent down his head a little, watched the horse from the corner of his eye and thereafter backed away.

Coyle, who did not know any other way of controlling the horses than by using the tools on hand, stared at him. Approaches were followed by retreats until the animal was finally so close that James could put a hand on its back. When Coyle once more looked at his watch, more than an hour had passed. It was with a certain amount of surprise that he found he had been so fascinated by the display, he had forgotten about time.

It did not escape Coyle that the youth looked uncomfortable as their eyes met again. For a moment, James had forgotten that he was being watched. The work with calming the horse had taken up his full attention.

The tension had left traces in the form of wet spots on his shirt. The palms of his hands were flayed and shone pink. His one leg shook until he put his foot to the ground.

"Is it the new stable master who has taught you this?" Coyle asked and nodded at the horse. For a moment, the man looked surprised, but gathered himself quickly. He seemed unsure about whether to reply or not.

"No, it was Edward," James said finally.

Chapter 49

It had not escaped any of the employees that Coyle had seemed more short-tempered over the last few days. Apart from the usual surliness, there were more than once hints of disciplinary actions, reporting to Mr Darcy and talk of how the one concerned should be mindful of their employment.

James kept out of the way; he had not forgotten Coyle's expression when he had mentioned Edward's name.

Coyle's temper was often of this character: ready to blow up suddenly before it abated. Sometimes he overreacted; but it was only his mother who had dared tell him this was so. That he furthermore lacked the ability to say sorry further decreased any sympathies one might have for his person. Coyle knew that he was not well liked.

He had never suffered from his solitude. For a long time he had sought it; it was not until recent years that he at times felt it was less welcome to him.

He had always had trouble socialising. If it did not concern work, he did not know what to speak of. Rather than running the risk of having his inadequacy confirmed, he had avoided both male and female society.

The surliness had served him well; it was an efficient way of keeping people at bay. If anyone made an attempt to come too close, he had passed a few sarcastic comments that made the other back off in alarm.

When they had not repeated their efforts, it had confirmed what he already knew to be true: he was a person whose company others could not abide.

Unlike what was generally believed, it troubled Coyle that his moods became more and more difficult to regulate. Even if his actions gave him peace for the moment, he found it harder and harder to forget the facial expressions of those he had frightened or hurt. This had become more evident with age.

The feeling was unknown to him; he did not know whence it came and he was not sure he liked what was happening to him. His habit of ignoring uncomfortable emotions did not work any longer. The strategy had been effective and reliable; what he had not thought or allowed himself to feel had not existed. Up until now, Coyle had never understood those who complained about not being able to think about anything else than that which worried them.

Coyle, who had never had any trouble sleeping, had, for the last few mornings, awoken at dawn. Although he had not thought any more about Edward since his visit to the stables, the thoughts and memories had come over him.

The images had been clear: Beth's bulging eyes; Edward's face when he had raised his arm to protect himself; the gaping wound; the hay stained red and stuck together by the blood.

The first time it had happened, he had thought it was a nightmare and had turned both his body and his pillow to go back to sleep. An unpleasant feeling had presented itself when he had discovered that he could neither go back to sleep or rid himself of the impressions. That he remembered details enough to be able to commission a painter for the picture was curious, as he had not made any effort to do so. Although he closed his eyes and thought about something else, the images returned again and again: they gave him no peace.

The anxiety made him shift his position in the hopes of going back to sleep. Not until he was tired out and rose from the bed to take on the morning's chores was he able to focus on what was at hand. During the day, he was freed from brooding. His activities left no room for thought.

As evening crept closer, however, the worry increased. Apart from the question whether he would lie sleepless another night, he wondered where these thoughts came from.

One morning the insight had suddenly struck him with full force. That he had lost his self-control, acted badly and abused his power, situation and strength was nothing new. The difference was that this time the shame had not budged, despite his attempts at rationalisations, explanations or self-justifications. For the first time in his life, Coyle admitted that he disliked what he saw when he examined himself.

The fair-haired youth in the stable had not been unknown to him. Coyle remembered that Edward had introduced a new member of staff, shortly after the incident with Mr Wilbur. The official reason had been the addition of horses that demanded another man's work.

Unlike Mr Darcy, Coyle had immediately seen that the employment was unnecessary. The only new addition in the last six months had been the horse Mr Darcy had acquired for his wife.

Coyle had not said anything to his employer about this; it had been unlike him to withhold such information. Even if he would not have admitted it to himself at the time, he knew what had kept him from divulging it.

Immediately, when seeing that Edward had difficulties lifting his arm, he had realised that he had harmed him seriously. Despite this, he had not asked about his condition or inquired whether he could help him. Instead, he had thought that Edward had only himself to blame, and left him to his fate. Coyle had not cared to find out how the stable master had acquired assistance and from whom.

For those who had seen Edward at work, it was evident that he did not have the use of his arm during the healing process. Mr Darcy had never noticed it. When Edward's presence had been required, he had been cunning enough to send James in his stead.

Coyle wondered what he himself would have done in Edward's position. He doubted he would have remained silent. It was likely he would have talked to his employer about what had happened.

He would have wanted to be compensated by knowing that the wrongdoer was punished. Knowing of his antagonist's shame and submission in order to keep his work would have given him satisfaction. If he had not spoken to his employer, he would clearly indicate that this could happen at any time. Coyle was sure he would have used the situation to his own advantage.

Edward had not done any of this. Coyle wondered why. Edward could hardly have had any doubts whether Mr Darcy would listen to him. His family had been in the Darcy's service long enough for him to be heard. Even if Coyle did not understand the stable master, he was grateful that he had not spoken to Mr Darcy.

Coyle had decided to see if Edward was still at his house. The decision had surprised him; he was not entirely sure why he wanted to do so. He had never before cared about anyone else than himself.

Besides he was well aware of the risks of such an endeavour, which made the whole thing even more incomprehensible. As the steward at Pemberley, he was well-known in the village: if his dealings came to Mr Darcy's attention... He did not allow himself to think further than that.

The risk of being detected made the choice of day simple: on Sunday morning all conscientious people would be out of sight. Coyle doubted that Edward, if he was still in Lambton, would go to church.

The remaining days of the week seemed unusually slow to Coyle; such was his character that when he had once made up his mind about something, he immediately wanted to take action. Waiting, regardless of whether it was for a beer at the bar, a work task, or an important decision, always made him impatient.

Although he had begun to doubt whether it would, Sunday finally arrived this week as well. When he had woken up and heard the rain drops pelting the ground, he had first wished that Pemberley's ground would be watered all day. Not because their land was suffering from drying crops; the rain would, apart from washing away dust and mud, also remove any casual pedestrians from the streets.

The dampness did not affect Coyle: the hat, great coat, rough boots and his forward-leaning walk masked him well. With quick steps he wandered towards the village, unaware that the light brown mud splattered his dark trousers.

Since the steward lacked friends as well as the confidence to ask any of his colleagues about the way, he did not quite know where to begin his search. A glance at the rooftops that increased in number for each step he took, made Coyle stop and look about him.

Lambton, which had always struck him as tiny, suddenly seemed to harbour a considerable number of inhabitants – but then he had never before been determined to search through every house in the village before.

Quarrelling voices and children's screams made him hide behind a dilapidated shed. What had first seemed a gathering of people, but now revealed itself to be a family, caught his attention. The woman had secured her own and her children's bonnets tightly, and she half-ran with the little ones trailing behind.

The youngest child caught sight of Coyle and turned, only to fall into a puddle. The mother's sharp reprimands and her failure to attend to what the child was trying to make her aware of, made her son scream loudly with frustration and cold.

The woman was at least as wet as her son, and well aware of the risk that one of them would catch a cold during the following hours. She took the boy under her arm and hurried to keep up with her husband. The thought of turning back to see to it that they were all dry and warm did not enter her mind: the fear of what such a decision would bring down on them was greater. The metal clang of the church bells called: only heathens dared turn a deaf ear.

Coyle waited another few minutes as yet more families passed. He had never regretted not having children. Wailing, demanding and costly – the more he saw of them, the more convinced he had become.

In later years he had, however, observed such things he had failed to notice before. The confidences between a mother and daughter; a father's proud face when his son had received his first wages; the speed with which a land was tilled when many hands were at work.

The choices he had made had, however, been right at the time: and to question them now was futile.

Coyle shook the water off his body; a glance at his watch indicated he had four hours. At random, he went into the tightly housed streets of Lambton: he might just as well start at this end of town as any other.

The cottages that were dark inside he passed by quickly: when a flame flickered or a light filled the house, he slowed and looked through the window.

The clouds that covered the sky darkened what remained of the few light hours of this autumn morning: Coyle praised the rain and his own cunning. Despite the restricted light, the shadowlike figures, and the film of rain, he could make out the inhabitants of the cottages without trouble. Most of them were old or sickly: those who were too unwell to make it to church. There had never been anything wrong with his eyesight.

As far as Coyle knew, Edward lived alone: his parents were dead and he lacked any brothers or sisters. Coyle did not know whether he had any other relatives alive. It was unusual not to have more than once child; Coyle knew of only a handful of families where this was the case.

The thought of the deceased Mr Jones made him stop in front of a window rather than sweep past it. In the lantern light, an ancient woman sat munching a rotten apple: he flinched as she suddenly looked straight up at him with a toothless grin. He backed away in alarm: he hoped she was too confused to wake the man in the rocking chair to make him aware of his presence.

Another twenty cottages without a sign of the stable master drove him on, although he was soaked through by this point. Darkness, darkness and a few houses whose exteriors signalled they were inhabited by the town's tradesmen made Coyle turn right rather than wander down the tiled street.

A green door was suddenly thrown open, light streamed out, laughter and shouting was heard. Coyle looked about him; he had been so focused on the inhabitants of the cottages that he had not observed in what part of town he had ended up.

Another glance at his watch showed he had now been out for over three hours: it was time to head back. The water that had poured down since early morning had gathered into a rivulet that streamed towards him: a quick step to the side to avoid a dead rat floating by.

When Coyle had passed the passage, he could not help but to turn around and look back. How people could bear living in such conditions was beyond him. The stench from the waste that had been thrown out of the buildings made him wrinkle his nose and hurry along.

The cottages that followed on the upper crest of the hill stood, despite their simplicity, in stark contrast to the area he had just passed through. Coyle cast a quick glance at them: he was persuaded that he was once more in the wrong part of town.

After a few strides, he turned and went back: outside the door of one cottage hung a horseshoe. Even if he would not have guessed Edward to be the owner of such an abode, Coyle was immediately convinced that the little stone house belonged to the formed stable master.

Although it had grown dark, he decided to step in and turned quickly from the street into the little yard that was common to two of the neighbouring cottages. The door was open and glided silently ajar as Coyle pressed down the handle. He did not bother knocking.

Chapter 50

Coyle remained standing at the door. The room was dark and cold. The place looked deserted; perhaps the family was out of town. It surprised him that they had left the door unlocked; in these times, thieves and idlers ravaged worse than ever.

Just as he was about to leave, he became aware of a movement in the far corner of the room. At first, he thought it was some animal. There were plenty of rats. As he squinted, he discovered that someone was lying under a blanket on the pullout sofa. After a moment's deliberation, Coyle stepped into the room.

Edward, who had not moved as the door was opened, quickly sprang to his feet as he saw who the visitor was. Coyle was glad of the darkness in the cottage. He was ashamed that, not long ago, he would have been pleased that his presence induced a gaze like the one he just witnessed.

Fear was what he saw. If Edward had been afraid during their previous dealings, he had never let it show so clearly.

The steward, who had taken a few strides forward, stopped immediately; only the kitchen table stood between them now. They both stood still and waited for the other to make a move: neither of them spoke.

Edward's watchful eyes made Coyle lower his arms and thereby not know what to do with them.

"Always this darkness," he muttered finally and went up to the window and pulled away the cloth that hid the grey sky outside. When he looked back at Edward, who blinked in the sudden light, he swallowed his next comment. Although his mother had always told him it was impolite to stare, this was precisely what he did.

It would not have affected him much if Edward's face had merely been devoid of a smile, laughter or jocularity. Once upon a time, he would even have thought that this was an improvement upon a reckless character.

Coyle had never before seen a man in a state that differed so greatly from his normal self: it both scared and fascinated him that such a change was possible.

The intensity of the gaze that Coyle had often interpreted as impertinent was now replaced by grimness and indifference. Although Edward avoided eye-contact, the steward had a feeling that he was continually being watched.

The dark hair hung loose and shadowed the pale face. The sunk-in posture, the marked facial features and the rumpled, baggy clothes were all signs that the stable master had, for some time, been lacking in exercise as well as proper food.

Edward remained silent, which unsettled Coyle as he did not know what to say himself. Finally he grabbed hold of a chair and sat down with a thump that was the only sound heard in the darkened room.

"Sit down," he muttered.

The questions that Coyle had on the tip of his tongue were improper, and he found it best to stay silent. Words did not come easily when the matter was sensitive; the thought that someone would be helped by a few well-chosen words had never occurred to him on any but the rarest of occasions. Most often, he had left this up to others: there were always some woman or other who had a natural way with these things.

None who had heard him give orders or reprimands would claim, however, that he was without vocabulary. Few, if any, had heard Coyle say what he felt.

When his father had lain on his deathbed, the steward had gone out to chop wood. By sparing his aged mother the work that would otherwise be added to an already heavy burden, he had felt he was of more use to her than at the bedside.

Coyle was a man of action, more comfortable with something in his hands than sitting still. After having sat a few minutes on the chair looking around him, he got up and went out of the cottage.

The steward had not mentioned the reason for his visit, and Edward had not bothered asking. He presumed that Coyle had come at Darcy's request, and he could well imagine what this gentleman would want to know. The hasty retreat, as well as the fact that Coyle had seemed ill at ease upon beholding him, was a bad sign, but hardly surprising.

Mr Darcy was a man of great importance and it had been naïve of him to think that his actions would stop at simply dismissing him. Darcy would now be informed that he was still in the village. In all likelihood, he would suspect that the temptation would become too great, and that he and Georgiana would, despite assurances to the contrary, carry out an elopement.

The surest way of preventing this was, naturally, to remove the greatest threat: in this case, Edward himself.

The likelihood of his master having such plans seemed minimal, but when Edward remembered the way Darcy had looked at him during their last conversation, he did not feel entirely convinced. The two options available were either to await what was to come, or to escape.

After his last meeting with Darcy, his intention had been to immediately relocate. However, listlessness had gripped him, and he had allowed several weeks to pass without leaving the house except on a few occasions. As he lacked the energy, he did not make any effort to flee this time either.

Edward, who had drawn his legs up on the sofa and looked out the window, flinched as he heard steps in the room. Coyle had not been gone long, which indicated Mr Darcy's men were close at hand. He wondered who they were and where they would take him.

He turned slowly around. He closed his hands about his legs when he noticed they trembled.

Before him stood Coyle. Water dripped from his hat, moustaches and coat. A puddle formed on the floor; the mud from his boots dissolved and stained the water that seeped into the floorboards. He was alone. Edward swallowed; the feeling of nausea lifted a little.

His eyes were drawn to Coyle's right hand that held a wrapped parcel whose cover was about to dissolve in the moisture. A weapon, he had time to think, before he convinced himself of the improbability that Coyle would have obtained such a thing on a Sunday.

As Edward did not make any attempt at examining the object, which had landed on the kitchen table with a thump, Coyle tore off the string and folded back the paper. He blinked some stray drops of water from his eyelashes, looked straight at Edward and said:

"I will come back next Sunday."

Edward stayed mute and looked for a long time after Coyle after he had stepped out through the door. For a moment, he wondered if the food was poisoned.

Chapter 51

John Goose took the silver tray and lifted the dome that, when he had left it there, had covered a portion of guinea fowl, potatoes and greens. The fowl's breast lay dry and untouched in a puddle of the sauce that by now was covered by a thin film. The supple leaves of the greens had begun to wither, and only the potatoes had kept their original colour and shape.

It was with relief that John noted that Mr and Mrs Darcy were expected back at Pemberley the same day. The first time he had removed Miss Darcy's tray, and saw that the food was untouched, he had presumed that a mild indisposition had prevented her from eating. As the returns during the last week had increased, and Miss Darcy herself had not signalled any anxiety over the situation, John had thought it best to consult with Mrs Reynolds.

After a visit to Miss Darcy's chamber, Mrs Reynolds had confirmed what John had already suspected. Miss Darcy's lack of appetite was not grounded in any of those states that were generally the reason for such afflictions.

Even if Miss Darcy had not betrayed her thoughts with a single word, her slow movements, lassitude and inability to commit to any activities spoke their own language. Particularly noticeable was the lack of involvement in things that usually sparked her interest and joy. For weeks now not a note had been heard from the pianoforte Georgiana had been given by her brother.

Mrs Reynolds had only mentioned her opinion that Georgiana's choice to withdraw from the outside world was a greater cause for worry than her lack of appetite to John.

John sighed: although more than two decades had passed, time seemed to have stood still; Miss Georgiana Darcy did not only outwardly resemble her aunt Christine Darcy.

Mrs Reynolds could name the day that Georgiana had entered her chamber, thereafter to leave the room only on the rarest occasion.

The day after Mr and Mrs Darcy had left Pemberley to go to Newcastle, Georgiana had asked Mrs Reynolds to accompany her into town. At the time of departure, Mrs Reynolds had not noticed any signs that would have been cause for worry.

On second thought, however, she remembered that Georgiana had been impatient when they had been made to wait for the preparation of the carriage. She had thought that Georgiana's eagerness was due to her wish to buy a medallion she had looked out for her sister-in-law before it was put up for sale.

Once in town, however, Georgiana had doubted her choice, and begun to study the other jewellery of the shop. Mrs Reynolds, who admitted to having been mildly stressed about the other errands that had to be carried out before they went back, had welcomed Georgiana's suggestion about returning to the shop an hour and a quarter later.

When, on her return, she could not find Georgiana in the shop, Mrs Reynolds had been both surprised and frightened. Miss Georgiana had never before shown tardiness towards any of their appointments. Despite her escalating worry over Miss Georgiana's safety, Mrs Reynolds had decided to wait half an hour before she took any action. She had placed herself outside of Mr Harve's shop in the hope of catching sight of Georgiana, who had, perhaps, visited a neighbouring shop.

She had carefully observed the well-dressed ladies who strolled past, casting gazes into the shop windows; the farmers who pulled carts of grain and vegetables to the marketplace; the dogs that were shooed away by the butcher; the children who played under a gaslight. Finally, she had, to her surprise, caught sight of Georgiana who was coming out of a close-lying alleyway. In her relief to see her ward again, she had forgotten to ask where she had been.

Mrs Reynolds was well aware that this oversight had prevented Mr Darcy from gaining important information as to his sister's current frame of mind. She was sure that something had happened during the time they were separated. The more she thought on it, the more she condemned her actions. If Georgiana had been hurt in any way during her town visit, and this was the cause of her present condition, then Mrs Reynolds was alone responsible for what had happened.

John Goose and Mrs Reynolds had not yet decided which of them was to tell Mr Darcy about the situation that had occurred.

Chapter 52

Unlike some squires, Darcy's return to Pemberley was keenly anticipated by his servants. Darcy smiled when he saw the people who had gathered to welcome their return home; he knew that they did not do so merely out of a sense of duty. For all these years, he had returned alone. To step out of the carriage next to Elizabeth, made his return all the more enjoyable.

Although no one had said anything, Darcy was well aware that his servants had wondered if he meant to present a wife to them. More than fifteen years had passed since Pemberley's last mistress, his mother, had died.

Mrs Reynolds had trusted Darcy's judgment implicitly when it came to his choice of bride. She had refused to be intimidated by other housemaids' stories of how young women had shown less desirable qualities in their new roles. Although she had long, and with great success, had the sole responsibility of Pemberley, she felt that her memory and energy were not what they had been at the start of her career. According to Mrs Reynolds, Mr Darcy could not have chosen a better wife; something that she often and eagerly reported to him.

Darcy took his wife's hand; Elizabeth turned and gave him a kiss.
"They deserve something for having stood out in the wind and waited for us," she said, and laughed when she saw her husband's face. The contrast between his manner when others saw them, and when they were alone, was so marked that Elizabeth could sometimes not refrain from teasing him. When they were alone, he was anything but deliberate or prudish.

John Goose, Mrs Reynolds and Coyle, who had been in charge when their master was away, stood at the front of the line. Around them, in a half circle, stood a score of maids and servants who all served Mr Darcy; there were as many gardeners and stable hands.

The sight of the new stable master dampened Darcy's joy temporarily; it made him think immediately of Edward and Georgiana. Although he had not for an instant doubted his decision or his actions, there was one thing that had not left him unmoved.

Georgiana's suppressed anger had both shocked and frightened him, as he did not know how to respond to it. Although it was he himself who had once rejected Wickham, and thereby saddened her, it was still with him she had sought comfort. This time her reaction had been completely different; she had rejected him completely and he did not know how to approach her.

The thought that the confidence that had always existed between them was now gone made him frown.
"What are you thinking of?" Elizabeth said.
"That our return is not only a source of pleasure," Darcy replied and sighed. Elizabeth

did not reply but looked at those congregated in the yard. She searched their faces for an answer to the question that neither she nor her husband dared to ask one another.

Mrs Reynolds's move to touch John Goose's arm with one hand did not pass Elizabeth by. She told herself that the sudden instability was due to old age, rather than an effort to gather her strength. Although she had previously seen that Mrs Reynolds's hair had taken on a grey tone at the temples; it was as though she witnessed it for the first time.

Elizabeth was interrupted in her thoughts by Darcy opening to the door of the equipage and rising to dismount the carriage. Before he greeted his employees, he turned around, caught her hand and looked long at her.

Even if Elizabeth had thought he had treated Edward unfairly, it plagued her to see him sad. Together they began the walk towards those gathered: all Elizabeth could do was press her husband's hand and hope for the best.

John Goose took a deep breath and prepared to answer the question he knew his master would pose.

"Where are Colonel Fitzwilliam and Miss Darcy?" Darcy said as soon as he was within earshot. His voice was comparatively neutral; it was Darcy's inquisitive gaze that gave away his concern. He had immediately seen that his sister and cousin were missing from the company.

John gathered himself and said: "Mr Darcy." The deep, comforting voice reminded Darcy that he was in sight of more or less his entire staff of employees. Even if they could not hear what was being said at the front of the line, it was his duty to uphold a calm demeanour, even if this was far from his private emotional state at present. Darcy straightened, let his shoulders fall and looked straight at his butler.

"Miss Darcy is in her room." After a moment's consideration, John added in a low voice: "Your cousin is with her." Darcy looked at the old man.

"Why are they not here?" he said, with effort. The silence that fell was a bad sign; the sight of Mrs Reynolds clasping her hands together increased his concern.

"Miss Darcy has hardly left her room since you went away," John said dejectedly.

"We are all very grateful that you are back," Mrs Reynolds said nervously. Elizabeth stared at her.

"Is Miss Darcy very ill?" she said in alarm. Before anyone had had time to answer Elizabeth's question, Darcy said:

"I take it you have sent for Dr Barnes?"

"Of course, Sir," Mrs Reynolds said hastily. "The doctor has been here several times."

Darcy did not bother to conceal his alarm anymore; it was, after all, his closest servants who brought him the ill-boding news.

If Doctor Barnes had visited Pemberley on more than one occasion, it must be widely known among the employees.

"Every time he has been here, he has found nothing wrong with Miss Darcy," John replied calmly.

"If that is the case, I better take a look myself," Darcy said, and left the company. Despite Elizabeth's own concern, she let her duties take precedence over her impulse to immediately accompany her husband. After a short account of the most important things to have happened during their absence, Elizabeth felt she had enough information to have a clearer picture of Georgiana's condition.

Darcy knocked on the chamber door and opened it before having been given confirmation by those inside. At the sight of his sister he froze in the doorframe; it was not until Colonel Fitzwilliam requested him to do so that he stepped in and shut the door behind him.

He had not seen Georgiana in a sick bed since she was a little girl. Although more than ten years had passed, it struck him that she looked as small and frail as she had when at nine years of age she had been afflicted by a severe cold. At the time, Dr Barnes had found a cause for her pale skin, matted eyes and lack of strength. What the doctor would tell him now, Darcy did not know.

In two quick strides he was up at the bedside, sitting down by his sister's side and taking her hand.

"Georgiana," he said and let her hand glide out of his grip as she immediately shied away from him. Although he struggled to keep up appearances in front of himself as well as his cousin and sister, he felt powerlessness grab hold of him. For a moment, he had to train his eyes on the pattern of the sheet before he could look back at his sister. His effort went unnoticed by Georgiana, who had only looked at him for a short moment before she had closed her eyes again.

Darcy felt at a loss, and alarmed that she still pushed him away. During the time they had been away he had hoped that her ill will against him might diminish. He had hoped they would be reconciled.

"Darcy, let us leave Georgiana to rest a while," Colonel Fitzwilliam said, after having regarded them together. Darcy let himself reluctantly be lead out of the room by his cousin.

"I admit that I am very concerned over Georgiana's health," Colonel Fitzwilliam said after having shut the door behind them. The calm face he had worn inside the room had disappeared, and he frowned, lowered his voice, and said:

"Although I have been at her side every day since my arrival, I cannot say what is amiss. It scares me that Doctor Barnes has not been able to give us any information."

Darcy admired his cousin's ability to keep his outward calm under pressure. His own abilities seemed mediocre by comparison: if his choice of words did not give him away, he was sure his rigid posture did. The silence that fell went on for so long that Colonel Fitzwilliam wondered if Darcy had lost his powers of speech from the shock.

"I know what ails her," Darcy said finally, and looked out through the window.

Chapter 53

Elizabeth admitted to herself that she had been anxiously awaiting another missive from the vicarage. On more than one occasion when Elizabeth and Darcy had retreated to the bedroom, her thoughts had gone to Charlotte. Despite the benefits her friend had once mentioned in connection to her impending marriage, not even Charlotte could overlook the fact that she and Mr Collins would be living together as husband and wife after the wedding.

Mr and Mrs Darcy had spent their wedding night at Netherfield, and Elizabeth smiled as she remembered the first night they had spent together. Despite her own gratifying memories, she could not hold back a shudder when she bethought that if Mrs Bennet had had her way, Elizabeth would have spent her wedding night with Mr Collins.

Elizabeth knew that ever since her marriage, Charlotte had wished to become a mother; she also knew that for a long time, Charlotte had worried that she could not seem to fall pregnant. The thought that had troubled Elizabeth since her visit to the vicarage, once more came into her mind.

An infant's looks at such an early age was not something to be too concerned about, and if it had only been a lack of resemblance between the child and Charlotte's husband, Elizabeth would have felt at ease.

The letter Elizabeth had been expecting arrived two months after she and Darcy had returned from the vicarage.

Dearest Lizzy,

First of all, I want to thank you from the bottom of my heart for your and your husband's visit; it meant more to me than you can know. The happiness of seeing my best friend again, and the knowledge that Lady Catherine de Bourgh has accepted you as Darcy's wife, are sources of the greatest joy to me. Her unwillingness to countenance your marriage has plagued me for a long time, as you are as dear to me as any sister.

Lizzy, what I am now about to confide in you means that after you have read this letter you must immediately burn its contents. I am sure you must remember my previous fears that I had not, after a year's marriage, shown any signs of producing an heir. For a while, I feared that this was due to infertility on my part.
Nothing could have made me more miserable than the thought of going through life with only Mr Collins as my companion. I only mentioned this to you on one occasion, but it persistently nagged in my mind.
My feelings for Mr Andrew are not unknown to you, and the forceful attraction he has on me cannot be overlooked. The mere sight of Mr Andrew has sparked reactions that have made me blush in embarrassment.
On those occasions when we have touched each other when dancing, I have had to make the utmost effort to hide the tremor it produced.

After having read my letters, you can hardly doubt the sincerity of my emotions towards Mr Andrew. Perhaps this will lessen the condemnation I fear from you, as soon as you have read that which I mean to tell you.

My daughter is dearer to me than anything; judging by your gazes, I think that you, my friend, have spotted that which is unknown to others.

As you may remember, Mr Collins attended his good friend's inauguration as a bishop this summer. The inauguration, which was held eight months ago, meant that I spent a few evenings alone at the vicarage.

Dear Lizzy, I admit that my decision to visit Mr Andrew on one of those days was made as soon as I found out that Mr Collins intended to witness the inauguration. The impropriety and risk of such a visit could not compare to my wish to carry out that which I had decided upon.

My thoughts and feelings about that evening made it impossible for me to sit still for a minute; all I could think about was that I would enjoy the company of Mr Andrew for an entire evening. My preparations began during the afternoon. Most of the time I spent in my chamber; as you may understand, I was scared that the maid would discover my agitation and over-eagerness. Through my friend Miss Croft, it had come to my attention that Mr Andrew would be at home this night, and I arrived as planned. You are probably wondering how this was possible, and how Mr Andrew reacted to my unexpected visit.

My carriage was ordered for Miss Croft's, and I alighted from it at my friend's, whose entire family were, at the time, in Bath.

Alone, and with the knowledge that the carriage would not return until later that night, there was nothing for me to do but visit the neighbour who lived within walking distance of Miss Croft.

Mr Andrew was surprised when he opened the door and saw who the visitor was, but as always when we greet each other, he welcomed me with a smile that awoke my hopes and thereby did not leave me indifferent.

His tall figure, the amused expression in his eyes, as well as his warm greeting made me fall silent for a moment and just savour the sight of him. My intention had never been to confess my feelings in words to Mr Andrew. If her feelings are strong, however, a woman can hardly conceal them in the presence of the man she desires.

During the supper I was invited to partake in, it became more and more apparent that Mr Andrew saw the depth of my gazes. Even if his feelings were not of the same character, his response was the same as that of any man who is given a woman's undivided attention. Only a man who finds a woman repulsive can resist the enticement that a woman in love communicates with her entire being.

Do not let these words lead you to believe that Mr Andrew is a man who lacks morality or respect for female kind. The decision, the inclination, the will and the initiative were my own doing, and for this I am solely responsible.

Mr Andrew is everything a man should be; his tall figure, broad shoulders and firm arms would without a doubt make me feel safe even on the darkest of forest paths. My *reaction is perhaps not so strange; is it not so that the biggest and strongest of the lions wins the female's favour and is the one whose offspring she chooses to produce?*

A woman's choice of husband is based on his ability to provide for her. Perhaps, however, the reaction Mr Andrew sparks in me is Nature's true way of telling a woman which choice she ought to make?

My conscience is not heavy, although it should be weighed down by an impossible burden. The knowledge that my life is for ever linked to Mr Collins's means I allow myself to remember that which I have had the opportunity to experience. My daughter will always be a wonderful reminder of the man her mother loves; through her a part of Mr Andrew is for ever with me.

Again and again, I induce the memory and the sensations of the night it was decided that my daughter would be conceived. The night that Mr Wints was ordained, I neither wished nor found any reason to conceal my eyes, my body or my desire. Rather than feeling embarrassed, I felt, in Mr Andrew's presence, both beautiful and feminine. The sight of Mr Andrew, as well as his response, made me meet him eagerly rather than anxiously. Mr Andrew's masculinity, his exterior as well as his actions, confirmed what I already knew: no matter what the consequences would be, I would not regret my decision.

If this is similar to the man's experience of the union of man and woman, his perseverance does not surprise me any longer. That which, during my marriage, I had only seen as a wife's duty towards her husband, has proven to be a pleasure that is not reserved for the man.

A woman's thoughts, dreams and wishes can also be what would be considered improper. I am well aware that my advice to you upon your marriage spoke the opposite. If it had not been to you that the letter was directed, I would have worried that I had, in my ignorance, communicated a false, even frightening, view of marriage. I am convinced, however, that Mr Darcy is to you what Mr Andrew has proven to be to me.

As for Mr Collins, he has been given a daughter, and even if his wife's heart belongs to another man, she will remain his companion for life. Again, I want to urge you to burn these lines as soon as you have read them; from now on, what has been said will exist only in the memory of two fond friends.

Elizabeth put the letter down and remained seated with her eyes on the flames that slowly consumed the firewood in the fireplace. Charlotte's letter had confirmed her fears: Mr Collins was not the child's father.

Elizabeth dared hardly think what kind of actions Lady Catherine would take if it came to her attention that a child had been born out of wedlock at the vicarage. She knew she would hold her tongue; but Charlotte's actions jeopardised her entire future. Lady Catherine de Bourgh's character and previous conduct were, by now, hardly unknown to Mrs Collins.

Although Charlotte's actions were scandalous, Elizabeth could feel for her in her situation. She could not imagine what it would be like to love one man and be forced to spend the rest of one's life with another.

Mr Collins had, despite his non-existent role in the matter, had a daughter; judging by Charlotte's earlier account, Elizabeth did not think this would have happened without Mr Andrew's participation. If no children had been born in the vicarage, it would not have been because Charlotte was infertile. This fact would not be commonly known either, as the doctor had, after Charlotte's difficult labour, announced that no more children were to be expected at the vicarage.

Charlotte's assumption concerning Darcy had been more than accurate. Elizabeth had, considering her friend's situation, not had the heart to object to the information she had communicated in her first letter.

A scratching sound was heard at the door, signalling that Hamlet had been commissioned to find Mrs Darcy. Elizabeth quickly hid the letter and opened the door, whereupon the little puppy, who had been standing on its hind legs, fell into the room.

Darcy, who saw her face, and that her hand rested over her middle, put his arms about Elizabeth. They were both surprised by the sudden movement that could be felt.

"Hmm... Not that they are not eagerly anticipated, but a delay of a few days or weeks would probably be preferable," Darcy said and smiled.

"They probably just want to remind us of their existence, and what we have to expect from the future. I dare promise that they will not arrive before our family party," Elizabeth replied.

"I must once more assume that you are right; and if not, I suppose your mother will be of assistance, as she has great experience of what is to come," Darcy said calmly.

"My dear mother has experience enough. I fear that in such an event she would be more than helpful. As you surely understand, I would prefer to have Jane at my side," Elizabeth said and laughed.

Darcy's interruption had been welcome; his attention had made her forget Charlotte and Georgiana's troubles for a while. Although there was still one page left unread of the letter, it took several hours before Elizabeth could make herself read Charlotte's final words.

The fear of what would be revealed was greater than the curiosity; such a story could hardly end well. By not knowing, Elizabeth postponed the discomfort she feared would be the result of her friend's confessions. Her thoughts were, however, not as easy to escape.

Charlotte was in a deeply unhappy situation; however she acted, it would bring unhappiness to herself.

Later that night, Elizabeth asked once more to have the fireplace lit in Christine's room. Not until it burnt high did she take out the letter to carry out what Charlotte had asked of her.

If my actions have shocked you; you are right to be. Perhaps these final lines will remind you of the friend you know and set your mind at rest. Although my feelings for Mr Andrew remain the same, time has given me insights that have stilled the worry that so long ravaged my soul.

The daydreams that used to bring me such joy, hope and pleasure, finally also induced anxiety, sorrow and despondency. Such conflicting emotions can only be a burden in the end.

To dream, daily and nightly, of another man than he whom one has been given, will, finally, have devastating consequences for one's mind, mood and marriage. My feelings for Mr Andrew were of the character that I had to find out to what degree they were reciprocated. Despite the pain it would cause me to find out that my feelings were not reciprocated, this seemed the only way of letting go of the dream of Mr Andrew. My conclusion is that a force of such magnitude as the passion I felt for Mr Andrew is not only positive.

As my strength, will and courage increased, my judgement, moral sense and connection to reality was lessened. If Mr Andrew's wish had been the same as mine, it is still to this day my conviction that I had let my actions take me away from family, friends and marriage.

Although my life here at the vicarage can seem humdrum, I feel calm for the first time in months. Mr Collins's mind and character is the same as it has always been; my situation is unchanged in that respect. The calm did not come until I had accepted that Mr Andrew did not harbour the same degree of feelings for me as I did for him. As long as I denied this and through hope, conviction and prayer sought to change reality, my suffering was indescribable.

Tears, despair and despondency were for a long time the names of my companions. Always by my side, but well concealed by a calm exterior in those moments others were in my presence.

I am happy, grateful and proud that I carried my burden without falling prey to the temptation of telling anyone but you. There were moments when the desire to put my feelings into words enticed me in the shape of another possible confidante. My misery would, however, surely have been the greater if I had revealed myself. Once again, I find myself pleased with my decision.

My foremost and dearest task since the birth of my daughter is to give her the best in life. Mr Collins's position and our beneficial connections with Rosings will undoubtedly contribute to this.

With kind regards,
Charlotte Collins

Since the contents of the letters from the vicarage had changed in character, Elizabeth had been burning them. Although Charlotte had never before urged her in this, Elizabeth had destroyed them as soon as she had partaken of their contents.

Elizabeth studied the flames of the fire; slowly the ink and sheets melted together to finally disappear completely.

"Are you stirring the fire again?" Darcy said with a smile as he stepped into the room.

Chapter 54

After having lain and stared at the ceiling for several hours, Edward admitted to himself that he finally must have fallen asleep from the exhaustion that the thought of an encounter with Darcy had provoked in him. Although weeks had passed and he knew that these thoughts only made him more and more desolate, it was as though he could not or would not rid himself of them. He had put himself in this situation, and sometimes he thought he deserved his misery.

Suddenly he had an uncomfortable sensation of being watched: he woke abruptly. The fear that struck him when he saw that a tall male figure was present in the room, made him convinced that someone had broken into the house to rob him of his savings. Having fully awoken, his discovery that it was Darcy who stood in his chamber hardly eased his mind.

While he regarded his visitor and hastily arose from a prostrate to a sitting position, he noted that Darcy blocked the only way out of the room. If it came to a fight, Edward thought he would be inferior to Darcy in strength, but not in speed.

Darcy looked at the young man and wondered if Georgiana would have been shocked had she been there in her brother's place. In theory, his sister's love was blind to lack of comfort, luxuries and material things; but how would it be if she were forced to share this wretchedness?

Darcy tried to shut out the image of Georgiana in this environment and tried to look at Edward without paying any attention to his impoverished surroundings. He was suddenly embarrassingly aware that he had not given any thought to Edward's situation. The anger, frustration and worry he felt had overshadowed all. At their last meeting, Darcy had even thought that Edward had got what he deserved. With his own background, he was well aware that he could never understand what it was like to live under such conditions.

On reconsidering, he found, however, one experience that the two men had in common. As he observed Edward's silence and wait-and-see posture, he remembered the feeling he had had when Elizabeth rejected his first proposal of marriage.

Convinced of his own happiness, and brimming with confidence, he had approached the vicarage that morning. Elizabeth's complete refusal to accept him and her account of her emotions meant that the happiness he had felt only an hour before seemed forever out of reach. Before he decided to do everything to win her love, he had had a feeling of complete despondency; something he had seen in Edward during their latest conversation. This insight made it possible for him, for the first time, to see him as a man of feeling, rather than a stable master and subject.

Darcy had, during their latest interview, had his queries answered and acted on it. Edward had left Pemberley, and his sister had once more been saved from the consequences that her lack of judgment could have given rise to.

While Darcy had felt assured that he had once again acted in time to avert catastrophe, Edward had every reason to feel embittered and hurt by the accusations that had been levelled against him.

Darcy had always prided himself on being a good judge of character; not even when he had questioned the stable master had be been completely convinced that he had behaved indecently towards Georgiana.

Edward had always been a faithful worker, and Darcy had always held him in high esteem due to his honesty, trustworthiness and caring nature. Wickham, who had once intended to elope with Georgiana, had had his eyes on the girl's fortune, and a wish to avenge himself on her brother.

Rather than seeing to his own happiness, Edward had been prepared to forego this out of love. He had predicted that an elopement would have meant that Miss Darcy would have been condemned and her name fallen into dishonour.

It was not the words he would have expected from his stable master, and for a moment, he had been surprised. Darcy was aware that he had both hurt and humiliated Edward, and he admitted to himself that he did not feel good about it. At the time it had, however, been necessary.

The pride Elizabeth had at one point accused him of, had once more got the better of him. The thought of his sister living with a labourer had filled him with disgust.

His conviction that Edward had lured Georgiana into infatuation for the sake of his own prosperity had made Darcy furious. The anger he had felt had not been directed at Georgiana but at the object of her affection. It was in this state that he had sought out and confronted Edward with what had come to his attention.

Reflecting upon it later, however, it was clear to Darcy that it was Georgiana's feelings that had come to his attention; it was not until his conversation with Edward that he found out that her feelings were reciprocated.

Darcy had thought hard and long on the matter. Even if he was not satisfied with it, he was determined to follow his inner conviction. The events of the last months had undoubtedly affected his thoughts in a direction he would not have thought possible.

However much he wanted what was best for his sister, Darcy admitted that he would never have thought himself capable of accepting a situation like this.

That Georgiana had rejected Lord Malcolm was not a matter of great importance to him. Even if the man was wealthy and possessed a happy disposition, he was almost twice as old as Darcy's sister.

This was not an obstacle in itself, older, wealthier men often married women decidedly younger than themselves. Darcy had always been determined not to force or advice Georgiana into a marriage that she did not give her full consent to. Of course, his wish that Georgiana should marry for love had never led him to consider that the object of her affection might be a worker.

As a person, he had no objections to Edward: he was possessed of all the requisite characteristics, and Darcy did not doubt that the young man's feelings for his sister were sincere. It was, naturally, Edward's unfortunate position in life that was the major obstacle.

Darcy had himself married Elizabeth, whose station in life had been below his own; but that was a different matter entirely.

A member of the upper classes marrying someone of the common people was virtually unheard of. Darcy admitted to himself, however, that there were a few stories of one or two beautiful farmer's daughters who had succeeded, to their own and their parents' great joy, in marrying a man of a considerably elevated position.

Chapter 55

Darcy, who had wandered to and fro in the room with determined strides while he had twisted his hat in his hands, said suddenly:

"You have every right to blame me for the accusations I levelled at you: they were unjust and only served one purpose."

Edward's confused expression brought a smile to Darcy's lips. Darcy scrutinized a chair whose top was anything but clear of dust. After a moment's consideration, he swept off the thin grey layer with his glove and sat down.

"I admit that Georgiana surprised me when she revealed her feelings for you; it was entirely unexpected on my part, even if my dear Elizabeth did not seem as surprised."

Darcy sighed and continued while looking at Edward with a scrutinizing gaze:

"You are a man of many good qualities, and I do not doubt that you would make my sister happy."

Edward observed every movement Darcy made; this gentleman's sudden friendliness made him suspicious. This was not what he had expected to hear from a man who, when last he saw him, had hurt him more with his accusations than Edward was willing to admit.

Even if Edward sometimes allowed himself to fantasize about his and Georgiana's situation, he had always been well aware of what was really to be expected. Darcy's reaction had thus been expected inasmuch as he had openly and vehemently expressed his dislike of the situation. What he had not expected was that Darcy thought him capable of the dishonourable deed of which he accused him.

Edward admitted that after their long cooperation and knowledge of one another's characters, he had been shocked as well as hurt that Darcy did not have higher thoughts of him than that.

Several weeks had passed since Edward had left Pemberley; the little news he had received was that which Coyle had saw fit to inform him. During his first couple of visits, Coyle had not mentioned anything of the life or people of the estate, out of consideration for Edward's feelings. Finally, Edward had asked him how the horses were, and after a while Coyle had begun to tell him of the everyday proceedings they had once shared.

Darcy's extreme swings in his judgement of him meant that Edward did not know what to think, and for a while he wondered whether Darcy was entirely well.

"Sir, your observation of my good character and your lack of doubt that I would make Miss Darcy happy, do not correspond with the words I received from you earlier," he said at length.

"Your doubt is understandable, but I had to make sure about your intentions towards Miss Darcy," Darcy replied calmly.

"Sir, with all due respect, could you not have asked me about the matter rather than accusing me of the most shameless of conducts?" Edward said. His insecurity had been superseded by anger as he remembered the humiliation he had felt at their last meeting.

The intensity of Edward's dark eyes and the speed with which he had countered Darcy's words revealed that one of his most distinguishing characteristics had once more been awoken. It was only the thought of the severity of the situation that kept Darcy from commenting upon what he had observed. He had often been astonished that his stable master never seemed to be at a loss for words.

"It was not without reason that I acted as I did, and perhaps you will be more understanding when I tell you what lies behind my apparently brutal way of assuring what your intentions are towards my sister," Darcy said, resisting the impulse to immediately blurt out what he was most eager to say.

Edward admitted that his curiosity was sparked by Darcy's glance at the door, as if to assure himself yet again that they were alone.

The two men remained in the positions they had taken when Darcy entered the room. Edward sat in the bed and let the wall support his back, leaning forwards with his elbows on his knees. Darcy could not but sit straight in the wooden seat. Even if he would not have admitted it, he had no intention of letting his clothes become even dustier by moving to a more comfortable spot.

"What will be said between us will be in greatest confidence," Darcy said solemnly.

"Of course, Sir," Edward said.

The silence that followed was lengthy, and he feared that Darcy might have changed his mind. Suddenly he spotted what the other had expressionlessly been regarding: a small shrew in the furthest corner of the room. None of the two men said anything, but both followed the little animal with their eyes.

Darcy was suddenly struck by the absurdity of his present situation. For a moment, he allowed himself to look upon the matter from Lady Catherine's perspective; it was only the thought of what he meant to confide in Edward that kept him from laughing.

"A couple of years ago George Wickham, the son of my father's former steward, took it as his foremost goal to win Georgiana's fortune," Darcy said, when he had finally gathered himself and managed to train his gaze on a picture of a sinking ship. Edward looked at Darcy but said nothing; he knew Mr Wickham's character and mind well.

As the son of Pemberley's steward, and being well-liked by the owner of the estate, Wickham had had privileges during his upbringing that few servants would dare dream about. In spite of this, he had been anything but humble and it was to Edward that Wickham had most clearly established his privileged position.

The fact that he was not the only one gifted with the powers of speech and an exterior that tended to attract the ladies' eyes, had not left him unshaken. Not even his privileged position had stopped him from refusing to accept that a woman would rather rest her eyes on one of the workers. That it had only been the servant girls' eyes at stake was beside the point.

Even though Wickham had never meant anything by his flirtations, he had had a hard time coping without the affirmation that the young maids' hopeful gazes had communicated. Visiting their chambers had not meant more to him than the pleasure of the moment. More than one of the maids had cried over George Wickham, who they had hoped – momentarily – would lift them to a more prosperous situation in life.

Darcy had never been part of this contest; Wickham had never been sorry that this gentleman's character forbade involvement in such activities. If it had not been for Edward, Wickham would have had the exclusive right to any women who were willing to oblige him.

The fact that Edward was naturally the better rider of the two had given Wickham another reason to make it clear to both of them – and certain others – who was of higher rank.

It had been worst when Wickham had been visited by his friends. Like Coyle, he had found several chores to carry out that were not motivated, urgent or necessary. Edward had never understood the motive for Wickham's ill-will towards him, and his decision to remain unruffled no matter what he felt had hardly alleviated the situation.

Even if Edward still felt that Darcy had treated him unjustly, he admitted that this gentleman's suspicions were not completely unfounded based on his previous experiences.

"Sir, my position has not changed in the last weeks. For what reason…"

"For what reason do I seek you out to tell you this." Darcy interrupted him and smiled.

Edward nodded.

"Miss Darcy's mood and behaviour have changed so decidedly the last few months, your positive effect can hardly be denied, even if I have tried to do so for a long time," Darcy said and continued in a serious tone of voice: "Neither can I deny Georgiana's deterioration for the last few weeks."

"Is Miss Darcy unwell?" Edward said anxiously and met Darcy's eyes.

Darcy arose, went up to the table, took the half-eaten loaf of bread and knocked it against the table-end. With his eyes trained on Edward, whose brown skin had paled in the interceding weeks, he said: "No more than you."

Chapter 56

Coyle leaned back in the chair and regarded the feast in front of him. The meat with its redbrown tone and shiny surface looked delectable; it had been nice of Jocelyn to cut it up for him.

Jocelyn was a round, cheerful maid who usually wore her thick, brown hair braided in two long plaits. Her eyes were round and slightly bulging; they twinkled with characteristic glee. Like Coyle, she had passed her youth a couple of years ago.

To his surprise, Coyle had discovered that he had greater patience with Jocelyn than he usually had with people. He had learnt to appreciate traits in her that he usually saw as weakness in others.

The change had happened gradually; at first, he had met her smiles and cheerful greetings with scepticism and a stern face. The usual and expected reaction did not appear however. Rather than falling into place, straighten her clothes and keep silent, this woman had continued to be as friendly and happy whenever they met.

He had felt uncomfortable, irritated, and, after a while, bemused by this. The curiosity, interest and welcome these smiles now evoked in him had sneaked up on him, and he had been aghast the first time he had caught himself reciprocating her smiles.

When Coyle had discovered that he had begun to run pointless errands in the hope of catching sight of Jocelyn, he had become seriously worried.

Despite stern rules of conduct, self-admonition and efforts to dissuade himself, he had not been able to resist the temptation of being in her company whenever the opportunity arose. These thoughts left him no peace; he looked forward to their daily encounters, but worried, too, that her happiness at seeing him would diminish.

Sometimes Coyle had wondered how it would be to have a woman like Jocelyn by his side; he had even considered whether or not to talk to her about it.

In the next moment he had baulked at the thought – what if she would not have him? No woman had ever wanted him before, so why should one want him now? He had always lived alone, and this was how things would remain. Despite this conviction, he could not let it go – what if it were possible that she liked him?

Jocelyn was always happy to see him, and she showed her consideration through actions that he knew were not part of her work tasks. Today she had prepared a meal for him; she had known that he had been out since the early hours of the morning and had only brought a few sandwiches for sustenance.

Hope mingled with doubt; he found it hard to judge whether her care was specifically directed at him or whether she was just good-natured and showed the same consideration to the other employees.

During one of his visit at Edward's, he had been tempted to bring up the subject. Not that he considered Edward to be the right man to ask, but he was the closest he came to calling anyone a friend.

Coyle's gaze fell on the tankard with its golden contents, the foam of which still fizzed at the surface. As he reached for it he anticipated the calm, relaxation and carefree mood that would soon settle over him. The evening meal was the best of meals: the working day was over, the chamber door closed, and he could finally allow himself to relax.

A knocking sound caught his attention for a moment; without paying it any further attention he went back to his food. The number of times someone had knocked on his door when he was not on duty could be counted on the one hand; at Mrs Dandore's in the room next-door, however, there was a constant toing and froing. Another knock made him fall silent and still for a few minutes, in the hopes that whoever was there would go away.

At the third knock, Coyle sighed, arose reluctantly and opened the door.
"Edward," he said in surprise, and stared at the stable master. He quickly gathered his wits and pulled the young man into the room with such speed that he almost fell over. The steward let go of Edward's shirt and slammed the door shut.
"What are you doing here?!" he hissed.
Before Edward had time to reply, Coyle had stuck his head out through the window to see if anyone was out there.
"I came here unseen," Edward said quickly when the window was once again closed.
"I sincerely hope so," Coyle muttered and gave him a quick glance.

Edward looked about the room; when he saw the crackling fire, the newly-poured beer and the half-eaten meal, he stopped his next sentence. His decision to visit the steward in his home had been carefully considered; in spite of this, he had hesitated more than once on the way.
Coyle's reception of him and his grumpy demeanour signalled as clearly as the food on the table that he had come at a bad time.
"Please excuse me, I can see that you are busy," Edward said and made to go.
"Stop right there," Coyle hastily thrust a rough, scarred hand against the door. The words as well as the tone of voice made Edward stop in his tracks.
"I thought you wanted to be left alone," he said in surprise.
"As you are risking your own as well as my safety, I am assuming that what you have come here to say is important," Coyle said gravely and pointed to an armchair for Edward to sit in.
"Get to the point: what on earth brings you here?" he said.

Edward, who had sunk into the armchair, righted himself so that he was sitting with his back straight. He pondered the older man opposite him. Coyle had also sat down, crossed his legs and was drumming his fingers against his thigh. A frown was added to the already furrowed face. He pointedly fixed his eyes on the steak.

The hour of this visit was the worst possible; if Mr Darcy found out that Edward was on his grounds, they would both be in trouble. Mr Darcy's strange behaviour had not passed any of his employees by. According to reports from several of them, he seemed troubled and had spent many hours in solitude. Matters of the estate seemed hardly to be the object of his ponderings, or the reason for his annoyance in encountering employees. According to a trustworthy source, something was the matter with Miss Darcy.

Edward's words brought him back to reality.
"I have a problem," he said thoughtfully and turned his gaze on the fire. Coyle regarded him and raised his eyebrows. "One problem?" he said emphatically, "I would dare say you have a dozen."
The hint of a smile disappeared as he saw Edward's discomfited expression.
"Let's hear it," he said smoothly.
"It concerns Mr Darcy…" Edward said and interrupted himself when he saw the steward stiffen. During his visits, Coyle had never mentioned Mr Darcy's name, nor had they ever spoken of the reason as to why Edward had had to leave Pemberley so dramatically.
"So you are aware that Mr Darcy has returned?" Coyle said and cleared his throat.
"I met Mr Darcy this afternoon," Edward said as their gazes met once more.
Coyle regarded him sceptically: Edward looked whole and clean as well as unharmed.
"You met Mr Darcy?" he said without much conviction.
"Yes," Edward replied and swept a dark tress of hair out his eyes; it was a movement he performed unconsciously.
"Yes," Coyle repeated in annoyance, "how can you say such a thing and then fall silent?"

Edward smiled; even if Coyle would never have admitted to it, he thought his annoyance was due to worry rather than anger. Although he was still brusque in his choice of words and tone of voice, his actions showed that his intentions were harmless.
Through his association with Edward, the steward risked his reputation as well as his employment. They were not related, they had never been friends and Coyle owed him nothing.

Coyle's worry was not without reason as he was unaware of what had taken place. However dreadful the news, uncertainty was always worst. Edward had not forgotten his own reaction when first Coyle and later Darcy had come to visit him in his home.
During Coyle's first visit, Edward had been both suspicious and afraid. He had been convinced that the steward had acted on Darcy's orders. He had not relaxed until a week later, when there had been no further visit and no sign of food poisoning.

Coyle's next visit had surprised rather than alarmed him. Soon, he had begun to look forward to these visits. It was not until he was in company that he had realised how lonely he had been.

Eventually, he had also begun to see beyond Coyle's grumpy façade.

Edward, who had tactfully looked away, could not help being astounded by how much his opinion of this wilful man had changed. Once he had genuinely abhorred Coyle and not thought him capable of doing anything that was not in his own best interest. Edward was well aware of what Coyle had risked by visiting him. Perhaps this was why he had appreciated the visits so much. He had never asked him about the reason. It was an unspoken agreement, just as Coyle had not asked him about Miss Darcy.

"Well," Coyle said impatiently. "I am still waiting to hear what you have to say on the matter."

"I doubt you will believe what I have to tell you," Edward replied with a smile.

"For my own part, I see nothing whatsoever amusing in the situation," the steward muttered as he regarded Edward who had sunk back into the chair. "And what makes you think I misjudge your trustworthiness?" Coyle asked. He fell silent as he remembered all the times he had questioned Edward's opinions, statements and actions.

Edward did not reply but instead told Coyle that Darcy had come to see him. Before he had completed the first sentence, however, Coyle sat up with such force that the armchair creaked.

"Darcy visited your home?" he exclaimed in astonishment. It was only the thought of the gravity of the situation that kept Edward from laughing when he saw the steward's face. The stable master nodded and continued, but Coyle immediately interrupted him.

"And Mr Darcy did not come to avenge himself on you?" he said with a frown. Edward shook his head and opened his mouth to reply. Coyle's words silenced him, however.

"You have Mrs Darcy to thank for that," he said abruptly. "If it hadn't been for her, it is hardly likely you would be sitting here today."

Edward was not sure he wanted to hear about the discussions that had preceded Mr Darcy's decision and he hurriedly continued his account of the visit.

It was with the utmost effort that Coyle managed to keep from interrupting him; he even had to get up and fetch a sandwich in order to listen without speaking. At intervals, he shook his head and muttered something inaudible. When Miss Darcy's name was mentioned he could no longer keep his countenance.

"Are you pulling my leg?" he exclaimed in a loud voice. Taken aback by the unexpected reaction, Edward fell silent.

"Did you really think I would believe that Mr Darcy would make such a decision?" Coyle continued in dismay. "No, I cannot believe it, the consequences would be too…" he silenced as he saw Edward's expression.

"Don't take it personally, it is Mr Darcy's station, reputation and respect I am referring to," he said with a half-smile.

"Is that so, well that makes it all right then," said Edward and crossed his arms.

Coyle arose, went up to the table and grabbed his tankard. With a swift movement he had emptied half the contents in another mug, whereupon he returned to his armchair.

"I think we are in need of something strengthening," he said and handed Edward a mug. "Continue; I have a feeling that you will have to repeat this story many times, and not everyone will appreciate what they hear."

On that point no clarifying words were needed; Mr Darcy had said something similar as he was leaving. Edward looked at Coyle; even if the man's straightforwardness could cause discomfort, he appreciated his honesty.

When the stable master had finished his story, Coyle sat stock still; his voice was serious as he spoke.

"And it is your opinion that Mr Darcy's intentions are honest? I do not mean to frighten you, it is just that..." Coyle paused and took a great swig of beer before he said: "Knowing the Darcy family, your story seems most improbable."

"You will hardly be alone in this opinion," Edward said and looked at him.

"For once, I think we are of the same opinion," Coyle said and drank the contents of his tankard in a single gulp. Edward, who had not touched his beer, gave him his mug and said:

"Mr Darcy wants me to join him at Pemberley tonight." Coyle looked Edward over, frowned and said:

"Dressed like that?"

"They're my best clothes," Edward said and sighed.

"That may well be, but they are barely fit for the maids' chambers," Coyle said and grinned.

"I feared you would say something of the sort," Edward said and smiled.

With a nod towards the table, Coyle got up and Edward joined him. It was not until now that he had had the time and peace to notice that the entire day had gone by without a morsel of food. He wondered if he would be invited to stay for dinner.

Coyle sat down at the table and took a healthy slice of the meat in front of him. As Edward remained standing at the fire, Coyle looked up at him.

"You better put some weight on you if you are to show yourself with Miss Darcy," he said and pushed over a plate. Edward sat down and looked at the bread for a moment, before cutting himself a thick slice. After he had taken a few bites, he looked thoughtfully at his clothes.

"If you have had Mr Darcy's blessing, everything else will be taken care of," the steward said. "Suitable clothes are a triviality in this context."

Chapter 57

Elizabeth and Georgiana were sitting in the drawing room when the door was suddenly opened and Darcy strode in.

Georgiana looked quickly at her brother, but then turned her gaze away. Although she had been upset when he turned away Wickham, that turmoil was as nothing compared to what she felt when she had understood that Edward was no longer at Pemberley. For the first time in her life she had felt genuinely furious with her brother.

Darcy's expression was grave, yet at the same time there was an amused glint in his eyes that confused Elizabeth and she was impatient to discover what he had to say.

"I have the honour of announcing that we have a visitor here at Pemberley; it is a man who is most keen to meet Georgiana," Darcy said solemnly.

Georgiana did not look up, but continued to stare into the fire, which had been her only occupation while sitting in the drawing room. She was not the least interested in seeing Lord Malcolm. He had paid particular attention to her during her stay in London, and Georgiana knew that he had confessed to Mrs Alcot his admiration for the calm, beautiful girl who was so shy in comparison to the ladies of London society. Lord Malcolm had genuinely made an effort to strike up conversations with her, and it did not surprise her that he had come all the way to Pemberley to try to win her favour once more.

"Well, shall I ask our guest to come inside?" Darcy asked and looked at Elizabeth with a smile.

"No, I am not the least bit interested in seeing anyone," Georgiana said coldly.

"That's a shame as he is just outside the door, and I dearly hope he did not hear you," Darcy said and opened the door.

Georgiana felt the anger rise again; her brother obviously thought he could dictate her life to her. She did not intend to stay and receive any guests, and she did not care if it was improper to leave the room. Although she was angry, she felt the tears rising and she set her jaw against them. To avoid meeting the guest, she turned to the door the servants used. Just as she was about to go, she felt Elizabeth's hand on her arm.

"Georgiana, stay," she whispered, "I believe it is the man from the masquerade."

Georgiana stiffened and spun around. She followed her sister-in-law's eyes and for a moment the room was perfectly quiet. Darcy smiled as he noticed their expressions when they saw who the guest was.

Georgiana, who was pale from the shock, let her gaze wander between her brother and Edward. When Darcy made no attempt to upbraid them for their former behaviour, she slowly rose and went to meet them.

Elizabeth, who was observing Edward, saw that he was happy as well as tense and shy, and that, like Georgiana, he seemed to have suffered a loss of appetite. It was the first time Edward had been inside the manor house of Pemberley, and it was clear that he did not feel as comfortable as he would have on his own turf; but then, he was aware he was being scrutinized from several quarters.

Darcy nodded to the servants who bowed and reluctantly left the room; Elizabeth smiled at her husband's gesture and caught his eye. She was sure that the maid who had been the last to leave would have happily sacrificed a month's wages to stay and see what would unfold. Like her husband, Elizabeth knew that the conjecture would start as soon as Mr Darcy opened his drawing room door to Pemberley's stable master.

Edward soon regained some of his usual sunny disposition. Even if he did not speak much, his eyes expressed the same happiness and liveliness as they had always done before.

Georgiana, who understood that Darcy had accepted their love, turned to her brother and threw her arms about him. Darcy reciprocated her hug and when he saw his sister's joy, he was convinced he had done the right thing, even if the price would be high for them all.

If Edward was to marry Georgiana, he could not stay on as a stable master at Pemberley. Darcy was of the opinion that there were good chances of finding him alternative employment, as he, like his father, had a good head for business. A respectable occupation would make the match less unseemly, even if Darcy was well aware that there would always be talk of Miss Darcy having married the stable master. This would come about regardless of Edward's profession, but it was the price they would have to pay for their love.

Elizabeth and Darcy soon left the room, on the excuse of changing for dinner. As they opened the door, four servant girls and a man backed away in fright and hurriedly resumed their business. John Goose, who showed great interest in a waistcoat that had been left hanging over a chair outside the door, cleared his throat.

"Sir, I apologise," he said and bowed.

Darcy regarded him with a serious expression, whereupon he took Elizabeth's hand and walked up the stairs with determined strides. Not until they were out of earshot of the servants did he allow himself to smile.

"Were you very surprised by my decision to give them my permission?" Darcy said finally.

"No one who has seen them together can be in any doubt that their feelings for each other are sincere, and as I know that more than anything you want your sister to be happy, I did not think you would deny her that happiness once she had found it," Elizabeth replied.

"Behind that decision lay many hours of agony. I must admit that a union between the two of them was for a long time out of the question," Darcy said.

"In a situation such as this, a few weeks' time for consideration is understandable," Elizabeth said and smiled. "What was it that finally made you change your mind?"

"Georgiana's obvious distress… and the unfairness of denying her the happiness I myself have been given," Darcy said quietly.

"I dare say your sister is the happiest woman in Derbyshire tonight," Elizabeth said. After a moment's silence, she added, "as are the gossip-mongers."

"Thank you for reminding me," Darcy said.

"You're welcome," Elizabeth replied and smiled.

As they passed the picture gallery, Darcy stopped and beheld the painting of Elizabeth and himself. The painting portrayed Mr and Mrs Darcy who stood together in the park at the very spot where they had chanced upon one another when Elizabeth had visited Pemberley the first time in the company of Mr and Mrs Gardiner. Darcy liked the painting, and every time he gazed upon it, he remembered the emotion that had filled him when, to his great delight, he met Elizabeth in a place where he would have least expected it.

After a long time lost in memories, Darcy looked at Elizabeth and observed with a smile:

"I have at least learnt that you women refuse to marry for any other reason than love, no matter how rich or poor the man in question is."

"The knowledge that a woman marries a man only for his fortune can hardly give true happiness, no matter how dear she is to him," Elizabeth said.

"You are right, and I suppose that you mean that I should really be grateful that you refused me the first time," Darcy said and embraced his wife.

"You must agree that our happiness is the greater now than what it would have been had I accepted your first proposal of marriage," Elizabeth replied.

"This I cannot deny. When you finally accepted me, I knew that this was truly your wish, and nothing could have given me greater joy than this knowledge," Darcy said seriously.

After a while, Elizabeth said:

"You must not forget that you have an important letter to write. Lady Catherine will surely receive the news of another improper marriage with pleasure."

"By now I think Lady Catherine has probably given up on the Darcy family. Possibly, she still nourishes some hope for Colonel Fitzwilliam," Darcy admitted with mock gravity.

"Perhaps it is also time to notify her Ladyship of that which will soon no longer be concealable," Elizabeth said.

"Even if your figure has always been petite, I must regrettably inform you that if you thought your condition was still unknown, you are mistaken: every servant is speaking about it," Darcy said and smiled.

"Is that so," Elizabeth said. "Then there is nothing left to do but to invite everyone to share in our and Georgiana's happiness."

Chapter 58

As Edward now required a higher position than that of stable master, he began training, with Darcy's aid, at an attorney's in Sheffield.

Darcy had sought out his father's good friend Mr Winslow and explained that he needed assistance in finding an apprentice position for one of his employees. Mr Winslow had accepted the commission and asked when the man in question intended to start.

"Right away," Darcy had replied, which confused Mr Winslow as Darcy had arrived in the sole company of his stable master. Laughing, he had asked whether it was Edward who was to be re-educated. The assenting reply had provoked further hilarity as it seemed completely unlikely to Mr Winslow that Pemberley's owner would take such a measure.

Mr Winslow knew that Darcy, like his aunt, was well aware of his position in society. One's standing in society was given at birth and followed one to the grave, the exception being those few who succeeded in obtaining a fortune through business. These nouveaux riches, as they were called, would however, despite their money, never be on equal footing with those who had been born into money. That a rich man like Darcy was a good employer and took care of his underlings was to his credit: to raise them above their station could at best be consider imprudent.

When it became clear to Mr Winslow that Darcy was serious, he had been so astounded that he had forgotten to ask for what reason the stable master was to be trained for the bar. The question thus remained unanswered, but not unconsidered. As the promise had been given, and Darcy was a man whom one did not refuse, Edward had begun his apprenticeship the same day.

At first Mr Winslow had been annoyed at himself for saying yes without having asked those questions he customarily posed when hiring new staff. Mr Winslow had assumed that Darcy was seeking employment for a man who was more or less already educated and simply needed the practical experience an experienced man could offer. A stable master, however, was unlikely to know how to read and write, and was not what Mr Winslow had had in mind; he admitted that his attitude towards Edward at the time left something to be desired.

Mr Winslow had, however, been relieved and surprised to find that Darcy's protégé could read as well as write. Before the end of the first week, Mr Winslow had been so astonished by his apprentice that he had to re-evaluate some of his prejudices where the servants were concerned.

If Mr Winslow had not witnessed Edward's position at Pemberley with his own eyes, he would have thought that Darcy had tricked him somehow.

Pemberley's stable master lacked education; his work was among the horses. His father had taught him to read and write, but that was all. Mr Winslow soon discovered, however, that Edward had an ability that was rare indeed.

One evening the elder man had sighed over the fact that he did not remember the exact circumstances of a case, and therefore had to search through the archives for a small but not unimportant detail. Smiling, he had confided in Edward that Mrs Winslow would not be pleased that the dinner would be delayed yet another evening.

Edward had interrupted his reading, written a few lines and passed him the note.

"How could you know that it was the supplement to Mrs Dobbenham's testament I was referring to?" Mr Winslow said in surprise.

"Sir, Mrs Dobbenham's papers were among the cases you assigned me to read," Edward replied.

"If I am not mistaken, you have read more cases than Mrs Dobbenham's, isn't that so?" Mr Winslow said thoughtfully.

"That's correct," Edward said and met the old man's eyes.

"How many cases have you had time to read?" Mr Winslow asked curiously.

"About two hundred, sir," Edward replied. Mr Winslow took off his spectacles and looked at him in amusement.

"You have read through two hundred cases and can deliver a detail like that without further thought?"

Edward, who was unsure whether it was a question or an observation, reciprocated his smile and went back to read the textbook Mr Winslow had provided him with.

At one point he chuckled, and asked Mr Winslow what year the book had been published. The answer that it had just recently left the press, made him regard the author's name with scepticism for a moment. He did not ask Mr Winslow if he really thought that the law first considered the crime and not the perpetrator's social standing.

After having regarded his apprentice with rising curiosity, Mr Winslow suddenly put down his file.

"Which is the fourth paragraph in the seventh part concerning libel?" he whispered.

"What?" Edward said in surprise, but soon found himself and answered Mr Winslow's question.

"Hmm," said Mr Winslow and reached for his favourite pen, whose tip soon dove into the ink flask. The white feather's upper tip vibrated in the air; Edward could not help but be amazed by the old man's speed with the pen. While the sheet was filling with flourishing, neat characters, he delivered a cascade of questions that Edward answered.

Edward did not think that Mr Winslow had forgotten the answer to all of them; if that was the case the future of the firm Winslow & Sons was uncertain indeed. Despite what the sign communicated, after two generations Mr Winslow was the only one who remained. Mrs Winslow had given her husband two daughters and a son, who, to his father's disappointment, had insisted on a career within the army.

When Edward had replied to what seemed to be the last question, he had remained seated and listened to the scraping sound of Mr Winslow's pen that had by now filled three sheets of paper. Mr Winslow crumpled up one of them and threw it at Edward.

"You have been blessed with the memory of a horse," he said and laughed. Edward did not respond; for as long as he could remember he had found it easy to recall things he had read once. By the light of their sole kerosene lamp, his father had taught him to read. Edward had been the only one among his friends in the village who knew how to read. Although he had at the time been more interested in chasing rats with his friends, he was forever grateful to his father for passing on his knowledge.

"To know how to read and write is everything," his father had said, and once more told the story of the good Mr Darcy, who had seen to it that his stable master had acquired these skills.

Mr Winslow took his task of training Edward very seriously, and it was with delight and surprise that he found that his least well-educated apprentice was the one who gave him the most pleasure.

When the old man had discovered Edward's considerable powers of recollection, he had ascribed a number of talents to him that he did not yet possess. To remember what one had read and be able to account for it did not necessarily mean that one understood the core of what was being communicated. Edward had to work hard to read those textbooks that were available on the subject and, to complete a task, he often had to interrupt his work in order to look for some piece of information.

Chapter 59

Although Edward had easily settled down in town and took a certain pleasure in his new work tasks, he admitted that he longed to be back at Pemberley. The distance meant that it was considerably further between visits than either he or Georgiana wished.

Every time Edward visited Pemberley, he began his visit by going to the stable master's residence under the pretext of seeing whether the new stable master had any queries he might be able to answer. These visits continued long after the new stable master, who was not without experience, was well-acquainted with the work. Elizabeth guessed that Edward missed his old employment, even if it was not something he would admit to her or Darcy.

Georgiana, who was just as pleased every time she saw Edward, always hurried to meet him. Edward was most comfortable in natural settings, and the two young people could often be seen roaming about the park or riding over the meadows. Sometimes he had dinner with them at Pemberley, but he had yet to dine in a larger company than that of Georgiana, Elizabeth and Darcy. Even if he knew this would be unavoidable, he dreaded it, and every time there had been a visitor at Pemberley, Edward had sent a message saying he could not be spared from his work in Sheffield.

Edward had not forgotten Darcy's reaction when he had questioned him at the stable master's residence. Where one came from, where the estate lay, who one's father and mother were – these were questions that always arose at such gatherings.

Edward had never before been particularly entertained by Georgiana's descriptions of such events. When he was expected to join in, he knew he had heard enough to be able to predict the outcome of it. The situation could easily become humiliating for Georgiana; the thought that he would be the reason for it gave him no peace.

Marrying Georgiana meant his own life would be enriched; but Georgiana risked having to give up things she would never have had to give up had she chosen a man of her own social standing.

Edward was well aware of some of the rumours that circulated in the village. What aggrieved him the most was that some of those he had thought were his friends could think his love stemmed from Georgiana's fortune. Sometimes, Edward wished that he and Georgiana could take up residence in some other part of the country, where they would be received and accepted as Mr and Mrs Jones without further speculations, rumours or surmise as to the grounds of their mutual affection.

The masked ball they had attended a couple of months prior had strengthened his vision of what the future held in store. At that event he had been masked and no one but Georgiana and Mr Wilkins had known his true identity. Thus shielded, he had been able to move in circles where people of his standing never had access other than as servants.

During the evening he had heard a conversation that took place between two elegant ladies in stylish dress. The two women had expressed their dismay at a young man from a neighbouring estate who intended to wed a merchant's daughter. They had spoken at length about the girl's failings and the fact that she lacked a fortune seemed to provide her with a number of inappropriate characteristics. Edward had been sickened by the conversation and when he had caught sight of the poor girl he had felt genuinely sorry for her.

Naturally, all the servants spoke of Miss Darcy's engagement to the stable master and the rumour had soon spread to the village. To Georgiana, the important thing was that Darcy had given them his consent; what other people thought she cared less about. She knew that some of their acquaintances were of the opinion that her brother had lost both his wits and his judgement. She was disappointed, however, that Edward so assiduously avoided all social gatherings at Pemberley; sooner or later he would be forced to confront her friends and relatives.

Georgiana confided in Elizabeth and Darcy and together they decided that Edward should be present at the gathering that was soon to come. Knowing about it would in all likelihood result in him feeling forced to spend the weekend in Sheffield. Edward was thus invited to the social event without his own knowledge of it; he was likewise happily unaware that it was to take place.

Georgiana feared that Edward would be angered with her when he discovered what was afoot, but Darcy convinced her that it was the only way to overcome his resistance.

Elizabeth felt a bit sorry for the young man who would be forced to meet all these people for the first time when he was present at a gathering where the number of guests would be greater than four. Even if he had never said anything, Elizabeth suspected that the reason he had avoided these gatherings was insecurity about his own role in this new situation; a feeling she was herself well acquainted with.

Chapter 60

The case of Mr and Mrs Crook was, at the moment, Mr Winslow's most prioritised case, and as new evidence had emerged, he had decided to immediately travel to London. It was the first time Mr Winslow had entrusted Edward to run the office, and he had every intention to live up to his employer's expectations.

After having completed the note-taking he had been assigned, put the books in the shelves and filled the ink-well with ink, Edward looked at the feather pen that awaited having its nib sharpened. He remembered how Mr Winslow had laughed as he had commented on the clever business idea of dipping gull feathers in colour. The feather pen, it would seem, came from a bird whose feathers could also be of a blue or green colour.

Edward looked around and thereafter sat down in Mr Winslow's chiselled armchair with the lion paws. For a moment, he tried to imagine what a cat with these kinds of paws would look like. Mr Winslow had said that there was a living specimen on display in London.

Deep in musings about African wildlife and thereafter in a chapter about applicable consequences of embezzlement, Edward was unaware of the carriage and its passenger who stopped outside the office.

A passing couple looked curiously at the black carriage; one glance from the man who had stepped down from the seat caused them, however, to hurry along.

The rough man, whose back was humped due to a spinal curvature, went up to the door with determined strides. He aimed a few well-aimed punches at the large wooden door. At the second, more forceful series of raps, Edward reacted, closed the book and went to see who the visitor was.

On the threshold stood a tall man in a dark greatcoat with his hat at an angle so that the shadow of the wide brim masked his face. More than this he was not able to distinguish through the peep-hatch Mr Winslow had installed after having had an unwanted visitor at one point.

Mr Winslow had on his departure exhorted Edward to lock the door on closing and make sure who was outside the door before he opened it. The inhabitants of Sheffield knew about Winslow & Sons' opening hours. The firm that had been started by Mr Winslow's father had been around for sixty years and the opening hours had remained constant.

"Mr Winslow is not available, please return again in the morning," Edward said through the hatch.

"We are aware that Mr Winslow is unavailable, that is why we are here," a male voice replied.

"What can I do for you?" Edward said calmly.

"For a start, you can open the door so that we can have a talk," the man replied.

213

Mr Winslow had never mentioned the circumstances around the last unwelcome visitor, or if there were any reasons for caution. Edward chose to await the man's next move; he had no plans to invite someone in who had not introduced himself.

A long moment's silence occurred, as the man on the other side did not seem to have any intentions of further discussing the matter. The silence was broken by the sound of a carriage door opening. Edward saw a glimpse of another person approaching the door; this face was likewise concealed by a hood.

The man in the greatcoat suddenly stretched out his arms, moved them slowly up and down along the sides whereupon he gave out a cawing sound. Soon thereafter Edward heard to his surprise a rumbling laughter and saw the man put his hands to his stomach in an effort to control the wave of laughter that broke forth.

"Edward! … What has living in town done to you…? I thought it was only women who didn't open the door to a visitor?" The man said, still laughing.

Edward smiled as he recognised the voice. He opened the door and looked over Pemberley's coach-driver.

"I didn't recognise your voice," he said with relief and held out his hand.

"That was intentional, I hope we gave you a fright – but it is nothing compared to what is to come," the driver said and pounded Edward's back.

"We?" Edward said with a smile. "Do you mean there is someone accompanying you?"

"I do indeed," the driver replied and stepped aside.

"Georgiana!" Edward said in surprise and took two steps forward to embrace her. For a moment he held her from him and smiled. "What on earth has brought you to Sheffield?"

Before Georgiana had time to answer Edward's question, the driver said: "I must say it is very odd to see you two together."

"You'll just have to look the other way, then," Georgiana said and smiled.

"Edward, imagine if your father could see you now," the man continued unabashedly and shook his head.

"Miss Darcy, it is lucky that your father can't see you now," he added in a chuckle. Georgiana and Edward looked at each other, well aware of how their respective fathers would have reacted to their engagement.

"On second thought, perhaps it is Edward who should be glad that your father can't see you now," the man continued in amusement.

"You certainly have a talent for bringing a man down to earth," Edward said and smiled. "But I am very grateful to you for driving all this way, whatever the reason may be."

"You're welcome, what would you not do for a former colleague?" the driver said and with a bow took three steps backwards.

Georgiana looked at him in amused amazement. In Edward's company, some of the servants showed sides to them that she had never seen before. The alteration from one moment having been one of the servants of the Darcy's to becoming Miss Darcy's fiancé would hardly go any of the employees by unnoticed.

The silence that fell when the driver had stepped away was so apparent that they both remained still. It was just the two of them. Nothing felt frightening or threatening.

The social events and occasions, with all their demands, seemed distant. Despite the sparing light, it did not escape her that his eyes reflected what she herself felt. None of them said anything.

"That felt good," the driver shouted; he had appeared from behind the bend where he had sought refuge to relieve himself of the drink that had by now passed through its host's passages. Edward shook his head when he saw that the man lifted his hat and set off for the closest pub at the end of the street.

Georgiana looked at Edward for a long time. The gaze that from the first had thrilled her still provoked the same emotion although they had not seen each other for a few days. Just the thought of being close to him effected a similar sensation. The thought of what it would mean to become Mrs Jones made her blush. She reminded herself yet again to ask Elizabeth's advice upon the matter. Although she was ignorant in such matters, her brother's and sister-in-law's behaviour towards each other revealed that they were happy in all aspects of their marriage.

The thought of Elizabeth made her remember why she was in Sheffield.

"You are hardly unaware of the joy I have felt since my brother gave us his blessing," Georgiana said and stroked a strand of hair from her forehead. Edward, who still had his arms around her waist, nodded and silently awaited the continuation.

"There is, however, one thing that would make me even happier," she added after a moment's silence.

"If it is anything I can affect, I will take it upon me at once," he replied gravely and held her away so that he could see her face. "So what is it?" he said as Georgiana looked at the ground.

"I want you to come to Pemberley so that I can introduce you to my friends and relatives," she replied and looked straight at him without flinching.

"Yes, I suppose it is time now, I have avoided it long enough." He hesitated before adding: "I have not been able to disregard how our different backgrounds will affect your acquaintances: that is why I have been reluctant to be presented to them."

"I can hardly blame you after everything I have told you about various gatherings," she replied and smiled.

"If this was meant to assuage my worries, I must regretfully inform you that you will have to try again," Edward said and laughed. Georgiana loosened her other arm, grabbed the collars of the white shirt and pulled his face towards her. Edward reciprocated her kiss.

"That's better; I feel completely at ease now," he said contentedly.

"The stories are often worse than reality, and people can change," she said and hoped it was the truth. That he, despite the circumstances, was so cheerful encouraged her to continue.

"Has not my brother given us his blessing? A few weeks ago, I think that was more than you could ever have imagined," she said and smiled.

"I could not have imagined it; if you'll pardon me I think I would have laughed aloud if anyone had suggested it," the coach-man, who had turned up again without them noticing, said.

"The situation for the both of you could have looked very different, I can assure you," he said seriously.

"Thank you, I feel much better now!" Edward said. "Don't you have a horse to attend to?" he added and smiled.

"That's your job; I beg your pardon, that was your job," the driver said and grinned.

Edward turned back to Georgiana and said: "I suppose you are right; if your brother could give us his consent, there are few people left to fear."

The coachman, who had taken up his position by the horses, discretely turned his gaze away and smiled as he saw Miss Darcy's reaction to Edward's decision to accompany them to Pemberley.

It was with new-won respect that he had seen Miss Darcy defy convention and enter into an engagement with a man far below her own social standing. Love, courage and stubbornness were characteristics that would stand them in good stead; there was more talk about them in the village than he had any intention of letting Edward know.

Georgiana's happiness that Edward had accepted her invitation had a calming effect on his nerves about the impending evening. The elaborate descriptions of those invited made him rather curious, and at the end of the journey Edward had begun to look forward to the affair.

Mr Bingley seemed to him a light-hearted man, and Edward looked forward to make his acquaintance in particular. The description of Lady Catherine de Bourgh did not unexpectedly come to be about her estate, Rosings, rather than her personal characteristics.

Chapter 61

Lady Catherine de Bourgh's decision to accept Mr and Mrs Darcy's invitation was not only due to her wish to continue the reparations that had commenced where their relations were concerned. The overwhelming reason was that she wanted to see how Elizabeth handled the role of mistress at Pemberley. That a simple girl from the country could run such a large estate and maintain its good name, traditions and style was more than she could imagine.

Darcy's choice of wife undoubtedly showed a lack of judgement. It might be said that his marriage to Elizabeth had spared Miss de Bourgh the misery of being wed to a man of ill judgement. This newfound insight had dampened Lady Catherine's resentment that her long-standing plans for her daughter's future had been thwarted.

She could only hope that the brother's actions had not had too great an effect on his younger sister's chances of making an eligible match. Georgiana was of a quieter and easily lead disposition, and had, according to Lady Catherine, never shown signs of headstrongness, foolhardiness or thoughtlessness. If it was necessary, she would herself introduce her niece to the better circles of society.

Considering the girl's fondness for her sister-in-law, it was probably best if this happened as soon as possible. Elizabeth would hardly emphasise the importance of marrying within one's sphere, and who knew into what company Georgiana risked being introduced. Lady Catherine sent a grateful thought to Mrs Bennet, who had had the sense not to bear any sons.

Mr Wilkins felt happy that his friend had invited him to share in a family gathering. His own happiness had not made him forget Georgiana's situation, which he was convinced he was the only one to know about.

In a situation such as this, neither advice nor well-meaning words or encouragement could fill any real function. It was his conviction that love could not be a malaise, however inappropriate the surroundings might find it. When Georgiana had confided her emotions for Edward in him, he had spoken and acted from the heart; if it had been a service or a disservice to her, he did not know. The fact that her letters had stopped for the last two months suggested the latter, which was the only thing that dampened his delight at the upcoming visit. Mr Wilkins wondered if Edward was still at Pemberley.

Not even Darcy knew the reason for Mr Wilkins' liberal view of love across class barriers.

Mr Wilkins' father was a cousin of the king. Apart from owning one of the greatest estates of southern England, he often spent time at court.

In his youth he had, like other young men of good families, let his gaze remain within the innermost circle when the time had come to wed. At the age of twenty-four, Mr Wilkins' father had married his sixteen-year-old cousin.

When four years had passed and Mrs Wilkins had still not born her husband any children, she had begun to despair. Her fate had, however, not been to walk through life childless.

During a trip to the continent, Mrs Wilkins had, on one of her walks through the French countryside, beheld a farmer raking his hay. Although her style of dress was different from that which the French upper classes wore, the farmer had immediately realised that it was a well-born lady who had crossed his path. He had interrupted his work and looked at her with an inscrutable face.

At the sight of the man's green gaze, Mrs Wilkins had had such a forceful notion that she remained, for a moment, paralyzed. The next day she had come to the same spot and waved to him to approach her. He had come closer and nodded as she showed him five gold coins and in almost perfect French whispered: "You will give me a son."

Nine months later, Mr Wilkins' father had recommended a good friend to let his childless wife partake of the French cuisine, the mild wind and the many sunny days that France had to offer.

Mr Wilkins had always wanted to visit the place in France that his mother had told him about on her deathbed. This had never come about, as he had not been able to bring himself to do so for as long as his father was still alive. When Mr Wilkins had been told of his son's engagement, he had called him to his side and said: "Your and Miss Byron's wedding trip must go to France... to Montpellier."

Angelina had long known about the circumstances surrounding her biological parents. She had not been meant to find out about it at such a tender age, but when she had accidentally heard a conversation that touched upon the matter, there had been nothing to do but to tell her the whole story. At first she had felt tricked, by her parents as well as Darcy's father, and reacted with anger towards the two that were still alive. Eventually, the anger had been replaced by a sorrow that her biological father had never had a chance to know that she knew the truth.

Wickham returned to Pemberley with mixed emotions. Darcy had forgiven him, which was more than he could have asked for. He doubted that in such a situation, he himself could have been as forgiving. The joy at once more being part of the family was intermixed with agony and worry. Wickham felt ashamed at the thought of meeting Georgiana again. He was painfully aware of the grief he had caused to others through his way of life. Apart from his history with Georgiana, the memory of the times he had slandered Darcy to Elizabeth likewise pained him.

On their most recent meeting, Elizabeth had pointed out that this was the price he had to pay for his former ill-living; but she had also said that it was his salvation. If he did not feel guilt and agony, there would be nothing to stop him from carrying on as he always had.

Chapter 62

Mrs Bennet had in her reply to her invitation let it be known that she would like to see Mary and Kitty introduced to some of Darcy's friends in Derbyshire. They all stood to gain from a favourable outcome of such introductions. For Elizabeth, it would mean a family member within a day's journey of Pemberley, and Mr and Mrs Bennet's visits would be easier the more daughters they had in the same part of the country. At the end of her letter, Mrs Bennet had added that if the gentlemen in question were well off, it would be a further advantage.

Elizabeth had not passed her mother's wishes on to her husband, and she hoped that no such requests would be put forward during their stay at Pemberley.

Ever since the invitation had arrived at Longbourn, Mrs Bennet had speculated about the good news that was to be announced. During the entirety of their journey to Derbyshire, her husband had to listen to the monologue that he would otherwise have taken respite from in his library, the only place where his wife left him in peace.

"A child! Naturally it is a child! Anything else is unthinkable!" Mrs Bennet cried in an eager voice. "My dear Lizzy is with child."

"Don't be so sure of that. Darcy may reveal his plans to renovate Pemberley – I think it has long been his intention," Mr Bennet replied.

"Renovate Pemberley! Why would they want us to come all this way to announce such a trifle?" Mrs Bennet exclaimed.

"It is no mere trifle – a renovated Pemberley would give you twice the material to brag about to your friends," Mr Bennet said and sighed. As his wife opened her mouth again, he leaned forward and nodded towards the building that was just visible between the trees. He hoped that the sight of the splendid estate would silence her for a moment.

"My dear, we are going to have our first grandchild!" Mrs Bennet chuckled, after a hiatus of about two minutes, in Mr Bennet's estimation.

"Lizzy, dearest child. Tell me when I will have the pleasure of greeting my next grandchild," Mrs Bennet blurted out as soon as she had alighted from the carriage.

"Are you to tell Elizabeth that she is pregnant? What if this is not the case – but then, you are her mother, so naturally you would know better than she herself," Mr Bennet said and looked at his daughter.

"Of course we will soon let you all in on our secret, but I would ask you to have patience and wait until we are all gathered this evening," Elizabeth said and smiled.

"This evening! Pray tell who the guests are that would keep a daughter from telling her mother the news she has so long been expecting?" Mrs Bennet said indignantly. When she did not receive a reply, she eyed Darcy.

"I am convinced it will be a fine boy child." No one chose to comment on this, but Darcy looked at Elizabeth with an amused expression on his face.

The guests who had arrived during the morning spent the greater part of the day inspecting Pemberley's magnificent architecture. No one who was in the same room as Mrs Bennet could avoid hearing her judgement upon her next-to-eldest daughter's home. From her descriptions, a stranger would have assumed that it was Elizabeth, and not Darcy, who was the rightful owner of the estate.

It was not without reason that Mr Bennet and his wife had been placed in the one wing and Lady Catherine de Bourgh in the other. Neither was it a coincidence that the two women had no opportunity to meet before dinner. Elizabeth felt more worried about the evening than she was willing to admit, either to herself or to her husband.

Georgiana's happiness overshadowed any concern she might have felt, knowing as she did about Lady Catherine's reaction to her brother's engagement. The night that Georgiana had told Elizabeth about her feelings for Edward, she had expressed concern about what her brother's reaction would be. Despite this there had been something defiant and determined in her gaze, and Elizabeth's thoughts had unintentionally gone to Georgiana's aunt Christine. She had been determined to marry the man she had chosen for herself. Whether Christine would have gone through with her plans to elope with her beloved there was no way of knowing.

At one point Elizabeth had asked Darcy how he thought Lady Catherine would receive the news of his sister's engagement. Darcy had replied that he hoped that Lady Catherine would in time – say twenty years – come to accept Georgiana's choice.

Darcy had told her he intended to introduce Edward as Mr Edward Jones. If Lady Catherine insisted on knowing Edward's position, he would say that he was employed by Mr Winslow. His aunt had great confidence in Mr Winslow, who had helped the de Bourghs alter the inheritance of Rosings so that it would fall into the hands of Miss Anne.

In Derbyshire, the odd alliance was a widely debated topic, among servants as well as the upper classes. Edward's hunger for riches, Miss Darcy's disrespect of her brother and ancestors, the great risks that mixing over social borders entailed.

Elizabeth was glad that neither Georgiana nor Edward had heard the more malicious gossip. Naturally, there were also those who spoke of love defying all boundaries, Miss Darcy's courage in defying social conventions. Edward's bravery in confessing his love for someone who was unattainable, and in mixing in circles where he could hardly be met as an equal. The strength of these voices were, however, not as evident, particularly not in those circles that the Darcy family moved.

Chapter 63

Lady Catherine de Bourgh was still as high-minded and reserved as ever; but she was not as malicious or condescending towards Elizabeth or her family, and even conversed for a while with Mr Bennet as they happened to be placed next to each other at the table.

Mrs Bennet, who was eager to share the joyous news, impatiently counted off the guests and discovered to her consternation that four chairs remained empty. When Wickham and Lydia stepped into the room she forgot about Elizabeth, Darcy and Pemberley for a moment, and focused all her attention on her favourite daughter whom she had not seen in half a year.

"Oh, Lydia, what a surprise to see you! Come here, dear child, and let me embrace you – and you too, dear Wickham!"

Mr Bennet looked at Elizabeth with a surprised expression, and when he thereafter saw Darcy's easy conversation with Wickham he didn't know what to think. Darcy, who saw his face, smiled and shrugged his shoulders, which hardly dispelled the confusion. Mr and Mrs Bennet were still unaware of Wickham's duel, or the change of temperament that it had brought about.

Lady Catherine, who had looked around and sighed as she saw the assembled guests, asked in a loud voice:

"Where is Miss Darcy?"

Jane, who sat next to her father, immediately fell silent; her respect, or rather, her fear of this highborn lady had not abated. Although Lady Catherine was of a slight build, there was something in her eyes and general demeanour that made her uncomfortable. She is not kind, Jane thought, and looked about her in alarm to ascertain that she had not spoken aloud.

It was not only Jane's conversation that had been interrupted by Lady Catherine's comment; all assembled guests apart from Mrs Bennet were awaiting Darcy's answer.

"My hopes where your sisters are concerned are high – with a son-in-law like Mr Darcy…" Mrs Bennet's twittering voice went into falsetto at the last words, and only fell silent when Lydia's shushing had reached her consciousness. Not unexpectedly, she looked unperturbed that which had been intended for Lydia's ears only had now been brought to everyone's attention.

Mrs Bennet's self-satisfied face revealed, rather, that she was proud of what she had accomplished. Mr Darcy could hardly have misunderstood her hint. As he had been given their permission to marry their daughter, it was his duty to introduce his wife's unmarried sisters among his friends.

Darcy neither had time to reply to Lady Catherine's question, nor introduce another topic for discussion before a discrete gesture from John Goose signalled that the absent party were on their way. A look at Elizabeth revealed that she was more stressed by the situation than he himself. Darcy hoped that his calm would have a dampening effect on her anxiety.

If she had previously mastered Lady Catherine, her current position hardly made the outlook worse. Perhaps it was her condition that made her vulnerable; Darcy looked at his wife and smiled.

At that moment, the door was opened and Georgiana stepped into the room: her companion immediately drew everyone's attention. Apart from Elizabeth, Darcy and Mr Wilkins, there were only two of the guests who recognised Edward from before.

Wickham looked in astonishment at the man by Georgiana's side. For a moment he wondered if his eyes were deceiving him: her companion looked eerily like one of Pemberley's employees.

What he thought he had seen seemed too unlikely to be true; but as Darcy introduced the man as Edward Jones, Wickham could only confirm that his senses had not failed him. He could not help staring at Edward. As to his clothes, he did not stand out in particular – if one were not, as Wickham was, used to seeing him in attire that would definitely have been unsuitable for a drawing-room.

Edward was dressed in a dark blue coat with a white shirt and waistcoat; with these he wore a pair of light grey trousers. There were more than one in the assembly, however, who noted his sunburnt face that also held traces of freckles. The eyes communicated a calm expression, and the unknown man looked quietly at those gathered. When he discovered Mr Wilkins, he struggled to hide a smile.

Darcy, who had seen both Edward's smile and Mr Wilkins' amused expression, looked at his sister in surprise; as far as he knew, the two men were not acquainted. Darcy, who was convinced that they had recognised each other, decided to further investigate the matter during the course of the evening.

After Darcy had introduced the guests to Georgiana's companion, he took up his seat between Georgiana and Darcy. The stranger's placement at the table suggested that he was a guest of honour, and the curiosity about him grew. Lady Catherine looked at Darcy with irritation; that neither her nephew nor her niece had told her that a new guest was to be introduced was quite reproachful. A guest by Miss Darcy's side should have been introduced and approved by the family's oldest and thereby most important member. It was a bad sign that Darcy had chosen to ignore this, despite his knowledge of her views on this matter.

Edward had been surprised when he had seen Wickham at the table, and he wondered what had persuaded Darcy to invite him to Pemberley. Darcy's account of Wickham's prior behaviour to Georgiana had hardly surprised Edward; he was well acquainted with Wickham's character. The servants often witnessed aspects of their superiors that were hidden from their equals. Many families would be surprised if they discovered how well known their family business were among their employees. Wickham had been known as a man who, through cunning, acquired whatever amused or pleased him. Among some of the servants there had been jealousy and envy over his privileged position. His lack of consideration, respect or gratitude had, together with his arrogant attitude, given rise to feelings of contempt and anger.

Edward assumed that Wickham's marriage to Elizabeth's sister was the reason he` was now present at Pemberley. Darcy obviously let his love for his wife and his desire to make her happy override the betrayal and anger he had felt over Wickham's former actions.

Edward had always respected Darcy, who was a good employer and took care of his employees. During the last months he had witnessed sides to Mr Darcy that had made him stand out from his peers. Edward cast an anxious glance at Georgiana; apart from the light blush that often appeared when she felt herself be the centre of attention, she seemed, to his relief, untroubled by the situation.

Georgiana had been made privy to the story of Wickham's duel as soon as Darcy and Elizabeth had returned from Hunsford. Once she had accepted his excuses for his prior behaviour towards her, she had no qualms about him being at Pemberley. She had, as Elizabeth and Darcy, felt that his apologies were genuine, and therefore accepted them. The feelings she had once harboured towards Wickham had been a slight infatuation; her feelings for Edward were so different that the past did not matter to her.

Although it discomfited him, Wickham could not help but look at Edward and Georgiana. The past made itself felt as soon as his surprise at seeing them together had abated. When he remembered his former attitude towards the stable master's son, he was filled with a discomfort that made him want to withdraw from the company.

Wickham felt his face take on a darker shade as he remembered how he had once seduced one of the maids whom he knew was fond of Edward. He had been convinced that Edward had returned the girl's feelings. Through admiring gazes, encouraging words and seemingly innocent brushes against her, he had transferred the young woman's adoration onto himself. The knowledge of his success had not been enough; he had wanted Edward to see his triumph. Wickham avoided Edward's eyes as he remembered that Edward's discovery of the two of them in the hay, had given him more pleasure than the maid's services.

Chapter 64

Edward, who sat opposite to Bingley and Jane, soon found his place, and discovered, to his delight, that his companions were perfectly agreeable. Mr Bingley was, as Georgiana had suggested, a man of an easy disposition, and his wife Jane was so mild that Edward dared believe that there were at least two among those assembled that would accept the odd situation Miss Darcy had placed herself in.

Edward had immediately won Bingley's approval. Among Darcy's acquaintances it was rare to find people who saw laughter as something liberating rather than something that should be checked. Although Bingley was sure he had not been introduced to Mr Edward Jones before, he seemed familiar to him. He assumed it was due to their similar dispositions.

Lady Catherine had studied the young man during the entire dinner, and she could not ascertain his origins. Judging by his speech, he was a local, but she could not remember if any of the estates in the vicinity were indeed the home of a Mr Edward Jones. The name meant nothing to her, and immediately excluded the possibility that Georgiana had met a man of a noble family.

Georgiana and the young man looked at each other often enough to tell anyone that they were in love, which sharpened the mistress of Rosing's attention. The placement at the table, Darcy's open manner towards the newcomer, the gazes that, without an ounce of discretion, were exchanged between Georgiana and Mr Jones, were alarming.

Lady Catherine impatiently awaited an opportunity to have her fears confirmed; that they would be allayed was not likely. When the guests had gathered in the drawing-room and found themselves in smaller groups, she saw her chance.

Mary, who had immediately taken up her station at the pianoforte and commenced a dolorous tune, had made Mr Bennet raise his eyebrows and discretely ask for a display that was meant to lighten rather than oppress the mood of those gathered.

Mrs Bennet and Lydia had placed themselves in the sofa where the former informed her daughter about the events in Merryton over the last six months.

Mr Wilkins, Angelina and Wickham had sat down at the games table and were about to lure Kitty into a game of whist where the stakes were two coins each.

Miss Anne de Bourgh sat alone in an armchair near the fireplace so that the draught from the windows would trouble her as little as possible.

The timing was well chosen; neither Darcy, Elizabeth nor Georgiana were in sight at the moment. With the intention of having her glass refilled, Lady Catherine approached Edward who had just made Bingley laugh with some comment or other. Jane, who saw her draw near, unconsciously took her husband's arm.

"Mr Bingley, Mrs Bingley… and… Mr Jones…" Lady Catherine said, whereupon she scrutinised the three of them. Jane took a firmer hold of Bingley's arm and tried to give an impression of the calm she wished she could feel. Lady Catherine's piercing gaze, her pursed lips and frowning forehead, clearly signalled that she disliked what she saw.

Jane promised herself to have greater patience with Miss Bingley who often could take a critical attitude towards people in her surroundings. In comparison to Darcy's aunt, she seemed positively friendly.

Lady Catherine de Bourgh's gaze lingered at Edward. She looked suspiciously at his sunburnt face.

"Young man, would you care to enlighten me about your origins; I can tell from your dialect that it must be in the vicinity."

"That's right: I am born and brought up in Derbyshire," Edward replied calmly. The highborn lady looked at him in surprise and drew the conclusion that Mr Jones must be the owner of one of the lesser estates, whose owners she was not familiar with.

"Which of the estates in Derbyshire is your family residence?" she asked and fluttered her feather.

"None of the estates in Derbyshire belongs to my family," Edward said. His repetition of her question both surprised and annoyed her.

"You mean to say, I assume, that your family residence is not situated in Derbyshire but in one of the neighbouring counties." Lady Catherine squinted at the young man in a way that unsettled him. Although he felt his pulse increase, he held on to his calm exterior.

"I am not the owner of an estate, either in or outside Derbyshire," Edward said finally.

Lady Catherine, who had immediately suspected that Mr Jones was a man on unfamiliar territory, was determined to find out exactly how unfamiliar this environment was to the young man at Georgiana's side. It could of course be that Mr Jones had inherited a fortune and recently begun moving in the upper circles.

"What is the name of your relatives?" Lady Catherine said, with a fawning smile.

Edward, who had felt rather relaxed in the enjoyable company of Mr and Mrs Bingley, had almost begun to hope that people would look beyond his poor background if they had a chance to know him better. That this woman, who was a close relative of Darcy and Georgiana, was of a different opinion, he had felt the moment their eyes met. Although she could not know anything about his person, and reasonably, nothing about his background, her entire being communicated a dislike that could not be disregarded.

"Since my father's demise, I have no living relatives," Edward said after another few seconds of silence.

The older lady looked as though this was exactly the reply she had expected; she nodded and looked him up and down. Edward reddened and thought that the inspection of horses was done in a more dignified manner than this. For Georgiana's sake, he remained silent. Lady Catherine looked thoughtful.

"How have you acquired your fortune if you have neither estate nor relatives of noble origins?"

Although he had not intended to look away, his gaze was drawn to the door. He wished Georgiana had stood by his side.

"I have no fortune," he said quietly.

For a moment, his gaze stopped at the young woman by the fireplace. She was a frail figure, who would have been easily overlooked if it hadn't been for the shimmering dress that contrasted against the sofa she sat in. The jewels she wore glistened as the light from the flames reflected in the precious stones. Edward had never seen so many precious jewels worn by the same person; he guessed that the earrings alone were worth more than a farmhand earned in the course of a year.

Despite all this splendour, he thought that a simple farmer's daughter could have attracted more attention. This woman's eyes were tired and lack-lustre. Although her eyes were downcast, Edward had the impression that she had witnessed the exchange. He remembered that Georgiana had said that Miss Anne was Lady Catherine's daughter.

"Where have you received your education, and in what profession do you utilise it?" Lady Catherine asked. There still remained the possibility that he was a younger son, who had to earn his living.

Those who had been closest to Edward and Bingley during their conversation had fallen silent. Although they all understood how exposed Edward must feel, they were too afraid of Lady Catherine to interrupt the exchange. In addition, several of those assembled were too interested in Edward's reply to continue their own conversation or pretend as though they had not heard anything.

Edward, who was not normally shy or scared, found himself in a situation where he had no reply. It was easy to see where the questions were leading, and his worst fears about this kind of assembly seemed to have come true before the evening had drawn to a close. Edward had told himself that he had been loath to meet people in Georgiana's circles because the situation might be embarrassing to her. He admitted that for the first time in his life, he was ashamed of his origin, and the feeling filled him with self-loathing.

"I have no formal education, and I earn my living as assistant at a lawyer's office in Sheffield," Edward said and met Lady Catherine's eyes.

"How can it be possible to gain employment at a lawyer's without any education?"

Edward's lack of reply was answer enough; the expression in Lady Catherine's eyes did not need to be clarified in so many words. For a moment he wondered what her reaction would have been if he had instead informed her that he was Pemberley's stable master. The reaction such as it was, however, was more than adequate; he did not intend to let her humiliate his family.

Although Edward was deeply hurt by her treatment of him, he realised that this was what his future held in store for him. There would always be those who saw themselves as above others in consequence, and who enjoyed their own power at the expense of others. Edward did not doubt Georgiana's love for him; but he wondered if it would stand up to these continual tests.

A voice from among the crowd broke the silence that had been complete since Lady Catherine's last words.

"Is there any other purpose to your questions than to put Mr Jones in a bad light?" More than one of the party were grateful that someone had finally spoken; they were likewise ashamed that it had not been them who had come to Edward's defence. The rustle of dresses and clearing of throats showed that the guests once more dared to make themselves heard. Heads were turned in the direction of the sound; a few surprised eyebrows were raised as they saw who had spoken. The silence turned into mumbles and whispers.

Edward looked around; he was grateful that someone had seen his predicament and dared to interrupt the unwelcome exchange. Even if the outcome was unavoidable, it felt less exposing to know that someone was giving him their support. To stand up to this woman took a great deal of courage, and he guessed that only an equal would dare something of the sort.

"Have you heard me answer my own questions? If the replies put Mr Jones in a bad light, it is hardly my doing," Lady Catherine replied.

"My words were not well chosen. What I should have asked was: is there any other purpose to your questions than to make Edward, I mean, Mr Jones, uncomfortable?" the man said and took a step forward.

Edward looked up in surprise; Wickham was the last person he would have expected support from.

In a situation such as this, he would rather have expected him to be gloating.

Chapter 65

Elizabeth, Darcy and Georgiana had been in the next room trying to decide how best to announce their news to the assembly, while Lady Catherine had been cross-examining Edward. When they returned, the mood in the room was perceptibly dampened, and Elizabeth needed only to look at Lady Catherine and Edward to guess what had taken place between the two.

Darcy looked about the room: Bingley met his gaze whereupon he took hold of his wife's hand. Jane put a handkerchief to her face, ostensibly to cover a sneeze; her glossy eyes revealed, however, that she had been crying. From the farther end of the room, Mrs Bennet's woeful voice could be heard: "My poor nerves, Mr Bennet, my poor nerves..."

Mr Wilkins and Angelina stood stock still by each other's side; the latter was red-faced and stared at Lady Catherine in distaste. The lady in question stood with her head held high; her facial expression was the same as when she had won a bet.

Miss de Bourgh avoided Darcy's eyes; he saw that she blushed and swallowed repeatedly, although there was no sign of anything edible in front of her. Lydia was the only one in the room who seemed to be in high spirits; she held her husband's arm in a steady grip and regarded him with pride.

"Would anyone care to enlighten me as to what is going on?" Darcy said in such a tone of voice as to draw everyone's eyes to him.

Edward, who hardly dared think how humiliating the situation must be for Georgiana, remained silent. The other guests shifted in their seats and hoped that someone else would reply to Darcy's question.

"Lady Catherine has, without any trace of discretion, carefully questioned Mr Jones as to his assets and business, and I dare say that she has signalled her view on the matter to us all," Wickham said finally. He turned to look straight at Lady Catherine, whose eyes were dark with rage.

"It is my opinion that Lady Catherine owes Mr Jones an apology," he said matter-of-factly. Lady Catherine's loud snort echoed in the otherwise silent room.

"Do I need to remind you that you of all people in this room should be the last to demand apologies of others? Your own motives, actions and deeds have hardly been above blame," she said in disdain.

"As I am well aware," Wickham said gravely and added: "I admit that you are in the right; I have been and still owe certain people my apology," he said thoughtfully and looked at Edward.

"Would Lady Catherine care to enlighten us as to why Mr Wickham feels she owes Mr Jones an apology?" Darcy said tensely.

"Would you be so kind as to tell me why you are allowing your sister to enter into an engagement with a man without a trace of fortune, connections or education! Your own union was bad enough; how this is even possible is beyond comprehension," Lady Catherine said and fell silent. She knew that she had gone too far, but as the oldest member of the family it was her duty to tell the truth.

"I cannot see that I owe you any explanation as to why Georgiana's choice of husband, like my own choice of wife, is guided by the axiom of obtaining the greatest possible happiness through marriage. I rather believe it is you who should ask Mr Jones, Georgiana and Elizabeth for forgiveness," Darcy replied, as he by now found it difficult to control his anger.

Lady Catherine looked at him with incredulity and said, an added sharpness to her voice:

"You can be certain I will do nothing of the sort."

Jane watched the scene in the drawing-room in alarm; the mood was so tense, she feared that at any moment a fistfight would erupt. Mr Bennet looked at his daughter and shook his head; despite everything, he had to admit that the situation partly amused him.

"You have insulted more or less every guest in this room, and I cannot see any other way out than that you leave Pemberley!" Darcy said and eyed his aunt sternly. Lady Catherine stared at him and did at first not seem to think she had heard him correctly: he had advised her to leave Pemberley.

Her eyes were brimming with rage, and after a final disdainful glance at those gathered, she left the room with bad-tempered strides. In anger, she slammed the great oak doors with such force that more than one of those assembled jumped. The contrast between the sharp exchange that had occurred and the silence that now fell was so perceptible that they all needed a moment to gather their wits.

It was Bingley who first spoke, by turning to Edward.

"Allow me to congratulate the both of you. Do not pay too much attention to Lady Catherine's judgement; as far as I now she has been opposed to all but one marriage in this room."

"I suppose you are not unaware of the circumstances surrounding my own matrimony," Wickham said and nodded his agreement.

"Lady Catherine once sought me out to let me know how unworthy I was of becoming Darcy's wife; I suppose it is a test each person marrying into the Darcy family must undergo," Elizabeth said and put a hand on Edward's arm.

"Poor Miss de Bourgh; if so, who could be good enough for Lady Catherine's daughter?" Jane said quietly.

"No one other than the crown prince! As it stands, it seems she must remain unwed for as long as her mother is alive!" Wickham said.

"Allow me to add my congratulations to Mr Bingley's. Do not be cast down by Lady Catherine's harsh words," Mr Bennet said and added: "There are more than one couple in this room whose fortunes are widely disparate."

At these words, Lydia could no longer stop herself.

"But – is it really true that you lack a fortune entirely?" she exclaimed.

"Lydia!" Elizabeth snapped.

"I am allowed to ask a question – it is up to the one questioned whether he or she wants to reply to it or not," Lydia said defiantly.

"I admit that a small house and an even smaller sum of money can hardly be called a fortune," Edward replied and looked at Lydia.

"What good luck for you then that Mr Darcy is such a generous and kind man! With his help, I am sure that no one will notice that you are without a fortune," Mrs Bennet opined. Elizabeth and Jane looked at each other; the former sighed, the latter blushed at their mother's thoughtlessness.

"But where did you meet?" Lydia asked curiously.

"How can Miss Darcy have made your acquaintance? I assumed she only moves in the best of circles," Mrs Bennet added, without any intention of being condescending.

"Mama! Lydia!" Jane exclaimed in embarrassment and looked at Edward, who in his turn looked at Darcy.

"My sister and Mr Jones met here at Pemberley," Darcy said and met everyone's surprised eyes.

"But did you not say that you worked at a lawyer's office in Sheffield – or was that just to mollify Lady Catherine," Lydia laughed.

"I do indeed," Edward looked uncertainly at Darcy and added: "Up until a few months ago, I lived here in Derbyshire."

"That's right, we have seen each other many times over the years, and I want to apologise for my previous behaviour. I used my position and acted wrongly; it was wrong of me to treat you the way I did," Wickham said.

Elizabeth glanced at her husband and wondered how he would react to Wickham's words. Darcy's decision to forgive and invite him to Pemberley did not mean that their newfound friendship should be tested too severely. If anyone was to reveal Edward's true identity, it was Darcy – Wickham's comment could easily lead to questions.

"Wickham is right; since childhood, Edward has been acquainted with both of us, as he, like his father, served at Pemberley for many years," Darcy said finally.

At these words, even Mrs Bennet fell silent and stared at Edward. Every time she opened her mouth to say something, it was as though the words had disappeared. The story just became better and better: who would have thought that Mr Darcy would let his only sister marry one of the servants? She shivered as she imagined what Mrs Phillips would have to say on the matter.

The silence that had fallen among those assembled revealed noises that would otherwise have been lost in the hum of voices. A stomach growled, someone swallowed, and outside the door the servants' footsteps and low conversation could be heard. It was John Goose's comment to Mrs Reynolds that finally broke the silence: "I better go in and see if someone has died in there."

Bingley looked at Edward and realised suddenly why he had seemed familiar to him, and why he had not been able to determine where this feeling came from. Dressed for a party rather than work in the stables, in a drawing-room rather than in a stable building, and with Miss Darcy by his side, were all factors misleading enough in their own right.

But this time, Darcy had surprised him more than usual, and Bingley regarded his friend in silence before he said:

"So you have given your sister permission to marry Edward, who was formerly an employee here at Pemberley?"

"That's right," Darcy replied and met Bingley's amused gaze.

Chapter 66

Edward soon gathered his wits after the shock of Lady Catherine's cross-examination and entered into a conversation with Bingley, who was fascinated that Darcy had given Georgiana and Edward his consent. It was wonderful to him that he would allow his sister to enter into engagement with a man of a social standing so far below their own station that it was not possible to overlook, when he had once upon a time dissuaded Bingley from marrying Jane.

Mrs Bennet sat and pondered whether she would remember all that had been said: it was a mighty story she must be able to relate to the neighbouring wives on her return to Merryton.

"Mrs Bennet, I expect you, as a member of the family, will respect that what we say to each other in confidence is to remain between us," Darcy said and looked severely at his mother-in-law.

"But of course," Mrs Bennet replied, without the least intention of keeping the story of Miss Darcy's fiancé from her friends.

Georgiana looked at Darcy and smiled, which made him remember his own unanswered question and turn to Mr Wilkins.

"Have you met Edward before?" he said and regarded his friend intensely. Mr Wilkins laughed and said that he would leave that to Edward to reveal. Darcy's gaze found Edward, who looked uncomfortable as he heard the question. It was Georgiana's expectant eyes that finally prompted him to speak up.

"The night before Georgiana's departure to London you were all invited to a masked ball at Mr Wilkins's; I knew nothing about this at first."

Mrs Bennet, who was at the other end of the party, immediately interrupted him.

"Speak up! We don't want to miss out on any details just because our hearing is not what it used to be – isn't that so, Mr Bennet?" she said delightedly and looked expectantly at Edward. Mr Bennet, who saw Elizabeth's expression, put a hand on her arm.

"Let her be: the thrill of the news will abate soon enough. Tomorrow there will be other things to talk about," he whispered with a smile.

"If only it were so," she muttered and exchanged a glance with Jane.

"Young man, do continue your narrative, we are all eager to hear it," Mr Bennet said kindly.

Edward looked at Darcy, who nodded.

"One night there was a knock on my door," Edward said and fell silent as he remembered the conversation that had taken place that afternoon.

"As I was not expecting any visitor, I did not intend to open it; thankfully, I changed my mind.

Outside was a strange man who introduced himself as Mr Wilkins, a good friend of

Darcy's. I suppose it was my alarmed face that presently made him add that he was also a close friend of Georgiana's. This hardly did much to calm me down. All I could think was that this man was probably Georgiana's intended, and that he had sought me out, at best, to let me know this. At the time there was no one who knew about my feelings for Georgiana, but in my state of my mind, I could not think clearly.

It was some time before Mr Wilkins managed to persuade me that what he had to say came from Georgiana and not her brother. It soon became clear that Mr Wilkins knew something about us. I hardly dared believe that he was serious when he invited me to the masquerade he was to hold that night. He explained that Georgiana would be very surprised and pleased if I accepted the invitation. I could very well imagine that she would be surprised.

Mr Wilkins offered to arrange all the practical matters and had even brought an outfit which he showed to me. At first, I was sceptical, and thought it was all a conspiracy. Mr Wilkins, however, made such an impression on me, that I finally let myself be persuaded to believe him. A masquerade was a golden opportunity to see Georgiana a final time before she left for London."

"How brave of you!" Lydia said, and looked admiringly at Edward.

"Well, I must admit that I hesitated when I saw all the well-dressed ladies and gentlemen. It was probably the cold that finally persuaded me to enter. Happily, there were so many guests that most only seemed to know a few of those invited. As a newcomer, I therefore attracted little attention."

"I noticed you and asked who you were," Angelina said and looked at Mr Wilkins in amusement.

"I'm glad I wasn't aware of that then," Edward said and smiled.

"But how could you know who Georgiana was if everyone was in disguise?" Lydia asked curiously.

"Mr Wilkins had informed me that she would wear a white dress and a mask of the same colour. I saw her soon after I arrived; but although I was certain that it was Georgiana, I dared not reveal myself immediately. After a while, she noticed that she was being observed and it was obvious that my presence made her uncomfortable. Not until she was about to leave did I take courage and began to speak. She refused to believe me at first, and demanded I lift my mask and show who I was."

"And did you?" Lydia said, who had moved closer to Edward to catch all the details. This story was almost as exciting as the adventure she and Wickham had been on before their wedding.

"Of course not; not with Darcy in the same room," Edward said and smiled.

Darcy looked at him.

"So you were the man in the silver mask. I did in fact remark to Elizabeth that it was curious how you avoided our company for the entire evening."

"My foremost goal was to avoid you, Darcy. At one point I was in the same company as Elizabeth and was certain that my bluff would be called. Elizabeth was too caught up in her own thoughts, however; she hardly noticed what was going on around her."

Darcy looked at Elizabeth, who blushed as she remembered the thoughts she had had that night; she had been convinced that Darcy and Miss Byron harboured feelings for one another.

Darcy was still amazed by Mr Wilkins' part in Edward's and Georgiana's relationship. At the time, he himself had been completely unaware of the young people's attachment to one another. That Mr Wilkins had sought out and welcomed Edward to his party, and that he, in turn, had entered upon alien territory made Darcy regard the two men with a certain wonderment and respect.

"One question for you, my friend, who takes such liberties," Darcy said to Mr Wilkins.

"Knowing me as you do, did you really think I would give Georgiana my consent?"

"Did… did you not d-do so just now?" Wilkins said and smiled.

"This may well be, but you could hardly have predicted that at the time," Darcy said.

"Per…perhaps I was not as… as sure of you as of Georgiana," Mr Wilkins replied.

"We who weren't there would like to hear more," Lydia said stubbornly and turned to Georgiana: "How did you react when you discovered that it was Edward behind the mask?"

Georgiana blushed when everyone's eyes were turned on her, whereupon she looked at Edward and smiled.

"At first, I did not think it possible – I just could not imagine it. As he refused to take off the mask, it was not until I came close enough to see his eyes that I recognised him."

"Your fear was not wholly unwarranted," Darcy added and smiled.

"Even if I saw that it was Edward, I still could not understand how he came to be there. But when Edward told me about Mr Wilkins' visit earlier that day, it all became clear. He was the only one who knew about my feelings for Edward, and I will always be grateful to him for what he did that night. It was the happiest night of my life," Georgiana said and looked once more at Edward.

"But how did you learn to dance? If you were at a ball, you must have danced?" Lydia exclaimed impatiently and turned to Edward.

"Mr Wilkins showed me a few steps, and then I carefully studied the other couples before I ventured onto the dance floor. It was lucky that there were so much people, no one noticed that I only took part in two kinds of dances," Edward said.

"But how…" Lydia's start of yet another question prompted Mr Bennet to finally speak.

"We now seem to have straightened out all the questions surrounding Edward; let us move on to dear Elizabeth and Darcy. Was there not another joyous piece of news that you were to announce to us this evening?" he said diplomatically.

"Yes, is it not time that you tell us the happy news that you are expecting an heir to Pemberley!" Mrs Bennet exclaimed delightedly, and then put a hand to her mouth.

"Forgive me, dear Lizzy, it was not my intention to reveal your secret!"

Darcy looked at his mother-in-law in amusement and said after a while:

"I am afraid I will have to disappoint you by telling you that an heir is not to be expected." Mrs Bennet had a long face and could not utter a word for several minutes. Elizabeth met Darcy's gaze and smiled.

"As Darcy said, it is true that in the nearest future there is no reason to expect a child. But there may, on the other hand, be two."

"Oh… Lizzy!! To think that you will have twins, oh, how happy I am," Mrs Bennet exclaimed, whereupon she looked at her husband and in a euphoric tone of voice added: "My dear, our Lizzy is expecting twins – can you imagine anything more delightful!"

"I can… that she would be expecting triplets," Mr Bennet replied, looked at Elizabeth and shook his head.

"Mr Bennet," Mrs Bennet said indignantly, "whatever do you mean by suggesting that you would be happier if Lizzy expected triples – are not twins more than good enough?"

Mr Bennet could not be bothered to answer his wife, but instead congratulated his son-in-law and Elizabeth on the happy news.

Epilogue

Darcy and Elizabeth were alone in their bedroom: he was just about to take the clasps out of her hair. The long, brown tresses that had taken the shape of corkscrews, curled over her shoulders. She knew that he liked her hair to fall free, and now that they were alone they were free to behave as they wished. She regarded her reflection and went through the evening's events in her mind.

Despite the drama with Lady Catherine, the rest of the party had passed in a pleasant spirit. Elizabeth doubted if Lady Catherine would ever speak to them again, but it did not matter to her.

"What a night!" she exclaimed and looked at Darcy.

"It must have been a shock to Lady Catherine to come here and discover that Georgiana is engaged to a man of the people," Darcy said and laughed.

"I wonder what she would have said if she had stayed long enough to hear about Edward's actual background." Elizabeth sighed and added: "Some people are just so prejudiced."

"Yes, some people are just so prejudiced: it's a good thing you have never suffered from such notions," Darcy said and held onto a strand of hair. Elizabeth looked up and a light blush tinged her cheeks before she found herself and replied:

"It's fortunate that some of us are of the opinion that prejudice is to be overcome."

"In my experience, the prejudiced sometimes need a little help on the way," Darcy said and locked his arms about his wife.

"Don't you think we are the happiest couple in the world – just as we set out to be?" She asked and met Darcy's loving gaze.

"There is not a doubt in my mind about it," he replied, and kissed her.